Praise for *New York Times* bestselling author Carla Neggers

"Carla Neggers is one of the most distinctive, talented writers of our genre."
—# 1 *New York Times* bestselling author Debbie Macomber

"A writer at the absolute top of her craft."
—*Providence Journal*

"Well-drawn characters, complex plotting and plenty of wry humor are the hallmarks of Neggers's books."
—*RT Book Reviews*

Praise for Beth Andrews

"Ms. Andrews can take any story line and make it unforgettable. Her characters are so strong and powerful and unique."
—*Fresh Fiction*

"Andrews' story contains well-drawn characters that readers will surely root for. Both Allison and Dean are flawed—and that only makes them more appealing."
—*RT Book Reviews* on *His Secret Agenda*

CARLA NEGGERS

is a *New York Times* bestselling author of more than sixty novels, novellas and short stories. Her work has been translated into twenty-four languages and sold in more than thirty countries. Ever since she first climbed a tree with a pad and pen at age eleven, Carla has drawn on her keen sense of adventure and love of a good story in creating her plots and characters. A distinguished member of the writing community, she is a popular speaker around the country as well as a founding member of the New England Chapter of Romance Writers of America, past president of Novelists, Inc., and past vice president of International Thriller Writers.

An avid traveler, Carla enjoys exploring new places and has a special fondness for Ireland, but she always appreciates coming home to her small town in Vermont and to her family homestead on the western edge of the Quabbin Reservoir in rural Massachusetts. She and her husband, Joe, live in a house they bought as a fixer-upper on a hilltop not far from picturesque Quechee Gorge. "I look out at a sugar maple much like the one I used to climb as a kid," Carla says. "It's inspiring. Every story I write is its own adventure!"

BETH ANDREWS

Romance Writers of America RITA® Award winner Beth Andrews saw a big dream come true when she sold her first book to the Harlequin Superromance line. Beth and her two teenage daughters outnumber...oops...live with her husband in northwestern Pennsylvania. When not writing, Beth can be found texting her son at college, video-chatting with her son at college or, her son's favorite, sending him money. Learn more about Beth and her books by visiting her website, www.bethandrews.net.

New York Times Bestselling Author

CARLA NEGGERS

Bewitching

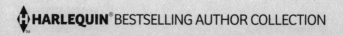
HARLEQUIN® BESTSELLING AUTHOR COLLECTION

Recycling programs
for this product may
not exist in your area.

ISBN-13: 978-0-373-18076-9

BEWITCHING
Copyright © 2013 by Harlequin Books S.A.

The publisher acknowledges the copyright holders of the individual works as follows:

BEWITCHING
Copyright © 1993 by Carla Neggers

HIS SECRET AGENDA
Copyright © 2009 by Beth Burgoon

Printed in U.S.A.

CONTENTS

Dear Reader,

Can you believe it's been more than 300 years since the Salem witch trials? I don't know anyone who isn't fascinated by them, including me. *Bewitching* might be inspired by that dark period in colonial America, but the story is just plain fun. My determined heroine, Hannah Marsh, sets out for Boston to prove that her ancestor was not a witch. The cramped Beacon Hill apartment where she stays is also inspired by real life—the Beacon Hill apartment where my husband and I lived when we first married. I promise you, though, that wasn't 300 years ago!

Joe and I have long since departed our basement apartment for a hilltop house in Vermont, but Boston is still "my" city, the setting for more books since *Bewitching* was first published. Emma Sharpe, an art crimes expert in my Sharpe and Donovan series, is part of a special FBI unit based in Boston, and Phoebe O'Dunn meets her swashbuckler at a Boston masquerade ball in *That Night on Thistle Lane,* the second book in my Swift River Valley series.

Read on to find out how a bewitching heroine casts a spell over her hero....

Take care,

Carla

BEWITCHING

New York Times Bestselling Author

Carla Neggers

CHAPTER ONE

THE PINKS AND ORANGES of dawn sparkled on the bay beyond Marsh Point, off a stretch of southern Maine that was still quiet, still undiscovered by tourists. Hannah Marsh stood on a boulder above the rocky coastline. The wind blew raw and cold, although the calendar said spring had arrived. In defiance of the weather, daffodils bloomed in the little garden outside her cottage.

In Boston the tulips would be out, perhaps even a few leaves budded. It wouldn't be so bad.

"You're going," a gruff voice said behind her.

She turned and smiled at Thackeray Marsh, aged seventy-nine, owner of Marsh Point, fellow historian and her cousin several times removed. He was a stout, fair-skinned, fair-haired man, although not as fair as herself, and kept in shape with dawn and dusk walks along a loop-shaped route that took in most of Marsh Point.

"I have no choice," Hannah said. "Most of the documents I need to examine are in Boston, and anything new on Priscilla Marsh will be there. It's where she lived and died, Thackeray. I have to go."

He snorted. "The Harlings catch you, they'll string you up."

"You said yourself there's only one Harling left in Boston, and he's even older than you are. I'll be fine."

Her elderly cousin squinted his emerald eyes at her. He was wearing an old tweed jacket patched at the elbows and rubber boots that had to be older than she was. His frugality, Hannah had learned in her five years in Maine, was legendary in the region.

"The Harlings and the Marshes haven't had much of anything to do with each other in a hundred years," he said. "Why rock the boat?"

"I'm not rocking the boat. I'm going on a perfectly ordinary, honorable research expedition." She tried not to sound defensive or impatient, but she had gone over her position—over and over it—with Cousin Thackeray. "It's not as if Priscilla Marsh died yesterday, you know."

Judge Cotton Harling had sentenced Priscilla Marsh to death by hanging three hundred years ago. Hannah hoped to have her biography of her ancestor in bookstores by the anniversary of the execution. Not only would it be good business, but it would pay a nice tribute to a woman who had defied the restrictions of Puritan America—of the Harlings of Boston.

And paid the price, of course. Hannah couldn't forget that.

The wind picked up, and she hugged her oversize sweatshirt closer to her body. Her long, fine, straight blond hair was, fortunately, held back in a hastily tied ponytail. Otherwise it would have tangled badly. Cousin Thackeray barely seemed to notice the cold.

"Hannah, the Harlings resent that we won't let them

forget it was a Harling who had Priscilla hanged. We, of course, say they *shouldn't* ever forget. The feud has been going on like this for three hundred years."

She refused to let his dark mood dampen her enthusiasm for what was, after all, a necessary trip—and no doubt would prove boring and routine, involving nothing more than musty books and documents and hours and hours in badly lit archives.

He made her trip sound like some kind of espionage assignment. "At least," her cousin went on, "don't let anyone in Boston know you're a Marsh. It's just too dangerous. If Jonathan Harling finds out—"

"That's the name of the last Harling in Boston?"

Cousin Thackeray nodded somberly. "Jonathan Winthrop Harling."

She grinned. "I look at it this way. What could one little old man who happens to be a Harling do to me?"

J. WINTHROP HARLING climbed the sloping lawn of the gold-domed Massachusetts State House above Boston Common with a sense of purpose. He had come to look at the statue of the infamous Priscilla Marsh. Her tragic death three hundred years ago at the hands of a Harling still colored his family's reputation. It was a part of what being a Harling in Boston was all about.

The wind off the harbor was brisk, even chilly, but he didn't feel it, though he was only wearing the dark gray suit he'd worn to the office.

Although he'd been born and raised in New York and had lived in Boston only a year, he was a stereotypical

Harling in one sense: he made one hell of a lot of money. Sometimes the size of his income, his growing net worth, staggered him. But the Harlings had always been good at making money.

Priscilla Marsh's smooth marble face stared at him in the waning sunlight. She looked very young and very wronged, more innocent, no doubt, than she had been in fact. The sculptor had managed to capture the legendary beauty of her hair, supposedly an unusual shock of pale blond, fine and very straight. She had been hanged on the orders of Cotton Harling when she was just thirty years old.

"Good going, Cotton," Win muttered.

But had she lived and died an ordinary life, Priscilla Marsh would never have inspired an oft-quoted Longfellow poem or a famous 1952 play. Nor would her statue have stood on the lawn of the Massachusetts State House, either.

Win brushed his fingers across the cool stone hair and felt the tragedy of the young Puritan's death. She had been dead less than a day when evidence of her innocence had arrived. Priscilla Marsh hadn't been teaching the young ladies of her neighborhood witchcraft, but how to cure earaches.

Her death should have been a lesson to future Harlings.

A lesson in patience, humility, faith in one's fellow human beings. A warning against arrogance and pride. Against believing in one's own infallibility.

But, Win thought, it hadn't.

HANNAH ARRIVED IN Boston without incident and set up
housekeeping in a cramped apartment on Beacon Hill.
She had traded with a friend, who would get two weeks
in Hannah's Maine cottage come summer. The friend, a
teacher, was off to Paris with her French class. Things,
Hannah decided, were just meant to work out.

Her first stop, bright and early the next morning, was
the New England Athenaeum on Beacon Street, across
from the Boston Public Garden. It was a private library,
supported by just four hundred members and founded
in 1892 by, of course, a Harling.

Hannah indicated she was a professional historian and
would like to use the library, a renowned repository of
New England historical documents.

Preston Fowler, the director, a formal man who appeared to be in his mid-fifties, informed her that the
New England Athenaeum was a private institution. Ac-
cordingly, she would be permitted into its stacks and
rare book room only when she had exhausted all other
possibilities and could prove it was the only place that
had what she needed. And even then she would be carefully watched.

Hannah resisted the impulse to tell him other private
institutions had opened their doors to her in her career.
Arguing wouldn't get her anywhere. She needed something that would work. She sighed and said, "But Uncle
Jonathan said I wouldn't have any trouble with you."

"Who?" Preston Fowler asked sharply.

"My uncle." She paused more for dramatic effect than

to reconsider what she was doing. Then she added, "Jonathan Winthrop Harling."

Fowler cleared his throat, and Hannah was amused at how rigid his spine went. Ahh, the Harling factor. "You—your name is…?"

"Hannah," she said, not feeling even a twinge of guilt. "Hannah Harling."

WIN SETTLED BACK in his soft leather chair and took the call from the elderly uncle whose name he bore. "Hey, there, Uncle Jonathan, what's up?"

Jonathan Harling, who had just turned eighty, got straight to the point. "You going to the New England Athenaeum dinner on Saturday?"

"Wild horses couldn't drag me. Why?"

"Friend of mine says he saw a Harling on the guest list."

"Well, it wasn't me," Win said emphatically. "I haven't even been inside that snooty old place. Your friend must have been mistaken. What about you? You aren't going, are you?"

Uncle Jonathan grunted. "Some of us don't have unlimited budgets, you know."

"I would be happy to buy you a ticket—"

"Damned if I'll accept charity from my own nephew!" the old man bellowed hotly. "Why don't you go, meet a nice woman who'll inspire you to part with some of that booty of yours? How much you worth these days? A million? Ten? More?"

Win laughed. "It's more fun to keep you guessing."

Still grumbling, his uncle hung up. Win turned his chair so that he could see the spectacular view of Boston Harbor from his fourteenth-floor window. He watched a few planes take off from Logan Airport across the water. It was a clear, warm, beautiful May afternoon, the kind that made him wonder if he shouldn't call up the New England Athenaeum and get a ticket to its fund-raising dinner, just to see who showed up.

But meeting women was not a problem for him. Contrary to his uncle's belief, Win did not live the life of a monk. No, he had no trouble at all finding women to go out on the town with him, occasionally to share his bed. It was finding the *right* woman....

"Romantic nonsense," he muttered.

BY HER FOURTH DAY in Boston, Hannah had settled into a pleasant routine of research. Preston Fowler himself had invited her to the New England Athenaeum's fund-raising dinner and she'd accepted, despite the rather steep price. But she was supposed to be a Harling and therefore have money. Besides, Fowler himself had begun to help her ferret out information on the Harlings; she had told him she was researching one of her ancestors, Cotton Harling. No point in stirring up trouble by mentioning Priscilla Marsh or the truth about her own identity. She was enjoying the perks of being a Harling.

"Is this your first trip to Boston?" Fowler asked on a cool, rainy morning. He had brought a couple of books to the second-floor table he had reserved for her at a window overlooking the Public Garden.

"Yes," Hannah lied, not without regret. He was being helpful, after all.

"Are you a member of the New York Harlings?"

The New York Harlings? Fowler's eagerness was impossible to miss—the New York Harlings must be rich, she thought—but she had never heard of them. She would have to remember to ask Cousin Thackeray, who still didn't know she was running around Boston claiming to be a Harling. But he had been the one to tell her not to reveal she was a Marsh.

She shook her head. "The Ohio Harlings."

"I see," the New England Athenaeum's director said. He was dressed in a Brooks Brothers suit today, a white on white shirt, wing tip shoes. There was never a hair out of place.

Hannah had invested in a couple of Harling-like outfits in an hour of rushing around on Newbury Street. Now she was afraid to dig out her charge-card receipts to see how much she'd spent. Would the IRS accept them as a business deduction? Preston Fowler would never believe she was a Harling if she kept showing up in her collection of jeans and vintage T-shirts. Once or twice she might get away with it, but not every day.

As for any real Harlings…well, there was only one in Boston, and she wasn't worried about him. Jonathan Winthrop Harling would be old, knobby-kneed and nasal-voiced, with a wardrobe of worn tweeds and holey deck shoes that he would be too cheap to replace. He would have bony hands with a slight tremble, and he'd wear thick glasses with finger smudges on the lenses.

She had him all pictured.

Fowler told her about a painting at the Museum of Fine Arts that she must see, a portrait of Benjamin Harling, the eighteenth-century shipbuilder. Hannah promised to have a look.

Finally he left.

She resumed her scan of a late-nineteenth-century newspaper account of a fistfight between some Harling or other and Andrew Marsh, Cousin Thackeray's grandfather. It involved their divergent opinions about the Longfellow poem on Priscilla Marsh, the Harling insisting it clearly romanticized her, the Marsh insisting it did not. A big mess.

Half paying attention, Hannah suddenly sat up straight. "What's this?"

She went back and reread a blurred, yellowed paragraph toward the end of the article.

In a long-winded way, it said that the Marsh had challenged the Harling to open up "the Harling Collection" to public inspection.

The Harling Collection?

Hannah's researcher's heart jumped in excitement. Now this was news. Something worth checking out. She read further.

Apparently Anne Harling, deceased in 1892, had gathered the family papers from the past three centuries, since the Harlings' arrival in Boston in 1630, into a collection.

What Hannah wouldn't give to get her hands on it!

She carefully copied the information into her notebook and sat looking out at the rain-soaked tulips and budding trees of the Public Garden, wondering what her life had come to that locating a bunch of old documents excited her.

"MR. HARLING?"

Win looked up from his computer and sighed. His young administrative assistant, fresh out of college, was clearly determined to shape him into her idea of a suitable executive. He wasn't sure just what his failings were. "You can call me Win, Paula," he said, not for the first time. "What's up?"

"It's the impostor again."

"Where?"

"The Museum of Fine Arts."

"Uncle Jonathan called?"

"While you were in a meeting," Paula confirmed, all business. Win wondered if it had been a good idea to tell her about the unknown Harling who was supposedly attending the New England Athenaeum's fund-raising dinner. She had been convinced right from the start that they were dealing with an impostor. "He said to ask you if you had signed up for the lecture series on seventeenth-century American painting that is being offered by the museum. A friend of his knows the instructor and—"

"Yes, I understand. Uncle Jonathan knows everyone." Win tilted back in his chair. "He doesn't think it's a practical joke?"

"No." From her look, neither did Paula. She was

tawny-haired and twenty-two and very good at what she did. "It's a woman, Mr. Harling. Trust me."

"Why would a woman pose as a Harling?"

Paula made a face that said what she wanted to do was groan, but groaning didn't fit her code of conduct. "May I speak freely?"

"What is this, a pirate ship? Of course you may."

She took a step closer to his desk, a black modern thing his decorator had picked out. "Mr. Harling, if you don't mind my saying so, I've been with you almost a year now, and it seems to me you don't have much of a clue as to how people around here view your family."

"The Harlings, you mean," he said.

"That's right." She was very serious. "Lots of people, given the chance, would like to take advantage of your wealth and reputation, your position in the financial community. You have breeding—"

"Breeding? Paula, I'm not a horse."

She was too sincere to be embarrassed. "As I said, you don't have a clue."

"Okay, suppose you're right. Suppose someone is trying to take advantage of me. First, why me and not my uncle? Second, why a woman?"

"In answer to your first question," she said, obviously disgusted by his ignorance, "because you are thirty-three and single and your uncle is eighty. Ditto that for the answer to your second question."

"Why can't there be a third Harling in Boston?"

"There isn't."

Win glanced at his computer; his work was beckoning. "So, a supposed Harling signed up for a class at the MFA and plans to attend a fund-raising dinner. That doesn't make a conspiracy."

"You wait," Paula said confidently, heading for the door. "There'll be another."

WIN ARRIVED a few minutes late for his weekly lunch with Jonathan Harling at his elderly uncle's private club on Beacon Street, just below the State House. It was a musty, snooty old place with cream-colored walls, Persian carpets, antique furnishings and an aging, largely male clientele. Win would bet he was the youngest one in the place by forty years. The food, however, was passable, if traditional New England fare, and he always enjoyed his uncle's company.

"Sorry I'm late," he said, approaching Uncle Jonathan's table overlooking a stately courtyard. "It's been one of those days. No, don't get up."

Jonathan Harling sank gratefully into his antique Windsor chair. Always a model of integrity and responsibility for his nephew, he was a tall, thin man with eyes as clear at eighty as they had been thirty years ago when he had been an acclaimed professor of legal history at Harvard. Win knew it had almost killed his uncle when he'd opted for Princeton.

"Name me one day in the past six months that hasn't been 'one of those days,'" the old man grumbled.

Win decided to sidetrack. "It's a busy time of the year. Is the chowder good today?"

Uncle Jonathan already had a bowl in front of him. "It's never good."

"Then why do you keep ordering it?"

"Tradition," he said in a tone that indicated he damned well knew his nephew had no patience with such things.

Win deftly changed the subject. "Any news on our Harling friend?"

"The impostor, you mean. Nothing yet. He's taking his time, making sure he doesn't make a mistake."

"My assistant is convinced it's a she."

Uncle Jonathan mulled that one over. "Good point. I've alerted a number of my friends to keep on the lookout. We don't want him—or her—to start charging diamonds and fast cars to our name. *You* might be able to afford such things, but I can't."

Win let that comment pass. "Have you talked to Preston Fowler at the Athenaeum?"

"Not yet. I just heard about the Museum of Fine Arts incident today. I don't want to start ruffling feathers and end up looking like a fool if it's all just a coincidence."

"But you don't think it is," Win said.

Uncle Jonathan shook his head, serious. "No, I don't."

The waiter came, and Win ordered the roast turkey, his uncle the scrod. Out of the corner of his eye, Win spotted the maître d' leading a lone diner to the table directly behind him.

It was all he could do to remember to tell the waiter to bring coffee.

The lone diner was young and female, so that automatically made her stand out. But in addition she had hair that was long and straight and as pale and fine as corn silk, hair that would make her stand out anywhere. She was slender and not very tall, and she wore a crisp gray suit.

Uncle Jonathan had also noticed her. "Where did she come from?"

"I don't know," Win replied. "I've never seen her before."

"I don't think she's a member. Must be related to a member, though. I wonder who?"

Win shrugged and eased off the subject, having seen the sparkle in his uncle's eye. There was nothing he'd like better than to have his nephew attracted to a woman whose family belonged to the same prestigious private club the Harlings had been members of for all the one hundred fifty years of its existence. Lunch arrived, and Win brought up the Red Sox.

It didn't work.

"Look," Uncle Jonathan said, "she ordered the lobster salad."

The lobster salad was the most expensive item on the limited menu. Win couldn't resist turning in his seat. Her back was to him, maybe three feet away, but he could see her breaking open a steaming popover. Her fingers were long, feminine but not delicate, the nails short and neatly buffed. There was something strangely familiar about her, yet he knew he had never seen her before. He would have remembered.

Their meals arrived, and he turned back to his uncle. "The Red Sox," he said stubbornly, "had a terrible road trip. They're at home this weekend with the Yankees. Are you planning to go?"

"She must not eat lobster very often. She wouldn't stay that thin."

Win sighed. "Of course, the impostor could try to take over our box seats…."

That brought Uncle Jonathan around. "No, I doubt it. He's only left tracks at the Athenaeum and the Museum of Fine Arts. Probably not a baseball fan."

"I don't know, it's possible. I suppose there's not much we can do at this point, except remain on alert. As you say, it's too soon to act." Win tried his turkey; it wasn't very good. "But if there *is* an impostor running around Boston, capitalizing on our name…well, I'd like to get my hands on him. Or her."

Uncle Jonathan concurred.

By the time the waiter cleared their plates and brought fresh coffee, their conversation was back to the blonde. "Why don't you turn around and introduce yourself? It's not as if you're shy. Invite her over for coffee. Let's find out who she is."

"Uncle Jonathan…"

But he pushed his chair back and grabbed his cane, half getting up. "Miss, excuse me. Our saltshaker's stopped up, and I hate to bother the waiter. Mind if we borrow yours?"

There was nothing Win could do but indulge the old goat. He turned around, and the blonde was there facing him, her eyes huge and green and luminous. She looked a little startled. Who wouldn't? Win took in the high cheekbones and straight nose, the strong chin. Combined, her features made an angular, curiously elegant face. Her skin was pale and clear. Her arresting eyes and hair, however, dominated.

She looked intelligent enough to notice that their table had been cleared. Their waiter was approaching with the coffeepot and Uncle Jonathan's ritual dish of warm Indian pudding, which always looked to Win as if it had come from a cat box.

"Of course," the woman said, and handed over her saltshaker. Win took it.

She turned away.

So much for that.

Win shoved the saltshaker at his uncle. "You're incorrigible."

"Don't you think she looks familiar?"

"Yes," Win said, interested, "I do."

"I can't figure out why. Anyway, she's pretty. Invite her to dinner."

"Uncle…"

"You might never see her again. What if she's the one? You'll have missed your chance."

"If she's 'the one,'" Win said, speaking in a much lower voice than his uncle, who apparently didn't give a damn who heard him, "then there'll be another chance. I believe in fate taking a hand in matters of the heart."

Jonathan snorted. "Romantic nonsense." He waved his spoon. "There, she's leaving. Catch her."

"She's not a trout."

"If she were a tempting stock option you'd never let

her get away. Can't you get excited about something that doesn't involve dollar signs?"

Win could. He most definitely could. He was right now. Watching the blonde's hair bounce as she left, the movement of her shapely legs, was not something that lacked consequences. Physical consequences, even. But he didn't share his reaction with his uncle. Instead he said sanely, "I won't come on to a perfect stranger. That could be construed as harassment."

"Only after she tells you to chew dust and you persist. The first time it's just an invitation to dinner."

"On what grounds do I invite her to dinner?"

"Who needs grounds?"

Win groaned. "If she had wanted to meet someone, she wouldn't have come here. This club's known for its elderly membership."

"It's no secret you and I have lunch here on Wednesdays, you know," Uncle Jonathan said thoughtfully. "Maybe she wanted to meet you. That ever occur to you?"

"If she'd wanted to meet me, don't you think she would have said something when you bellowed at her about the salt?"

His uncle was undeterred. "Maybe she would have if you'd said something first."

Win gave up. His uncle was the one indulging in romantic nonsense. The woman had given no indication she was interested in, had recognized or indeed cared if she ever saw either Harling again.

But those eyes. They were unforgettable. And her hair.

What was it about her that was so damned familiar?

Their waiter slipped Win the bill, which he would quietly sign and have put on his account. It was an arrangement they had, in order to keep his uncle from insisting on paying his half, which was just for show. Win knew Uncle Jonathan wouldn't part with a dime if he could get someone else to pay first.

Financially secure though he was, Win found the tab a bit staggering. "Wait just a minute! You've put an extra meal on my bill."

"Well, yes, your...Ms. Harling indicated..."

Win jumped to his feet. *"Who?"*

"The woman." The waiter nodded to the table just vacated by the silken-haired blonde. "If there's been a mistake..."

Uncle Jonathan was reaching for his cane. He was an intelligent man. He plainly knew what was going on. "She's our impostor!"

"Yes," Win said through gritted teeth. He looked at his uncle. "You all right?"

Uncle Jonathan waved him on with his cane. "Go, go. Track down the larcenous little wench."

Win didn't bother arguing with his uncle's choice of words, but simply signed the bill for the entire amount and went.

CHAPTER TWO

HANNAH WAS BREATHING hard and hoping she was sane
again by the time she reached the modern building in
the heart of Boston's Financial District. Her name was
Marsh, she repeated under her breath. Hannah Marsh,
Hannah Marsh, Hannah Marsh. She *wasn't* a Harling.

This little visit would straighten everything out. She
would go up to Jonathan Winthrop Harling's office, introduce herself, confess if she had to and explain if she
could. She had put herself down for the New England
Athenaeum's fund-raising dinner to keep Preston Fowler
happy, had signed up for the lecture series at the Museum of Fine Arts on the spur of the moment, and realized only after she'd committed herself that she'd better
be consistent and go as a Harling.

She didn't know how she'd explain lunch.

The Beacon Street club was one of Jonathan Winthrop Harling's hangouts, and she'd gone there hoping to
meet him. Hoping to explain. Hoping to ask him about
the Harling Collection. But she didn't even know if he'd
been there because she'd frozen up, plain and simple.

That black-eyed rogue behind her had done it. Something about his looks had rattled her. Two hundred years
ago he would have run guns for George Washington.

Three hundred years ago Cotton Harling would have had him hanged. He had looked, she thought, decidedly unpuritanical. How could she think, much less confess, with him around?

So she hadn't. And then the waiter had asked if she wanted to put her lunch on the Harling account— she'd had to pretend to be one, of course, to get into the place—and not wanting to blow her cover, she'd said yes.

Now she was a criminal. If the Harlings were all as miserable as Cousin Thackeray had said they were, she could be in big trouble with Jonathan Winthrop.

Then she'd never get a look at the Harling Collection.

The time had come, she told herself as she went through the revolving doors, to come clean, plead for mercy and hope that an eighty-year-old man, even if a Harling, would understand that she was a legitimate, professional biographer. She would make him understand.

She glanced around the elegant wood and marble lobby, then bit her lip when she spotted the armed guards. There were four of them. One behind a half-moon-shaped desk, two mingling with the well-dressed businesspeople flowing in and out of the elevators and revolving doors, another on the mezzanine. He had a machine gun.

An easygoing place, Jonathan Winthrop Harling's office. Hannah had expected a nice old brownstone on Beacon Hill. But probably the old buzzard liked being surrounded by men with guns.

She approached the guard behind the half-moon desk. He was a big, red-faced man, tremendously fit-looking, with curly auburn hair and a disarming spray of freckles across his nose. He didn't look as if he would shoot a woman for pretending to be a Harling, but this was Boston and Hannah just didn't know.

He listened without expression while she explained that she had an appointment with Jonathan Winthrop Harling, but had forgotten which floor he was on.

"Your name?" he asked.

She gulped.

"Ma'am?"

"Hannah," she said. "Jonathan's expecting me."

His eyes narrowed. "Who?"

She'd made a mistake. "Jonathan Winthrop Harling. I'm—I'm Hannah Harling. From Cincinnati. The Midwest Harlings. We…"

She hated lying to men with guns.

The guard picked up the phone. "I'll call Mr. Harling."

"No!"

The old buzzard would swallow his teeth if the guard said one of the Midwest Harlings was here to see him. There were no Midwest Harlings.

"I just need his floor number," Hannah added quickly. "Really."

"And I need to call," the guard said coolly. "Really."

Good, Hannah. Get yourself shot.

She backed away from the desk. "Never mind," she told the guard, manufacturing a smile. "I'll come by another time. Don't bother telling Mr. Harling I was here. I—I'll call him later."

No one followed her through the revolving doors. Her

heart was pounding when she reached the plaza in front of the building, but when she looked over her shoulder she didn't see any armed men coming after her.

But she didn't relax.

She wondered what had become of play-by-the-rules Hannah Priscilla Marsh. Cousin Thackeray had warned her about Boston. Maybe she should have listened.

Not wanting to look totally guilty, in case the guard was watching, she lingered at the fountain. It was a warm, beautiful day. Yellow tulips waved in the breeze and twinkled in the sunlight all along the fountain, which sprayed thin arcs of water every few seconds. The effect was calming, mesmerizing.

But she still had half an eye on the revolving doors. A flurry of activity, some shoving, people moving out of the way caught her eye. She turned.

And there he was.

"Oh, no!"

She was off like a shot, adrenaline surging. She didn't know who he was or what he thought she'd done, but she knew instinctively that he was after her, that she couldn't let him catch up with her.

It was her black-eyed rogue from lunch.

He looked fit to be tied. Determined. Dangerous.

Did he work with Jonathan Harling? Were they friends? Did he know she was running around town pretending she was a Harling?

There was no time to think.

She moved fast, pushing her way through a crowd and around the block, vaguely aware that Jonathan Winthrop Harling's building occupied the corner. She came to a side entrance.

She had no choice. None whatsoever. Looking back, she saw her pursuer pounding around the corner, straight for her. She had no idea if he had spotted her, was only aware that this wasn't her city and she didn't know where to hide, didn't want to meet him in a dark, unpopulated alley.

So, back into the building she went.

WIN SPOTTED HER going through the revolving doors at the side entrance and moved fast to intercept her.

But when he got back to the lobby, she was gone.

He searched the place with his eyes. The red-haired guard came up to him. "Lose her?"

"She's in here," Win said.

"One of my men must have seen her."

"It's okay." This was his place of business, his space. He couldn't have a green-eyed blonde creating chaos here. "I'll find her myself."

"She doesn't know what floor you're on," the guard informed him. "I wouldn't tell her."

"Thanks."

Where could she have gone? The guard would have seen her if she'd tried to circle back to the front entrance. Win would have seen her if she'd doubled back through the side entrance. The only other options were the ladies' room and the elevators. Surely a guard would have questioned her if she'd tried to get onto an elevator. His was a financial building with moderately tight security.

Hannah Harling of the Midwest Harlings.

The blonde from lunch.

The larcenous little wench, Uncle Jonathan had called her. Win could think of other names.

He posted himself outside the ladies' room just off the lobby and waited.

HANNAH FINISHED BOOKING a trip for two to Vancouver. Her plans, she told the agent, were tentative. The small travel agency off the main lobby was as good a hiding place as any and better than most.

She hated lying, but felt she had little choice.

"When I have everything finalized," the agent, a pleasant woman in her mid-fifties, said, "I should send it up to Jonathan Winthrop Harling. Is that correct?"

"Yes."

"And you're Hannah Harling," she went on.

Hannah didn't respond. She was going to get herself arrested if she wasn't more careful, but avoiding the truth about her real name was certainly preferable to facing the black-eyed man who was after her. He didn't look as if he would listen to any excuses she might have. Had he heard her say she was a Harling at the Beacon Street club? Was he protecting Jonathan Harling?

What if the old man with him at lunch had been Jonathan Harling?

She wished she had never listened to Cousin Thackeray. She wouldn't have been predisposed to say she was a Harling if he hadn't insisted so adamantly that a Marsh was doomed in Boston, "Harling country." But she knew her elderly cousin wasn't responsible. She was responsible for her own actions.

"I hadn't," the agent resumed, "realized Mr. Harling was married."

Married?

To some eighty-year-old man?

Hannah smiled and left without correcting the woman on any of her misconceptions. Surely she would be able to explain Vancouver for two to Jonathan Winthrop Harling. *Yeah, right. Given what you've demonstrated of your character so far, he'll just be delighted to give you access to his family's papers.*

She'd dug one very deep crater for herself.

But what was done was done, and she couldn't hang around in the travel agency forever. Venturing carefully into the corridor, Hannah peered toward the main part of the lobby where the security guard was posted behind his half-moon desk. She was out of view of the man on the mezzanine with the machine gun. *Thank heaven for small favors.* The other two she couldn't see. They didn't worry her nearly as much as her dark-eyed stranger.

Spotting him, she inhaled sharply.

He was posted at the women's bathroom at the far end of the corridor, not fifty feet from her.

Lordy, she thought, but he was a handsome devil.

Did he think she was hiding in the bathroom? Was he waiting for her? Maybe she was just being paranoid. Either that or she'd outwitted him, she thought, with a welcome surge of victory.

You're not out of here yet, she reminded herself.

She saw him glance at his watch and march toward the bank of elevators, his back to her. She held her breath at the sight of his clipped, angry walk. He did have broad shoulders. And his suit was so well cut it moved with him, made him seem very masculine indeed.... A modern pirate.

Telling herself she was playing it safe, not behaving like a coward, she ducked back into the travel agency to give the elevators time to whisk him back where he belonged.

The travel agent said happily, "I just emailed the information to Mr. Harling's office."

Oh, good, Hannah thought.

She decided to cut her losses for the day and darted out the side entrance before anyone so much as saw her, never mind pinned her to the nearest wall and called the police.

"I WARNED YOU," Paula said, handing Win the printed email from the travel agency off the main lobby.

"What is it?" he asked, still too angry to focus on anything other than his frustration at having lost the blonde.

"Reservations for two to Vancouver next month."

"What?"

"You're going to Vancouver for a week. The agency's working out the details of your stay, but from what I can gather, it's going to be very luxurious."

"Paula, I'm not going to Vancouver."

"I know that." She jerked her head in the direction of the offending email. "But tell Hannah Harling."

Win's eyes focused. He saw two names: Jonathan Winthrop and Hannah Harling. Then the little note from the travel agency downstairs, congratulating him.

On what? For what?

"She's not satisfied with being a long-lost cousin from Cincinnati," his assistant said scathingly. "She wants to be your wife."

THAT EVENING, HANNAH opened up a can of soup for dinner, still too stuffed from lunch and too frazzled by her day to want a big meal.

She ate standing up, pacing from one end to the other of her borrowed, Beacon Hill apartment. It wasn't very far. At eye level, three shuttered windows looked onto the brick sidewalk and offered an uninspiring view, nothing like her view of the bay off Marsh Point. The friend who'd lent her the apartment kept a powerful squirt gun on the kitchen windowsill. Hannah had discovered the hard way that it was meant as a handy deterrent to particularly bold dogs, who occasionally did their business without benefit of leash, manners or master.

But the apartment was a quiet, functional place to work, and that, she reminded herself, was her purpose in Boston. Work. Nothing more. She had nothing to hide. She had no bone to pick with the Harlings.

Now she realized she'd blundered badly; she'd let Cousin Thackeray's hyperbole and paranoia get to her. She should never have posed as a Harling.

There was nothing to do but make amends. She had to confess.

First, however, she would lay everything out for her elderly cousin and see what he had to offer by way of advice. Her soup finished, she started for the wall phone in the kitchen.

And stopped, not breathing.

She was sure she recognized the charcoal-covered legs. The deliberate walk. The polished shoes. They were on her sidewalk, directly in front of her middle window.

She moved silently across the linoleum floor and leaned over the sink, balancing herself with one hand on the faucet. She peered up as best she could, trying to get a better look at the passerby as he moved toward the kitchen window.

It was him!

Her hand slipped off the faucet and landed in the sink, wrenching her elbow. Her soup pan, soaking in cold water, went flying. The thud of stainless steel on linoleum was loud enough to be heard at Boston Public Garden. There was water everywhere.

Hannah swore.

She heard the fancy shoes crunch to a stop on the brick sidewalk. Saw the handsome suit blocking her window. All he had to do was bend down and he'd see her.

She didn't breathe, didn't swear, didn't yell in pain. Didn't make a single, solitary sound.

He moved on.

I'm haunted, she thought, getting ice out of the freezer for her elbow. She threw towels on top of the spilled water and dumped the soup pan back into the sink. How many people in metropolitan Boston? Four million? What were the odds against seeing the same man at lunch, in the financial district, and now, on Beacon Hill at dinnertime?

Hannah waited an hour before going out. She tied a scarf around her head, tucking in every blond hair in case her black-eyed rogue was still out and about and might recognize her. She had to risk it. She needed to walk, to think. She couldn't even concentrate enough to call Cousin Thackeray. What on earth would she tell him? How could she explain her peculiar day, even to him?

Beacon Hill was a neighborhood of subdued elegance, a lovely place to be at dusk, with its steep, narrow streets, brick sidewalks, black, wrought-iron lanterns and Federal Period town houses. Louisa May Alcott had lived here, the Cabots and the Lodges, Boston mayors and Massachusetts senators—and, of course, the Harlings.

Hannah barely noticed the cars crammed into every available parking space, the fashionably dressed pedestrians, but imagined instead the picturesque streets a hundred, two hundred years ago. She knew her ability to give life to the past was the central quality that, critics said, made her biographies not just scholarly, but intensely readable.

Less than a week in Boston, and already her reputation was in jeopardy.

When she came to Louisburg Square, one of Boston's most prestigious residential addresses, she turned onto its cobblestone circle. Elegant town houses faced a small private park enclosed within a high wrought-iron fence. Hannah made her way to the house the Harlings had built. It had a bow front and was black-shuttered, its front stoop ending right on the brick sidewalk. Any yard would be in back, one of Beacon Hill's famous hidden gardens.

According to her most recent information, now several years old, the house was owned by a real-estate developer. The Harlings had sold it during the Depression.

Hannah sighed and stared at the softly illuminated interior that was visible through the draped windows. Would the current owner let her have a look at the place? Would she have better luck as Hannah Marsh, biographer, or Hannah Harling of the Midwest Harlings?

She wasn't quite sure why she cared. After all, what did a house built more than a hundred years after Judge Cotton Harling had sentenced Priscilla Marsh to death have to do with her work?

The cream-colored, brass-trimmed front door opened, startling her. She jumped back.

Then felt her heart jump right out of her chest.

Her black-eyed rogue bounded out, wearing running shorts and a black-and-gold Boston Bruins T-shirt.

Never mind getting to blazes out of there, as any sensible woman would have done, Hannah barely managed not to gape at the man's thighs. The muscles were hard and tight, and a thick, sexy scar was carved above the left knee. He looked tough, solid, masculine.

And he recognized her immediately, scarf or no scarf.

"Don't move," he said. "I wouldn't want to have to chase you."

Given that she'd only slipped on a pair of flats and

he was wearing expensive running shoes, she doubted she'd get far. And his legs were longer.

She was at a profound disadvantage.

His eyes bored into her. They were black, piercing, intelligent, alive, the kind of eyes that sparked the imagination of a woman more used to examining the lives of dead people. "I won't have you arrested—"

"Good of you," Hannah retorted, just lightly sarcastic.

He was unamused. "You will stop posing as a Harling."

She blinked. "Posing?"

Still no sign of amusement. Whoever he was, he took her little ruse this past week seriously—too seriously for her taste. "Posing," he repeated.

His lean runner's body was taut, and he seemed very sure of himself.

Hannah couldn't let him get the better of her.

"I don't know what you're thinking," she began, doing her best to sound indignant, "but I am a Harling. I'm from Cincinnati. I'm in Boston on a genealogical expedition and—"

He leaned toward her. "Give it up."

"Give what up?"

"You're not a Harling, and if I were you, I'd cut my losses while I still could."

His words grated. "And just who are you to be telling me to do anything?"

He raised his head slightly, looking at her through half-closed eyes.

Something made her swallow and think, for a change.

"You're not…" she mumbled, half to herself, "you can't be…"

"I'm surprised," he said cockily, "you don't recognize your own husband."

For the first time in her life, Hannah was speechless. A hot river of awareness flowed down her back, burned into every fiber of her.

The black eyes had thrown her off. Cousin Thackeray had said the Harlings were all blue-eyed devils.

But this black-eyed devil said, "Name's Harling."

She swallowed hard, preparing herself for the rest of it.

"J. Winthrop Harling."

He wasn't eighty. He wasn't knobby-kneed. He didn't wear smudged glasses. And he sure as blazes wasn't harmless.

What had she done?

You'll be in Harling country, Cousin Thackeray had warned her. *Just never forget you're a Marsh.*

She pulled off her scarf, letting her hair fall over her shoulders, feeling a small rush of pleasure at the sight of J. Winthrop Harling's widening eyes. But the pleasure didn't last when she realized what she saw in them. Lust. It was the only word for it.

Right now, at that moment, he wanted her.

Cousin Thackeray would croak.

She tossed back her head. "You Harlings will never change. You're the same arrogant bastards you were three hundred years ago. I'm surprised you haven't threatened to have me hanged."

He frowned. "Hanged?"

"It's the Harling way," she quipped, and about-faced. She headed for her street, daring J. Winthrop Harling to follow her.

WIN LET HER GO.

He jogged down to the Charles River and did his three-mile run along the esplanade, his mind preoccupied with the fair-haired, green-eyed impostor. She had as much as admitted that she was no Harling.

Then who was she? A con woman? A nut? Had one of his friends put her up to this charade as part of some elaborate practical joke?

What was that nonsense about hanging?

Her eyes had seemed even more luminous in the soft lamplight, their irises as green and lively as the spring grass. Half of her had seemed humiliated by having met a real Harling, but the other half had seemed challenged, even angry. She hadn't, he would guess, chosen the Harling name out of admiration.

So, what was her game?

Sweating and aching, Win returned to the drafty house he had bought a year ago. It needed work. He could hire the job out, but he wanted to do it himself, with his own hands.

He grimaced, turning on the shower, trying to erase from his mind the image of his hands, not smoothing a piece of wallboard, but the impostor's soft, pale skin... touching her lips...stroking her throat....

He turned the faucet to cold and climbed in, welcoming the shock of the icy water on his overheated skin. But the heat of his arousal was not easily quenched, and the image remained. Fund-raising dinners, art lectures, his uncle's club, Vancouver, even his own street. The woman had invaded every corner of his life. And now his mind, as well. His body was responding to the simple thought of her tongue intertwined with his.

"She must be a witch," he muttered.

Then he had it.

He no longer felt the cold of the shower. He shut off the water and reached for a towel. He barely noticed the continued swollen state of his arousal.

A witch.

Of course.

The pale, silken hair…the green eyes…the anger… the accusation about threatening to have her hanged…

His impostor was a Marsh.

CHAPTER THREE

HANNAH WAITED until morning, when she'd fully collected her wits, before calling Cousin Thackeray in Maine. "Jonathan Winthrop Harling," she announced to him, "is not the only Harling in Boston."

Her elderly cousin didn't comment right away, and Hannah used the moment of silence to quickly close the shutters, an easy process, since she was on a cordless phone. There was no point in inviting trouble, in case her black-eyed Harling decided to search Beacon Hill for her. She didn't trust him to be above looking into people's windows to find a woman posing as a Harling.

"Well," Cousin Thackeray said carefully, "I could be a bit out of touch. I haven't been to Boston myself in… oh, it must be fifty or sixty years."

Hannah gritted her teeth. "Then for all you know Boston could be crawling with Harlings."

"No, no, I doubt that."

"Thackeray," she blurted, "I'm in big trouble."

She told him everything, start to finish. He listened without interruption, except for an occasional gasp or sigh. It wasn't a pretty story.

When she finished, he said, "You've been posing as a *Harling?* Oh, Hannah."

"What's done is done, Thackeray. And now I need to talk to the elder Harling—this Jonathan Winthrop. I still want to examine the Harling Collection."

"Hannah, I want you to listen to me." Her cousin sounded very serious. "The Harling Collection doesn't exist. It never existed. The Harlings made it up to drive folks like you crazy."

"But I have reason to believe—"

"Trust me on this one, Hannah. It doesn't exist."

"If it does, Thackeray, it could well contain information that could provide insight into Cotton Harling's thinking when he signed the order for Priscilla's execution."

Her cousin was apparently unmoved. "It doesn't exist. Give up your search for it at once. Come home, Hannah. If the Harlings find out a Marsh is in town…"

"I'm not finished with my research here," she countered stubbornly.

Cousin Thackeray sighed, clearly not pleased. "You have a plan, I presume?"

"No, not really. I just want to find this old Harling— Jonathan Winthrop—and try to explain everything to him."

"He won't understand."

"Just because he's a Harling?"

"And because you're a Marsh," Thackeray Marsh added.

"Well, I'll have to take my chances with him. I suppose I could have explained to this younger Harling last night…." She inhaled, remembering the black eyes fixed on her, the arrogance. "But it didn't seem the time or place."

Her cousin grunted. "What, was a good hanging tree nearby?"

Hannah made a face. "That's not very funny."

"It wasn't a joke." He sighed. "You'll do what you'll do. You always do. If you need help, give me a holler. You know where I am."

"Thanks." But she could feel her heart thumping, and knew she should heed his advice. "I know I can always count on you."

He muttered something under his breath and hung up. Hannah gathered her materials and stuffed them into her canvas bag, promising herself an ordinary day of research at the New England Athenaeum. No hunting down Harlings today…unless, of course, she got a really good lead on old Jonathan Winthrop, one that would allow her to bypass the black-eyed Harling. She suspected that he was most likely devising his own plan to track *her* down.

As HE ENTERED the Tiffany reading room of the New England Athenaeum, Win noticed the dour portrait of an ancestor above the mantel. He had to admit there was a family resemblance. Although not a member of the venerable institution, he doubted he would be turned out on his ear.

He introduced himself to the middle-aged woman behind the huge oak front desk. She showed Win back to Preston Fowler's office immediately.

"Mr. Harling," Fowler said, rising quickly from a chair

old enough to once have belonged to Ben Franklin, "what a pleasant surprise. What can I do for you?"

"Win, please." He turned on the charm. It was mid-morning, and he had already shocked his assistant by phoning in to say that he'd be late and she should re-schedule his morning appointments. "I believe one of my relatives is in town."

"Well, yes, of course. I assumed you knew. I under-stand she's your cousin...."

"We're not close." His wife in one place, his cousin in another. She should keep her story consistent, Win thought.

"So I've begun to gather. She's been trying to locate your uncle. I haven't given out his private address, of course, but I did tell her she might find him at his club. I hope there's no problem."

"Not at all."

So, she was after Uncle Jonathan. No wonder she'd been so shocked when she'd run into him yesterday in-stead. They were both called Jonathan Winthrop Har-ling, something Win would guess she hadn't realized.

"She's from Ohio—Cincinnati, I believe."

Like hell. "I see. And she's attending Saturday's fund-raising dinner?"

"Yes, she is. She's not officially a member of the li-brary and wants to repay us for permitting her to use our facilities for her research."

"Her research?"

"She's a historian. I'm not sure precisely what her

project is, but she's very interested in the Harling family."

No doubt, Win thought. The more she knew about the Harlings, the better chance she'd have of continuing her ruse of posing as one of them. "Do you have any idea what she wants with my uncle?"

"Just to meet him, I should imagine."

"And she hasn't mentioned me," Win said.

Fowler shook his head. He obviously didn't want any trouble with the Harlings. Win didn't judge the man. He had a tough job, trying to maintain an aging building and a priceless collection on what he could beg from a bunch of tightfisted Boston Brahmins. Uncle Jonathan's idea of a generous donation wouldn't keep the rare book room climate-controlled for a day.

"I'm not sure she's aware you're in Boston," the library director said carefully.

Undoubtedly not. Win spun an old globe, from the days of the British Empire. "Is it too late to purchase a ticket for the fund-raising dinner? I'd like to attend."

Fowler obviously struggled to contain his excitement: it was no secret Win had a hell of a lot more money than his uncle did.

"We would love to have you—I'll attend to the details myself. Oh, and if you would like to meet your cousin, she might be in the stacks. I'm sure I saw her earlier this morning."

Win felt his adrenaline surge, but said nonchalantly, "Really? If you don't mind, I'd like to see her."

"I can send someone after her…."

"No, that's all right. I'll go myself."

HANNAH WAS FLIPPING through a book of fasting sermons from the seventeenth century when she heard footsteps below her. The old-fashioned stacks had been formed by dividing the space between the tall ceilings in two, then making a floor in between of translucent glass and adding curving, wrought-iron stairs and bookshelves. It was easy to detect another person wandering about. Only, she thought, this person sounded very purposeful…even sneaky.

She closed her book and set it back upon the shelf. She was sitting cross-legged on the thick glass floor at the far end of a row of shelves. Below her, through the translucent glass, she could see the shadow of a tall figure. It wasn't one of the library staff. She was sure of that.

Listening carefully, not moving, Hannah heard the figure walk steadily up and down the stacks below her. The footsteps never paused, never varied their pace. It was as if whoever was down there was looking, not for a book, but for a person.

Me.

The figure reached the end of the row below her, then she heard the sound of footsteps on metal as it started to climb to her level.

Instinct brought Hannah to her feet. Launched her heart into a fit of rapid beating. Tightened her throat.

The footsteps came closer.

She slipped down to the end of her row and moved

soundlessly past the next one, and the next, until she was at the far end, near the stairs.

The figure climbed the last stair and stepped onto her level. It was her black-eyed rogue of a Harling.

Oh, no....

Hannah slipped back behind the shelves and waited, not breathing, while he moved all the way to the end of the stacks. She knew he would then methodically walk up and down each row until he found her.

Then what?

Sweat breaking out on her brow, she heard him start on the far row. She ducked up her row so that he wouldn't spot her when he reached the end of his. She could try to keep this up, but he'd eventually catch up. Why not just pop out and hope she scared him to death? Why not just explain herself? Apologize?

Yeah, and you can get on your knees and beg a Harling for forgiveness while you're at it.

Priscilla Marsh hadn't begged. She'd gone to her death with her pride and dignity intact.

Hannah decided to take what little pride and dignity she had left and get the blazes out of here. He'd hear her on the stairs—no question about it. But she'd have a head start, she knew her way around the library, and if she was lucky...

Since when can a Marsh count on luck around a Harling?

She had to count on her wits...and maybe on a little gall.

Speed being more critical than silence, she darted

down the row and hit the stairs at a full gallop, taking them two and three at a time.

Above her, she heard her pursuer curse.

She swung down to the next level and scooted through the stacks, zigzagging her way to the small corridor in the far right corner. Preston Fowler had loaned her the key to the rare book room. She came to the heavy door that marked its entrance, stuck in the key, and, relying on stealth, quietly pulled the door open and slipped inside.

Without turning on the light, she pressed her ear against the door and waited.

WIN FIGURED she'd locked herself in the rare book room. He also figured his uncle would never forgive him if he made a scene in the venerable New England Athenaeum by hauling a pretty, blond-haired Marsh out by her ear. Preston Fowler would have questions that Win couldn't answer and Hannah Marsh, if that was her name, no doubt wouldn't answer.

So, he rapped on the door and said, "I know you're in there."

Naturally she didn't answer.

"You haven't stopped pretending you're a Harling," he went on. "Until you do, I have no intention of leaving you alone."

He waited, just in case she had something to say.

Apparently she didn't.

"By the way, I would say you have my uncle and me confused. We're both named Jonathan Winthrop Harling."

He heard a muffled thud. Had Ms. Hannah pounded her head against the door? He would guess he knew more about her and her devious plans than she expected him to know. Certainly more than she wanted him to know.

"You'd better leave my uncle out of this," he said in his deadliest voice. "I won't warn you again on that score."

Her voice came to him through the door, sounding very clear and surprisingly close: "What're you doing? Tying the noose even now?"

The woman was incorrigible.

In no mood to make her life any easier, Win tiptoed away, so she wouldn't know he had gone.

HANNAH SWEATED IT OUT in the rare book room for another hour.

There were two Jonathan Winthrop Harlings in Boston. All her leads had pointed her in the direction of the wrong one, and as far as she could tell, she was doomed.

Doomed.

But when she went back down to the main reading room, no one treated her like an impostor. Preston Fowler and his staff apparently continued to believe she was a Harling, which was a relief, if a small one. It meant, she knew, that the younger Jonathan Winthrop Harling planned to deal with her himself in his own good time.

Hannah had no intention of waiting like the proverbial lamb for the slaughter.

On her way out, Preston Fowler said, "We'll see you tomorrow night at the dinner, Ms. Harling."

She smiled. "I'm looking forward to it."

She realized she would need a dress. Her Harling clothes were all for day, and her Hannah Marsh clothes— *my clothes,* she reminded herself—were too casual. So, she headed off to Newbury Street, just a few blocks down from the New England Athenaeum. It was one of Boston's most chic and high-priced shopping districts. There wouldn't be much she could afford.

Her black-eyed Jonathan Winthrop Harling, however, could probably buy out the whole street and have plenty left over.

WIN HAD A HELL OF A TIME trying to concentrate that afternoon, and it was almost with relief that he greeted a grim-faced Paula bringing him news of another bit of larceny performed by Hannah of the Midwest Harlings.

"Is she my cousin today," he asked, "or my wife?"

His assistant didn't seem to appreciate his wry humor. "Your wife. The owner of the shop on Newbury Street where you buy your ties just called. A woman fitting the description of the impostor was in earlier and bought a black evening dress on your tab. He faxed me the bill." Paula handed it over. "You will note that she signed her name as Mrs. Hannah Harling."

"Arnie didn't believe her?"

"Oh, no, he believed her. He just called to congratulate you on your wedding. I think he's hurt he wasn't invited."

Win looked at the bill and inhaled, controlling an urge to pound his desk or throw things. The price of the dress was staggering. It was, he knew, Hannah Marsh's way of thumbing her nose at him.

"I was the one who had him fax the bill," Paula said.

"Did you give him a reason?"

She shook her tawny curls. "He should have asked for identification or at least called you before he let her have the dress. She must be awfully convincing."

For sure. Arnie was no pushover. Still, he wasn't alone in not wanting to annoy a Harling. "Call Arnie back," Win instructed her. "Tell him Hannah jumped the gun and we're not married yet."

Paula's eyes widened. "Yet?"

"The point is, I will pay for the dress. This impostor isn't Arnie's problem. She's mine."

THE DRESS WAS AWFUL, and Hannah decided she couldn't wear it. It was too…Boston. Too matronly. Too something. She stood in front of the full-length mirror in her borrowed bedroom an hour before the New England Athenaeum dinner and tried to figure out what wasn't right about a dress that had cost as much as this one.

She had bought it in a fit of pique when she'd only wanted to strike out at Jonathan Winthrop Harling. Now the Harlings really had grounds for throwing her in jail. But better to hang for a three-thousand-dollar dress, she'd decided, than a fifty-dollar lunch.

Was she crazy?

Not only was the dress not her style, it also wasn't, in fact, hers. Never mind that it was in her possession.

Harling money had—or would—pay for it. She hadn't even removed the tags.

And wouldn't. She would take the thing back on Monday. Twenty-four hours of sitting alone in her borrowed apartment, doing her work, being the studious, law-abiding biographer she was, had enabled her to think. Not even a Harling would turn her into an out-and-out thief.

A smarter decision would have been not to go tonight. The prospect, however remote, of bumping into her black-eyed Harling on his own territory didn't thrill her. But how could she just drop everything and head back to Maine? It just wasn't in her to run.

She rummaged around in her closet and found the dress she'd picked up at a vintage clothing store in Harvard Square. It was not a Harling dress, and it hadn't cost three thousand dollars. It hadn't even cost fifty.

But it was her.

"YOU'RE SURE SHE'S A MARSH?" Uncle Jonathan asked when Win picked him up. Naturally his uncle had insisted on going to the Athenaeum's fund-raising dinner, once he knew their impostor was potentially a Marsh and would be there.

Win nodded grimly. "I'm positive."

"I should have guessed it myself. The blond hair's a dead giveaway."

"You can hardly suspect every blonde you see of being a Marsh without further evidence."

"You'd better watch yourself, Winthrop." Uncle Jonathan climbed into the front passenger seat. "If she's a Marsh, she's after something. Any idea what?"

"None."

"The Marshes have never let us forget Priscilla. They refuse to understand that Cotton was a man of his times, a flawed human being just doing his job."

Win frowned at his uncle. "He had an innocent woman hanged."

"He wasn't the first, nor the last."

There was no point in arguing. Win pulled into traffic, trying to concentrate on the road and not on what was coming up this evening.

"Think she'll risk showing up tonight?" his uncle asked.

Win had already considered the question, given what had transpired yesterday morning, but it had only one answer. "She wouldn't miss it."

HANNAH ARRIVED EARLY at the exclusive seafood restaurant on the waterfront where the New England Athenaeum's fund-raising dinner was being held. Preston Fowler greeted her warmly. Before he could introduce her to anyone as a Harling, she slipped off to the bar, ordered a glass of white wine and found her table. Mercifully, it was at the far end of the room, but still had a good view of the entrance.

She sipped her wine, watching Boston's upper crust filing in, dressed in its spring finery. She saw a dress much like the one she had rejected. It looked curiously right on its owner, just as it had looked wrong on her.

What a long night she had ahead of her, she thought, if all she had to do was notice what people were wearing....

An old man with a cane shook hands with Preston Fowler. Hannah shifted in her chair, her interest piqued. She had seen him somewhere before.

Salt, she thought, for no apparent reason.

Lunch at the private club on Beacon Street.

Her heartbeat quickened, her fingers stiffened on her wineglass, and she said to herself, "The old man with—"

But she didn't finish.

Across the room, the younger Jonathan Winthrop Harling's black eyes nailed her to her seat.

"Oh, no," Hannah whispered.

Her first impulse was to tear her eyes away and pretend she hadn't seen him, but she resisted just in time and met his gaze head-on. She even smiled. She made everything about her say he didn't intimidate her. She could take on him—a Harling—and win.

If ever a pair of eyes could burn holes in someone, it would be the two fixed on her. Hannah felt an unwelcome, unbidden, primitive heat boiling up inside her. There was something elemental at stake here, she thought, something that had nothing to do with Harlings or Marshes or three-hundred-year-old grudges.

She raised her wineglass in a mock greeting, then took a slow, deliberate sip.

He was past Preston Fowler in a flash, threading his way through the crowd, aiming straight for her. His steps were long and determined, as if he'd just caught someone picking his pocket.

Then he was upon her.

The man, Hannah thought, strangely calm, was breathtaking. His dark suit was understated, sophisticated, highlighting the blackness of his hair and eyes, making him look all the richer and more powerful. To be sure, he was a descendant of robber barons and rogues, but also of an infamous seventeenth-century judge who'd hanged one of her own ancestors.

"I like the daffodils," he said in a low, dark voice.

"Do you?" She fingered the two she'd tucked into her hair; it was an un-Brahmin-like touch that went with her cream-colored, twenties tea dress. "I thought they were fun."

"They didn't go with your Newbury Street dress?"

So, he knew already. She licked her lips. "Not really, no."

"You're a thief," he said simply, "and a con woman."

She tilted her head to a deliberately cocky angle. "You know so much about me, do you?"

His eyes darkened, if that was possible. "I should, shouldn't I? We're supposed to be married."

Her mouth went dry. "I never said…"

"You didn't have to, did you? People assumed." He moved closer, so that she could see the soft black leather of his belt. "I wonder why."

The old man with the cane stumbled up to them, saving Hannah from having to produce a credible response when she could still barely speak. "So, you're our Cincinnati Harling," he said.

She managed a smile. "Word travels fast."

"This is my uncle," his nephew said, his tone daring her to persist. "Jonathan Harling."

She put out a hand to the old man. "I'm Hannah. It's a pleasure."

"Delighted to meet you. Welcome to Boston." He surprised her by placing a dry kiss upon her cheek, his eyes—Harling blue—gleaming with interest, missing nothing. He turned to his nephew. "You two have met?"

"Not formally," Hannah replied.

"No?" The old man clapped a hand on the younger Harling's shoulder. "This is my nephew, Win. J. Winthrop Harling."

So, it was true. There *were* two Jonathan Winthrop Harlings in Boston. Oh, what a mistake she'd made.

"It's a pleasure," she said, refusing to let the situation get the better of her.

But Win Harling murmured, "The pleasure's mine," and bent forward, kissing her low on the cheek. To all appearances, no doubt, it was a perfunctory kiss, not unlike his uncle's. Hannah, however, felt the warm brush of his tongue on the corner of her mouth, his hard grip as he took her hand. And she felt her own response; it was impossible to ignore. Her mind and body united in a searing rebellion, imagining, feeling, that warm brushing, not discreetly, against the corner of her mouth, but openly, hotly, against her tongue, against other parts of her body.

"If Priscilla Marsh was anything like you, Hannah Marsh," Win Harling said in a rough, low voice, "I can see what drove Cotton Harling to sign her hanging order."

CHAPTER FOUR

THE WOMAN WAS QUICK. Win would give her that much. She gave him a haughty look and threw back her shoulders regally, or as regally as anyone could manage in a silk tea dress from the twenties. The daffodils in her hair didn't help matters. But she said, "I don't know what you're talking about."

He laughed. He couldn't help himself.

She thrust her chin at him. He could still see the flush of pink, high on her cheeks, from his kiss. Obviously it had as powerful an effect on her as it had on him. "Why did you call me Hannah—who?"

He decided to indulge her. "Marsh."

"And Priscilla—it was Priscilla, wasn't it?"

"Yes."

"This Priscilla Marsh. Who is she?"

"Your great-great-great-great—oh, I don't know, I'd give it five greats—grandmother. She was hanged by a Harling three hundred years ago."

"I see," she said, apparently trying her damnedest to sound confused. Win knew she wasn't confused at all.

"Her statue is on the State House lawn."

"Oh!" Hannah smiled suddenly, as if finally getting it. "You mean the witch."

Look who was calling who a witch, Win thought, but kept his mouth shut. He was already out several thousand dollars, thanks to Priscilla's great-whatever and was beginning to feel the bewitching effects of her eyes, her luscious, pink mouth.

"I've read about her," Hannah said.

"Every real Harling knows about Priscilla Marsh and Judge Cotton Harling."

"I don't."

"You're not a real Harling. You're a Marsh."

She sighed. "Well, I'm not going to argue with you. Shouldn't you and your uncle be finding your seats?"

Uncle Jonathan had busied himself tracking down a couple of drinks. Win sat down in the empty chair next to Hannah Marsh. "Preston Fowler thought the Harlings should sit together."

"How nice," she said, clearly not meaning it. She pursed her lips, trying to buy time, Win suspected, to think of a way to wriggle out of the tight spot she'd squeezed herself into. "If you're so certain of who I am, why haven't you told anyone?"

"You're a smart woman. Figure that one out for yourself."

"With a Harling, it usually boils down to reputation."

Win indicated his uncle, who was making his way through the crowd, carrying two drinks. "If it weren't for him, I'd stand right up on this table and expose you to everyone here for the lying thief you are. But Uncle Jonathan..." He narrowed his eyes on her and saw the spots of pink in her cheeks deepen under his penetrating gaze. "He deserves better."

"I can explain, you know. Or won't you give me the chance?"

"What mitigating circumstances might there be for you to charge an expensive dress to my account?"

Her lips parted slightly, her eyes shone. She dragged her lower lip under her top teeth, a habit, Win guessed, when she was caught red-handed. "You asked for it," she challenged him. "There isn't a court in the country that would convict me—unless a Harling was the presiding judge."

"You have to be a Marsh. Only a Marsh would hold someone responsible for what one of their ancestors did three hundred years ago."

She shrugged, neither accepting nor denying his accusation.

Uncle Jonathan arrived with the drinks. "Here you go, Winthrop. Did I miss any excitement?"

"No, not at all." His eyes didn't leave Hannah. "We were just discussing genealogy."

"Boring stuff." Uncle Jonathan sniffed. "Let the dead bury the dead, I say."

Since when? No one was more adamant on the subject of the Marshes' long-standing grudge against the Harlings than Win's uncle. Win glanced at him but said nothing.

"Well, Miss Harling," his elderly uncle said, "how do you like our fair city so far?"

She graced him with one of her beguiling smiles. Her

eyes skimmed over Win, as if he were a cockroach she was pretending she hadn't noticed. "Please," she said, "just call me Hannah."

"My pleasure."

Win scowled at his uncle; he knew the woman was a liar and very likely a Marsh, yet he was still trying to charm her. She might look innocent, and she certainly was attractive, but Win wasn't fooled. She'd already cost him too much time and money.

Hannah gestured toward the glittering view of Boston Harbor. "Boston's a lovely city. I'm glad I can appreciate other places without wanting to give up my own life. I know people too afraid to appreciate somewhere else, because they believe it might make them think less of where they live, and others who can only appreciate places they don't live."

Uncle Jonathan stared at Hannah for a few seconds, blinked, sipped his drink and looked at Win, who from years of experience with his uncle already knew what was coming. "What did she say?"

"She likes Boston but doesn't want to live here," he translated, turning to Hannah. "Uncle Jonathan's a bit hard of hearing."

"I'm not. I just didn't understand what in hell she was saying."

Win wondered if he'd be as blunt in his eighties or have as tolerant a nephew. What Hannah was doing, he knew, was saying whatever popped into her head to keep the conversation going before one of the real Harlings at the table decided to call her bluff in public.

"I'm sorry," she apologized quickly, "I've had a long day."

"You're not going to plead a stomachache and make a fast exit, are you?" Win challenged her with an amused grin.

Her luminous eyes fastened on him, any hint of embarrassment gone from her cheeks. There was only anger. The zest for a good fight. "You'd like that, wouldn't you?"

"Just wondering how hot it will have to get before you bow out."

"I don't care what you think. I know who I am."

"And who is that?"

She gave him a small, cool, mysterious smile. "That's for me to know and for you to find out."

Before Win could respond, Preston Fowler came up between them and clapped a hand upon each of their shoulders. "You found each other all right, I see. Glad you could make it. People are delighted to have the Harling family active in the New England Athenaeum again. Hannah, have you talked to your cousin and uncle about your family history? Jonathan here is quite an authority. He might have family papers pertinent to your research that aren't part of our collection."

He spotted another couple entering late and made his apologies, quickly crossing the restaurant.

Uncle Jonathan looked at Hannah. "Didn't know I had a niece in Cincinnati."

Win watched her smooth throat as she swallowed. She

said, "I sort of exaggerated our relationship, so I could use the library for my research."

"Sort of?" Win asked wryly.

She scowled at him. "Believe what you want to believe."

"I will."

"What kind of research?" Uncle Jonathan asked.

"Oh, I'm just looking into my roots."

"Why?"

"Curiosity."

Uncle Jonathan sniffed. He pulled at Win's sleeve and whispered, "She's a Marsh, all right. I know just what she's after."

Hannah was frowning, obviously certain Jonathan Harling wasn't saying anything positive. Win, seated between them, turned to his uncle. "What's that?"

"The Harling Collection."

Win had never heard of it.

"I'll explain later," Uncle Jonathan told him, just as Hannah Marsh saw her opening and jumped to her feet.

Win grabbed her by the wrist with lightning speed. "Don't leave," he urged amiably. "You paid for dinner with your own money."

She licked her lips guiltily.

Win gritted his teeth.

"I started to pay with my own money," she explained, "but then I…well, one of the staff asked me if they should just send the bill along to you, and I said sure, why not?"

He didn't release her wrist. He didn't know how she managed to look so damned innocent. So justified.

"I also put you down for a five-hundred-dollar donation," she added.

"Sit."

"You won't make a scene. I know you won't."

"Sit down, *now*."

She batted her eyelids at him, deliberately, cockily.
"Shall I beg, too?"

"It could come to that."

He spoke in a low, husky voice, and it was apparently
enough to drop Hannah Marsh back into her chair. The
spots of pink reappeared in her cheeks. Her breathing
grew rapid, light, shallow. She drew her lower lip once
more under her top teeth.

"I'm going to find out what you're after," Win said.
"And if I have to, I'll stop you."

She gave him a scathing look. "Spoken like a true
Harling."

It wasn't a compliment.

HANNAH GOT OUT her checkbook the moment she returned
to her Beacon Hill apartment and wrote out a check to J.
Winthrop Harling for every nickel she owed him.

When she had refused their offer of a ride home, Win
Harling and his uncle had insisted on getting her a cab.
She was quite sure they'd heard her give her address
and wished, belatedly, she'd lied. But she was getting
tired of lying.

She was not a liar. She was not a thief.

She had merely adopted an unwise strategy, that was
all. Pretending to be a Harling had been a tactic. An

expedient. She wasn't out to get the Harlings. She just wanted to write the definitive biography of Priscilla Marsh. She, Hannah Marsh, had always played by the rules. She didn't look for trouble.

But she'd found it in spades, hadn't she?

Her check made out, her bank account drawn down to next to nothing, she called Cousin Thackeray in southern Maine. She was still wearing her twenties tea dress.

Thackeray answered on the first ring.

"I'm in trouble," she began, then told him everything.

Her cousin didn't hesitate to offer his advice when she finished. "Come home."

It was tempting. She could picture him in his frayed easy chair, with rocky, beautiful Marsh Point stretched before him. From her own cottage nearby, she could see the rocky shoreline, tall evergreens, wild blueberry bushes, loons and cormorants and seals hunting for food. Even now she could conjure up the smell of the fog, taste the salt in it. Marsh Point was the closest thing she had ever had to a real, permanent home. She would go back. There was no question of that.

But not yet.

"I can't," she said before she could change her mind. "I have a job to do and I'm going to do it. I won't be driven from Boston by anyone."

"Driven?" There was a sharpness, a sudden protectiveness, in Thackeray's voice that made her feel at once wanted and needed, a part of the old man's life. He was family. "Have the Harlings threatened you?"

"Not in so many—well, yeah, in so many words. But don't worry. I can handle myself."

"Shall I drive down?"

Just what she needed. An eighty-year-old man who hated cities, particularly hated Boston, and really and truly hated the Harlings. He would, at the very least, get in the way. And she doubted he could do anything to get her out of hot water with Win Harling.

"No, I'll be fine."

He hissed in disgust. "You're not still after that Harling Collection, are you?"

She sighed. "I'd like to know at least if it exists."

"Can't you take my word for it that it doesn't?"

"Cousin Thackeray…"

"Come home, Hannah. You've done enough research on Priscilla. Just pack up and come home."

Although he was over a hundred miles away, and couldn't see her, Hannah shook her head. "You yourself have said that for the past three hundred years the Harlings have been tough on Marshes who don't kowtow to their power and money. Well, I won't. I'll leave Boston when I'm ready to leave Boston and not a minute sooner."

Cousin Thackeray muttered something about her stubborn nature and hung up.

Hannah was too wired to sleep. Work, she knew, was always the best antidote for a distracted mind. But when she sat at her laptop computer, she thought not of Priscilla Marsh and Cotton Harling, but of J. Winthrop Harling. His searing black eyes. His strong thighs. His sexy, challenging smirk.

Such thinking was unprofessional and unproductive.

Definitely not scholarly.

And as for objectivity… How could she be objective about a man who made her throat go tight and dry, even when she just looked at him? Win Harling could have passed for a rebel who'd helped rout the British, dumped tea into Boston Harbor, tarred and feathered Tories. He was tough and sexy and didn't fit her image of a Harling at all.

Clearly she needed to restore her balance and perspective. But how?

"Give the bastard his money," she muttered, "and hope it makes him happy."

"IT'S A SHAME," Uncle Jonathan said, having agreed to meet his nephew for Sunday morning breakfast, "that an attractive woman like that—bright, gutsy, clever—turns out to be a Marsh."

Win blew on his piping-hot coffee, then took a sip. The café at the bottom of Beacon Hill wasn't crowded, but he had still chosen a table at the back, in case Ms. Hannah, apparently also a Beacon Hill resident, blundered in. He needed to concentrate; he'd found he couldn't when she was near.

"If she wasn't a Marsh," his uncle continued, "she just might be the woman for you, Winthrop. She'd make you think about something besides work, I'd allow."

She already had, but Win said, "Uncle Jonathan, I didn't ask you here to discuss my love life. Now…"

"You need a woman."

Win sighed. "That's a rather blunt statement."

"It's true. You're waiting for fate to take a hand and present you with the woman of your dreams. I say she's out there somewhere and you need to hunt her down."

"Like a buffalo?"

"More like an antelope, I think. Maybe a tigress."

"Uncle Jonathan…"

"Well, Win, what can I say? You work too hard. You don't pay enough attention to your personal life. Dating women isn't the same as finding the woman meant for you. And don't tell me that's romantic nonsense, because it's not."

Win knew a change of subject was in order. He didn't want to argue, and not just because he didn't want to sit through another of his uncle's lectures on marriage and little ones. Anything Win said would bring up, however indirectly, Uncle Jonathan's own unhappy life. He had lost his wife to cancer twenty-five years ago, his only child, a daughter—a cousin Win had adored—to a car accident ten years back. The kind of life Jonathan wanted for his nephew meant that Win would have to set himself up for tragedy. Right now he preferred to keep his risks financial.

"Tell me about the Marshes," he said.

That distracted his uncle. He poured cream into his coffee and began a lecture on the Marsh-Harling feud of the past three hundred years, sounding like the history professor he'd once been. Win listened carefully.

"I wouldn't think," he said after a while, "that reasonable people would blame an entire family for the conduct of one of its ancestors. Right or wrong, Cotton's been dead a long time."

"The Marshes will capitalize on his mistake whenever they see an opening. That's how they ended up with a chunk of prime southern Maine real estate that's rightly ours."

"Ours? What do you mean?"

"About a hundred years ago the Marshes swiped a lovely piece of coastal land from the Harlings. They stole the deed from us and claimed they'd bought the land first. No one could prove otherwise. It's theirs to this day." He grimaced. "They call it Marsh Point."

"And the Harling Collection," Win said. "Tell me about it."

"About the same time the Marshes appropriated our land in Maine, a Harling—Anne Harling—gathered the family papers together into a collection."

"I never knew—"

Uncle Jonathan held up a hand, stopping him. "It's never been proven to exist. It disappeared not long after Anne finished putting it together. Nobody's ever produced a credible theory of what happened to it."

"And you think our Hannah Marsh is after it?"

"Yep."

Win shook his head. "It doesn't explain her behavior. Why would she lie to us and steal from us if she expected us to hand over the Harling Collection for her to examine?"

His uncle lifted his bony shoulders, then let them drop; he sighed heavily. "She doesn't expect us to hand it over."

"What do you mean?"

"I mean," his uncle announced, "she plans to *steal* it."

HANNAH ENDURED A disturbingly quiet Sunday. Twice she ventured into Louisburg Square. Nothing seemed out of the ordinary. But then, how would she know? The Harling House stood bathed in spring sunshine, giving away none of its secrets. She debated venturing up the steps and sticking her check into its mail slot. It would mean a lean winter ahead, but would restore her sense of pride. But she decided against leaving it. It had her name imprinted at the top, and she wasn't sure she wanted Win Harling to have her name confirmed for him, at least, not yet. First she had to find a way of explaining what she'd done, making him—or his uncle—understand her motives.

By Monday morning she'd decided Win Harling couldn't learn much more about her than he already suspected. But she remained on her guard. She couldn't relax. If anything, the fund-raising dinner on Saturday could only have stimulated his desire to best her.

Stimulated his desire?

She cleared her throat, reacting to the unfortunate choice of words, and tried to dismiss the possibilities, but dozens of images flooded her mind.

Work. She had to keep working.

But when she arrived at the Athenaeum for a morning of what she'd promised herself would be disciplined research, a message was waiting for her. It was a note scrawled in black marker on a scrap of paper.

I suggest you come by my office in the Financial District today at noon. We need to discuss the Harling Collection and Marsh Point. If you value your reputation, you won't be late. I know who you are.

It was signed, arrogantly, just with Win Harling's initials, JWH.

Hannah stood rock still, feeling every drop of blood drain out of her. She read the note twice.

First of all, she now knew why he'd been in the well-armed building in the Financial District the other day; *his* office, not his uncle's, was there. Probably his uncle was retired and no longer had an office. Hannah hated making a mistake in her research, but never had one been as costly as this one.

"Well, no use crying over spilt milk," she muttered, reflecting that a lot more than milk could be spilled by the end of this affair.

Second, the Harling Collection. He'd figured out she was after it. Well, that she could understand. She had made no bones about looking into the Harling family history, and so could be expected to want to examine the Harling Collection, if it existed. Still, she would have preferred to have a chance to explain her real reasons for wanting access to it before Win Harling found her out. But so be it.

The mention of Marsh Point, however, she didn't understand. Why would he want to discuss Marsh Point? Did he know that was where she lived?

And just who did he think she was?

The library assistant who had handed her the note said, "He also left a book for you."

It was a copy of her biography of Martha Washington.

The bastard knew.

He knew!

"Well," Hannah muttered under her breath, "it's not as if you didn't see it coming."

But to threaten her reputation…

How like a Harling.

"Is something wrong, Ms. Harling?" Preston Fowler asked, emerging from his office.

"No. Not at all." She crumpled the note, stuffing it into the pocket of her squall jacket, and turned the book so that Fowler couldn't see the name of its author. She forced a smile. "Thanks for asking."

"Did you enjoy the dinner Saturday?"

"Yes—yes, I did. The food was wonderful, and I enjoyed having the chance to be with my relatives." She smiled, hoping she didn't look as flustered as she felt, but knew she'd always been particularly good at thinking on her feet. A Marsh trait, according to Cousin Thackeray. Of course, if she had listened to him, she might not be in the crummy position she was in right now. She'd be home in Maine, where she belonged. "If you'll excuse me, I'd like to get to work."

"Of course. Let me know if I can be of any assistance."

Would he be so willing to help if he knew she was Hannah Marsh and not Hannah Harling?

But she had a couple of hours before noon and refused to fall victim to obsessions about J. Winthrop Harling. Instead she tucked her notebook under her arm and proceeded to the second floor to the rare book room; the small, secure, climate-controlled space where Win Harling had trapped her the other day.

Amid her musty books, she began to relax. Come what might in her life, she always had her work.

She had already examined the most pertinent documents stored in the room, but there were several peripheral books and documents she wanted to look at. She got started.

After a relatively peaceful hour, disturbed only by moments of having to stomp on her unruly thoughts, she located a history of colonial Boston written in the early nineteenth century. On the inside front cover she spotted, in a faded handwriting, the name Jonathan Winthrop Harling and an address in the Back Bay section of Boston, just around the corner from where she was right now.

Win's uncle Jonathan. The old man with the cane. The man Hannah had intended to find in the first place, the only Harling supposed to be still in Boston. He must have donated the volume.

He had seemed reasonably charming on Saturday evening, and was still her best lead to the Harling Collection. If he hadn't moved, she could look him up herself, instead of going through his black-eyed, suspicious nephew. He might listen to her explanation of her behavior during the past week, to her legitimate reasons for wanting to examine the Harling Collection. He wouldn't threaten her reputation.

Neither would he threaten her peace of mind, create the kind of mental and physical turmoil his nephew did. He wasn't young and good-looking and too damned sexy for *her* own good.

She had time, if she hurried, to try and see Jonathan Harling before her summons to the Boston Financial District and the offices of J. Winthrop Harling. She gathered her papers, stuffed them into her satchel and headed out, hardly stopping to say goodbye to Preston Fowler.

Built on fill from the top of Beacon Hill, the Back Bay consisted of a dozen or so streets beyond the Public Garden, within easy walking distance. Jonathan Harling lived in a stately Victorian brownstone on the sunny side of Marlborough Street. Once a single-family dwelling, the building had been broken up into apartments, probably shortly before or during World War II. The name HARLING was printed next to a white doorbell, which Hannah rang.

There was no answer.

Her spirits sagged. Just her luck. She had hoped she could explain her situation and get him to contact his nephew to have him call off his witch hunt. If she were particularly persuasive, she might get the old man to talk to her about the Harling Collection and forgive her for her many transgressions. She *would* pay back his nephew.

She considered waiting on his front stoop until he returned, then realized that if she did, she would never make the Financial District by noon. Win Harling would only hunt her down. She owed it not to him but to herself to find out what he knew about her, how he'd learned it, whom he'd told and—most important—what he'd meant by his reference to Marsh Point.

Uncle Jonathan would have to keep.

CHAPTER FIVE

BY THE TIME she reached the modern federal building
and its armed guard, an appropriately blustery wind was
blowing off the water and dark clouds had rolled in.
Springtime in New England. Hannah hunched her shoulders against the cold. She had on a lightweight black
squall jacket, black pants and a pale yellow silk shirt,
a little less the proper Bostonian than on her previous
visit to the Financial District, but still not quite herself.
Cousin Thackeray, she remembered, had insisted the
Harlings and their crowd were a bunch of tightwads who
considered new clothes tackily nouveau riche. Dowdy,
worn-out, once-expensive clothes were the mark of a
true Boston Brahmin. They'd accept her a lot quicker,
he'd maintained, if she could show off a few moth holes.
Hannah had refused his offer to beat her clothes on the
rocks to make them look more authentically "old money."

Cousin Thackeray...

She couldn't have her feud with Win Harling touch
him.

The red-haired guard grinned at her, not making a
move for his gun as he might have been expected to,
given their last meeting. "Go right on up. Fourteenth
floor."

Hannah gave him an I-told-you-so smirk, but there was nothing in his expression that indicated he thought she had the upper hand. She dashed for the elevator and blamed its fast ascent to the fourteenth floor for the slightly sick feeling in her stomach and her sudden light-headedness. *Win knows about the Harling Collection... about Marsh Point....*

What could he have found out about Marsh Point?

Had Cousin Thackeray neglected to tell her something that he should have?

Checking the floor directory, she found her way to Win's office suite, entering a large, airy, L-shaped room, arranged so that both the reception area and corner office had windows with views of the city and the fountain plaza below.

A young woman greeted Hannah, who was a good ten minutes late. "Mr. Harling's waiting."

Hannah sensed the administrative assistant's disapproval; she obviously didn't like anyone keeping Mr. Harling waiting. The younger woman led the way, pushing open his door in an exaggeratedly professional manner she'd probably seen in old Joan Crawford movies.

J. Winthrop Harling's office was spacious, modern and spare, and Hannah was struck by its contrast to her own rustic, cluttered space overlooking Marsh Point. It was just more evidence that the two of them led totally different lives, and that she was an intruder. She was on his turf, and she wasn't the only one who knew it.

"Welcome." Win rose smoothly, his graciousness belied by the dark, suspicious expression in his eyes. He gestured to a leather chair in front of his gleaming desk. "Have a seat."

His assistant silently withdrew, shutting the door behind her.

Hannah shook her head. "Thank you, I prefer to stand."

"As you wish."

"I got your summons," she said coolly.

His mouth twitched, and he sat down, eyeing her. He was wearing a white shirt, its sleeves rolled up to mid-forearm, its top button undone, and had loosened his tie. Very sexy. His suit jacket was slung on a credenza to his right. His jaw looked even squarer than usual, but if Hannah could change only one thing about him, it would be his eyes. She'd fade them out, water them up a little, add some dark shadows and red lines. That done, surely the rest of him wouldn't seem nearly as appealing...or as dangerous.

"So," she said, crossing her arms over her chest, "who am I?"

"Hannah Marsh, the biographer."

She shrugged, neither confirming nor denying, but her heart was pounding. The man was relentless. But at least by leaving the Martha Washington biography for her, he'd given her fair warning of just what he knew.

He pushed a slender volume across his immaculate desk. It was her biography of three women married to famous robber barons of the nineteenth century. Like the study of Martha Washington, it had not been a bestseller. Win Harling would have had to dig to find her out.

"Okay," Hannah said unapologetically, "so I lied. In my position, wouldn't you have done the same?"

He made no apparent attempt to disguise his outright skepticism. After their rocky start, he was going to have a tough time believing anything she said. "Just what is your position?"

"Simply put, I'm a Marsh in Harling territory."

"There are just two Harlings in Boston." His tone was even and controlled, and all the more scathing for it. "My eighty-year-old uncle and me. Neither of us was disposed to harm or impede you in any way."

Hannah duly noted his use of the past tense. She decided she should keep her mouth shut until he finished.

Win sprang up and came around his desk, black walnut from the looks of it. Expensive. The man did know how to make money. "In my position, what would *you* do?"

She shrugged. "Leave me alone."

A smile, not an amiable one, tugged at the corners of his mouth. Hannah pushed aside the memory of that whisper of a kiss the other night.

"Wouldn't you want to find out what a woman posing as a member of your family was up to?" he asked. "Especially given the history between our two families."

"A lowly biographer? Nope. I wouldn't waste my time with her."

His eyes narrowed. In her mind, she washed out his black lashes. It didn't help. She still had to contend with the black irises.

"Wouldn't you think your behavior suspicious?" he asked.

"I'm not of a suspicious nature." She tilted her chin at him, unintimidated. They were fourteen floors up, in a well-guarded building. What could he do to her? "I'm a Marsh, remember? I don't think like a Harling."

He moved forward, so that they were only inches apart. She could smell his clean, expensive cologne and see a tiny scar at the corner of his right eye. It did not detract from the intensity of his gaze. "You're working on a biography of Priscilla Marsh."

"So?"

"So, it's a nice cover for what you're really after."

"The Harling Collection," she said calmly. "I don't know what nefarious purpose you have attributed to me, but I only want to examine it for research purposes. I want to do as thorough a job as possible on Priscilla Marsh's life. Examining the Harling Collection could be very helpful in understanding Cotton Harling's thinking when he had her hanged."

Cotton's descendant stared at her in dubious silence. It was outrageous, Hannah thought, how sexy she found him. What would Priscilla have thought?

"That's the truth," she continued. "I didn't know it was even rumored to exist until I'd arrived in Boston and started doing my research, identifying myself as a Harling so I wouldn't arouse suspicion and might get better treatment. When I came here the other day, I tried to get in to see you without giving a name. I wanted to talk to you about my research first and explain. Of course, I thought you were your uncle. I had no idea..." She took a breath and glanced at him. "You don't get it, do you?"

"Oh, I get it. Your devious plan backfired."

She scowled. "No, you don't get it. You think I'm up to no good and I'm telling you I'm not. I was just doing my best under difficult circumstances."

"Of your own making. How do you explain the dress?"

"That was personal," she snapped. "I owed you for hunting me down like a dog."

His mouth twitched again, and this time she was sure he wanted to smile. At what? *She* wasn't having any fun.

She reached into her pocket and produced the check, by now wrinkled, she'd written on Saturday night, and thrust it at him. She could still return the dress, but she'd included its price in her check. "Here, take it. It's reimbursement for the lunch, the dress, the dinner, the donation to the New England Athenaeum—everything."

"I don't want your money, Hannah."

"Then what do you want?"

His eyes darkened and she stopped breathing. *Stupid question, Hannah. Stupid, stupid.* His answer was obvious in the heat of his gaze, the tenseness of his body.

What he wanted was her.

Just as she wanted him.

Their physical attraction was a fact, unpleasant, distracting, constant. And just as there was nothing they could do about their relationship to Cotton Harling and Priscilla Marsh, there was nothing they could do about the primitive longing that had erupted between them.

Well, Hannah thought, there was something....

But that was crazy. He was a Harling. He was the enemy. She couldn't think about going to bed with him!

Did he know that was what she was thinking? Could he even guess it?

"Okay, okay, fine," she said quickly, before he could respond. "Have it your way."

She spun around, preparing to leave. Wanting to leave. She would return to Marlborough Street, talk to Jonathan Harling about the Harling Collection, and by-pass his know-it-all nephew altogether.

She got almost to the door before Win said, "The Harling Collection has been missing for at least a hundred years. Uncle Jonathan insists a Marsh stole it, just like a Marsh stole our land in southern Maine. Marsh Point, you call it now."

Stole Marsh Point? Damn, Cousin Thackeray! He must have known that was what the Harlings thought.

"Of all the—" Hannah whipped around, even more furious when she saw Win sitting calmly on the edge of his desk, watching her, waiting for her reaction. She pounded over to him, slinging her satchel. "That's what you think? That we've had the damned collection all along? Then why in hell would I risk life and limb try-ing to get in to see you to talk you into giving me ac-cess to it?"

"You tell me."

She groaned, itching to knock him off his high horse.

"So, you no longer deny that you're a Marsh," he said, rising.

It wasn't a question, but she said, "I never did deny it. I just didn't acknowledge it."

He touched her hair, wild from her mad dash across Boston, from the wind, from her anger. She fought the tingling sensation it caused. "A direct descendant of Priscilla Marsh?"

"The last."

He tucked a stray lock of hair behind her ear, letting his finger trace the outline of her jaw and creating a heat in her like none she'd known before. Then he dropped his hand to his side. "You're not from Ohio."

"I'm not from anywhere. I live in Maine now."

"Marsh Point."

"We didn't steal it." Her reply was based more out of loyalty to her cousin than on any certain knowledge.

"We have a case, you know. I've been looking into it. If we can prove the Marshes stole our deed, we can establish our right to the land." He remained close to her. "Until you showed up, I never paid much attention to Harling family history."

Hannah thought of Cousin Thackeray, who had been born on Marsh Point and wanted to die there. It was his home. Had he fried to talk Hannah out of going to Boston out of fear that she would rekindle the Harlings' claim to his slice of Maine?

Now Win Harling was on the case.

Thanks to her.

She faced him squarely. "What do you want from me?"

She saw the immediate spark of desire in his eyes and

held her breath, wondering if he could see it mirrored in hers. But he didn't touch her, didn't act on the sexual tension hissing between them like a downed and very dangerous electrical wire. Neither did she.

"All I want," he said, "is the truth."

"I've told you everything I know." Her voice was hoarse; she paused to clear her throat. She wondered if his uncle had been filling him with the same kind of nasty tales about the Marshes that Cousin Thackeray had told her about the Harlings. "I understand you have no reason to trust me, but I'm not here to reignite the Marsh-Harling hostility. I'm just doing my work."

"If I knew you better, maybe I'd find it easier to believe you."

She tried to ignore the sudden softness of his voice. The fox coaxing the chickens to open the henhouse door. "Does your uncle know about me?"

"He suspects you're a Marsh, but that's all."

"He won't approve of my writing Priscilla's story, will he?"

"I'm sure he'll question your objectivity."

"Do you think he knows what happened to the Harling Collection, if it ever existed?"

Win smiled. "If he does, he'd never tell a Marsh."

She hoisted her satchel onto her shoulder, preparing once more to leave. She'd see what Jonathan Harling knew and didn't know, and what she could talk him into doing. "Truce?"

"Cease-fire. I'll talk to Uncle Jonathan this afternoon." Win stared at her for a moment. "Dinner tonight?"

It was more a challenge than an invitation. Hannah felt her throat tighten, but nodded. "Okay."

"You're not staying at any hotel in Boston," he said. She assumed he remembered the address she had given the cabdriver after the fund-raising dinner.

"No, I borrowed a friend's apartment on Pinckney Street, right around the corner from you."

His eyes held her. "So we are neighbors."

"I guess so," she said cheerfully and fled, wondering what she had got herself into. Why hadn't she listened to Cousin Thackeray to begin with and steered clear of Boston altogether?

"WIN HARLING KNOWS EVERYTHING," Hannah told Cousin Thackeray from the kitchen phone. Her nerve endings were still on fire from her encounter with the wealthy Bostonian. She tried not to think of him simply as Win. That was too…personal.

Cousin Thackeray sniffed. "I told you this would happen."

"So, you did."

"You coming home?"

"Not yet. Thackeray, what do you know about a Harling claim to Marsh Point?"

Silence.

"Thackeray?"

"They don't have one."

"Not a legitimate one, I'm sure. But—"

"But nothing's ever settled with a Harling," he grumbled, half under his breath. "Win Harling's after my land?"

"I don't think so. He says he doesn't know much about Harling family history, so all this stuff's fresh for him. He could laugh it off, or he could decide to take up the Harling cause. I just want you to be prepared." Not, she thought, that her dear cousin had paid her the same favor.

Cousin Thackeray laughed without amusement. "I'm always prepared for a Harling."

Hannah wished she could say the same for herself.

HOURS AFTER HANNAH MARSH had left his office, Win was still trying to get her out of his mind. He walked home, hoping for distraction. The gusting wind, the traffic, the bustle of rush hour.

Nothing worked.

He made his way to Tremont Street off Boston Common, walking past the shaded grounds of Old Granary Burial Ground behind the First Congregational Church. Established in 1660, it was one of New England's oldest cemeteries. Thin, fragile, rectangular headstones stood at odd angles. Paul Revere was buried here, John Hancock, Samuel Adams, Ben Franklin's parents, the victims of the Boston Massacre.

And the man who had condemned Priscilla Marsh to death, Judge Cotton Harling.

He continued across Boston Common, welcoming its green grass and fluttering pigeons, its history. He crossed Charles Street and went through the Public Garden, where tulips and daffodils were in bloom. He didn't stop until he was in Back Bay, on Marlborough Street, letting himself into his uncle's brownstone with his key.

The door to his uncle's first-floor apartment was slightly ajar. Win creaked it halfway open. "Uncle Jonathan?"

He tensed when no response came.

Although Uncle Jonathan was not paranoid about city life, he was cautious and consistent about his personal security. He would never just step out for a quick walk and leave his door ajar, never mind unlocked. Had he been on his way out and stepped back inside because he'd forgotten something?

"Uncle Jonathan," Win called, raising his voice.

Still no response.

He went inside the apartment; its faded elegance made him feel as if he were taking a step back in time. Not wanting to startle his uncle, who might just be fine, Win shut the door hard and called him again as he headed from the small entry into the living room. Its bow windows looked onto Marlborough, and its Victorian style contrasted with the earlier Federal Period architecture of Beacon Hill.

"Good God!"

The place was a wreck.

Sofa cushions, drawers, shelves, the antique secretary; everything had been pulled out, tossed, scattered and left.

Win's heart pounded. *"Uncle Jonathan!"*

He leaped over books and magazines and papers and

pounded down the short hall to his uncle's two bedrooms and bath.

Jonathan Harling was sitting on the edge of his fourposter bed, staring at the small fireplace. He looked unharmed, if gray-faced and stunned. He rubbed a hand through his thin hair and peered at his nephew. "I heard you."

Win squatted beside the old man. "Are you all right?"

His blue eyes focused on Win, betraying not fear, but anger. "She could have asked."

"What?"

"Your Hannah Marsh. She could have asked. I'd have told her no one's seen hide nor hair of the Harling Collection since around 1892."

Win jumped to his feet, stifling a rush of anger. He wanted to go out and track down Hannah and wring the truth out of her beautiful, lying lips. But he resisted the temptation. He had his uncle to see to. "Come on, Uncle Jonathan. I'll make you some tea and we'll talk. You're sure you're all right?"

"Oh, yes. I came in after the damage was done. Nearly had a damned heart attack on the spot. Wouldn't that have delighted the Marshes no end?" He reached for his cane, which lay on the bed, and used it to pull himself upright. He appeared, indeed, remarkably steady. "They'll never be satisfied until they've killed off one of us, the way they say we killed off Priscilla."

"Uncle…"

He shook his cane at Win. "She's a witch, I tell you!"

"Are you saying Hannah trashed your apartment looking for the Harling Collection?"

"Now you're getting it."

Win indulged his uncle's crotchety mood, given the scare the old man had just had, not to mention the circumstantial evidence that appeared to point to her. "Did you see her?"

"Nope. She's too clever by far for that. But I called the neighbors upstairs. They saw her. I gave them a description. She's easy to spot, you know."

Win knew.

"They said she came by this morning while I was at the club."

"Have you called the police?"

"Nope." He shook his head and pointed his cane again at Win. "This is between her and us Harlings."

Leaving it at that for the moment, Win helped his uncle, who kept grumbling he didn't need any damned help, into the kitchen, which had been spared the upheaval of the other rooms. Win filled a kettle with water and put it on the old gas stove.

Uncle Jonathan sat at his little gateleg table and heaved a long sigh. "And such a pretty woman to be such a scurrilous thief. I thought she was the one for you, Win, Marsh or no Marsh. Those eyes of hers...well, I should have known. She's got nothing but larceny in her heart."

"I'm having dinner with her tonight."

"Good. You can fleece the truth out of her."

Win thought he already had. He pictured Hannah Marsh standing in his office, proud, indignant, sexy, a woman to be reckoned with, who wouldn't project her own insecurities onto him. She hadn't looked as if she'd just ransacked an old man's apartment.

But then, what did he know about the real Hannah Marsh? She had already proved herself capable of lying and scheming to get her way, no matter how honorable her cause or understandable her reasoning. If indeed they were honorable and understandable. He had only her word to go on.

The kettle whistled, and Win made his uncle a pot of tea and even had a cup himself, though he was not a tea drinker.

"We need to talk," he said. "Then I'll clean up the place."

"Don't cancel with Miss Marsh on my account."

"Oh, no." He regarded his uncle's pale face with growing anger. What was worth terrifying an eighty-year-old man? "I'll keep our date on your account."

Uncle Jonathan grinned feebly. "That's the spirit."

HANNAH SIPPED AT the glass of wine that Win had poured her and watched him whisk together raspberry vinegar and olive oil for the mixed green salad he'd thrown together. She hadn't expected dinner would be at his house. "What?" she'd asked upon entering the historic Beacon Hill mansion. "No maids?"

Win had smiled over his shoulder. "No furniture, either."

He wasn't exaggerating by much. Although the place retained its regal lines and potential, it needed work.

Win Harling clearly could afford to have it done. Why didn't he?

There was a lot, Hannah admitted, she didn't know about the man. A lot mere prejudice couldn't explain.

"I haven't been here that long—I wanted the house back in the family and snapped it up when I had the chance. I keep thinking I'd like to do the work myself, but I haven't gotten around to it."

He swirled the contents of the glass carafe, then added pinches of dried herbs from small unmarked containers. "How do you know what's what?" Hannah asked.

"Who says I do?"

A seat-of-the-pants cook. "Dinner should be interesting."

"Always."

The kitchen was large and drafty, this morning's dark clouds now pouring forth a cold, steady rain. Expecting a restaurant, Hannah had put on a simple dress and flats. Now she wished she'd brought a sweater.

"You're shivering," Win observed.

"Not really."

He pulled off his cardigan and tossed it to her. "Here, put this on."

"Won't you get cold?"

"Nope. Cooking always makes me hot." He had his back to her, but Hannah didn't need to see his expression to guess what he was thinking.

The sweater was old but bulky, a thick, cotton knit still warm from his body. She slipped it on. He was wider through the torso than she was, and his arms were longer. She pushed up the sleeves, the fabric soft and well-worn, like a caress against her skin. She licked her lips, suddenly feeling self-conscious, even somewhat aroused. Wearing his sweater was too much like having him hold her. Dinner maybe hadn't been a good idea, but she had to find out what he knew—what he intended to do—about Marsh Point. If anything. She'd stirred up this trouble; she'd see to it that it didn't reach Cousin Thackeray.

Win glanced back at her. "Better?"

"Yes."

He did not, she observed, look the least bit chilly himself in his close-fitting jeans and dark purple, short-sleeved pullover. She would bet it wasn't just the cooking that kept him warm, or even his all too apparent physical desire for her. There was also the fact that they were in his house, his city, on his turf. Easy for him to stay nice and toasty.

"What did you do today?" he asked casually.

"Not much. I spent most of the morning at the New England Athenaeum, met you, then headed up to the Boston Public Library. After that I went back to the apartment and entered my notes into my laptop."

Win got a small paper bag from the refrigerator and withdrew from it a mound of fresh linguine, which he promptly dropped into a pot of bubbling water. He scooped a cupful of the boiling water into a plain white pasta dish and swirled it around while the linguine cooked. "You didn't happen to wander over to Marlborough Street, did you?"

"Mmm…why would I?"

"I don't know." He stopped what he was doing and regarded her, his expression hard, challenging. "Why would you?"

Hannah licked her lips. "Am I being set up here?"

"Just tell the truth, Hannah."

"All right. I found your uncle Jonathan's address this morning in the rare book room. Before answering your summons, I took a walk over to Marlborough Street."

"Why?"

"To talk to him about the Harling Collection. I thought he'd know more than you would, and that he might be more reasonable than you would."

"Did you see him?"

"No, he wasn't in."

"How do you know?"

"What do you mean, how do I know? I rang his doorbell and he didn't answer. I assumed he wasn't home."

"Then you didn't go into his apartment?"

"No."

"What about this afternoon? Did you go back to Marlborough Street?"

She shook her head. "I decided to wait until we'd talked before trying to see your uncle again."

Win didn't say a word. Instead he picked up the bubbling pot and dumped the contents into a colander in the sink, steam enveloping him. He set down the empty pot. Hannah noticed the muscles in his back and upper arms, felt the raw sexiness of the man. Her careful preparations for dealing with the Harlings of Boston had been way off the mark.

He transferred the pasta to the warmed dish, then spooned on a herb and oil sauce and sautéed vegetables, tossing them with two forks.

"Why the interrogation?" Hannah finally asked.

"Because I don't know you." He brought the bowls of pasta and salad to the table, which wasn't set for dinner. "I don't know you at all, Hannah Marsh."

Suddenly he turned and lifted her by the elbows, slipping his hands under the heavy sweater and drawing her toward him. She didn't resist. To maintain her balance she let her palms press against his chest. It was even harder than she had anticipated. He drew her even closer, until she had little choice but to let her arms slide around his back. Now her breasts were pressed against his chest. She could feel the nipples turning into small pebbles. How much more of this could she stand?

How much more did she want?

Their eyes locked, just for an instant. She knew what he wanted. What she wanted.

Then his mouth closed over hers, hot and hungry, his tongue urged her lips apart, as if its probing would find all her secrets, answer all his questions. She felt herself responding. Her mind said she was crazy. He was a Harling, Cousin Thackeray had warned her, but her body didn't care. Her tongue did its own probing, its own urging. Her breasts strained against the muscles of his chest. He pushed one knee between her legs, pressing his hard masculinity against her, kneading her hips until she moaned softly, agonizingly, into his mouth. *Don't stop,* her body said, over and over. *Don't ever stop.*

But he took her by the shoulders and disentangled himself, pulling himself away. She felt swollen, frustrated, a little embarrassed. She couldn't read his expression. His eyes were masked, dark and mesmerizing.

"Did you ransack my uncle's apartment?" he asked hoarsely.

"What?"

"You heard me."

"No, I—of course I didn't!"

"You never went back to Marlborough Street?"

"I said no. What happened? Is your uncle all right?"

"Someone broke into his apartment. He's shaken up but otherwise fine."

She stepped back, increasing the physical and psychic distance between them. "So, that's what this is about. You're trying to weaken my defenses and get me to admit to something I didn't do. Well, you're way off base, Win Harling. I've told you the truth."

He nodded curtly. "Fair enough." He picked up the two bowls that stood on the table. "We'll eat in the dining room."

"I don't know how I can have dinner with you after— My God, I can't believe you'd think I could rob an old man!"

"Why not? Think of all the things you believe I'm capable of doing." He grinned at her over his shoulder. "Come on, Hannah. My doubts about you aren't upsetting you nearly as much as that kiss."

She grew cool. "I've been kissed before."

"But have you ever responded like that?"

It was only nominally a question. He had got it into his head that she hadn't. That he'd been the first man she'd let get to her like that with a first kiss. The problem was, he was right. Ordinarily she held back. Deliberately, easily. She had never before permitted herself to respond with such abandon, such openness.

A serious mistake, perhaps?

Well, what was done was done. He had used her. Manipulated her. Lowered her defenses so that he could pose his nasty question and catch her off guard. He hadn't been anywhere close to out of control.

But he had been aroused. No doubt about that.

As he led her down a short hall, she noticed its cherry floor needed sanding. They entered a chandeliered dining room with the ugliest wallpaper she'd ever seen. Parts of it had been peeled back, revealing a clashing, but prettier, paper underneath. The only furnishings were an antique grandfather clock, a massive, gorgeous, cherry table and a couple of folding, metal chairs that decidedly didn't match. The walls were wainscoted and the ceilings high, the windows looking onto a darkened courtyard. The table was set with cloth place mats and simple white porcelain plates.

"I'll get the wine," Win said and disappeared.

Alone in the dining room, Hannah took the opportunity to restore her composure. She wiped her still-sensitized mouth with a soft cloth napkin and listened to the ticking of the grandfather clock, letting it soothe her. Although the Harling House was in the middle of the city, it might have been on Marsh Point itself for all its quiet and sense of isolation, its potential for loneliness.

Suddenly she wondered if she and Win Harling had more in common than either wanted to admit. Perhaps what had them groping for each other wasn't just a physical attraction gone overboard, but a subconscious understanding of that commonality.

He returned with their two glasses and the bottle of wine.

"I should go," she said.

"I know. I should make you go." He refilled her glass. "But there's another matter we need to discuss."

She could think of several. "What's that?"

"A rare copy of the Declaration of Independence, possibly worth hundreds of thousands of dollars."

CHAPTER SIX

"I DON'T KNOW what you're talking about," Hannah said simply.

Win lighted two tall, slender, white candles and sat on the folding chair at one end of the table, watching her in the flickering light. She was, he thought, a bewitching woman. "I figured that was what you'd say."

"It's the truth."

"Tell me," he said, pausing to sip his wine. "How did you learn about the Harling Collection?"

"It was mentioned in passing in something I read. I can't remember offhand exactly what it was, but I keep exhaustive records. I could look it up."

"Why don't you?"

"I don't like your tone, Mr. Harling." Hers was assertive, bordering on angry. "And I'm not under any obligation to obey any orders from you."

He set down his wineglass and passed her the pasta bowl, noting the slenderness of her wrists, the unselfconscious femininity of her movements. "Tell me again why you want to get your hands on the Harling Collection."

"I don't want to 'get my hands' on it. I want access

to it—a chance to study it for anything it might contain pertinent to my work."

"Meaning anything on Priscilla Marsh or Cotton Harling."

"That's right."

"Then you're saying you didn't realize the Harling Collection is rumored to include a valuable, rare copy of the Declaration of Independence."

He could see his words sinking in, along with all their ramifications, and was suddenly glad they'd kissed before he'd brought up the touchy subject.

"Oh, I see what you're getting at." She bit off each word, anger visibly boiling to the surface. Her green eyes were hot, almost liquid. "You're accusing me of breaking into your uncle's apartment in an attempt to find the Harling Collection or some clue as to its location, in order to steal this Declaration of Independence and make a handy profit for myself at Harling expense."

Win scooped pasta onto her plate, and then onto his, maintaining his calm. "Only Uncle Jonathan doesn't know where the Harling Collection is. No one does. No one can even verify it exists, or ever did." His gaze fell upon her; it would be easier if she weren't so damned attractive. "Unless you have a new lead you're keeping to yourself."

She gave him a haughty look. "Why would you think that?"

He shrugged. "You're a scholar. You're good at doing research. Who knows what you might have ferreted out in the last week?"

"We're in quite a position, aren't we?"

Her voice rasped with not very well-suppressed fury, although, given her behavior this past week, Win couldn't understand why she was so irritated. Under the circumstances, he felt his suspicions were quite natural.

"By pretending to be a Harling," she went on, speaking tightly, "I shattered any trust you might have had in me, no matter how innocuous my intentions or how understandable my reasons. You still can't believe me. Won't believe me. Then there's the impact of three centuries of Marsh-Harling conflict...."

"It hasn't had any impact on me." Win tried his pasta; not bad. Hannah might calm down if she ate some. "Maybe it's had an impact on you, but not on me. I was hardly even aware of the extent of the grudge you Marshes hold against us."

"You're a Harling...."

"But not a Bostonian. I was born and raised in New York. I only came to Boston last year, when I bought this house and moved my offices."

She didn't seem particularly interested in his personal history, but he found himself wondering about hers. Where did Hannah Marsh live? How? And what made her tick?

"You had to know about Cotton and Priscilla," she said.

He smiled. "You talk about them as if you know them."

"That's my job, to feel as if I know the people I write about. It's pure arrogance to believe I do, but I have at least to have some sense of who they were. I have to feel that if they suddenly came to life in my kitchen, I'd recognize them." She caught herself and took a breath. "Not that I have to explain myself to you."

"Of course not. Yes, I was aware of Cotton and Priscilla, but I haven't participated in perpetuating three-hundred-year-old grudges."

"Well, aren't you high and mighty? I've been doing everything I can to maintain my objectivity. I don't have a personal grudge against the Harlings. And if you don't have anything against the Marshes, why check into your family's absurd claim to Marsh Point?"

"It's not absurd," he said offhandedly. "Actually, it's rather well-founded."

Her look would have shot holes in him if it could have. "There, you see? You're no saint, Win Harling."

"Oh," he said playfully, "that I'm definitely not."

He could see her recognizing his words as the multipronged threat he'd intended them to be. Even with the pasta and more wine, he could still taste her mouth, imagine the taste of her skin.

"The point is," she said a little hoarsely, "where do we go from here?"

His gaze held hers. In the old, candlelit room, she could have passed for her doomed ancestor. But Win couldn't make up for the wrongs of Cotton Harling. He had his uncle to consider. "Trust is earned."

Hannah sprang to her feet, visibly indignant. "I didn't break into your uncle's apartment. I had no idea until tonight the Harling Collection might include anything of monetary value." She threw down her napkin, resist-ing an impulse, Win thought, to try to whip his head off with it. "There's nothing I can do to make you believe me. I'm not even going to try. Good night, Win. Please tell your uncle I hope he's all right."

And that was that.

Off she stomped to the front door, yanking it open and slamming it shut on her way out.

An angry woman, Hannah Marsh.

She hadn't eaten so much as a pea pod of her dinner. Win sighed and got up. He supposed he ought to go after her and apologize. But for what?

And what bothered her more? he wondered. His ac-cusing her of breaking and entering or kissing her? Wanting her as much and as obviously as he did?

How the hell was he supposed to know for sure what she was up to? His first loyalty was to Uncle Jonathan, not to some fair-haired scholar with a bee in her bonnet about his ancestors.

Yet Hannah Marsh was so much more. He sensed it, knew it. There was a depth and complexity to her he hadn't even begun to probe.

He gritted his teeth at the unbidden thought of just how much of Ms. Marsh he wanted to probe....

"Damn," he muttered. Now it was his turn to throw down his napkin and pound from the room. He'd lost his appetite.

The doorbell rang.

"Hannah?"

He headed for the entry and pulled open the heavy

front door, only to find his elderly uncle leaning on his cane and looking none the worse for wear for his day's ordeal. Without preamble the old man said, "The damned thief did get away with something."

"What? You don't have much of value…."

"Anne Harling's diary."

Win stared. Now what? "Who the hell's Anne Harling?"

"Your great-great-aunt, remember? The one who gathered together the Harling Collection. She died in 1892."

Wonderful. "Uncle Jonathan…"

"Invite me in, Winthrop. We need to talk."

THE NEXT MORNING, Hannah arrived at the New England Athenaeum within five minutes of its opening and asked to see Preston Fowler, in private. He brought her into his office, where she admitted to him that she was not Hannah Harling of the Ohio Harlings.

"I'm a Marsh," she said baldly.

He paled.

"Hannah Marsh."

"The biographer?"

At least he'd heard of her. She nodded.

He sighed, looking slightly ill. "My, my."

"I'm sorry I lied to you. It was just an expedient. I didn't think I could use the facilities here if you knew I was a Marsh." She swallowed. "I didn't think you'd risk offending the Harlings."

Fowler winced. "Your two families…the Harlings and the Marshes…"

"The history between us hasn't affected—and won't affect—my work," she said crisply, trying to sound like the professional she was. "I didn't want my being a Marsh to come into play. Hence my ruse. I'm very sorry."

"Oh, dear."

"The Harlings know the truth now, and I've made it clear to them that you were in no way a party to my deceit." She sounded so stuffy and contrite, but in fact she was neither. What she wanted to do was tell Win Harling to go to hell and Preston Fowler to have a little more integrity than to suck up to rich Bostonians for donations. "That's all I came to say."

Fowler tilted back his chair, placing the tips of his fingers together to make a tent. He sighed again. "How awkward."

"It's not awkward, Mr. Fowler. Not at all. I'm leaving Boston today. All you have to do is carry on with your work and pretend I never existed."

He nodded. "Very well. What about your biography of Priscilla? Will it go forward now that this has happened?"

"Of course. Why shouldn't it? Most of my research is completed."

"But the Harlings…"

Hannah sat forward. "I don't care what the Harlings want or think."

With that she apologized once more, assured him no harm had been done to his venerable institution and headed out. Yesterday's clouds and rain had been pushed off over the Atlantic, leaving blue sky and warm air in their wake. Hannah breathed in deep lungfuls of it before crossing the Public Garden and cutting past the Ritz Carlton Hotel into Boston's Back Bay, straight for Marlborough Street.

Jonathan Harling asked for her name twice over the intercom. "Marsh," she said both times. "It's Hannah Marsh."

He buzzed her in, anyway.

"Come on in," he said, opening his apartment door. "I've been wondering when you'd show up. Think the roof'll cave in with a Marsh and Harling under it? Though I suppose if it didn't last night, with you and Win, we should be all right."

The glitter in his eye suggested—although Hannah couldn't be certain—he had a fair idea that she and his nephew had more than simply shared the same roof. But she had vowed to stop thinking about Win's mouth on hers, his hard maleness thrust against her. She would not be at the mercy of her hormones.

Nonetheless, every fiber of her body—of her being—said she wanted more from Jonathan's nephew than a kiss, more than a heady embrace. She wanted to feel his skin against hers, his maleness inside her.

She wanted him to make love to her…with her.

There was no point in denying the obvious. Her abrupt departure last night had had less to do with his disgusting suspicion—his talk of the Declaration of Independence and of larceny—than with her ongoing, unstoppable, outrageous physical response to him. His dark, penetrating gaze had filled her with erotic notions. His hands, as he'd lighted the candles, had left her breathless, conjured up images of his touch on her mouth, her breasts, between her legs. Just looking at him had made her think of the two of them together in bed, or just right there on the dining room floor.

Such wild, irresponsible thinking had to stop.

It just had to. It was perverse to want a man she couldn't possibly have. A man who, even as her body ached for him, believed she was a thief, a grudge-holding Marsh, a woman he couldn't trust.

Jonathan Harling's apartment looked tidy, if cluttered, no evidence of a thorough ransacking still apparent. He offered Hannah a seat on an overstuffed, overly firm sofa. He himself flopped into a cushioned rocker. He was casually dressed, in a cardigan frayed at the elbows and chinos that must have seen Harry Truman into office. Hannah didn't feel the least bit out of place in her jeans and giant Maine sweatshirt.

"What can I do for you?" Jonathan Harling asked.

"I wanted to tell you how sorry I am about yesterday. Win told me. I hope you know I wasn't involved. I—" She broke off awkwardly, then decided she might as well get on with it. "You know by now I'm a Marsh and there are no Ohio Harlings."

He grunted and waved a hand. "I knew that days ago."

"Do you hate me for being a Marsh?"

"Nope. I don't trust you, but I don't hate you."

A fine distinction. Hannah let it pass.

"Be stupid to trust you," Jonathan added.

"I suppose, given the history of our two families,

that's not unreasonable. Also given my own behavior. I'm leaving Boston today—"

"Win know?"

She bristled. "Why should he?"

"I didn't say he should or shouldn't," the old man replied, matching her gruffness. "Just asked if he did."

"No. I haven't seen him since last night."

"You going to tell him?"

"I don't see any reason to tell your nephew anything, and I didn't come here to discuss him. I…" She frowned. "What are you looking at?"

"You. Trying to figure you out. How come you go all snot-nosed professor when someone asks you a personal question?"

"I'm not a professor."

He rocked back in his chair. "You and Win got something going?"

"Mr. Harling…"

"He threw me out last night after I started asking him personal questions. I do it all the time. Pride myself on being able to say anything I want to my own nephew, but I mentioned you, and out on my ear I went." He folded his scrawny hands in his lap. "Must be you two got something going."

Only Hannah's years of dealing with her exasperating Cousin Thackeray kept her from gaping at Jonathan Harling or throwing something at him. Or politely leaving. "Dr. Harling, I suspect your rather salty speech pattern is a total fake. You're a scholar yourself."

He waved a hand dismissively.

"Legal history. You taught at Harvard for fifty years."

"What, you writing a biography of me? I thought your only subjects were dead people."

She couldn't suppress a smile. "You're not dead yet."

"Glad you noticed."

"Look, I just came by to tell you I had nothing to do with yesterday's break-in. I only wanted to look at the Harling Collection for research purposes. I didn't know it might include a valuable copy of the Declaration of Independence. And I'm going home." She climbed to her feet. "It's been interesting meeting you. Should I send you a copy of my biography of Priscilla Marsh when it comes out?"

He lifted his bony shoulders, clearly feigning disinterest. "If you remember."

"Oh, I'll remember."

She told him not to bother seeing her to the door, but halfway there she felt his presence behind her and spun around. He was leaning on his cane, alert, still handsome in his own way. "Will you be mentioning Anne Harling?"

"Who?"

"You heard me."

"Yes, I did, but I'm not familiar…" She paused, searching her memory. "Cotton Harling's brother was married to a woman named Anne, wasn't he? She died before Priscilla was executed, as I recall."

"I'm talking about my great-aunt."

Hannah frowned, uncertain where he was leading her.

"She never married. Lived in the Harling House on

Louisburg Square until her death, late in the last century. Interesting woman. She's the one who supposedly gathered the family documents together into the Harling Collection."

"I see," Hannah said, although she didn't.

Jonathan smiled knowingly. "Her diary was stolen from this apartment yesterday."

His words only took a few seconds to penetrate. "Oh, my. And you think…it would seem logical that I…"

"That you stole it, yes."

"But I didn't."

"So you say."

"Win… Have you told your nephew?"

"Told him last night."

And he hadn't broken her door down at dawn to demand an explanation. Maybe he didn't care nearly as much about her supposedly larcenous tendencies as much as he claimed. Or maybe hadn't liked the idea of dragging her out of bed at the crack of dawn. With his blood boiling and hers about to boil, who knew where it would have lead?

"I thought perhaps that was why you were leaving town," Jonathan Harling said, looking decidedly smug.

Hannah threw back her shoulders. "It isn't."

"Win's not going to scare you off, eh?"

"Nobody will."

"Then you're going to stay?"

She felt Jonathan Harling's trap snap shut around her and knew all she could do was wriggle and complain.

Or chew her leg off. Figuratively speaking. "You haven't left me any choice."

He grinned. "That was the whole idea."

WIN WAS WAITING, slouching against Hannah's apartment door, when she rounded the corner of Pinckney Street. He could hear her sharp intake of breath when she spotted him. His own reaction was more under control; he'd had a few extra seconds to adjust to her imminent presence. He watched her slow down, saw a wariness creep into her gait. He also noticed how her hair tangled in the afternoon wind and glistened in the bright sun.

"I thought you'd be working," she said, coming closer.

"I left early."

"Is it costing you?"

He smiled. "In more ways than you probably would want to know."

"Try me."

Oh, lady, he thought. "I'd better resist. Let's just say I don't take many afternoons off. Mind if I come in?"

Without answering, she unlocked the heavy black door that led to the two basement apartments. The main entrance to the building was up the steps to their right, the first floor elevated, so that Hannah's borrowed apartment was almost at ground level. She unlocked that door, too. The apartment was predictably small, cluttered with her laptop computer, index cards, spiral notebooks, folders, papers, books.

"Look," she began, going straight into the kitchen area and filling a kettle with water, "if this is about Anne Harling's missing diary, I've already spoken to your uncle. He told me everything. I don't know what happened to it. I honestly don't. I didn't steal it."

"Did he tell you she was the one who gathered together the Harling Collection?"

She nodded, setting the kettle upon the stove. She dried her hands and headed back into the living area, where Win was clearly considering just where he might sit. Not one surface was free. She settled the matter for him, lifting a pile of folders from a chair and dropping them onto the floor. "Have a seat. Would you like tea?"

"No, thank you."

What a life she must lead, he thought, sitting down. Steeped in the past. Inundated with books, documents, paper. Did she have friends? Romances? Or was her strength the past, not the present? He wondered about her and men.

"I borrowed this place from a friend of mine. She's taking my cottage on Marsh Point sometime this summer." Hannah returned to the kitchen area, banging around as she pulled out a cup, saucer, strainer and teapot—anxious, he thought, to stay busy. "I can always stay with Cousin Thackeray if I can't get away when she wants the place."

"Who's he?"

"Thackeray Marsh. He reminds me somewhat of your Uncle Jonathan."

"Lucky you," Win said, amused.

She laughed. "Thackeray would hang me out to dry for saying that. He's not much on Harlings. But..." Her shoulders lifted, as if she couldn't quite express her feelings. "I owe him."

"For what?"

"Saving me."

And she yanked open the refrigerator, blocking Win's view of her. She had said more than she'd meant to. More, certainly, than she felt he deserved to know. But it wasn't enough. He wanted to know more, everything.

"You're sure you don't want tea? I can make coffee, too. I have one of those one-cup drip things."

"I'm fine. Thanks. How did your cousin save you, Hannah?"

"After my mother died five years ago—my father was already dead—I found myself wanting to see Marsh Point, and I met him. He's a historian, too. He understood me, knew I needed roots, a place to belong." She shut the refrigerator door and glared at Win. "I won't let you take Marsh Point away from him."

He said nothing. Her relationship with her cousin, he sensed, was much like his own with his uncle. What else might they have in common?

She set about her tea making. Win hated the stuff himself, but any more coffee today and he'd spin off to the moon. After Hannah's abrupt departure last night and Uncle Jonathan's peculiar visit, Win had taken a long walk up and down the meandering streets of Beacon Hill, trying to piece his thoughts and feelings into some kind of rational whole. But there were too many variables, too many bizarre, uncontrollable longings. Back home, he'd slept for a couple of hours, but had been up again at dawn, making a pot of coffee, seeing Hannah Marsh with him in his kitchen, imagining them up together at dawn after a night of lovemaking. Wondering if she really was a lying thief.

"So, why," she said thoughtfully, carrying her tea into the living area, "do you think Anne Harling's diary was stolen?"

"I don't know."

"Come on. You have a dozen reasons why you think I stole it. I presume that's why you're here, to interrogate me on the possibilities."

"I'm here to talk to you. That's all. No accusations, no offensive questions, just straightforward talk."

"We'll be logical and rational."

He ignored her sarcasm. "Right."

"Is that what you tell your clients? Let's be logical and rational about your financial portfolio?"

"Sometimes. Other times logic and rationality aren't at issue. Emotion is, wants and needs that go to the heart of a client's being, what he or she is about, what makes them feel alive. Sometimes a client just needs my encouragement to go for the impulsive and outrageous."

"All in a day's work, I suppose," she said lightly, but he could see that his words had had an effect. Their kiss had been impulsive and maybe even outrageous. It was still on her mind, just as it was on his.

She dropped to the floor and sat cross-legged amid her scattered research materials. Uncle Jonathan's apartment hadn't looked much worse than this yesterday, after it had been ransacked. But she seemed relaxed enough, setting her cup and saucer upon an enormous dictionary, muttering something about computer dictionaries just not being the same, no comparison. She ran her fingers through her hair, working out several small tangles.

"If I were going to break into your uncle's apartment specifically to steal Anne Harling's diary," she said, "don't you think I'd have gone out of my way to make it look like a real robbery and stolen a bunch of other stuff?"

"Not necessarily. You might have thought Uncle Jonathan wouldn't miss the diary until too late, if at all. You might have thought he didn't even realize he had it."

"Quite a risk."

"Maybe, maybe not. If Uncle Jonathan did realize the diary was missing, he would assume the other things had been taken as a smoke screen. If you were going to get caught, better with just an old diary in your possession than the family silver, so to speak."

"The 'you' here being a hypothetical you, not me."

He smiled. "Of course."

"So, the thief took a chance."

"Possibly."

"It's also possible, wouldn't you say, that the diary isn't missing, that your uncle got rid of it years ago, or maybe never had it to begin with and just forgot."

"Obviously you don't know Uncle Jonathan, but never mind. How do you explain the break-in?"

She shrugged. "He's on the first floor of a nice building. He, or someone else in his building, could have left the front door ajar, and our would-be thief took advantage. He got into your uncle's apartment, pulled the place apart, didn't find any ready cash or easily fenced valuables and took off, cutting his losses."

"Highly coincidental, don't you think?"

"Life is full of coincidences." She drank some of her tea, watching him over the rim of her cup. "What's so special about Anne Harling's diary?"

"Nothing, so far as I know. That's the point. It's what *you* think is special about it that's important." Win stretched his legs. "Suppose you believe it contains a clue as to what happened to the Harling Collection."

She shook her head. "Ridiculous. The Harlings being the Harlings, they'd have discovered the clue decades ago and skimmed off anything of value in the collection themselves."

"I can't argue with that. But maybe it's a clue you—"

"Our thief."

"As you wish. Maybe you're the only one who understands the significance of the clue."

"Pretty far-fetched."

"But the risk of breaking into Uncle Jonathan's apartment would have to be worth the potential benefit. Don't you agree?"

"I still like my idea about it being a coincidence."

"That's because it lets you off the hook." Win rose and walked over to where she sat, looking so casual and honest with her cup of tea. So unselfconsciously sexy. He lifted a manila folder marked Puritan Hangings of the 1690s. Charming subject. "You've been steeping yourself in Marsh-Harling history for how long?"

"I began work on Priscilla's biography last September."

"And you've been in Boston over a week, immersing yourself in three centuries of history that you can feel and touch. You've traveled the same streets Priscilla Marsh traveled. You've seen what Cotton Harling's descendants have become."

She set her teacup upon the floor beside her, a slight tremble in her hand. "I don't know what you're getting at, but I'm a professional historian. I don't get emotionally involved in my subjects."

"You're human, Hannah," Win said softly, reaching out and touching her hair. "Your mother's mother's mother's mother. How far back does it go? Does it even matter? Priscilla Marsh was wrongly hanged, and here in Boston you've been immersed in that wrong. It would be understandable if you let yourself get carried away."

"Into ransacking an old man's apartment?"

"And other things," he said deliberately.

She wriggled her legs apart and shot up. She appeared ready to bolt. But there was nowhere to go. This was her apartment, her space. And he hadn't moved an inch. To get past him, she would have to leap over stacks of books and files, a fact he could see her assessing, processing.

"You can't run from what's going on between us," he said, hearing his voice outwardly calm but laced with tension, desire—and determination. "Neither can I."

"I'm going back to Maine," she blurted.

"I figured as much."

"If you want to search my things before I leave…"

"If you did take the diary, you'd be too smart to leave it here. You wouldn't risk my showing up and tearing apart the place until I found it."

"Was that your plan when you came here?"

She held her chin raised, haughty and unafraid—or at least she was trying to appear so. Her eyes gave her away. But she wasn't afraid of him. He could see that. She was afraid, he thought, only of herself, of their muddled feelings about each other, on top of the very clear, obvious and tenacious physical attraction between them. Emotions, not just overexcited hormones, were at work and at stake.

"No," he said. "This was."

He tucked one finger under her chin, giving her a chance to tell him to go to hell, but she didn't. He breathed deeply, knowing he was crazy. They both were.

"Hannah," he whispered, and closed his mouth over hers.

Her lips were smooth and soft and if not welcoming him, at least not turning him away. He tasted them. She tasted back.

"I wish I didn't want this to happen," she whispered into his mouth.

"I know."

But it was happening, and neither of them wanted it to stop. He pulled her to him, felt her hands around his middle, her slender body pressed against him. Her tongue slid into his mouth, tentatively at first, then more boldly. He could feel every fiber of him responding... aching...wanting....

And then it was over.

He couldn't say if it was he or she who pulled back. He wasn't sure it mattered. He only knew that within too short a time he was back on Pinckney Street's brick sidewalk, looking at the Charles River in the distance and wondering what in blue hell had happened.

She had wanted him. He had wanted her.

So, why the devil wasn't he in there, making love to Hannah Marsh?

He raked one hand through his hair and heaved a sigh. He hadn't been motivated by any false nobility or nebulous impression that making love to her wasn't, deep down, what she wanted, as well. And it sure as hell wasn't the missing diary of some aunt who'd been dead for over a hundred years or his eccentric, crotchety old uncle that had stopped him.

It was, he thought, very simple.

He was falling for Hannah Marsh and didn't want to make a wrong move.

And right now, taking into account not only the history that had brought them to this moment but all he didn't know about this woman, who could seem so outrageous and cocky one minute and so prim and proper the next, scooping her up and carting her off to bed would be a mistake. Never mind how much he wanted it. Never mind how much she wanted it.

First things first, he told himself. First he had to learn more about Hannah Priscilla Marsh. Find out what made her tick. Then...

By God, he thought. Then there'd be no stopping him.

CHAPTER SEVEN

"YOU'RE HOME EARLY," Thackeray said when Hannah reported in upon her return to southern Maine. "I knew your common sense would prevail."

She smiled. "It wasn't common sense, it was self-preservation."

"Whatever works."

When Hannah looked at her elderly cousin, she couldn't help but think of Jonathan Harling in Boston. On the surface all the two old men had in common was their age, but Hannah suspected they were much more similar deep down than either would care to admit.

He shoved a cat off the chair near the fire in his front room. It was cold, dank and foggy on Marsh Point, but Hannah had already been out to the rocks and tasted the ocean. She was home.

While she had a small winterized cottage close to the water's edge, Thackeray had a bona fide house, built in 1880, with high ceilings, leaded glass windows and four fireplaces. His wife, a native of Maine, had died ten years ago and they'd had no children, but still he'd managed to clutter up the place. He persisted in subscribing to a dozen magazines, plus the *Wall Street Journal* and the *New York Times*. He refused to read any of the Boston papers, lest he run across the Harling name, be it a reference to a live one or a dead one. Boston, he maintained, had never been kind to the Marsh family.

"Tea?" he offered.

"No, thank you. I just wanted to say hi."

"Anything to report?"

She decided not to tell him she had kissed a Harling, but filled him in on everything else, including the two Jonathan Winthrop Harlings' suspicion that she was after the rumored copy of the Declaration of Independence. Cousin Thackeray snorted at the very idea. She laughed, appreciating his unconditional support. But it had always been there, as consistent as the tide.

"What're you going to do now?" he asked.

Exorcise Win Harling from my mind....

"Start writing, I guess," she said, hating the note of melancholy in her voice. Her life would never be the same after Boston and her brush with the Harlings. "I've done more than enough research to get started, at least. I can't help but feel I ran away from Boston, but I hope that will pass."

"You exercised good judgment, that's all. You didn't run away from a thing."

No, not from a thing. From Win.

"You're not the type," Cousin Thackeray added, clearly convinced, as always, that any Marsh who deliberately avoided a Harling was just doing the right thing.

Hannah wished she shared his certainty. Instead she could only think about the desire Win Harling stirred up in her with his kisses, his touch, his very presence.

And it was not just a matter of physical desire. In spite of their differences, she had felt an emotional connection starting to grow between them, something beyond flaming hormones.

But staying had become impossible. She simply hadn't been willing to risk the Harlings finding some way to blame her for Jonathan's ransacked apartment and the missing Anne Harling diary. She couldn't risk reigniting their outrage over having lost their beautiful point in southern Maine to a Marsh. She couldn't risk their finding some loophole—and Win was just the high-minded, bulldog type to find one—that would put it back in their hands.

She couldn't risk falling in love with Win Harling.

She shook her head. No. She really couldn't. She had her work. It would fill her mind, once she got into it.

"Hannah?"

Smiling, she kissed her cousin on the cheek and patted his hand. "It's good to be back."

UNCLE JONATHAN HAD spread a detailed map of Maine on Win's table when he arrived home from work, the evening after Hannah Marsh bolted. It was after eight. He could see his uncle had helped himself to the leftovers of the aborted dinner. The old man had also polished off the last of the wine.

"Trying to drown your sorrows in work, eh?" Uncle Jonathan said, cocking his head at his nephew.

Win slung his suit coat over the back of a folding chair. "I had to catch up on a few things."

"Distracting woman, that Hannah Marsh. If I didn't know better, I'd say old Cotton offed her ancestor, just so he could get his mind back on track."

"That's ridiculous," Win said.

"Of course it is, but if Priscilla Marsh looked anything like your Hannah, she made one hell of a Puritan." Uncle Jonathan abruptly turned his attention back to his map, running one finger down Maine's jagged coastline. "There's another helping of that anemic spaghetti in the refrigerator."

"Thanks, but I'm not hungry."

"Going to starve yourself over a woman?"

Win sighed. "I had a late lunch with a client. Uncle Jonathan, what are you doing here?"

"Besides acquainting myself with the pitiful existence you endure here?"

"Besides that," Win said, unable to stop his mouth twitching. He never quite knew when to take his uncle seriously.

"For heaven's sake, how much do decent chairs cost? You know, the Harlings have never been cheap. Frugal, yes, but not cheap."

"This from a man who hasn't bought a suit since 1980?"

"Don't need one."

"The map, Uncle Jonathan."

"Oh, yes." Placing one hand on the small of his back, he stretched, clearly a delaying tactic. He put the half-moon glasses he had hanging around his neck upon the end of his nose and peered more closely at the map.

Then he tapped a spot in southern Maine. "That's Marsh Point."

Win leaned over and took a look. "So it is."

"You can take Interstate 95 north to Kennebunkport, then get off on Route 1. There'll be signs you can follow."

"'You' as in me?"

"Of course."

"Why would I go to Marsh Point?"

Uncle Jonathan exhaled, pursing his thin lips in disgust. "Do I have to spell everything out for you, Winthrop? Hannah Marsh is there."

"I know, but what—"

"She's probably curled up by the fire with her stolen view of the ocean, studying Anne Harling's diary for clues about where she can lay her greedy little hands on the Harling Collection and our copy of the Declaration of Independence."

Win stood back and crossed his arms over his chest, trying to figure out his uncle. "I thought you liked her."

"Did I say that? I'm strictly neutral. I don't like her or dislike her. I can objectively admit she's an attractive woman who might discombobulate a stubborn monk like yourself, but that's not to say I trust her." He yanked off his smudged glasses. "She can't help being born a Marsh. It's in her genes to want whatever she can get from us."

"How do you know what she wants is the copy of the Declaration of Independence?"

"I don't. Maybe it's just you."

Win scowled.

"The point is," Uncle Jonathan went on impatiently, "you can't wait for her to make the next move."

"Uncle, Uncle," Win said, "who says I'm waiting?"

WITHIN TWO DAYS Hannah knew she would have to take another crack at the Harlings of Boston. Specifically, at J. Winthrop Harling.

Although she'd resolved to put him out of her mind, she had done a little research on him, thanks to Google, her local library and Cousin Thackeray's pack-rat habits. Most interesting was the article on him she'd unearthed in the *Wall Street Journal*. It painted the picture of a financial wizard even richer than Hannah had guessed. He had surprised no one by leaving New York for Boston. It was apparently his destiny to restore the Harlings' position as an active financial and social force in the community. Having a prestigious name wasn't enough for him. His purchase of the Harling House on Louisburg Square was, he was quoted as saying, only the beginning, a small step.

Cotton Harling's hanging of an innocent woman wasn't even mentioned. Steeped as she was in Priscilla's story, Hannah found this omission insulting. "How 'bout a little perspective?" she complained to Cousin Thackeray.

He sniffed. "Precisely what the Marshes have been saying for three hundred years. One doesn't begrudge the Harlings their successes or overly enjoy their failures, but putting them in context, it seems to me, isn't too much to ask."

She had also learned that J. Winthrop Harling had never been married. And when he did marry, he would—according to rampant speculation and unnamed sources—likely choose a woman who could further his dream of reclaiming his family's lost heritage. It sounded pretty calculating to Hannah, but then, Win Harling could be one formidably calculating man.

Except for their kiss. That hadn't been calculated.

Or had it?

"Thackeray," she said, "there's something I've been meaning to bring up. It's about the Harling Collection."

He groaned, throwing down his newspaper. He had the business section out, but Hannah knew he'd been reading the comics. "I thought you'd given up on that angle."

"Did you know a Marsh had been accused of stealing it?"

"Even were we all dead and gone for a hundred years, the Harlings will blame us for anything that happens to them that they don't like."

"I'm not talking about us. I'm talking about your Uncle Thackeray, the man you were named for. Not long after the Marshes moved to Maine, the Harlings accused him of having stolen a collection of valuable family papers."

"Where'd you hear this?"

"I found mention of it in an old Maine newspaper."

Her elderly cousin snatched up his paper and flipped back to the comics, not bothering to pretend he was reading about the latest stock market tumble. "So?"

"So, I'm just wondering if things between the Harlings and the Marshes aren't exactly what they seem."

His eyes, as green as hers, narrowed at her over the top of his newspaper. "What have I been trying to tell you these past weeks?"

"Thackeray, did the Marshes steal the Harling Collection?"

He didn't even look up. Chuckling, he wagged a finger at her and made her read a comic strip he found particularly amusing. Hannah didn't laugh. She thought her cousin was being deliberately obtuse.

To clear her head and sort out her thoughts, she headed out to the rocks. The tide was coming in, and the wind out of the north was brisk and cold, but the sun glistened on the water. Hannah climbed down below the waterline, out of sight from Thackeray's house or her own cottage. Careful not to slip on the barnacle-covered rocks, she squatted in front of a yard-wide tide pool soon to be inundated. Waves swirled and frothed all around her. Wearing her jeans, sweatshirt and sneakers, she felt more like herself than she had in weeks.

A crunching sound on the rocks behind her startled her, and she started to fall backward, putting out a hand to brace herself. She felt barnacles slicing into her palm and cursed. It was probably just a damned seagull. Obviously she wasn't used to being back in the country yet, away from the city of the Harlings.

"I thought for a minute there you were heading for the sharks," Win Harling said above her.

"You!"

He jumped lightly from a dry rock, landing next to her tide pool. He grinned. "Me."

Hannah regained her balance and shot to her feet, the wind whipping her hair. Caught completely off guard and seeing Win, so damned breathtaking, so incredibly sexy, so *unexpected,* she needed a few extra seconds of recovery time. "I thought you were a seagull...."

He laughed. "I suppose people have thought worse about me. Are you all right?"

"Fine."

But he took her hand into his own and examined the scrapes from the barnacles. The skin hadn't broken. His touch was gentle, careful.

"I'll stick it in the ocean," she said, still breathless. "Ice-cold salt water's a great cure for just about anything."

"Anything?"

She saw the heat in his eyes. "Win, we need to talk...."

But talk, she knew, would have to come later. He lifted her into his arms while the wind churned the waves at their feet, spraying them with a fine, cold mist, but all she could feel was the warmth of wanting him.

"I'd hoped I could think with you out of town," he murmured, "but I couldn't. All I could think about was you—and this."

She tilted up her chin until her mouth met his, their lips brushing tentatively at first, then hungrily, eagerly. His hands slipped under her sweatshirt to the warm skin at the small of her back, and she sank against his chest, trying, even on the cold, windswept rocks, to meld with his body.

Then a wave crashed into the tide pool and soaked them to their ankles, its icy water a shock to their over-heated systems.

Win swore.

Hannah smiled and brushed strands of hair from her face. "Welcome to Maine."

HANNAH'S COTTAGE WAS about what Win had expected. Its cedar shingles weathered to a soft gray, it stood amid tall pines above the rocks. In the tiny living room, the picture window provided a view of the ocean. A fire in the stone fireplace was just dying down as they entered. Hannah pulled off her wet sneakers and socks and set them in front of the fire while she stirred the red-hot ashes. She threw on some kindling while Win, also barefoot by now, wandered down the short hall, taking note of the two small bedrooms and bath, then back up the hall and into the kitchen, all knotty pine and copper-bottomed pans. The entire floor area would probably fit into his dining room and foyer. It would be sort of like sticking a map of New England inside a map of Texas.

In contrast to the sparsity of his furnishings and the impersonal, motel-like quality of his spacious rooms on Louisburg Square, every inch of Hannah's cottage was crammed with stuff. Pot holders, hummingbird magnets, wildlife wall calendars, samplers cross-stitched with silly sayings, old quilts, throw pillows, odd bits of knitting, photo albums, pottery bowls and teapots; all of it vied for space with the mountains of books, files, notebooks, clippings and office equipment.

The only order he could sense was indirect: Hannah Marsh seemed absolutely at home here. She padded about with an ease that he hadn't sensed in Boston.

He spotted a yellowed newspaper picture of himself, then saw that it was the vile profile from the *Wall Street Journal.* He hadn't agreed with the writer's highly subjective, not to mention uncomplimentary, slant on his motives for making money. Couldn't a man simply be drawn to a job that he did well and that also happened to pay well?

The fire caught and Hannah stood back, appraising her handiwork with satisfaction. Or relief? Perhaps it had occurred to her that he might have suggested they manage without a fire.

"Nice place," Win said. "How long have you lived here?"

"Almost five years."

"Before that?"

"Oh, here and there. I traveled a lot."

She wasn't so much being evasive, he thought, as cryptic, holding back a part of herself from him. But that was all right. He had conducted his own research into the life of Hannah Priscilla Marsh, finding a thorough, if brief, biography of her in the *New York Times Book Review*'s critique of her study of Martha Washington. Hannah, the only child of an army officer and his would-be artist wife, had led the peripatetic life of a member of a military family until her father's death in a helicopter crash when she was fourteen. She and her mother had then wandered from art school to art school, until Hannah had finally gone off to college. Her mother had eventually settled in Arizona, making her living as a painter and teaching as a volunteer in low-income neighborhoods. Her death five years ago had left Hannah alone, until she'd found her cousin and Marsh Point...and that elusive sense of belonging Win thought he understood.

These details were just a few important pieces of the puzzle that was Hannah Marsh.

"How's your uncle doing?" she asked, her tone conversational.

"Just fine, thanks."

"Did he ever report his break-in to the police?"

Win thought he detected a note of suspicion in her tone. "No, why?"

"Just curious."

More than curious, he decided. "You have a theory, don't you?"

"Nope."

She shoveled free a space on the sofa for him and disappeared into the kitchen without another word. Win sighed and sat down. The fire crackled, and he could hear the rhythmic crashing of the waves on the rocks. It was an almost erotic sound. Or maybe his mind was just being driven in that direction.

Hannah, Hannah.

She wandered back in a few minutes with a tray of mugs, teapot, English butter cookies and crackers. She set them down upon an old apple crate she used as a coffee table, atop a stack of overstuffed manila folders. "Be back in a sec," she said, and disappeared again. When she returned, she held a pottery pitcher, sugar bowl and a tea strainer, which she set over one of the mugs.

She poured the tea, and he immediately noted that it was purple. Honest-to-God ordinary tea was bad enough.

She smiled. "It's black currant—very soothing."

"Do I look as if I need soothing?"

Color spread into her cheeks. Seeing her discomfort— her awareness—was almost worth having to drink purple tea. "It's great with milk and sugar," she added quickly, "almost like eating a cobbler."

The "almost" was a stretch, but at least he could drink the stuff without gagging.

"Do you like it?" she asked, seating herself on a rattan rocker.

"It tastes like tea with something that shouldn't be in tea."

"I've been drinking more herbal teas lately."

"Not sleeping well?"

Her eyes, shining and so damned green, met his, and she smiled, knowing, he guessed, what he was thinking. "You flatter yourself, Win Harling."

"I'm not keeping you awake nights?"

"Nope."

He laughed. "That's two lies—or at best half truths— so far. Want to go for a third?"

She scowled at him, sipping her tea, clearly savoring it, rather than gulping it down, as he was his, in an effort to finish the job.

Leaning forward, he said, "Tell me you're not glad to see me."

"Are you asking me?"

"Yes, I'm asking you. Are you glad to see me?"

A smile tugged at the corners of her mouth. "What'll you do if you believe I'm lying?"

"That would be three lies in a row. I don't know. I guess I'd figure something out."

"Then the answer is yes. Yes, I'm glad to see you." She set her mug upon one knee, everything about her challenging him. "Now it's for you to decide if I'm lying or not."

He took one last swallow of the purple tea and set down his mug, then leaned forward again, so that his knee touched hers, and brushed one finger across her lower lip. It was warm and moist. Her eyes were wide with desire.

"I think a part of you isn't lying," he said, "and a part is."

"Do you know which part is which?"

He could hear the catch in her voice, the breathlessness. She had pulled off her sweatshirt; underneath it she wore a long-sleeved navy T-shirt. The fabric wasn't particularly thin, but he could see the twin points of her nipples, whether still from the cold or in reaction to him, he couldn't be sure. He made no attempt to disguise his interest.

"I think I do," he said, and this time he could hear the catch, the breathlessness in his own voice. He raised his eyes to hers. "Time for one part to listen to the other, wouldn't you say?"

"Should my mind listen to my body or my body listen to my mind?"

"Decide, Hannah. Decide, because your purple tea hasn't soothed me one little bit."

He skimmed her nipples with his fingertips, inhaling deeply, wanting her more than he'd ever wanted any woman. But he knew he had to hold back. Knew he couldn't touch her again, because if he did, he would be lost. He would never get Hannah Marsh out of his system.

Her breathing was rapid now, and he could see the pulse beating in her throat. But she didn't draw closer.

"It's your decision, Hannah. It has to be."

"Why?"

"You didn't invite me here. I came. I thrust myself back into your life. It's your decision if I stay."

She licked her lips, but pulled her lower lip under her top teeth. Didn't move.

"How long do I have?" she asked.

He tried to smile. "Now, Hannah." He knew how tortured he must sound, but couldn't help it. "Decide now."

CHAPTER EIGHT

HANNAH JUMPED UP, spilling her tea. She raked her hands through her hair. Every millimeter of her wanted to fall to the floor with Win Harling and make love with him, until neither of them had the strength left to accuse the other of anything. Instead she said, "You need to meet Cousin Thackeray."

Win remained seated on the couch. She wasn't deceived by his outward composure. His eyes were half-closed, studying her. His mouth was set in a grim, hard line. The muscles in his arms and legs were tensed. Everything about him was taut, coiled, ready for action.

And she knew what kind of action.

She wondered if his scrutiny would ever end. She watched the tea seep into her dhurrie carpet and wondered if the purple stain would forever be a visible reminder of her encounter with a real, live Harling. A warning of the perils of her own nature. A symbol of regret, of what might have been.

She should have stuck to dead Harlings.

Finally he slapped one hand on his knee and rose with a heavy sigh. "Okay, let's go."

"You're sure it's okay?"

"Hell, no. I'd rather carry you into your bedroom and make love to you until sunup, but—"

"That's not what I meant." She felt heat spread through her. "Cousin Thackeray—are you sure you want to meet him? He doesn't care for Harlings."

"Has he ever met one?"

"He says he did decades ago, but he won't give me a straight answer."

Win nodded thoughtfully, and Hannah grabbed her squall jacket, glad to have the added cover. She could still feel the physical effects of wanting this man she had absolutely no business wanting. Even his gaze sparked pangs of desire in her. But she had to maintain control. She couldn't give in to her yearning…until she was sure she was doing the right thing.

"Well," he said, "let's go see if he decides to run me off with a shotgun."

"He doesn't own a shotgun. I'd watch out for a hot poker, though."

"A charming family, you Marshes."

They followed the narrow gravel path to the dirt road that connected Hannah's cottage to the main driveway. The wind made the air feel more like winter. Cousin Thackeray's few pitiful tulips seemed to be wishing they could close up again and come out when it was really spring. Walking beside her, Win didn't appear to notice the cold. Maybe he even welcomed it.

Thackeray's truck was still outside, but he didn't answer his door. Hannah pounded again. "Thackeray, it's me, Hannah."

No answer.

"He must have gone for a walk," she guessed. "Or maybe one of his buddies from town picked him up for a game of chess, although he usually lets me know when he's going out."

"He could be taking a nap."

"Are you kidding?" But she pushed open his back door, unlocked as always, and poked her head inside. "Thackeray?"

"We can look around out here," Win suggested, "or try again later. What have you told him about your trip to Boston?"

"Everything." She cleared her throat, feeling hot and achy with desire, and added quickly, "Except about you, of course."

He smiled. "Of course."

"It would only upset him."

"I understand."

She wondered if he did. "Does your uncle—"

"He knows to stay out of my private life. Not that it stops him."

"Does he really think I broke into his apartment and stole Anne Harling's diary?" But she didn't wait for an answer, springing ahead of Win to reach the driveway again. She cut over the side yard, heading toward the rocks. "You know, we only have your uncle's word for what happened."

"Meaning?"

"Meaning it's possible he made up the whole thing."

"You mean he pulled apart his entire apartment himself?" Win said dubiously.

Hannah knew she was on shaky ground; she could just imagine how she'd react if Win said something similar about Cousin Thackeray. "I'm not saying it's likely, just possible. I know *I* didn't do it."

He caught up with her. "What would be his motive?"

She shrugged, proceeding with caution. "Nothing devious, for sure. Cousin Thackeray would probably pitch me onto the rocks for saying this, but I actually like your uncle. I wouldn't want to believe he was up to anything truly underhanded."

"Such as?"

Inhaling, she went ahead and said it. "Getting Marsh Point back into Harling hands."

She continued walking, but Win stopped, not speaking. Up ahead, she could see Thackeray among the low-lying blueberry bushes with his binoculars, looking out at two cormorants diving for food.

"Thackeray!" she called, and waved.

He lowered his binoculars and turned, spotting her and waving back. She could see his grin.

"I've got somebody for you to meet!"

Behind her, Win said, "No."

She whipped around. "What do you mean?"

"I mean I'm not going to wait and see if I pass Thackeray Marsh's inspection. I'm not going to let you let him decide for you whether or not we—you and I, Hannah, no one else—go forward. I won't make it that easy for you." His black eyes searched hers for long seconds, and she saw in them not only physical longing, but a longing that came from his heart, maybe even his soul. "You're going to have to decide this one for yourself."

He about-faced and marched down the path toward her cottage.

Hannah gulped, not knowing what to do.

Cousin Thackeray was heading in her direction. Not fast—he never moved fast. Had she dragged Win out here to meet him, just so she could avoid making any decision about their relationship herself? What if Thackeray didn't like Win?

What if he did?

She sighed. It shouldn't matter how Thackeray felt. Win was right. "The bastard," she muttered.

But she didn't chase down the path after him. Instead she trotted across the windy point, toward the old man to whom she owed her loyalty, if not her life.

"YOU'RE SULKING."

"I'm not sulking."

Thackeray squinted at her in the bright sunlight, but didn't argue. He thrust his binoculars at her. "Look, a loon."

Hannah had no interest in his loon sighting and just pretended to focus the binoculars, while Thackeray gestured and gave instructions. "I see it," she said dispiritedly.

He hissed in disgust and yanked the binoculars away. "No, you didn't. There's no loon out there."

She pursed her lips. "That was a cheap trick."

"No matter." He gave her a long look. "Do you want to tell me about the Jaguar with Massachusetts plates parked at your cottage and that man I saw with the distinctly Harling build?"

Distinctly Harling build? What did Cousin Thackeray know? But she gave up before she even started. She was confused enough as it was.

"It's Win Harling," she told him.

"The younger J. Winthrop."

She nodded.

"Why's he here?"

"I'm not sure."

"They're after Marsh Point, aren't they, he and his uncle?"

Hannah hesitated only a moment. "It's possible. I have no proof, of course, but the uncle's story about his apartment being ransacked and Anne Harling's diary turning up missing strikes me as a bit fishy."

"Me, too. Think Win's a party to it?"

"It's hard to say. He's about as loyal to his uncle as I am to you."

Thackeray scowled and hung his binoculars around his neck. "What the devil's loyalty got to do with anything? A Marsh thinks for himself—or herself. You don't do what's wrong out of some skewed sense of loyalty. You do what's right for you."

But what if what's right for me is falling in love with J. Winthrop Harling?

"Hannah," Thackeray said when she didn't respond.

She turned to him. His nose was red in the cold air,

his ratty corduroy jacket was missing a button. He was like a grandfather to her, a father, an uncle. Most of all, he was a friend. "I won't do anything that would make you hate me," she said.

"What in hell could make me hate you?" he scoffed.

She looked toward her cottage.

Then Thackeray Marsh surprised her with a hearty, warm laugh, one that reminded her he had led a long, full life. Still laughing, he headed through the blueberry bushes that were just beginning to get their foliage.

"What's so damned funny?"

"You and that Win fellow. My God, wouldn't that set three centuries of Marsh and Harling bones rattling?"

"I don't give a damn. We're talking about my life here, you know."

He stopped and spun around so abruptly that for a moment she thought he'd lose his footing. But she had never seen him so steady. "That's right," he said intently, his laughter gone. "It's *your* life."

With that, he pounded back to his house.

When Hannah returned to her cottage, Win was staring out her picture window. She controlled a rush of desire at seeing his tall, lean body, at seeing him still there.

"I thought you might have cut your losses," she said.

He looked around, the corners of his mouth twitching. "Sounds a bit drastic, don't you think?"

She refused to blush. "Witty, witty."

"I try." But his humor didn't reach his eyes, and he asked, "Do you want me to leave?"

"No. No, I don't."

"Who decided?"

"I did."

He nodded. "Good."

"I owe Cousin Thackeray a lot, and I'd never deliberately hurt or disappoint him, but not making up my own mind about things..." She paused, searching for the right words, the courage to be honest. "Not making up my own mind about you—that isn't what he wants from me, even if it were something I could ever give."

Win was silent.

"Do you understand?"

"Yes," he replied.

"And you believe me?"

He smiled, the humor now reaching his eyes. "This time."

"Win Harling..."

"Shall we go talk to the old buzzard?"

She laughed. "I believe he used the same expression to describe your uncle. I thought we..." She felt blood rush to her face. "Never mind. I guess it's your turn to torture me."

"Hannah, Hannah," he said in a low, deliberately sexy voice, "you haven't seen anything yet."

THACKERAY MARSH PROVED as irascible as Win had anticipated. He and Hannah joined the old man at his drafty house for lemon meringue pie that must have been around for days and coffee that tasted as if it had been poisoned. Win later learned that Hannah's cousin had reheated it from his pot that morning. A waste-not, want-not family. Hannah, he noticed, drank every drop.

"So," Thackeray said, "how's that old goat of an uncle of yours?"

"He's quite well, thank you."

Win glanced at Hannah but couldn't will her to meet his eyes. She was sitting cross-legged on a threadbare braided rug in front of a roaring fire. Southern Maine's evening temperature had plummeted; there was even talk of frost.

"We met decades ago. He was a frosty old bastard even then. Heard a Marsh had dared set foot in Boston and hunted me down, warned me one day the Harlings would get Marsh Point back. He called it Harling Point, o' course." Thackeray fastened his intense gaze—his green eyes bore a disturbing resemblance to his young relative's—on Win, who didn't flinch. "That why you're here?"

Win worded his reply carefully. "I'm not interested in pressing the Harling case for Marsh Point, no."

Thackeray grunted. "They don't have a case."

"Then why worry?"

"Who said I'm worried?"

Definitely irascible. Hannah smiled, visibly amused, as she uncoiled her legs and rested on her arms. Win wished, not for the first time, that he hadn't been so damned noble and had instead made love to her before offering to chitchat with her elderly cousin.

Before heading out, she had insisted on taking a quick shower—he hoped she'd had to make it cold—and had twisted her hair into a long French braid that hung down her back. Win still didn't know how he'd stopped himself carting her off to the bedroom there and then. Even now it amazed him.

With her hair pulled off her face, her eyes seemed even bigger, more luminous. She had changed into jeans that conformed to every shapely turn of thigh and calf and left him imagining how her legs would feel entwined with his. Her top left much more to the imagination. It was a huge sweatshirt she must have picked up in Vermont; it had a Holstein's head on the front and its behind on the back, with Enjoy Our Dairy Air in black lettering. Apparently she collected T-shirts and sweatshirts. She had shown him one of the Beatles, circa 1967. It was another side of the scholarly Hannah Marsh, as was her Hannah of the Cincinnati Harlings. A complex woman.

"Win came to Maine to make sure I hadn't made off with Anne Harling's diary," she informed her elderly cousin, "which his uncle still insists I stole."

"He only wants to know the truth," Win amended. "So do I."

Thackeray waved them both off. "I'll bet you a day's work Anne Harling didn't keep a diary any more than I did."

Hannah shook her head. "It wouldn't surprise me. Upper-class women of that era quite commonly kept diaries…."

"*She* didn't."

But Hannah didn't give in, so Win sat back and observed while the two argued about the journal-keeping habits of late-nineteenth-century women. It was a spirited discussion, given, at least to Win, the dry nature of the topic. As far as he could tell, the two Marshes didn't even disagree.

"But back to Win's Uncle Jonathan," Hannah said, and Win's interest perked up. He saw the flush of excitement in her cheeks and smiled, not just wanting her, but liking her. "He indicated Anne Harling was the one who pulled together the Harling Collection, his theory being that I stole her diary to look for clues as to the collection's location."

"That's ridiculous," Thackeray said.

"Of course. The Harlings have had the diary—if it exists—for a hundred years, and certainly would have noticed any reference to a collection that could contain a valuable copy of the Declaration of Independence."

Win couldn't let that one go unanswered. "Maybe they never read it," he speculated. "Or maybe in your research you learned something that suggested to you a passage in the diary was really a disguised clue, something we wouldn't have recognized all these years. Maybe," he went on, ignoring Thackeray's snort of disgust, "you weren't looking for the diary itself, but stole it because it was the only thing of potential value in my uncle's apartment."

Hannah fastened her cool academic's gaze on him without an inkling, he suspected, of the elemental response it produced in him. He could have hauled her off to her cottage and made love to her all night.

He might yet.

No, he thought, not might. Would.

"I suppose," she said reasonably, "there are a number of reasonable theories to fit the supposed facts. But as I said, I'll manage my biography of Priscilla Marsh without the Harling Collection."

She climbed to her feet in a lithe movement that made him think of what they were going to be like in bed together. Considering her preoccupied state, Win thought, delaying the inevitable perhaps hadn't been wise.

"Thanks for the pie, Thackeray."

The old man jerked his head toward Win but addressed Hanna. "Is he going back tonight?"

Win shook his head, answering for himself. "No."

"You're going to stay at Hannah's cottage?"

She nodded, answering for her guest.

Thackeray Marsh thought that one over. "This fellow thinks you're a thief, and you still want to put him up for the night?"

"We've called a cease-fire," Hannah said steadily. "I've paid him back for every nickel I...appropriated."

And Win had already burned her check. Its ashes were in his fireplace in Boston.

Thackeray grunted. "I'll keep my shotgun loaded by my bed. You just give a yell if you need me."

Hannah had the gall to thank him.

On their way out, Win whispered into her ear, "I thought you said he didn't have a shotgun."

She grinned. "He's full of surprises, isn't he?"

Outside it was pitch-dark, the air downright cold, the wind gusting at at least thirty miles an hour, but Hannah Marsh seemed at ease, in control, downright perky. Win heard the gravel crunch under his feet. She seemed hardly to be hitting the ground at all. She darted ahead of him, familiar with every rock, every rut in the road to her cottage, while he stumbled along behind her.

He caught up with her. "I suggest," he said, slipping his arm around her slender waist, "you watch your yelling tonight, unless you want me blown to bits."

She turned her eyes upon him, luminous now in the starlight, and smiled softly, playfully. "Now what could possibly make me yell in the middle of the night?"

"I can think of several things."

He slipped one hand under her sweatshirt, touching the hot, smooth skin.

"Your hand's cold!"

"Serves you right."

But she didn't pull away. "Of course," she said, "*I* won't be the one Cousin Thackeray will shoot."

"Then the risk is all mine, isn't it?"

She shrugged, leaning against his shoulder. "I wouldn't say that."

"What's your risk?"

The gravel crunched under her feet as she came to a stop, staring at him with wide, serious eyes. "Falling for a Harling."

"Is that a bigger risk than getting shot?"

"It could be."

"Hannah…"

"But I'll take it," she said quickly, and darted away, into the night.

CHAPTER NINE

NOW THAT DARKNESS enveloped the cottage, Hannah felt even more alone with Win Harling...and surprisingly content with the situation.

He lay stretched on the floor in front of the fire, staring at the blue-and-orange flames. She was on her rocking chair, rummaging through tins and old cigar boxes filled with scraps of paper, clippings, coupons and recipe cards. Mostly she was trying not to think how damned appealing Win's thighs looked.

"What are you doing?" Win asked finally.

"Looking for a recipe. I've got one last pint of wild blueberries from last summer in the freezer and thought I'd make blueberry scones. Thackeray gave me the recipe—it's from his mother. They're wonderful."

"Uncle Jonathan makes blueberry scones," Win said. "He insists they're only worth making with wild blueberries. The cultivated varieties won't work."

Hannah grinned. "Cousin Thackeray says the same thing. Do you suppose those two are twins, after all?"

"Don't ever suggest that to them."

"Scandalous, isn't it? They'd probably call a truce between the Marshes and the Harlings and string us up together."

"Hannah," Win said dryly, "no hanging metaphors tonight."

She felt a rush of warmth at the way he said "tonight," as if it were just one in a long string of nights they would have together. But she didn't want to dwell on thoughts of the future and the choices it might bring, only on the present. She concentrated on the familiar smell of oak burning in the fire, the familiar sound of the gentle ebbing of the tide just beyond her cottage. Then Win moved, adding an unfamiliar sound, an unfamiliar presence as he put another log onto the fire.

"Here it is," she said, withdrawing a yellowed three-by-five index card. On it, in black ink now faded by time, Cousin Thackeray's mother had neatly printed her recipe for luscious blueberry scones.

Hannah jumped up and headed for the kitchen.

Win followed.

"You don't have to help," she told him.

"Okay." As he leaned against the sink, she noticed his narrow hips, the muscles in his thighs. "I'll watch."

She scowled. "You're in my way."

So, he sat down at her small kitchen table, in front of a double window that looked onto her back porch. On the table itself stood only a wooden pepper grinder; there was neither cloth, napkins nor place mats. Hannah thought of Win's metal folding chairs and ugly dining room wallpaper and smiled, unembarrassed by her own simple existence. Never mind the fact that he could easily afford to turn the Harling House on Louisburg Square into a showpiece, that he wouldn't need a mortgage to buy Marsh Point.

He doesn't want to buy it, she thought suddenly. *He wants to prove the Marshes appropriated it from the Harlings....*

She wouldn't dwell on that little problem right now.

"Are you going to just sit there and watch me?" she asked somewhat irritably.

He shrugged, obviously amused, knowing just what kind of distraction he was. "Why not?"

Why not, indeed? She tore open the refrigerator door and dug around inside until she found a bottle of beer behind smidgens of leftovers of this and that she'd promised herself would go into a pot of soup. More likely they'd end up in the garbage.

She handed Win the beer. "It's my last one."

"Don't you want it?"

"I'm not much on beer. I bought a six-pack for friends who came to visit—oh, around New Year's, I guess it was."

"Your last company?"

"Hmm? I don't know...." She thought a few seconds. "No, I had friends over a couple of months ago."

"A couple of months ago," he repeated.

"I do more entertaining in the summer, and I've been so involved with my work I haven't had time for a lot of outside activities. I get out for dinner every once in a while with friends." She pulled her pint of wild blueberries from the freezer. "And I see Cousin Thackeray just about every day."

"Do you like living here in Maine?"

"Yes."

"Your cousin has no children," Win guessed.

She looked around. "Are you trying to ask me if I'm his heir? If so, yes, I am. He plans to leave me Marsh Point. Then, if you Harlings want to go toe-to-toe with me over who rightfully owns it, that's fine. I'll take you on. Just leave Thackeray alone."

Win didn't respond at once, but sat back in his oak chair and stretched his long legs, taking up more of her small kitchen than anyone had since she'd banished Cousin Thackeray's old Irish setter. The man simply wasn't built on the same scale as her cottage.

"So, you're protecting your cousin," he said at length.

"I'm not protecting anyone. I have nothing to hide. I'm just giving you fair warning: I won't let Cousin Thackeray lose Marsh Point."

"Especially to a Harling."

"Especially."

She set to work on her scones. She got out her chipped pottery flour canister and her sugar container, of airtight plastic so the ants wouldn't get into it, the salt and baking powder. All the while she was intensely aware of Win's eyes on her. Finally she thrust the blueberries at him. "There might be a few stems and leaves floating around," she told him.

He insisted on doing a thorough job, spreading the blueberries on paper towels and examining every single one of them for stems, leaves, brown spots, bird pecks.

Hannah was amused. "I usually just dump the lot into the batter and hope for the best."

"I'll keep that in mind," he said, "should I ever eat anything else I haven't supervised you cooking."

Besides the scones, supper included eggs, scrambled with fresh chives, and a carrot and raisin salad she threw together because she figured carrot sticks were too ordinary for company. Or maybe because she needed to do one more thing before sitting down kitty-corner to Win at her own kitchen table. She tasted none of the food, not even the scones. All her senses were focused on the rich, handsome, sexy rogue of a Bostonian who had come, it seemed, to dominate her very being.

"Are the scones like your uncle's?" she asked.

"Very much. It could be the same recipe."

But he was no more interested in discussing wild blueberry scones than she was. She could see it in his eyes, in the tensed muscles of his arms. He was as preoccupied with her as she with him.

It was not a comforting thought.

After dinner, they moved back into the living room, and for the first time in years, Hannah wished she owned a television set. She would have loved to turn on the news or have the idle chatter of a sitcom in the background. With just the crackle of the fire and the rhythmic washing of the ocean, it was as if there were nothing more in her world than the little cottage on Marsh Point and the man who'd come to visit.

Except that he hadn't come to visit. He had come to find out if her desire to examine the Harling Collection had prompted her to ransack his uncle's apartment and steal an old diary, so that she could later steal a rare and valuable copy of the Declaration of Independence.

He had come to find out if she was a thief.

"There are sheets in the bathroom," she said suddenly.

Win glanced at her from his spot in front of the fire. He had left plenty of room for her to join him, but she'd flopped into her rocker again, well out of reach. She could feel the warmth of the fire licking at her toes. Her fingers, however, were icy cold.

"For the bed in the guest room," she added.

"Ahh. I see."

She thought he did.

Still, she found herself trying to explain. "There's no point...your uncle...my cousin...this business about the Harling Collection and the Declaration of Independence..." She lifted her shoulders and let them fall again. "You know."

"I know," he responded. His voice was soft and liquid, filled with understanding. There was none of the hardness or defensiveness she would have expected.

Didn't he care?

She jumped up and snatched a tome on the Puritans from a pile of books next to her desk. "I'm done in. I've had a long day. I'll check the guest room and make sure everything's in order before I turn in. Do you want me to make the bed?"

"No," he said calmly, "I'll get it."

He doesn't care, she thought. She had been projecting her own desire onto him, thinking that because she wanted him that he must, therefore, want her. Which he had. Definitely. Only clearly not as much as she had him. Or at least he didn't now, which was the whole point.

I'm not making any sense.... I must be more tired than I thought.

As she flounced from the living room, she noticed he was hoisting a fat log onto the fire and arranging it with his bare hands, as if oblivious to the flames. "Don't set yourself on fire," she called over her shoulder.

"Too late," he said, half under his breath.

She slammed into the guest room. It was freezing. The curtains were billowing in the wind and the shade was flapping. Hannah quickly shut the window. When had she opened it? Not this morning. Yesterday? The day before? It had rained buckets one night.

She ran one hand over the twin bed.

Damp.

No, she thought, soaked.

She tiptoed out to the bathroom, got a couple of towels and hurried back, spread the towels on the mattress and patted them down so they could absorb as much moisture as possible. She let them sit a minute while she returned to the bathroom and grabbed sheets. If she made the bed, maybe Win wouldn't notice the wet mattress.

Her job done, she scooped up the damp towels and carted them off to her room, where her guest would be less likely to run into them. Given his suspicious mind, he'd think the worst.

"Making the man sleep in a wet bed *is* pretty bad," she admitted under her breath.

But what was the alternative?

She wouldn't think about it. The alternative, she knew, was too tempting...too much like what she really wanted. Instead she pulled on her flannel nightgown—it was a cool night, after all—and climbed into bed with her book on the Puritans. It was dry stuff. She gave up after a couple of paragraphs and picked up a mystery that lay on her night table.

About forty minutes later she was dozing between paragraphs, fighting nightmares, when footsteps in the hall startled her. Then she remembered she wasn't alone. It wasn't so much that she had forgotten Win's presence as that his footsteps were a tangible reminder of it.

"Good night, Hannah," he said softly.

"Good night. If you need anything, just give a yell."

In a few minutes he yelled, all right. *Hannah!*

He was back at her door in a flash, but Hannah casually dog-eared her page and yawned before she looked up. The door stood open now.

"Oh, dear," she muttered.

Send a man to lie on a cold, wet mattress, she thought, and pay the consequences.

J. Winthrop Harling was standing in her doorway in nothing but his shorts. As shorts went, they weren't much. But Hannah's attention was riveted on what they didn't cover. Long, muscular legs. A flat abdomen. A line of dark hair that disappeared into the waistband of his shorts.

He, of course, seemed totally unaware of his near-naked state.

"Is something wrong?" she asked innocently.

"The mattress is wet."

"It is?"

"Clammy, cold, wet."

"You aren't the sort of guest who would be too polite to point out something like that, I see."

His eyes seemed to clamp her against her headboard. "I'm never too polite."

"Well, I left the window open when it rained the other night. I suppose a little rain must have gotten onto your bed. I didn't notice when I made it up."

"Liar."

Succinct and accurate. She sighed. "Can't you make the best of the situation?"

"Oh, yes." He leaned against the doorjamb, suddenly looking quite relaxed, even more darkly sexy. "I can make the best of the situation."

Her heartbeat quickened. She waved her hand in the direction of the living room. "You can always camp out by the fire. I have a sleeping bag you can borrow. It's good to twenty degrees below zero."

"A good hostess," he said, "would give me her bed."

Her mouth went dry. "But I'm already in it."

As responses went, she could have done better. Win took a step into her room, her space. But just one step was enough. "Exactly."

There was no undoing, she thought, what she'd already done. She had told him he could stay. She had told him in effect that she wanted a relationship with him. A romantic relationship. A physical relationship. She had let him see a part of her she usually kept hidden. Oh, she could still send him packing. It wasn't too late. And he'd go. He'd already made it plain that he understood when no meant no.

But she didn't want him to go. She had made her choices and there had been reasons for them, even if there were also very good reasons for choosing the opposite.

She knew, with a certainty that had escaped her earlier, that she wanted him to stay.

Something in her expression must have told him so, for he took another few steps into her room. She didn't stop him.

Finally he stood next to her bed, staring down at her. "Flannel, hmm?"

"It's a year-round fabric in Maine."

"How practical."

"I bought Cousin Thackeray a nightshirt just like this one for his birthday last year. I've had this one for...I don't know, it must be going on four years. It's got a couple of holes." She held up one arm so he could see the burn hole in the sleeve. "The fire got me one morning."

"Hannah..."

"You know, don't make the mistake of thinking I'm a rube or anything. I've lived most of my life in the city. And here we're just a couple of hours from Boston. Just because I sleep in a flannel nightgown doesn't mean I'm unsophisticated. I've turned down teaching positions at Ivy League colleges."

"Hannah..."

"I'm sometimes torn between city and country."

"Hannah…"

"It's just that Marsh Point is the only real home I've ever known. My mother did the best she could after my father died, but she was chasing her own demons—and rainbows. We all do."

Finally Win just threw back the covers and climbed into bed with her. She stared at him. He grinned. "After getting into that snow cone you call a guest bed and standing here for ten minutes, I'm about to freeze."

She stuck out a toe and found his calf. "You don't feel cold to me."

"You're in the wrong place," he said, a little raggedly.

"Oh."

Even with the cold wind, Hannah had the curtainless windows in her bedroom open. Win said, "I guess I should have brought my own flannel nightshirt."

"Do you have one?"

He sighed.

"Well, they are toasty."

"I prefer," he said, "other methods of staying warm."

"Like electric blankets, I suppose. I don't believe in them, myself. I won't say they cause cancer, but they sure do waste electricity, and they're not very romantic. But I guess if you're allergic to down, or maybe if you turn down the heat in the house so low that you can justify the use of electricity…"

"Hannah."

"You had other methods of staying warm in mind?"

"Yes."

That silenced her. He looked so damned tempting and rakish beside her, a man who would stop at nothing to get what he wanted. Herself included? Did she dominate his list of wants tonight? But he was more complex than that. *They* were more complex than that.

But she didn't want to dwell on complexities now.

She moved closer, and he touched her mouth with his fingertips, just grazing her lips. "What do you want, Hannah Marsh?"

Without speaking, she caught up the hem of her nightgown and lifted it over her head, the cool night air hitting her warm skin. She tossed the nightgown onto the floor.

His black eyes were on her. She met his gaze head-on, without flushing.

"I've dreamed about this moment," she said honestly.

"So have I."

His mouth closed over hers, his hands skimming the soft flesh of her breasts, tentatively at first, then more boldly. She took a sharp breath when his thumbs found her nipples. The ache inside her was almost more than she could bear. But he didn't pause, merciless in his teasing and stroking, never letting up with either his mouth or his hands. She didn't want him to.

Still, it was a game two could play.

She reached forward blindly, a little awkwardly, but without embarrassment, until she felt him, already hot and ready, and before she could pull back or even hesitate, he thrust himself hard against her hand.

"I've never wanted anyone the way I want you," he whispered. "Never."

He drew back, just for a moment, sliding out of his shorts, then rolling back to her so that their bodies melded, so that she could feel the long length of him against her. She felt sexy, aroused.

"You're so beautiful," he whispered, before he began a deep, hungry, evocative kiss. He trailed his fingertips down her spine, captured her buttocks in his palms, then skimmed the curve of her hips until he found the hot, moist, ready center of her.

"Win...I..."

"It's okay," he whispered, "it's okay."

And it was. More than okay.

"I don't know if I can last...."

"That's two of us."

But he hadn't finished.

"You're not going to have mercy on me, are you?" she said playfully, already knowing he wouldn't.

She let him roll her onto her back. He moved on top, his torso raised while his eyes seemed to absorb every inch of her. She splayed her fingers in the hairs on his chest, feeling the lean muscle, then let them trail lower, until they closed around his maleness. He thrust against her with a rhythm that was as primitive as the crashing of the waves upon the rocks outside her window.

His mouth descended to hers, tasted, then moved down her throat, tasted some more, and to her breasts, tasting and nipping. She wouldn't release him. Then he moved down her abdomen, tasting and licking now, not stopping.

"Let yourself go," he whispered. "Just let go."

As if she could stop herself.

But then she realized she'd never felt anything so erotic, so achingly pleasurable as his caresses.

He drew away from her, only for a moment to take precaution, before coming inside her, hard and fast, murmuring his encouragement, his love, until her cries mixed with those of the cormorants and the seagulls and finally his body quaked with hers, rocking, shattering.

Afterward, in the stillness, she noticed the wind had died down, too, and the waves were making a gentle swishing sound, as if they had all the time in the world to get wherever they were going. Hannah listened to the ocean for a long time and smiled at the man beside her.

A Harling. In her bed.

"Do you suppose," she said, "three centuries of Harlings and Marshes are already planning ways to haunt us tonight?"

He grinned back at her. "If they are, we'll be ready for 'em, don't you think?"

After making love with him, Hannah figured she was ready for anything.

IN THE MORNING the only sign he'd been there was the blazing fire in the living room.

She was ordinarily not a heavy sleeper, so Hannah assumed that either their lovemaking at dawn had knocked her out or that Win had sneaked out on her very, very quietly. She made herself a pot of coffee, added another log to the fire, and told herself she didn't regret last night. If she had to do it over again, she would. The giving and taking, emotionally and physically, had been mutual, real, if also fleeting. She had decided last night to let tomorrow bring what it would.

And it had, hadn't it?

She called him a host of names, dumped the trash and changed her sheets, wanting a fresh start.

The name-calling didn't work. She kept seeing his dark eyes on her, hearing his deep laughter, feeling the strength and warmth of his arms around her. She kept remembering the things they had told each other in the night, about growing up and climbing trees and finding a rare piece of glassware at a yard sale for two dollars and not being able to take it, having to tell the new widow who was selling off her stuff to pay her property taxes with what it was worth. Mostly they had talked about little things. There had been nothing about Thackeray Marsh or old Jonathan Harling, nothing about the Harling Collection, the ransacked apartment, the missing diary or the Declaration of Independence.

"Oh, Hannah," Win had said, stroking her hips, the inside of her thighs. "There's never been anyone remotely like you in my life…never."

She remembered how she'd responded. Hotly, eagerly, more boldly than on the occasion of their first lovemaking, she had shown him where to touch her, let him show her where to touch him. They had made love with abandon. Without thought. Without inhibition.

Without commitment?

"Hannah, Hannah…I'll never stop wanting you," he'd added.

He had been inside her then, thrusting hard yet lovingly, and she'd had her hands on his hips, urging him on, thinking that her ache for him would never end, never be satiated, that he'd collapse first. But he hadn't. He'd murmured his encouragement, urged her to let go…and she'd felt his satisfaction when she'd exploded, rocked and moaned as he kept going….

Now, in the bright, cold light of morning, Win Harling was gone. Calling him names wouldn't bring him back or make her hate him.

Or regret a single second of what they'd done last night. It had been a deliberate, conscious, mature choice on her part. She'd known the potential consequences.

Just as she knew that, come what may, there would never be another man for her. Win Harling was it. She wasn't the sort of woman who jumped into bed with one man one night and just hoped for the best. She had gone to bed with him because she had wanted him and only him.

Now she had to pay the price.

"Damn," she swore under her breath. She grabbed a sweatshirt, anxious for the solace of the sea, the rocks, the tide…for the solace of Marsh Point itself.

Outside in the chilly air, the dew soaked into her sneakers and she saw that his Jaguar was gone, too. It wasn't as if he'd ducked out for an early walk and planned to be back soon.

She didn't know if he planned to be back at all.

"The scoundrel," she muttered.

But what had she expected? She'd seen the two sides

of Win Harling: the black-eyed rogue who'd chased her down in Boston and the sophisticated gentleman who hadn't pressed himself upon her yesterday, despite his plain sexual need. Had the rogue made love to her last night? The gentleman? Or some combination of the two?

"What does it matter? He's gone now."

She began her litany of names again, but none of them made her feel the slightest bit better.

CHAPTER TEN

At some greasy-spoon diner not more than two miles from Marsh Point, Win and his uncle Jonathan sat over weak coffee and runny eggs. "You need to let me sort out this mess on my own," Win said in an attempt to reason with the old man.

Uncle Jonathan shook his head, soaking up a pool of egg with a triangle of pale white toast. "It's not your mess."

"Look..."

"I'm here, Winthrop. Make the best of it."

It was pointless to argue and Win knew it. Shortly after crawling out of Hannah's bed that morning and building a fire, he had slipped out to refill the wood box. He had planned to spend the morning with her, going over all the details of her trip to Boston, her research into Priscilla Marsh and Cotton Harling, her discovery of the possible existence of the Harling Collection. Everything. In turn, he'd tell her what little he'd learned from Uncle Jonathan.

Instead, out in the woodpile, he'd caught his uncle prowling about Marsh Point. Why the crazy old coot hadn't fallen and broken his hip in a tide pool was beyond him. Now there was nothing to be done but gather his things and cart Uncle Jonathan off to town, before one of the Marshes awakened and called the police.

So far, his uncle had yet to satisfactorily explain what he was doing in Maine. He had, he'd said, taken a bus from Boston and then a cab out to Marsh Point that had cost him double, he insisted, what it should have. He'd spent the night in a "disreputable" motel and had risen early and sneaked onto "the disputed property," where Win had found him.

"Has your apartment been broken into again?" Win asked.

"Nope."

"Did you find the Anne Harling diary under a couch cushion or something?"

"Nope."

"Uncle…"

"That cottage where I found you," Jonathan said, pouring still another little plastic vial of half-and-half into his coffee. "Hannah Marsh's, isn't it?"

Win sighed. "Yes, it is."

"She and you…slept together, did you?"

"Uncle Jonathan, you know I don't discuss my private life."

The old man grunted. "I'll wager you did more than sleep. My word, Winthrop. Falling for a Marsh." He let out a long breath. "No wonder I had trouble sleeping last night."

"You had trouble sleeping," Win muttered, controlling his growing frustration with difficulty, "because you know damned well you should have been home in your own bed. Uncle Jonathan, there's nothing you can do here except cause trouble. Go home."

The old man slurped his coffee and said, without looking at his nephew, "I wasn't the one who slept with a Marsh last night."

Win was at the end of his rope. "Cotton Harling and Priscilla Marsh lived three hundred years ago. I won't let them dictate to me what I should do with my life. And I don't give a damn whether we have a legitimate claim to Marsh Point or not. I don't even give a damn if Hannah would lie to her grandmother to get her hot little hands on the Harling Collection! You," he said, knowing he was losing control, "are going back to Boston."

Looking remarkably unperturbed by his nephew's outburst, Uncle Jonathan flagged the waitress for more coffee. She was back in a jiffy. Win let her heat his up. It was dreadful stuff. Almost worse than Hannah's purple tea.

Hannah, Hannah.

He had to keep Uncle Jonathan away from Thackeray Marsh and Marsh Point, at least until he and Hannah had adequately compared notes.

His uncle began again. "I talked to a friend of mine from Harvard who deals in rare books and documents."

Continually amazed by the variety of people Jonathan Harling knew, Win indulged him. "About what?"

"The copy of the Declaration of Independence in the Harling Collection."

"Allegedly."

Jonathan waved off Win's correction. "It's worth even more than I had anticipated."

"You'd anticipated a lot. How much more?"

"If it's in mint condition…"

"And if it exists."

Uncle Jonathan sighed. "It would be worth seven figures."

"Seven—"

"A million dollars."

At that moment, with Win gritting his teeth at the figure his uncle had just named, Thackeray Marsh wandered into the diner.

Directly behind him, spotting the two Harlings at once, was his cousin, the blonde and beautiful Hannah Marsh.

HANNAH GLARED AT Win and his uncle, while Cousin Thackeray gave a victorious sniff. The two Harlings looked remarkably guilty. Still, Hannah felt a rush of excitement at seeing Win, though she had to fight back memories of last night. At the same time, she didn't regret one nasty name she'd called him.

"Thackeray Marsh," Jonathan Harling declared, eyeing his contemporary with exaggerated disdain. "So, you're still alive. I'd heard you were killed in the war. Nothing heroic, of course. Drowned stepping over your own feet."

Win scowled at his uncle who, Hannah was sure, had heard no such thing.

It was equally clear that Thackeray wasn't in the mood

to help matters. "At least I fought in the war, instead of using privilege to get me a safe stateside job."

Jonathan Harling reddened and nearly came out of his chair, but Win clamped a hand on the old man's arm and held him down.

"Thackeray!" Hannah admonished her cousin.

He gave her a smug look for her trouble.

The diner was filling up with fishermen, in from their morning rounds. *All we need now is to start a brawl,* Hannah thought. "You two keep on like this," she told the two old men, "and you'll get us all arrested."

"Just stating the facts," Cousin Thackeray said loftily.

Jonathan Harling grunted. "A Marsh wouldn't know a fact if it smacked him in the face."

"Perhaps," Hannah said through clenched teeth, "we should go back to Marsh Point and discuss things."

Cousin Thackeray shook his head. "I don't want them on my property."

"*Your* property," Jonathan sneered. "Why, back in 1891—"

Win cut him off, his eyes pinned on Hannah. "How did you find us?" he asked quietly.

Before she could answer, Thackeray said, "That damned ostentatious car you drive sticks out around here like—"

Now it was Hannah's turn to do some cutting off. "My cousin found evidence of a prowler while on his morning walk and insisted it had to be a Harling. I indulged him in a spin around town, the result of which is our presence here."

"What evidence?" Jonathan demanded.

Thackeray gave him a supercilious look. "Nothing *you* would notice. I, however, who was raised out here, wondered if an elephant hadn't been through."

Win was on his feet, laying bills upon the table. His jaw was set, hard. He moved with tensed, highly controlled motions. An unhappy man. Obviously hadn't got enough sleep last night. Hannah watched him, pleased with herself. At least she wasn't the only one suffering.

"Let's go," he said, taking in both Marshes and his uncle.

"Oh, no, you don't," Cousin Thackeray replied, shaking his head. "I'm not letting you two sneak off before I get a chance to search your car and your persons."

"Fine." Win's tone was steely, but had no apparent effect on anyone. "You and my uncle can drive together. I'll take Hannah."

The two old men argued all the way out to the parking lot, but Win was adamant. He opened the passenger door to Thackeray's 1967 GMC truck and told his uncle it was his choice: he could be helped in or thrown in. Jonathan squared his shoulders and climbed in without anyone's help. Thackeray muttered something about wanting to ram the passenger side of his truck into a tree, except for the fact that it had another five or ten years left in it, might even outlast him. Win just looked at Hannah in despair.

"We'll follow you," he told his uncle and her cousin. "No tricks."

He turned away before either could say any more.

Hannah had opened the passenger door to his Jaguar. "Any orders for me?" she asked coolly.

He glared at her. "Just get in."

She did so, slamming the door shut. He followed. His tall, lean body filled the interior, instantly making her aware again of last night, of her unceasing attraction to this man. She tried not to show it.

"I take it," she said as he started the car, "that you found your uncle snooping around this morning and sneaked out."

A muscle worked in his jaw. "That's about it."

"You made your choice, didn't you?"

"The way I see it," he said tightly, rolling into position behind Thackeray's truck, "I didn't have a choice."

"I'm not saying you shouldn't have gone with your uncle. All I'm saying is, a note or a quick goodbye would have been…courteous."

"And what would you have done?"

"If I knew your uncle was snooping around Marsh Point? I don't know."

"You'd have raised hell, Hannah. At the very least you'd have hauled your cousin over, and he'd have called the police and had Uncle Jonathan arrested as a trespasser." He glanced at her. "Like me, you would have felt you had no choice."

He was crowding Cousin Thackeray on the winding, narrow road out to Marsh Point. Thackeray braked hard and Win cursed, just missing the truck's rear end. But he backed off. Hannah could almost hear her cousin's satisfied chuckle.

She sighed. "I don't know if you're right or you're wrong, and I guess we'll never find out. Did your uncle tell you why he's here?"

"We were just getting into it when you and Thackeray barged in. Nice timing." He exhaled, running one hand through his wild hair. His day obviously hadn't started out very well. Neither, however, had hers. "Hannah, I'm doing the best I can. Will you believe that much?"

She didn't answer right away. They had just rounded a bend, and she could see white-capped waves pounding the rocks of Marsh Point. The sun was shining. The temperature had begun to climb. It would be a splendid day in southern Maine. But her life here, Hannah thought, would never again be the same.

Finally she said, "I'll believe that much, yes."

In a few moments, he turned into Thackeray's driveway and followed the truck up to the house. Jonathan Harling seemed to jump out before the truck had even come to a full stop. He was waving his arms and shouting.

"This should be interesting," Win said grimly.

"Think I should keep a bucket of cold water handy, in case things get out of control?"

He looked at her and grinned. "A woman after my own heart." He nodded toward the house. "Shall we?"

"As I see it," she said, paraphrasing his earlier words, "we have no choice."

HANNAH, THACKERAY MARSH and Uncle Jonathan were arguing a point of early-American history that held no interest for Win, but at least, he thought, no one had yet come to blows. He noticed that Hannah held her own in the argument with the two men, whom she accused of agreeing with each other, even if they wouldn't admit it. Being no historian, Win couldn't comment.

Finally he rose, feeling it was relatively safe to leave them alone, and wandered from the living room to the dining room, preoccupied not with Puritans but with a document potentially worth a million dollars. If it existed. If it could be located.

Uncle Jonathan could use the money.

So could the Marshes.

Win exhaled, walking through the French doors onto a deck that overlooked a small cove he hadn't noticed yesterday. Here the land sloped gently to the water, where waves lapped over sand and marsh grass. He squinted against the sunlight.

Something had been shoved into the brush. It was dark blue; he could see just one end.

A canoe. A wooden canoe.

His uncle was capable of many things, but not of paddling from Boston or even Kennebunkport in a canoe. He had said he'd taken a bus and a taxi, and Win believed him. Maybe it was Thackeray Marsh's canoe. Or Hannah's.

But he didn't believe it. A dark suspicion started to formulate itself in his mind.

Returning to the living room, he grabbed his uncle. "Let's go for a walk."

Uncle Jonathan was red-faced with arguing. "These

two—" he jerked his head at the Marshes "—know nothing about American judicial history."

"I'm sure they don't." Win didn't give a damn if they did. "Let's go."

"Hold your horses, there. I won't have you humoring me just because I'm an old man."

"Uncle Jonathan, we need to talk. I have a proposition I want to discuss with you before I present it to Hannah and Thackeray."

It was never easy for Jonathan Harling to abandon an argument, but he took the hint and followed his nephew outside. They left behind Hannah and Thackeray, grumbling and looking very suspicious, as well they might.

"What the devil have you got a bee in your bonnet about?" Uncle Jonathan demanded. "I was being civil to those two."

"I think I know who ransacked your apartment."

The old man narrowed his eyes, then nodded solemnly. "I was wondering when you'd figure it out."

"What do you suppose they're up to?" Thackeray asked.

Hannah sat cross-legged on the threadbare carpet, already contemplating just that question herself. "I don't know. But don't you get the feeling they're holding more cards in their deck than we are? And don't tell me it's the Harling way."

"Well, it is."

"Win's on to something." She climbed to her feet, feeling oddly confident. Not outmatched. Not outwitted. Not as if Win Harling and his cantankerous uncle were actual enemies. Not allies, perhaps, but definitely not enemies. "I think I'll take a walk, too."

"Don't let 'em catch you."

But he sounded distracted, preoccupied with something besides his natural inclination to doubt everything the Harlings said or did. His eyes weren't focused on her. She said goodbye, but he didn't answer, didn't even wave a hand.

Something was definitely up. Was she the only one who didn't know what?

Outside the air was still and so clear that everything seemed overfocused, outlined in sharp detail against a sky so blue that it made a body appreciate life. Hannah went through the side door, just as Win and his uncle had, but saw no sign of them. She had no idea where they'd gone. Had they wandered toward her cottage? She didn't want to eavesdrop, but her trust level wasn't what it had been only a few hours ago. She wanted to keep an eye on the two Harlings.

It was ridiculous, she thought, a Marsh like herself falling for a Harling, but there it was. And she wasn't falling, she knew that much. She'd already fallen.

She was in love with the man.

They weren't anywhere outside or inside her cottage. Hannah stared out the picture window in her living room, tapping her foot and cursing them. She forced herself to return to Thackeray's house, duly noting along the way that Win's car was still parked behind her cousin's old truck. Wherever they'd gone, it couldn't be far.

She headed back inside, determined to get some

straight answers out of Thackeray Marsh about the Harling claim on Marsh Point and about the missing Harling Collection.

She would not let him or Jonathan Harling sidetrack her with their inflammatory comments on some obscure historical fact. She wanted answers.

When she had them, then she would figure out what to do about Win Harling.

And find out what he meant to do about her.

Cousin Thackeray wasn't in the living room. She checked the kitchen, but he wasn't there, either. She was getting really irritated now.

"Thackeray?"

Silence.

Had he gone for a walk, too? Let them all go off, she thought. She'd be damned happy, living all alone on Marsh Point! Who needed two old men and one know-it-all, black-eyed rogue?

She groaned. How the hell could she have fallen in love with J. Winthrop Harling? He made too much money. He'd had his life handed to him on a silver platter. He probably didn't know anything about the Deerfield Massacre or the influence of covenant theology on American democracy.

"Thackeray! Dammit, where are you?"

She flounced upstairs to check the bathroom; surely he must have heard her, for all the racket she was making?

The attic door was ajar.

Creaking it open, Hannah stuck her head inside and

squinted up the dark, steep staircase. She could smell the dust and mold. "Thackeray, are you up there?" she called, lowering her voice for no particular reason.

When there was no answer, she reached along the wall for a light switch, but found none. She didn't relish walking up there in the dark. But if Cousin Thackeray was up there, surely he had a flashlight and was just off in some corner? And even if he didn't, even if he wasn't up there, what else—who else—could be?

Bats, she thought. Spiders, cobwebs, mice.

"Coward," she muttered to herself and headed up.

The steps creaked and the musty odor worsened as she climbed the steep staircase. She had never been up to the attic. It was unfinished, there was no rail or wall built up around the stairwell; as her eyes adjusted to the darkness, she could see silhouettes of boxes and old furniture, but no beam of a flashlight. She was probably on a wild-goose chase, while Win and Jonathan and her cousin were all doing the real business of the day elsewhere.

"Thackeray," she called irritably, "are you up here?"

A shuffling noise came from the far corner off to her right, then a strangled cry. Her cousin's voice croaked, "Run, Hannah!"

"Thackeray!"

She lurched up the last three steps. The silhouette of a man emerged from behind a huge armoire. It wasn't her tall, thin, elderly cousin. Hannah quickly grabbed whatever was at her feet—a soggy box of hats, it turned out—and heaved it at the figure. It went wide. She scrambled for a stack of old drapes and started heaving them, too, but in a moment the strange figure had her, one arm clamped firmly around her middle. She kicked. He cursed viciously.

"What have you done with Thackeray?" she yelled. "Who are you? *Help!*"

But with one last, violent curse, he threw her against the armoire. She hit it hard with her right shoulder and spun into the darkness, out of control, breaking her fall with her left arm and landing unceremoniously in a heap in the pile of drapes. Her entire body ached. She let loose a string of curses herself.

"Thackeray, for God's sake, get away!"

She flung drapes at the figure behind her and leaped over the open stairwell to the other side of the attic, away from her cousin. Her pursuer followed. She could hear him breathing hard. She grabbed a ladder-back chair and shoved it into his path, knocking him off his feet.

Thackeray Marsh slipped down the stairs.

The man swore, scrambled to his feet and came after her again. "Bitch!"

There was a small, dirty window at the far end of the attic that Hannah was eyeballing for size. Would she fit? Could she make it through before her attacker caught up with her?

What happened if she did?

What happened if she didn't?

She dodged behind a metal clothes closet and dived for the window, tripping over a rolled-up rug. Adrenaline kept her from feeling any pain, any fatigue. She refused to panic. She got back to her feet.

Something to break the window... She needed something hard and within reach.

An old cane. Perfect!

Iron fingers closed around her left ankle and pulled her off her feet, sending her headlong. A heavy body landed on top of her. She felt the air going out of her lungs. Her right arm was twisted around to the small of her back, under him.

"Don't move, don't talk. I wouldn't want to hurt you."

She nodded her understanding.

And recognized his voice. The pieces of the puzzle fell together.

Her captor was Preston Fowler, director of the New England Athenaeum, to whom she had confided so much. He took a deep breath, then laughed roughly. "I might want to do other things to you," he said, stroking her hair with his free hand, "but not hurt you."

She kicked his shin as sharply as she could.

He bore down upon her twisted arm, and it was all she could do not to cry out. "You just bought yourself some pain, Miss Marsh."

"What do you want with me?"

"Don't talk."

"Tell me!"

He brought his mouth close to her ear, and she felt his breath against her cheek. "You're my ticket to a million dollars."

"I don't—"

"Shut up." He settled himself more firmly on top of her, sliding his free hand down her upper arm and just skimming her breast. "Just be quiet and still and nothing will happen to you."

She didn't move, didn't even breathe.

"You see," he said, "you're my hostage."

"WHERE THE DEVIL do you suppose he is?" Jonathan Harling asked.

Win regarded him with growing exasperation, though the feeling was directed not so much toward his uncle as the situation. They had combed the point for any sign of Preston Fowler, but found only the canoe and a single footprint in the mud. Both, they decided, had to be his. It was too early for tourists, and they had no doubt that Preston Fowler very much wanted first crack at the Harling Collection and the Declaration of Independence.

Win and his uncle headed back onto the deck off Thackeray's dining room, figuring to tell the Marshes everything.

"I don't know where he is, but if—"

Thackeray Marsh burst around the corner of the house, his thin hair sticking up, his face ashen. His clothes were covered with dust, and a cobweb dangled off one arm. He could hardly speak. "Hannah...the bastard's got her...he..."

A cold current shot through Win.

"Calm down, man," Uncle Jonathan ordered impatiently. "We can't understand what in blazes you're saying."

Win had understood. "Where?"

Thackeray pointed to the house. "The attic…"

It was all Win needed to hear.

Behind him, Uncle Jonathan hissed in annoyance. "Now don't go barging in up there before you get all the facts!" He pounded his cane on the ground. "Winthrop—Winthrop, we need a plan!"

But Win was already through the French doors. He grabbed the poker from the living room fireplace and headed upstairs, the cold current now a hot rage.

Fowler. If the stinking bastard even touched Hannah…

He ripped open the door and took the stairs two at a time, ignoring the darkness. He thought only fleetingly about how Fowler might be armed, what he had planned. His main concern was Hannah.

Hannah…

At the top of the stairs he stopped and listened, let his eyes adjust to the lack of light. He heard nothing, could make out nothing that resembled Hannah or Fowler. Had the bastard already sneaked off with her?

To his left he heard a soft moan.

"Hannah?"

Holding his poker high, he moved toward the sound. He had to fight his way through scattered drapes and past overturned furniture, but remained alert. The sun was angling in through the dirty window now, casting a faint light upon a figure that lay sprawled on what appeared to be a rolled-up carpet.

It moved, and the sun hit strands of long, silken, blond hair.

"Hannah," Win breathed.

Within seconds he was kneeling beside her, pulling a nasty-looking gag from her mouth, fumbling at the drapery cord that was tied around her wrists. Her eyes were huge and frightened, and damned beautiful.

She spat dust and cobwebs from her mouth, coughing, and finally sputtered, "It's a trap."

No sooner were the words out than Win felt something cold and metallic against his lower jaw. "Now I have two hostages," Preston Fowler said.

"Now," Win said tightly, "you have one hell of a mess on your hands. Let us both go, before you get yourself in any deeper."

"You arrogant, insufferable prig." Fowler laughed nastily, never moving the gun. "God, I've wanted to say those words to one of you for years. No, do not move, I warn you. As you have so accurately pointed out—as if I needed you to tell me—I'm in one hell of a mess. I intend, however, to emerge from it intact."

"He thinks Cousin Thackeray has the Harling Collection," Hannah told Win hoarsely. "He wants the Declaration of Independence. He's the one—" She had to pause to cough, so merciless had Fowler been in applying the gag. "He broke into your uncle's apartment."

"I know," Win responded gently. "I should have known from the beginning. He knew what you were working on. With your blond hair and reputation as a biographer, he probably figured out you were Hannah Marsh—Priscilla's descendant—right from the start."

Fowler smirked. "It was a simple matter to blow her cover story straight to hell."

"So, he watched you, and knowing you were an expert researcher, he followed your leads to the Harling Collection...." Hannah shut her eyes, and Win could see pain and regret wash over her; it could be no worse than what he felt. He would give anything to see her smile. "Hannah, Uncle Jonathan knew it had to be Fowler who ransacked his apartment. Other than you, he was the only one who could have known about the diary or the Harling Collection."

"Oh, stop, both of you," Fowler ordered. "Let's get this over with. The Harling Collection, Miss Hannah. Where is it?"

She shook her head, not, Win could see, for the first time, and said wearily, "I told you, I don't know."

Keeping the gun pressed to Win's jaw, Fowler leaned over him and said to Hannah, "Suppose I start blowing holes in your lover boy here? Do you think that would improve your memory?"

Win made himself chuckle. "You've got that one wrong, Fowler. Give her the gun. She'll blow holes in me herself."

"Shut up!"

Win thought he heard a small, creaking sound on the attic stairs. Footsteps? Old men's footsteps?

Dear God, he thought.

He looked at Hannah and saw her eyes widen slightly. Had she heard the creaking sound, too?

Uncle Jonathan and Cousin Thackeray coming to rescue them.

It was almost more than Win could bear.

His fingers closed around the poker. One small opening was all he needed. He longed to knock Preston Fowler onto his greedy ass. But he had to cover for the two down on the staircase. Hannah, he noticed, was noisily shifting around.

"Can I untie her wrists?" Win asked.

"No, leave them. She's a vicious bitch, you know. Practically emasculated me. I'm sure you're disappointed she didn't succeed. But I won't be diverted from my task. The Harling Collection, Miss Marsh."

Behind them, Jonathan Harling's voice broke through the darkness. "It isn't hers to give away."

Then Thackeray Marsh said, "Drop the gun, Mr. Fowler. I have a loaded Colt .45 pointed at your lower spine and would be glad to pull the trigger to repay you for the thrashing you gave me alone."

"You're bluffing," Fowler sneered.

"So, call my bluff. Find out what happens."

"He's a mean shot," Uncle Jonathan said. "He taught me how to shoot when we were at Harvard together. I remember he could hit a weasel from fifty yards, right between the eyes—"

"I can blow your nephew's head off," Fowler interjected.

Thackeray sniffed. "Go ahead. He's a Harling. I'll get a bullet into you before you get to Hannah."

Win's eyes locked with Hannah's. He could see she realized her cousin was having a hell of a time.

"Drop the gun," Thackeray Marsh drawled. "Slowly."

He seemed to be taking his lines from old Clint Eastwood movies, but Fowler, biting back what sounded like a curse, removed the gun from Win's jaw and slowly lowered it to the floor.

"Bastards," he muttered, "all of you."

Then he whipped around, roaring like a madman, catching everyone by surprise; he shoved the two old men aside and leaped for the stairs.

"Shoot him!" Uncle Jonathan yelled. "Shoot the greedy bastard!"

"I can't bloody see him! I'm not twenty anymore, you know, you old snot. Why the hell don't you go after him?"

"I'm eighty years old!"

"So? I'm seventy-nine."

"Take care of Hannah," Win growled. "*I'll* go after him. Mind if I borrow your gun, Thackeray?"

"Not at all, but you'd better take care. It's not loaded."

Win forced himself to refrain from comment.

"If you hadn't gone off like a decapitated chicken," Uncle Jonathan put in, "we'd have been able to take time to load the gun. As it was, Thackeray couldn't remember where he'd put the bullets. In fact, he'd almost forgotten he even had the gun. I had to remind him...."

"The hell with it," Win muttered and dashed off with the poker. Maybe Fowler hadn't loaded his gun, either.

He fought his way through the scattered drapes and overturned furniture, choking on cobwebs and dust, warning himself not to let his anger lead him into another trap. With a near-physical effort, he dismissed the image of Hannah bound and gagged. It must have been a devastating experience for her. And it was all his fault. Would she ever be the same? Would she ever forgive him for not having shared his suspicions sooner?

No. You'll have to deal with that later.

Fowler had shut the attic door. Win pushed against it, but it wouldn't give. The bastard must have blocked it. He reared back and threw all his weight at the old door. It bounced and cracked a little, but still didn't give.

"Here," Hannah said, suddenly beside him, as pale as a ghost, "let me help."

Win saw the raw, bloody wrists, the spreading bruise on her jaw, and felt rage boil up inside him, threatening once again to overwhelm him.

Then he saw the gun in her hand.

"What's that?" he asked.

She smiled a little. "Fowler's gun."

Win grinned, suddenly reenergized. He pointed a thumb at the door and smiled at Hannah. "Shall we?"

She set the gun upon a step, and Win turned it so it wasn't pointed at either of them. He was taking no more chances.

Uncle Jonathan and Cousin Thackeray appeared at the top of the stairs. "Heave-ho!" they yelled.

It took Hannah and Win three tries, and the door splintered into three parts before the chair Fowler had anchored under the knob gave way.

They were out.

CHAPTER ELEVEN

HANNAH IGNORED THE PAIN in her wrists and shoulders, her dry mouth, her fear. She concentrated only on keeping up with Win and trying not to shoot him or herself in the foot. Guns were not her thing.

They caught up with Fowler in Cousin Thackeray's truck. He must have snatched the keys from the hook by the back door; he was still fumbling with them when Win hauled him out of the cab and threw him onto the ground. Hannah controlled a wild impulse to fire the gun into the air.

"All right, all right!" Fowler yelled when Win twisted his arms behind his back. "I give up. Call the damned police."

Breathing hard, Win didn't let up. "You won't try anything?"

"Like what, running? You lunatics would shoot me like a dog." He spat a mouthful of grass and dirt. "Just let me go. I'll take what's coming to me."

"You're damned right you will."

Fowler glanced at Win, who still held his prisoner's arms pinned behind him. "I wouldn't have hurt anyone."

Hannah could see Win gritting his teeth. "You did hurt someone."

"She's a Marsh. One wouldn't think a Harling would go all soft over—"

He shut up when Hannah stepped forward, holding his gun. "One wouldn't think," she said, "a snooty Harling could knock you on your behind, either, but look at you now, Mr. Fowler."

"It's *Doctor* Fowler," he said loftily.

Win made a sound of pure disgust and let up, climbing to his feet. He looked at Hannah. "I'll call the police. You can keep an eye on him?"

"Sure. With pleasure."

Fowler sat up, his face red with anger, devoid of remorse. That was as far as Hannah would let him go. After her ordeal in the attic, she was taking no chances. But just as Win started for the house, they heard the wail of a siren, and Cousin Thackeray and Uncle Jonathan raced out of the back door, armed to the teeth with kitchen knives and skillets. They looked as if they were having the time of their lives.

"I've called the police," Thackeray announced.

"They're on their way," Jonathan added excitedly.

Fowler looked at his four captors and muttered, "Thank God."

The police came, explanations were made, and Preston Fowler was carted off. Charges were filed and the sorting-out process was begun. Through it all, Hannah noticed that Cousin Thackeray never once allowed that the Harlings and the director of the New England Athenaeum might be correct in their opinion that he knew the location of the long-missing Harling Collection.

She also noted that Win Harling never left her side.

The police seemed to be having a difficult time fathoming why a director of a prestigious institution like the New England Athenaeum would risk arrest to snatch a collection of old papers, even one that might include a valuable copy of the Declaration of Independence.

"How valuable?" the lieutenant in charge asked the group of people assembled in his small office.

The Marshes didn't answer. The Harlings, however, said, "A million dollars, give or take ten thousand or so."

The lieutenant, a rail-thin Maine native, whistled. "But there's no proof this thing exists?"

"None whatsoever," Thackeray Marsh replied, although the question wasn't directed at him.

Win smiled at Hannah, but said nothing. Then his gaze fell upon her bruised and raw wrists and his smile vanished, his expression darkening. The police had asked her if she needed medical attention, but she'd said no, largely because she didn't want to miss the Harlings' explanation of the day's festivities.

"And this Fowler character," the lieutenant went on, "learned about the collection—and presumably the Declaration of Independence—when Miss Marsh here was conducting research in Boston?"

"They weren't in cahoots," Thackeray put in.

"That's not what I was implying. I'm merely trying to establish the sequence of events. Miss Marsh, we'll need a statement from you on your trip to Boston and your association with Dr. Fowler."

"Certainly. I had no idea he would go to such extremes for personal profit. I myself had only an academic interest in the collection."

An eyebrow went up and the lieutenant asked, "Even though the subject of your new biography is one of your ancestors, who was wrongly executed by an ancestor of the Harlings?"

She smiled coolly. "Even so."

Jonathan Harling gave a small grunt that she managed to ignore.

Beside her, Win said, "Fowler broke into my uncle's apartment in an attempt to discover any materials that would provide him with a clue as to the location of the Harling Collection. He stole a diary written by——"

Win's elderly uncle cleared his throat and squirmed in his rickety wooden chair. "That's not quite the case. Fowler did break into my apartment, of course, and combed the place, but he didn't steal the diary. He just read it."

"He read it," the lieutenant repeated dubiously.

"That's right. It describes how the Marshes hood-winked us out of our land here in southern Maine and stole the Harling Collection."

Thackeray was on his feet now. "It was never your land! The Marshes are the legitimate owners of Marsh Point and have been for a hundred years!"

The lieutenant sighed. "Could we stick to current history? The diary, Mr. Harling. You say it was never missing?"

"That's right. I only claimed it was gone to keep my nephew on the case. He and Miss Marsh…well, their relationship was about to go sour unless Winthrop did something, and I felt he was of a mind to do nothing at all, and therefore..."

Hannah could feel Win stiffening beside her and smiled. His uncle, she thought, was every bit as exasperating as her cousin. "I wouldn't," he said, "have done nothing."

Jonathan Harling shrugged. "Couldn't take that chance, m'boy."

The lieutenant continued. "How do you know Fowler read the diary?"

"Common sense," Jonathan replied simply.

Thackeray snorted. "A damned good guess is what it was."

"If you knew the Harlings knew the Marshes had the Harling Collection," the lieutenant asked, "why didn't they come after it before now?"

"We didn't know. Anne Harling was an eccentric and...well, she didn't care for the Marshes. She was aware of their grudge against our family and—"

"You—meaning the Harling family—didn't take her accusations seriously," the lieutenant supplied.

The elderly Harling pursed his lips and remained silent.

Hannah noticed a ghost of a smile on Win's face and felt a rush of pure affection for him.

"But Preston Fowler did," the lieutenant went on. "What made you suspect him?"

Jonathan squirmed.

"Tell him," his nephew ordered.

The old man grimaced. "I didn't think—I didn't believe Hannah, although a Marsh, was capable of ransacking my apartment. I knew my nephew didn't do it, and I knew *I* didn't do it."

"Why not a random thief?"

"Impossible."

His tone was so supercilious and dismissive that even the lieutenant didn't argue. He proceeded with his questioning, finally sending them all home with orders to stick around, because he was sure to need further clarifications. They began to head back toward the house.

"By the way, Thackeray," the officer said to his retreating fellow townsman, "what's this about you holding a gun on Fowler? Seems to me you don't have a weapon registered."

It was Jonathan Harling who spun around and replied, "Thackeray Marsh hold a gun on anyone? Don't be absurd. That old buzzard couldn't shoot a hole through the side of a barn at fifty feet."

"But you all said…"

"A ruse, Lieutenant, a simple ruse."

Then Jonathan marched out, shoulders thrust back, as if he'd made perfect sense and hadn't told a huge lie. For once Thackeray didn't contradict him.

Win seized Hannah by the waist. "I just know those two are both going to live to be a hundred," he muttered.

Back at the house, Thackeray rattled around in the kitchen and emerged with cups of hot tea laced with brandy and insisted they all drink up. For once, no one argued.

"Are you certain you don't want a doctor to examine your wounds?" Jonathan Harling asked Hannah.

She shook her head. "I'll be fine, thanks."

"It's a wonder Winthrop permitted Fowler to leave the property relatively intact."

Only the darkening of Win's eyes indicated he concurred with his uncle. All things considered, he was being remarkably untalkative. He never, however, left Hannah's side.

"Winthrop, hell," she said spiritedly. "It's a wonder *I* let him leave intact. Did he hurt you at all, Cousin Thackeray?"

"Only my pride. I have never done anything so difficult as leaving you in the clutches of that man, but I knew he had a gun, and I would be of no use to you, dead or maimed." He swirled around a mouthful of tea and then swallowed; gradually his face regained its color. "He sneaked into the house while Win and Jonathan were off plotting. You had gone, and I'm afraid he took me quite by surprise. Clearly he had no idea the Harlings were about. He thought he would just have to contend with Hannah and me. Of course, we would have managed."

Jonathan Harling opened his mouth, but his nephew cut him off before he could speak. "I'm glad things worked out."

"I just have one more question," Hannah said, her gaze taking in both old men. "You two were at Harvard together?"

Thackeray's face took on a look of pure distaste and Jonathan's matched it.

"Cousin Thackeray, you never told me you attended Harvard!"

"I'm not proud of it," he stated.

"He graduated magna cum laude," Jonathan Harling added. "Damned near killed my father, having a Marsh outdo a Harling, but I wasn't much of a student in those days. I reached my potential later, in graduate school. Thackeray had gone back to Maine by then, intent on being a Marsh."

Thackeray nodded. "Jonathan and I should have been great friends."

"And were for a while," his former classmate reminisced wistfully. He grabbed the brandy and splashed more into Thackeray's teacup, then into his own. "To our lost youth, my friend."

They drank up.

Win leaned toward Hannah and whispered, "Don't believe any of this. Uncle Jonathan's just leading up to demanding what in hell your cousin's done with the Harling Collection."

Sure enough, a few minutes later, Jonathan Harling leaned back, looking smug and content. "So, Thackeray, where have you had my family's papers hidden all these years?"

WIN FILLED HANNAH'S tub with water as hot as he thought she could stand it and added white bath salts from a glass bottle. He had piled two fluffy white towels on the edge of the tub, where he sat, watching the water foam. He had abandoned Uncle Jonathan to dinner with Thackeray

Marsh. The two would, no doubt, argue about the Harling Collection well into the night or perhaps reminisce about their days at Harvard. One simply never knew with those two, Win had decided.

"Going to take a bath?" Hannah asked, appearing in the bathroom doorway.

He shook his head. "You are."

She half smiled. "By your order?"

"It'll be good for your bumps and bruises."

And her spirits, he hoped. Since returning to her cottage she had been uncharacteristically reticent, and her skin, though normally pale, seemed almost ghostlike now. He had left her standing in front of her picture window, staring at the sea, while he filled the tub. A gulf had opened between them. He sensed it, hated it, but didn't know what to do about it.

He turned off the water. The silence that surrounded them felt damned unbearable. He felt Hannah's luminous eyes on him. He turned to meet them. "Are you going to be all right?"

She nodded, saying nothing.

"It was a hell of a scare, Hannah, for all of us. You just got the worst of it."

She nodded again. He rose from the tub and started past her, but she touched his arm, just a whisper of her fingers. "When Fowler had me pinned down..." She stopped and cleared her throat. Win could see the pain in her eyes, a pain that had nothing to do with cuts and bruises. "I wanted you to come, Win. It scares me how much. I've always been so independent."

"You still are," he assured her, then gestured to the tub. "Relax for as long as you want. Call me if you need anything."

And he left.

HANNAH SOAKED IN THE TUB until her skin was as pink as a lobster's, but couldn't boil J. Winthrop Harling out of herself. The hot water swirling around her only served to remind her of how much she still wanted him.

Fatigue weighed down her eyelids, while stress and the heat of the water made her feel drained and limp, without energy or purpose. She wanted only to sleep and when she woke up, to find that her life on Marsh Point was as it had been before she'd gone to Boston. Except that it wouldn't be, couldn't be…and if it meant losing Win, she didn't want it to be the same as before. She knew that.

Such contradictions! She groaned at her own confusion and climbed out of the tub, the stiffness in her joints and muscles eased for the moment. She toweled off, pulled her terry-cloth robe from the hook where she kept it and wrapped it around her. Her reflection in the steamy mirror made her wince.

"You look like hell," she muttered.

Dark circles under her eyes made them appear even wider, nervous, afraid. Her skin looked splotchy and unnatural. Her mouth was raw from biting her lips. The bruises and cuts on her wrists had turned ugly shades of red and purple. She looked done in, as if the impact of what had happened earlier today had finally hit her squarely between the eyes.

And yet that was only a part of it.

The rest of what had hit her, she knew, was the impact of being in love with Win Harling…and of knowing she had no choice but to tell him to take himself and his uncle and head back to Boston, where they belonged.

WIN LISTENED TO Hannah's request without interrupting. She had emerged from the bathroom in a robe that was surprisingly sexy and feminine, given her penchant for androgynous flannel nightshirts. "I know I look like hell," she'd said. That was the first inaccuracy he'd heard from her lips. Others followed.

But he let her talk.

Finally she finished and looked at him expectantly. He knew what he was supposed to say. Yes, she was absolutely right. Yes, he would collect Uncle Jonathan and leave immediately. But instead he said, "Let me see if I've got this straight."

"Okay."

He moved over on the couch and made room for her. "Have a seat."

"I don't…"

"What are you worried about? Didn't you just say that last night was just the product of—how did you put it?"

"Adrenaline. The excitement of the moment."

"Right. Then you shouldn't be afraid of sitting next to me, should you?"

"I'm not."

He patted the spot beside him.

She flipped back her hair and sat down, as far from him as she could manage. He tried not to smile. *Adrenaline, my hind end!*

The tie on her robe had loosened, so it wasn't wrapped around her as primly and tightly as it had been. He could see the soft swell of one breast, still pink from her long, hot bath. Right now, even her feet looked sexy, designed just to torment him.

He wasn't leaving.

"Okay," he began. "You think Uncle Jonathan and I ought to leave because we belong in Boston."

"Yes."

"Does that mean we should never leave town? Never take a vacation? Nothing?"

She scowled. "It means you don't belong here."

"On Marsh Point," he concluded.

"That's right."

"And you and I. We don't belong together because I belong in Boston, I'm a Harling, I make too much money, I have a city job, and I would never live down falling in love with a Marsh."

She mumbled something that he had to make her repeat, which she did reluctantly, not meeting his eye. "I didn't say anything about falling in love with a Marsh."

"Ahh, correct. You said 'being with.' A fine distinction, don't you think?"

"No."

He leaned toward her. "Hannah, you're dead wrong on all counts."

She didn't say a word.

"I love Boston, but I didn't grow up there. I don't need to live there. I am a Harling. You're not wrong about that, but you are wrong if you think it determines my outlook toward you or anything else. I do make a great deal of money, but how much is too much? And I don't, as you implied, exist to make money. I could not make another dime my entire life and find ways to be fulfilled and happy. As for a city job… With computers, I can do my work from virtually anywhere. I just happen to prefer Boston."

Her top teeth were bearing down on her lower lip, already ragged from her ordeal with Preston Fowler. Win ran a forefinger gently over her lip, freeing it, while further tormenting himself. He shifted on the couch. Stupid to have made a fire; its heat was totally unnecessary, as far as he was concerned.

"And that last—never living down 'being with' a Marsh. Hannah, I don't give a damn what people think of who I want to be with. It's never mattered to me and doesn't now." He spoke in a low, deliberate voice. "And you know that."

"Win…"

"You know all of it."

She jumped to her feet. "I can't let you stay!"

"Fine. I'll go if you want me to go. Just tell me the real reason why."

"Can't you just leave?"

"Hannah…"

"All you have to do is get your uncle, throw your

stuff into your car and drive on out of here. It's really very simple."

He got up. "Okay, if that's what you want. I'll go pack up. Can you run over and tell Uncle Jonathan to be ready to leave in fifteen minutes?"

"Sure. I mean..." She narrowed her eyes at him, visibly suspicious. "You're going to leave, just like that?"

"It's not just like that. It's after listening to all your crazy reasons why I should and taking you at your word. You want me out. Okay, I'm out."

He started down the hall.

"Now wait just a minute!" she blurted.

Ignoring her—and his own incipient sense of relief— he walked into the guest room, where he'd deposited his overnight bag.

She was right behind him. "But you don't believe my reasons for wanting you gone."

"That's right," he agreed, shoving things back into his bag. "I don't."

"But you're not going to insist on the truth?"

"Nope."

"Why not?"

"Because I'm not a boor."

She was stunned into a momentary silence.

"If a lady orders me out of her house," he went on, "I go. It's the proper thing to do, you know. I don't plan to share a prison cell with Preston Fowler."

Hannah frowned.

Win resisted an urge to scoop her into his arms and carry her off. She looked so tired, so damned fragile.

And yet he knew it was an illusion. Hannah Marsh was a strong and independent woman who was struggling with the fact that that strength and independence had been challenged.

"I wish I'd knocked a few of the bastard's teeth loose when I'd had the chance," he said. "You?"

Surprise flickered in her green eyes, then she gave a small smile and nodded. "More than a few."

"Damned humiliating, having to be rescued by those two old goats."

She almost laughed. "At least we got Fowler in the end."

"Yes, we did."

Then the laughter went out of her eyes, and she said softly, "It was terrifying, Win, finding him up in the attic…. I didn't know what he'd done to Cousin Thackeray, and then, when he tackled me…and touched me…" She inhaled. "But we got him."

"I'm not Fowler, Hannah. I'm not the enemy."

"You were," she reminded him quickly. "For a while you were, and it was fun thinking that way, but after today…it's just not fun anymore."

Win zipped his bag and straightened, his body rigid. "Go warn Uncle Jonathan," he said.

She started to speak, then shut her mouth, nodded and went into her bedroom to get dressed.

Cousin Thackeray's house was locked up and empty.

Hannah peered through a living room window. The only light visible was from the dying coals in the fireplace. A stiff wind gusted at her back. The contrast between the cool night air and her still-overheated skin was enough to make her shiver.

Where the hell was he?

Had Jonathan Harling gone with him?

She made a hissing sound of pure irritation through her gritted teeth and went around to all the entrances, looking for an unlocked door or a note, courteously mentioning where in blazes they'd gone.

There was nothing.

Indeed, her life had been different since the Harlings had erupted into it. Of course, that had been her doing. She had gone looking for them. It wasn't as if they had decided to hunt up the Marshes and demand Marsh Point and the Harling Collection after a hundred years. Now she was taking responsibility for her own actions.

But how could she send the two Jonathan Winthrop Harlings packing if she couldn't even find one of them?

Muttering and growling, she marched back to her cottage. On the way she noticed that Cousin Thackeray's truck was gone.

Win had set his bag by the back door in the kitchen and was scrambling some eggs, apparently unaware of her presence. She could smell toast burning. He cursed and popped it up, just shy of being ruined. Hannah observed the fit of his sweater over his broad shoulders, the place where it ended, just above his hips. She imagined his long legs intertwined with hers.

It wasn't fair, this longing for him. Making love last night had only made her want him more. Made her even more aware of him—and of herself, of her own capacity for love and desire.

Her throat tightened. She cleared it and said, "They've absconded for parts unknown."

Giving no sign of having been startled, Win looked around. "I wondered if they'd end up plotting something." He divided the eggs in the pan and dumped half onto one plate and the other half onto a second. "Jam on your toast?"

"Don't you think we should go look for them?"

He smeared butter onto the two slices of toast and put another two into the toaster. "Where would you suggest we begin our search? For all we know, they've decided to go fishing in Canada."

"They've gone after the Harling Collection," Hannah said. "You know it and I know it."

"To what end?"

"I don't know!"

"Maybe they've just gone out for lobster." He put the toast onto the plates and carried them into the living room. "Let's eat by the fire. It's always easier to endure being shot out of the saddle on a full stomach."

Hannah followed him into the living room. Except for the fact that his bag stood by the door, he didn't look like a man intending to depart anytime soon. She remained standing. "You haven't been shot out of the saddle. I've just asked you to leave."

"Then you plan to continue our relationship," he said.

"Well, yeah, I guess so."

His eyes darkencd, looking as black and suspicious

as the day he had run into her, outside his house. "That's not good enough, Hannah."

It wasn't. She'd known it when she'd said it. She changed the subject. "What about Cousin Thackeray and your uncle?"

"They're big boys. They can take care of themselves."

"But why didn't they tell us where they were going?"

"Maybe because it's none of our damned business."

He sat cross-legged on the floor in front of the fire, placing her plate next to him. He'd forgotten forks. Hannah went into the kitchen and got them, along with the second batch of toast, which had just popped up. It, too, was nearly burned. She slathered it with spicy pear butter and felt a sudden gnawing of hunger in her stomach. Dinner, perhaps, wasn't such a bad idea.

She took up her plate and sat at her desk chair in front of her computer. Win turned so that he was facing her instead of the fire. She groaned inwardly. Why did he have to be so damned good-looking? So rich. So successful. So *Harling*.

"You look more yourself," he said softly, the hardness gone from his eyes.

She nodded. "I'm feeling better."

"Hell of a day. If you want, I'll take a spin around the area and see if I can find your cousin and Uncle Jonathan."

"No, I'll go. I know the area."

He said nothing.

Suddenly she knew she didn't want to go alone. If she

had to, she could do it. But she didn't have to. It was a choice, she thought, not a sign of dependence.

"We'll take my car," she said.

CHAPTER TWELVE

As CARS WENT, Hannah's wasn't much. She explained to Win that in a rural setting high mileage, reliability and durability were more important than speed and prestige. He realized she was contrasting her car with his—in essence, her life with his. Or at least her understanding of his life. There was a difference, he thought.

They bounced along the narrow road that led from Marsh Point into town. "This is nuts," she muttered.

"So, turn back."

She glanced at him; her hair seemed even paler in the darkness. "What about those two?"

"At worst, Uncle Jonathan is having Thackeray take him to the Harling Collection at gunpoint. It's far more likely they've gone into town for a drink after their ordeal today. Either way, if they had wanted us to interfere, they would have told us where they were going."

"Don't you feel responsible?"

"No."

The car slowed. Hannah gripped the wheel with both hands.

Win stretched his legs as best he could in the small vehicle. "You're not really worried, either. You're just looking for excuses, so you won't have to toss me, after all."

She shot him a look. "I am not."

"Then you still want me to head back to Boston tonight?"

"As soon as we find your uncle," she confirmed.

"Suppose he doesn't come back until morning. Suppose he and your cousin have taken off for Boston to see their old haunts in Harvard Square."

"Cousin Thackeray's not that crazy."

"Uncle Jonathan is," Win said mildly.

She braked hard, swerving onto the side of the dark road. The ocean was mere yards away. Win, however, assumed she knew what she was doing, and that whatever it was didn't include dumping him out for the seagulls to pick over.

After a few maneuvers, she had the car heading back toward Marsh Point.

"I'm not thinking straight tonight," she mumbled under her breath.

Win chose not to comment.

When they arrived back at the cottage, Win noticed that Thackeray Marsh's yellow truck stood in the driveway behind his house. He and Hannah looked at each other and sighed. "I wonder where they've been," she said, puzzled. "We were on the only road out of here."

The house's living room lights were on. Win climbed out of Hannah's car and started up the driveway without a word, assuming she would want to ease her mind and find out where the two old men had been.

She fell in beside him, not looking at him, not speaking. Watching her, Win nearly tripped over a rock. Her jaw was set…her eyes shining…everything about her was alive, focused, dynamic. The near depression, the preoccupation of earlier seemed to have vanished. And, Win thought, he hadn't even gone back to Boston yet.

As he'd suspected, he wasn't the problem.

He wondered if she'd figured that out yet.

On the stone path to Thackeray's side door, she darted past him and didn't bother knocking before bursting in.

"Ahh, the posse is back," Uncle Jonathan announced.

Hannah was having none of it. "Where were you two?"

Thackeray Marsh answered, "We took a spin out old Marsh Road. It's barely passable, but we managed."

"Thought we might see a moose," his contemporary added.

They were both seated near the fireplace, where Thackeray was poking at the coals, trying to restart the fire. Win saw that his uncle looked exhausted; he was also filthy and about as pleased with himself as his nephew had ever seen him. He doubted a moose sighting had done it.

Thackeray cursed the stubborn fire and gave up, flopping into his chair. He addressed his young cousin. "We'd have told you we were going," he said, "but didn't want to catch you…well, you know."

Win watched Hannah stiffen and her cheeks grow red. "I was asking Win to leave," she said starchily.

"Tonight? After what we have all been through today?" Thackeray snorted and waved a hand. "Even I wouldn't do that. Damned rude it is."

"It's okay," Win said. "She was bluffing."

"I was not bluffing!"

"Yeah, you were. You've just been slow to realize it." He smiled at her. "The perfect bluff is the one you do on impulse, when you're not sure it is a bluff or even why you're doing it."

Uncle Jonathan gave an exaggerated yawn. "Winthrop, what in hell are you talking about? Carry this woman off, will you? I'm tired. Thackeray and I have a big day tomorrow, and I need my rest. I'm not a young man anymore, you know."

Hannah threw up her hands. "These two are impossible!" she exclaimed irritably. "Carry me off, like he's some kind of Neanderthal. Moose hunting. Bluffs that aren't bluffs. Crazy Bostonians trying to kill me. Heck, I'm going to bed."

"Before you do," Thackeray said, "would you and your fellow here bring in the trunk from the back of my truck? I'm afraid Jonathan and I expended ourselves getting it into the truck in the first place. It's damned heavy."

"Set it in the kitchen," Uncle Jonathan added.

Thackeray nodded. "Yes, we'll have at it in the morning."

Hannah refused to play their game and started out without demanding an explanation, but Win didn't have her forbearance, or just hadn't reached total disgust the way she apparently had. "What trunk?" he asked.

"The one in the back of Thackeray's—"

"Uncle Jonathan…" Win warned.

The old man sighed. "See for yourself."

Thackeray sat forward and shook a finger at Jonathan Harling. "Now wait just a minute. We agreed to wait until morning."

"I'm not breaking our agreement. All Win has to do is look at the damned thing, and he'll recognize his name in brass letters on the front, don't you think? I sure as the devil did."

Hannah froze in the doorway.

"We'll be glad to get the trunk in," Win assured them.

He slipped his arm around Hannah's waist and urged her outside, where the wind was coming in huge gusts now. She had plenty of energy to jump up and into the truck bed, ahead of him.

Indeed, the name Harling was embossed in scarred brass lettering across the front of the trunk.

"The Harling Collection, I presume," he said.

Her luminous eyes fastened on him. "It must have been out at the old lighthouse on the other side of Marsh Point. It's been abandoned since 1900. I've never been out there because Cousin Thackeray insisted it wasn't safe."

Win decided not to mention the obvious: Uncle Jonathan was right. A Marsh had stolen the Harling family papers, just as Anne Harling had claimed in her diary of long ago.

"You know what's going to happen if we leave this thing in the kitchen," he said.

"Preston Fowler's in jail. He's no threat."

"Hannah, think about those two old men in there.

Once each thinks the other's asleep, they're going to sneak downstairs and skim off whatever they don't want the other to see."

"Cousin Thackeray wouldn't—" She stopped herself, stared at the trunk, then said, "Yes, that's exactly what he'd do."

"And what do you think Uncle Jonathan was making such a big deal about getting to bed for? He never turns in before midnight. It's not even ten o'clock."

Hannah pursed her lips. "They can't be trusted with history."

So, they each grabbed an end and lifted the trunk out of the truck. After that Win offered to carry it himself, but Hannah was having none of that. He grinned. "Don't trust me, do you?"

She held tight to her end of the trunk. "I do."

"But I'm a Harling."

"You can't help that. Look, it's not far to the cottage."

"Doesn't this hurt your wrist?"

"A little."

He could see in her expression that it hurt a lot. "Hannah, let go."

For a few seconds she did nothing except stare at the brilliant night sky. Then she looked at him, nodded and let go. Win carried the trunk into her kitchen and set it down next to his overnight bag.

"You were the one who was bluffing," Hannah said accusingly, pointing at the bag.

"Me?"

"You never had any intention of leaving tonight."

"If you asked me to…"

"If I *made* you."

"I'm not a cad. If you didn't want me around, I'd have gone."

"Ha!"

He straightened, breathing hard…from carrying the heavy trunk…from watching her prance ahead of him. From wanting her. "I was just hoping I could call your bluff before you called mine."

"Well, you didn't succeed."

"Yes, I did."

"How so?"

He picked up his bag. "Say the word, Hannah." His eyes held hers. "Right now. Tell me to leave and I'll leave. No arguments. Nothing. I'll go."

"Your uncle won't leave without seeing the Harling Collection."

"This is between us. Just you and me, Hannah. I'll deal with Uncle Jonathan if I have to. What's it going to be?"

She hesitated, staring at the floor, at anything but him. For an instant, Win wondered if he'd guessed wrong, if having him around was more than she could tolerate.

"You're making excuses," he said, "so I can stay."

Then she looked at him and grinned, the devil in her eye. "You noticed?" She glided toward him, confident. "You can stay, Win Harling, under one condition: I'm not going to let you sneak into the kitchen and have at that trunk before I do."

"How do you propose to stop me?"

"You know the saying: An Ounce of Prevention Is Worth a Pound of Cure." She slid her arms around him. "I propose that the only way for you to get to the trunk tonight is through me."

"Physically?"

She smiled. "Physically."

"TELL ME IF I HURT YOU," Win whispered, pulling her on top of him.

"You're not hurting…not at all."

Because of the thrashing she had received from Preston Fowler, Win was being gentle and cautious with his caresses, not that it was necessary. Hannah wanted him as much as she ever had. He stroked the curve of her hip, and she felt his maleness alive between them. The earlier fears had been dissipated by her desire for him, and his for her.

They kissed, a long, slow, delicious kiss that penetrated to her soul.

"I guess," she said teasingly, "old Cotton Harling would have us both hanged."

Win laughed softly, running his fingers through her hair, his eyes locked with hers. "I'm sure he could think of a number of offenses. Do you feel guilty?"

"Nope. You?"

He answered by lifting her gently, and she knew what he wanted. Slowly, erotically, she brought him inside her.

"I don't want to hurt you," he murmured close to her, "not ever."

Then he inhaled, letting her set the pace. She did so

eagerly, believing once more in her capacity to confront the future, however different it might be from the one she'd imagined for herself only a few weeks before.

DESPITE HER BEST efforts to avoid the predicament, Hannah had fallen asleep, her body mercilessly intertwined with Win's. It had been that kind of night. She woke with the first light of dawn, impatiently taking a minute to plan her escape.

Finally, carefully lifting his arm from her waist, she peeled her top half free and raised herself upon one elbow. He looked so innocent in sleep. But he was a competent man, strong-willed, caring, not one to cross. Locking the doors and pulling the shades and curtains had been his idea; he hadn't trusted their two elderly neighbors not to barge in on them.

She contemplated her next move. Somehow she had to extricate the lower half of her body. How had she got into such a position?

Then she remembered.

Oh, she remembered.

In the middle of the night she had stirred in the darkness, half-asleep, the nightmare still swirling around her...Preston Fowler on top of her...Cousin Thackeray in danger. She had cried out, and Win had been there, wide-awake, pushing back the shadows, he'd said, of his own nightmare. They'd clung to each other and fallen asleep that way.

How could she go back to sleeping alone? An occasional night or two, perhaps. But not permanently. Not because she had been unhappy before she met and fell in love with J. Winthrop Harling. But because she *had* met him and fallen in love with him.

Still, there were his legs and other things between her and freedom.

She bent down and listened to his steady breathing; he was definitely asleep. Slowly, biting down now on her lower lip, she eased her left leg free, holding her breath when he flopped over and lay on his stomach. His hair brushed against her breasts. She almost groaned, wanting him all over again.

Exhaling silently, she yanked out her right leg in one quick movement. It was the only way to go. Given its delicate position, anything else would have just started things up again and then she'd have been in a mess.

She was free.

On the wrong side of the bed.

With her spectacular view of the water and solitary sleeping habits, she had pushed her bed against the wall, so that she could just open her eyes and see out the window. It was almost like sleeping outside. Now, however, she was on the wall side of the bed.

Which meant crawling over her sleeping partner.

There'd be hell to pay if he caught her.

But how could she ever explain to Cousin Thackeray that she'd spent the night making love to a Harling, instead of doing her damnedest to get the first look at the Harling Collection? If there was anything in it that would cause him to lose Marsh Point, she owed it to him to find it and keep it out of Harling hands. Her biography of Priscilla Marsh was only a secondary concern.

She raised herself and carefully lifted one knee over Win's hips, his narrowest point. Quickly she lowered one hand to his side of the bed, all the while lifting her other knee. It was a tricky maneuver. She had to roll onto her side without rocking the bed and waking him up.

She kept on rolling, right out of bed, grabbed her robe and tiptoed down the hall to the kitchen.

The trunk was gone.

Gone!

"That sneaky old goat! Wait until Cousin Thackeray finds out. He'll…"

"He'll what?" Win asked languidly. He was leaning against the door frame behind her.

She whirled around. "Well, good morning. I was awake and thought I'd make coffee…."

"Then why the big production to get out of bed?"

"I didn't want to wake you."

"I'll bet the hell you didn't."

"Now, Win, I know what you're thinking, and I don't blame you…."

"Because I'm right."

"That's not the point. The point is, where's the damned Harling Collection?"

He came into the kitchen and leaned against the counter. She had already noticed he hadn't bothered with a robe or anything else, which made his presence even more distracting.

"Aren't you cold?" she demanded.

He smiled. "On the contrary."

Evidence to that fact was becoming increasingly apparent. Then Hannah realized she hadn't bothered tying her robe and it was hanging open, revealing everything. "The Harling Collection!" she cried hoarsely. "Where is it?"

"On its way to Boston."

"Boston! Win Harling, you double-crossing bastard! You took advantage of me so I'd sleep like the dead and you and that old goat of an uncle of yours could pull a fast one on us Marshes and—"

"And do you want the real story, or do you want to rant and rave for a while?"

She shut her mouth and tied her robe. Tightly. *So, there,* she thought.

Win smiled faintly. "I carted the trunk back to your cousin's truck while you were sound asleep. He and Uncle Jonathan promised to leave at the crack of dawn— which it is—to take it to the Athenaeum, where it can be catalogued by qualified, neutral historians."

"I'm a qualified historian!"

"You're not neutral."

No, she thought, *I'm not.* It was a point she knew she needed to concede. An objective biography of Priscilla Marsh had never really been possible for her, either.

"They both agreed?" she asked.

"Not without a hell of a lot of arguing."

Hannah sighed. "Will wonders never cease? Cousin Thackeray must not be too worried about the collection corroborating the Harling claim to Marsh Point."

"No, he's not."

"You sound awfully confident."

"I am." And he nodded toward a large, manila envelope on her kitchen table. "Open it."

She did so, her fingers trembling. Inside were several sheets of yellowed, near-crumbling paper.

"It's tough going," Win explained, "but basically it lays out the details of how the Marshes managed to hoodwink the Harlings out of Marsh Point. I showed it to your cousin before he left and promised I would keep it separate from the collection. You know what he said?"

"Win…"

"He said, 'What the devil! You know damned well you Harlings used your power and influence to get your hands on Marsh Point, just when we were set to make our purchase.' He claims whatever the Marshes did, it was not without justification. He also said—and again I quote—'We won't sort out the legal mess until after I'm dead and then Hannah will have Marsh Point and you can fight *her* for it.' And then he grinned—you know that grin of his—and suggested it'd be a hell of a fight." Win laughed. "He's an old cuss, Hannah. He wasn't worried one bit about those papers. You know why?"

She shook her head.

He came to her and undid the tie on her robe, letting it fall open before he slipped his arms around her waist. His mouth descended to hers and he kissed her briefly, flicking his tongue against hers. "Because he knows the Marsh and Harling feud ends with us. He knows we're going to be together forever." Win lifted her to his waist, while she held onto his shoulders and let him ease her onto him, welcoming his heat. He kissed her hair, whispering, "And so do I."

"Win…"

"Just say it, Hannah."

"Forever."

A MONTH LATER the Marshes and the Harlings made headlines once more.

It seemed, the newspaper reported, that the newly recovered Harling Collection included not only a rare copy of the Declaration of Independence worth over a million dollars, but an order signed by Judge Cotton Harling, exonerating Priscilla Marsh of the charges against her. She had, the judge said he'd come to realize, only been teaching young Boston ladies traditional herbal remedies, not witchcraft. But due to some unexplained mix-up, the order had come too late to save the doomed, fair-haired Bostonian.

The copy of the Declaration of Independence, it seemed, had been authenticated, its value assured. Its ownership, however, was in dispute. Jonathan Harling claimed it belonged to his family. Thackeray Marsh claimed it belonged to his. Neither would budge.

Reached for comment, Hannah Marsh, the newly appointed, part-time director of the New England Athenaeum—Preston Fowler was awaiting trial—had suggested the two elderly Harvard-trained historians sign a joint declaration donating the document to the prestigious institution.

Both men had replied, in effect, "In a pig's eye."

J. Winthrop Harling had had no comment, except to say he was planning to whisk Hannah Marsh away on a honeymoon, to a part of the world where they were not likely to bump into anything remotely historical.

Taking a break from her biography of Priscilla, Hannah read the entertaining article aloud to Win while he stripped wallpaper from the dining room of the Harling House on Beacon Hill. His parents were driving up next weekend from New York for a visit. Hannah was anxious to meet them. She and Win had invited Cousin Thackeray down for dinner, but he'd said that'd be too many Harlings in one room for him. Old prejudices died hard.

"Did you say 'historical' in a scathing tone?" she asked her husband.

"As scathing as I could manage."

She grinned at him. Marsh Point and Beacon Hill. Maine and Boston. A Marsh and a Harling. "It's a good thing we love each other, isn't it?"

He smiled. "A very good thing."

* * * * *

Dear Reader,

I'm a small-town girl. I've lived my entire life in my hometown in northwestern Pennsylvania surrounded by rolling hills, lush woods and familiar faces. It's where I grew from a child to a teenager to an adult. Where I had my first kiss, first love and first heartbreak. My children attend the same high school I graduated from, were baptized in the same church where I was married and spend at least one day a week with their grandparents and various aunts, uncles and cousins. Every important memory, every life-changing event I've ever had happened right here—and I wouldn't have it any other way.

Serenity Springs, the setting for *His Secret Agenda,* may be fictional, but everything about this quaint tourist town is based on all I know and love about my own hometown—the warm and friendly people, the security of knowing your neighbors, the joy of having family close by. My heroine, Allie Martin, returns to Serenity Springs when she gives up her promising career as an attorney. She needs a place where she can find peace, acceptance and forgiveness for her greatest mistake.

Or maybe she just needs a place to hide.

If you enjoy *His Secret Agenda,* I hope you'll check out the other books in my Serenity Springs series, *Not Without Her Family, A Not-So-Perfect Past* and *Do You Take This Cop?*

Happy reading,

Beth Andrews

HIS SECRET AGENDA

Beth Andrews

CHAPTER ONE

DEAN GARRET HAD TWO WORDS to describe the town of Serenity Springs, New York.

Freaking cold.

And to think just last week he'd been complaining about the weather in downtown Manhattan. Guess mid-February wasn't the best time to head north into the Adirondack Mountains.

Lesson learned.

The brisk wind blew through his coat—the coat that had kept him plenty warm during the past three winters in Dallas—and pricked his skin like shards of ice. Snow stung his cheeks and collected on his eyelashes as he made his way across the parking lot to The Summit bar.

When he'd arrived yesterday he'd thought the snow was sort of cool. The way it covered every available surface, all pristine white and fluffy, made the town look like a postcard. Or one of those snow globes his aunt Rita collected.

But still, enough was enough already. How did people live with this all winter?

Thank God he had no plans to stay in town longer than a few weeks. That is, if all went according to plan.

He opened the door, stepped inside the warm building

and took off his Stetson, hitting it against his thigh to dislodge the snow. He scanned the bar, noting the exits, plus a short hallway and swinging doors that must lead to the kitchen. A guy with a shock of wiry gray hair nursed a beer at the end of the bar. A couple of college-age kids were shooting pool, while three men in suits sat at a table by the jukebox, stretching their lunch hour into two. Or three.

A sharp-featured redhead in snug blue jeans and a long-sleeved black T-shirt, carrying a bottle of wine in each hand, pushed through the swinging doors. With her short, spiky hair and slim figure, she deserved the second look the college kids gave her.

Dean walked up to the bar. "Allison Martin?"

"Sorry to disappoint, but I'm not Allie," she said over her shoulder as she set the bottles with the rest of the stock in front of a large mirror. "I'm Kelsey Martin." She took one look at him, her green eyes shrewd, and grinned. "But don't worry, if you're straight, you'll get over any disappointment real quick once you meet Allie."

He blinked. *If* he was straight?

He switched his hat to his other hand. "I'm Dean Garret. I—"

"Hold that thought," she said, before crossing to the cash register, where one of the businessmen waited.

Dean drummed his fingers on the scarred wood, realized he was doing so, then stopped. He set his hat on the bar and studied her as she swiped a credit card through the machine. How should he play this? Over the past two years he'd had a number of jobs, each of which had required him to be an excellent judge of people.

A trait he used to his advantage as often as possible.

He jerked the zipper of his jacket down while Kelsey sent her customer off with a friendly goodbye. When she'd spoken to him, there'd been no personal interest or attraction in Kelsey Martin's eyes, so he'd save his patented I'm-just-a-good-ole-boy-from-Texas routine for the one woman who mattered to him.

"Sorry about that," Kelsey said. "You're looking for Allie?"

"She's expecting me."

"With Allie, that's debatable."

He frowned. "Sorry?"

"Sometimes…well…time gets away from her." The guy at the end of the bar raised his empty glass and Kelsey nodded at him. She pulled a draft and indicated the swinging doors with her head. "Allie's in the kitchen. You can go on back."

He picked up his hat and circled the bar. Opening one door a few inches, he heard the synthesized sound of a syrupy pop song. *Great.* He had a few simple rules, lines he didn't cross. He didn't cheat. He kept to the truth as much as possible. He didn't get personally involved with the people he worked with.

And he didn't listen to crappy music or even pretend to like it.

After all, a man had to have his standards.

He stepped into the large, industrial kitchen. She stood at the stove, her back to him, wearing a fuzzy, deep purple sweater that slid off her shoulder '80s style, as well as black, pointy-heeled, knee-high boots and a leather miniskirt. Her dark, straight hair was pulled into a high ponytail but still fell to the middle of her back, and when she did a little shimmy, it took him a moment to realize the harmonizing tones weren't coming from the radio. They were coming from her.

He clenched his fingers, bending the rim of his favorite hat.

Turning, she spotted him and took a step back. Then flipped the radio off. "Is that a real cowboy hat or just for show?"

"Excuse me?"

"Your hat. Real or no?"

He stared at the hat in question. "Real as it gets."

She clapped her hands together. "Am I imagining it or do I hear a hint of Texas twang?"

"I don't have a…a twang," he muttered. A twang was the nasal sound his youngest brother made when he tried to sing along with Brooks and Dunn. What Dean had was an accent that he could downplay or exaggerate depending on the situation.

"No offense," she said offhandedly. "I'm just so excited because you're exactly what I need."

"I'm Dean Garret," he said smoothly. "We have an interview? For the bartending job?"

She waved her hand in the air. "Yeah, yeah. We'll get to that, but first we have something more important to figure out." She glanced over her shoulder. "Just set your coat on the chair there."

Shrugging out of the garment, he laid it on the back of the chair, and crossed the room. "Ma'am, I'm not sure I—"

She shoved a triangle of quesadilla into his mouth. "What do you think of this?"

Since he had no choice, he chewed. It didn't taste like any quesadilla he'd ever had before. And for the life of him he couldn't figure out what she'd put in it—not shrimp or crab. Then, out of nowhere, the heat hit him.

His throat burned; his mouth felt as if he'd just chowed down on a fireball.

"I tried to get Kelsey's take on it but she wouldn't try it because it has tomatoes. Isn't that the craziest thing you ever heard? Who doesn't like tomatoes?"

His face flushed and sweat formed on his upper lip.

"I mean," Allison continued, "she eats pizza and pasta sauce—both of which, I shouldn't have to point out, are tomato based." The woman paused long enough to take a breath. "Well?"

He cleared his raw throat. "How much hot sauce did you use?" he wheezed.

Her eyebrows drew together. "Did I add too much? The recipe called for four tablespoons, but I got called away in the middle of making it and couldn't remember… I figured another tablespoon or two couldn't hurt, right?"

"You thought wrong."

"Are you sure?"

"I'm sure," he said. "Didn't you try it?"

She wrinkled her nose. "I don't like spicy food, which

is why I needed an opinion." She smiled, and it was like being struck by a bolt of lightning. "But maybe I should get a second one. Opinion, that is. Just in case you're like me and can't handle a little heat."

He scowled. Which he knew was damn intimidating—especially when combined with his size. Even with her high heels, he had a good five inches on her.

"Lady," he growled, "I can handle spicy food. That—" he jabbed a finger at the offending quesadilla "—isn't a little heat. It's a blowtorch. My lips are still tingling."

She burst out laughing.

Women. He'd spent a good deal of his life studying them, but he'd learned only one thing for sure.

They never did what you expected.

THE BIG COWBOY BRISTLED, but his hooded eyes gave none of his thoughts away. Allie swallowed the rest of her laughter. Some guys just had no sense of humor.

Too bad. He was seriously cute though, with his sandy-blond hair and aquamarine eyes. Cute in an earthy, masculine, too large and with a heavy dose of ride-'em-cowgirl way.

She preferred dark-haired guys who dressed more conservatively than jeans and a striped, button-down shirt.

He picked at the top layer of the remaining quesadilla on the plate. "What's in this, anyway?"

She turned her grill pan off. "Hot sauce—"

"Obviously."

"Tomatoes, some lime juice, onion, scallions…" She

ticked each item off on her fingers as she spoke. "Cheddar cheese, cream cheese and lobster."

He jerked his hand back. "Lobster?"

She stirred the big pot of tomato sauce simmering on the back burner. "Sure. Why not?"

He scratched his cheek. "I've never heard of a lobster quesadilla before, that's all."

"That's why I made it. I wanted something different."

"It's different all right," he murmured in his sexy drawl.

She tapped the spoon twice on the edge of the saucepan. It didn't matter what this…cowboy thought about her menu. The Summit belonged to her and if she wanted to liven things up with fancier fare, then she would.

Besides, if she had to cook one more boring cheese-chicken-and-mushroom quesadilla for the next Tex-Mex Monday, she'd stick a fork in her eye.

She slid the band off her heavy ponytail and combed her fingers through her hair. "Well, let's get on with your interview. Why don't we sit down?"

He pulled a chair out for her at the small table. She thanked him and took her seat. Studied him as he sat opposite. Okay, so he was polite. She couldn't help it if she had a weak spot for courteous manners.

She flicked her hair over her shoulder again as she picked up the file containing Dean Garret's résumé, as well as the job application he'd sent in.

"So, I guess we'll get right to the basics," she said. "I need someone to tend bar in the evenings from seven to three Tuesday through Saturday. We're closed Sundays…except during football season."

"Football's big here?"

"We have our fair share of fans. Although if I had to guess, I'd say we're packed Sunday afternoons because people go a little stir-crazy around here in the winter. They need to get out, and since social opportunities are limited to church functions or skiing, they wind up here."

He leaned forward. "Please tell me there are other things to do in this town beside church dinners and going a hundred twenty miles per hour down a hill on a pair of toothpicks."

"I take it you're not into religion or winter sports?"

He glanced around as if checking to make sure they were alone in the room. "If my mama happens to ask, I attend church every Sunday."

He was afraid of his mama. God, that was sweet. "So, it's just skiing you have a problem with?"

"I prefer warmer activities."

Her mouth went dry.

Oh, this wasn't good.

She got to her feet. And about fell back to her seat when he stood, as well. Yeah, those manners were mighty impressive. She went to the refrigerator. "Most guys avoid the ice rink—except for the Tuesday and Thursday night hockey league. And since we're on Main Street, we don't get any snowmobilers coming in, either. They all stop at The Pineview on the edge of town." She opened the fridge door and pulled out a diet soda. "Can I get you something to drink?"

"No, thank you, ma'am." He glanced out the window at the falling snow—and she could've sworn she saw him shudder. "Is there anything to do here that doesn't involve the threat of hypothermia?"

She couldn't help but grin. "Not too much. At least, not between the months of November and February." She pursed her lips as she opened the can. "And sometimes March." He winced, but covered it quickly. She sat back down and he did, too. "Since you're not a fan of cold weather, I have to ask—are you staying in Serenity Springs long?"

He leaned back, the picture of relaxed, confident male. "I don't plan on leaving anytime soon."

Talk about a nonanswer. "I need someone I can rely on. I've been through too many bartenders to count." He just nodded—in agreement? Pity? Who knew? "To be honest," she continued, "it's getting really annoying to hire someone, only to have them walk away a few weeks—or in one case hours—later. I need someone dependable who's not going to leave me in the lurch."

She sipped her soda and waited, but he didn't say anything. And the intense way he studied her made her squirm.

She cleared her throat. "Now, that's not to say if I hire you I expect you to stay forever...." The idea of staying at The Summit forever caused a chill to run up her spine. "But," she continued, shoving aside the uneasiness she always felt when she thought of her future, "I would appreciate at least two weeks' notice, not to mention a few months' worth of work first."

He remained silent.

She sighed. Why were good-looking men always such a trial? "I'm not sure if you understand how a conversation works, but that would be your cue to speak."

He hesitated. Her experience as a defense attorney told her he was readying a lie. But when she searched his expression, she saw no hint of deception.

Which just went to show she'd made the right decision to quit practicing law. She obviously wasn't as good at reading people as she'd thought.

"I'll be in Serenity Springs for a while," he said. "But I can't guarantee how long."

"If I hire you, I need to know you won't leave me in a bind."

Still no response. He didn't try to persuade her he was best for the job, didn't promise he'd stick it out as long as possible. He sure didn't seem all that desperate for work. So, why was he here?

She glanced over his résumé again. After graduating from Athens High School in Texas, Dean had worked at a Dallas establishment called Benedict's Bar and Grill for three years before joining the Marine Corps, after which he'd served in both Afghanistan and Iraq. "I see you tended bar before you went into the military, but your recent work record has quite a few gaps. Care to explain those?"

"I was trying to find something that suited."

"Since you're here, I take it you didn't find what you were looking for?"

"No, ma'am."

She picked up a pen and tapped it against the table. "See, this is where we get back to me being able to rely on you to stick around. And from what I can tell of your work history—or at least, your work history over the last two years—you don't stay in one place long."

He clasped his hands together on the table. "After my discharge I did some traveling. For personal reasons."

"Hmm…" He was hiding something. She could feel it. "So, you had a difficult time adjusting back to…what would you call it…civilian life?"

"No more than anyone else who served."

She tucked her hair behind her ear and studied him. Maybe he suffered from post-traumatic stress disorder. She was far from an expert on PTSD, but knew that a person affected by it could have trouble keeping a job. Or it could be something else. Wanderlust. The inability to get along with his employers or fellow employees.

And then it hit her why he was so secretive. Why he gave such vague answers. Why there were periods of up to three months unaccounted for in his work history.

"Have you ever been convicted of a criminal offense?"

He raised his eyebrows. "Excuse me?"

"The gaps. I'm just wondering…"

"Are you asking if I was in prison? Is that even legal?"

"In New York State, a prospective employer may ask if a prospective employee has been convicted of a criminal offense, just not if they've ever been arrested or charged with a crime."

Something flashed in his eyes, something like respect. But before she could be certain, he said, "That makes no sense."

"That's the law for you. Besides, being arrested or charged with a crime in no way means you were convicted of said crime."

"You could always run a background check on me."

She sipped her soda. "I could—after I informed you of that fact, of course. But I like to form my own impressions of the people I hire based on what I see and hear from them. Not what the state of New York tells me."

"Would you refuse to hire me if I had a criminal past?"

"Article 23-A of the New York Correction Law prohibits employers from denying an applicant employment because the applicant was previously convicted of one or more criminal offenses." She caught herself and shook her head. She wasn't a lawyer anymore. No need to talk like one. "I just mean that it's illegal, not to mention unethical, to refuse to hire you because of your past. So no, that wouldn't be a problem." She paused. "But you lying about it would be."

"You make a habit of hiring convicted criminals?" he asked, his accent so sexy it made her want to do whatever it took to keep him talking. She tilted her head in a silent question. "Just wondering what type of people I'll be working with if I get the job," he explained.

She took a long drink. "*If* you get the job, you can be assured that none of your coworkers have a criminal record."

After all, Kelsey's juvenile record didn't count, and

while Allie's kitchen assistant, Richie, had some past troubles with drug use, he'd never been formally charged with possession.

And Allie's sins hadn't landed her in jail.

Just her own purgatory.

"But," she continued when Dean remained silent, "if you have a problem with people who've paid their dues to society, reconsider if you want this job." And really, did she want someone so…judgmental working for her? "One of my good friends spent time in prison and he stops by quite often."

Dillon Ward, Kelsey's brother, had served time for manslaughter after killing their stepfather while protecting Kelsey. After his release, Dillon had battled prejudice and his own guilt. Luckily, he'd gotten past all of that and was now able to move forward in a relationship with local bakery owner Nina Carlson.

Allie smiled sweetly. "I wouldn't want any of his criminal tendencies to rub off on you."

"You don't have any problems with his past?"

"No," she snapped. She inhaled a calming breath. "I don't have a problem with anyone's past." Well, except her own—but that was what she was doing here, right? Her penance. "I have a bigger problem with people in the present. Out of the last three individuals I hired, one stole from me, one walked off the job and one…" Allie squeezed the can she was holding, denting the aluminum. "She was the worst of all. She lied."

"Lying pissed you off more than desertion and theft?"

"Deserters can come back," she said coolly. "A thief can return what he or she stole. But a liar? You can never take back a lie."

He inclined his head and slowly straightened. "I've never been imprisoned or convicted of a crime."

"And the gaps in your résumé?"

"As I said, I was traveling."

All the signs, everything she'd ever learned about being able to tell when someone was lying, said that Dean Garret was just what he appeared to be. Easygoing. Stoic. Confident. A sexy cowboy in need of a job. If he could mix drinks, he'd be an asset behind her bar. Once word got around about him, women would flock to The Summit just to hear his Texas drawl. And he wasn't so pretty as to put her male patrons on the defensive.

"I guess that's all the information I need then." She stood, and couldn't help but second-guess herself when he got to his feet, as well. Who knew manners could be such a turn-on? Still, she walked around the table and offered him her hand. "Thank you for coming in."

His large, rough fingers engulfed hers, and damn if a crackle of electricity didn't seem to shoot up her arm and jump-start her heart.

"When can I expect to hear from you?" he asked, still holding her hand.

She pulled free of his grasp and stepped back. "I'm sorry, but you won't."

"I don't understand," he said.

"Listen, I have to be honest. I'm going in a different direction." She met his eyes and told him what her instincts were screaming. "You're just not what I'm looking for."

CHAPTER TWO

D<small>EAN DIDN'T SO MUCH AS</small> blink. Hell, he was so stunned, he didn't even move.

He wasn't what she was looking for? What did that mean? His blood began a slow simmer. Damn it, he was perfect for this job. He'd worked for three years tending bar before joining up. What more did she want? A note from his mother?

"If anything changes," she said, the hint of pity in her tone causing him to grind his teeth together, "I'll be sure to let you know."

In other words, here's your hat, get your ass moving.

He forced himself to smile. "I appreciate your time." He pulled his coat on and set his Stetson on his head. Though his better sense told him not to, he stepped forward until she had to tilt her head back to maintain eye contact. Until her flowery scent filled his nostrils. "You be sure to let me know if you change your mind," he said, letting his accent flow as thick as honey.

Heat flashed in her eyes, turning them a deep, denim blue.

He tipped his hat. "I'll find my own way out."

He didn't slow until he'd pushed open the door and stepped out into the blowing snow and mind-numbing cold. He trudged across the parking lot, unlocked his truck and slid inside.

He didn't get the job? He slapped his hand against the steering wheel. Unreal. He always got the job. Always got the job done.

He started the engine and cranked up the heat. Allison hadn't believed he'd stay in Serenity Springs.

She didn't trust him.

He sat there, resting his forearms on the steering wheel, and stared at the swirling white flakes drifting down. His record of success was a direct result of his tenacity. He'd go back to his motel room and regroup. Come up with a plan to somehow convince her he was the best candidate for the job.

That she could trust him.

Even if she really shouldn't.

"YOU SENT HIM PACKING?" Kelsey asked. "But I wanted to keep him. I've never had a cowboy of my very own before."

Allie, perched on the top rung of the stepladder, snorted down at her sister-in-law. "You can't have one now, either." She climbed down, careful to keep her high heels from hooking on the rungs. Once both feet were safely on the ground, she moved the ladder next to the bar. "I don't think Jack would appreciate you wanting to keep this—or any—cowboy."

They were the only people in the bar. Allie hated this time of day—what Kelsey referred to as the dead zone.

The two hours in the afternoon after the lunch crowd left and before people got off work.

Allie knew she should be taking advantage of this lull to get caught up on the pile of paperwork on her cluttered desk. She had inventory sheets to go over. Bills to pay. Taxes to file. Liquor deliveries to schedule and grocery orders to submit.

All of which bored her to tears.

"I guess you're right," Kelsey said in mock disappointment, as if she wasn't completely gaga over Allie's brother, ever since the day they'd met, right here at The Summit a few months ago. Kelsey tapped her forefinger against her bottom lip. "Hey, I know. What if I slap one of those cowboy hats on the sheriff? And do you think spurs would be too kinky?"

"Eww. I think my brain just imploded. And if it didn't, I wish it would." Allie climbed two more rungs and reached down for the red paper heart Kelsey held up to her. "For one thing," she said, hanging the heart from a rafter, "could you please refer to my brother by his name? Or better yet, pick a better nickname for him. He's the police chief, and you calling him 'sheriff' is too weird. What about 'pooky bear'? Or 'snookums'?"

"You expect me to get down and dirty with a man called snookums?" Kelsey grimaced. "That is just wrong."

Allie glared down at her. "And that's the other thing. I don't want to hear anything about you and Jack playing dress up or getting down. Dirty or not. How would you like it if Nina told you all about her and Dillon's love life?"

Nina, a mutual friend, had been involved with Dillon since Christmas. Everyone around Allie had paired up. It was like Noah's ark.

With her all by her lonesome on a life raft.

Good thing that's how she wanted it, or else she'd be depressed as hell.

Kelsey waved another paper heart in the air. "Nina's far too sweet to ever discuss something like that."

Allie rolled her eyes and descended the ladder. She reached the last rung and slipped, twisting her ankle when she landed on the floor. "Ouch." She rubbed the sore spot through her boot. "Why don't you be a real friend and hang the rest of the decorations?"

"Take your boots off. Why are you climbing a ladder in that getup?"

"Because I don't have any other shoes with me. And if you think I'd walk around in here in my stocking feet, you're more delusional than usual."

Kelsey picked up the ladder and moved it to the end of the bar. "There. I helped. But I'm not hanging any froufrou hearts. You know how I feel about decorating for holidays. Especially ones as commercial as Valentine's Day."

What could Allie say? That she needed to keep busy? That if she stopped for even a minute she started questioning herself? Started wondering if she should've listened to Evan, her ex-boyfriend, and accepted the partnership at Hanley, Barcroft, Blaisdell and Littleton.

Or if her life would've been different if she'd never taken Miles Addison's case.

But she had taken it. And she'd been so determined to get ahead that she forgot all the reasons she became a defense attorney in the first place—to help people. People who needed it.

See why she hated this time of day?

"Hey," Kelsey said, rubbing Allie's arm. "You okay? Your ankle isn't sprained, is it?"

Allison rotated her foot while she cleared her thoughts. "No. It's fine. I just can't believe you don't like Valentine's Day, that's all." She climbed the ladder again. She was so counting this as her workout for the day. "Are you sure you're female?"

"Valentine's Day is a holiday made by the greeting card companies and retailers to trick poor saps into spending money on a bunch of useless crap." Kelsey's voice rose and she began to pace. "I mean, what's up with sending flowers? They just die. And if I want candy, I'll pick up a Hershey's bar at the convenience store."

Allie hung a set of pink hearts and climbed down. "What about jewelry?"

She sneered. "Do I look like someone who wants diamonds?"

No, she didn't. Well, except for that gorgeous engagement ring Allie had helped her brother pick out. "You poor thing," she said, wrapping an arm around Kelsey's stiff shoulders. "Have you ever gotten a valentine?"

"I never wanted one," Kelsey said haughtily.

"I'm sure Jack will get you something superromantic," Allie assured her. She gave Kelsey a little squeeze.

"He'd better," she mumbled. "And it better be expensive."

"At least now I understand why you want to host a speed-dating event on Valentine's Day. You're rebelling against romance."

Kelsey crossed her arms. "I'm all for romance. The speed-dating thing gives our customers a chance to find true love. And if they happen to find love while helping our bottom line, all the better."

Allie grinned and folded the ladder before carrying it back down the hallway to the supply closet. Her good humor faded as she realized what had become of her life. Instead of playing a very important part in the American legal system, she now spent her time hanging cheap decorations, preparing the same meals over and over, and avoiding paperwork.

She slammed the closet door shut. Well, she'd wanted to change her life. As usual, when she set out to do something, she'd succeeded. And while running a bar might not be as exciting as practicing criminal law, it was a lot less stressful.

And she wasn't unhappy, she told herself as she went into the kitchen. She loved Serenity Springs and had fabulous friends and the best, most supportive family a person could ask for. A family that didn't ask too many questions. Such as why she'd quit her job and moved back.

She owned her own business, which was growing

by leaps and bounds. Plus, she got to do something she enjoyed every day. Even if a year ago she hadn't considered her love of cooking to be anything other than a fun hobby.

Hey, she was nothing if not adaptable.

She gave her pasta sauce a quick stir, adjusted the flame under the pot and picked up her coat.

"I'm going home to change," she told Kelsey as she walked back into the bar. "The sauce is simmering, so could you check it once or twice? Oh, and I almost forgot, can you switch the appetizer on the specials board to grilled flat bread pizza? I'll do a veggie one and a chicken one."

Kelsey leaned against the bar and sipped from a bottle of water. "Sure. But hey, before you go, you never told me why you did it?"

"We've offered bruschetta twice this month," Allie said, pulling on her red leather coat, "and it hasn't gone over too well. I thought we'd try something different."

"No, why did you reject Mr. Tall, Not-So-Dark but Very Handsome? Didn't he pass your test?"

Well, damn. And here she thought she'd avoided the subject of Dean Garret.

"Actually," Allie said, lifting her hair out from beneath her coat, "he passed with flying colors. He didn't hit on me once."

Although she remembered how, right before he left, he'd stepped closer to her, how his eyes had heated and his voice had lowered.

Kelsey set her bottle on the counter and crossed her arms. "If he passed the test, what was the problem?"

Allie shrugged and picked up her purse. "He wasn't right for The Summit."

"Ahh." She nodded sagely. "In other words, he didn't need to be saved."

Allie narrowed her eyes. "What's that supposed to mean?"

"You only hire the downtrodden, the needy or, in a few memorable cases, the just plain pathetic. You're like the Statue of Liberty. All you need is a tattoo on your forehead that reads 'Give me your poor, your tired, your flakes who don't know the difference between a cosmo and a mojito....'"

"So?" Allie asked, sounding to her own ears suspiciously like a pissy teenager. "I don't know the difference between them, either."

"Which is why you need to hire a bartender who does. Besides, none of the people you've hired since I've been here have stuck around. What does that tell you?"

Allie pulled on her black leather gloves. "That my manager keeps firing them all?"

"Hey, I only fired three of them—and they all deserved it. The rest quit. And they quit," she continued, when Allie opened her mouth to speak, "because though you tried to save them from themselves, they weren't interested. All they wanted was to get on with their dysfunctional lives."

"Who was stopping them?" Allie zipped her coat.

"You act like I offered counseling sessions as part of a benefits package or something."

"Pretty close," Kelsey mumbled.

"Relax. I'm telling you, Dean Garret isn't right for this job. Trust me on this, I'm doing the right thing here."

"I hope so," Kelsey called after her as Allie walked out the door.

She shivered and hurried over to her car. Yeah, she hoped so, too. And Kelsey was way off base about her trying to save people. She was out of that game.

Because the last time she'd played, she'd saved the wrong person.

THE NEXT DAY, Dean held his cell phone between his shoulder and ear as he dropped a cardboard pizza box onto his motel bed. "Hey there, darlin'," he said when his call was picked up, "it's me. I need a favor."

"I'm not that kind of girl," Detective Katherine Montgomery said in her flat, look-at-me-wrong-and-I'll-kick-your-sorry-ass New York accent. And people thought he sounded funny. "And don't call me darlin'."

The corner of his mouth kicked up. He'd met Katherine over a year ago when he'd worked in Manhattan. The mother of three teenagers, she'd been married for twenty-five years and was built like a rodeo barrel. She was also one of the most savvy cops working in the anticrime computer network in the NYPD, and she didn't take crap from anyone—least of all him.

Was it any wonder he was half in love with her?

"Now don't be that way," he said, flipping the box

open and sliding a piece of pepperoni-and-onion pizza onto a paper towel. "I'm betting with the right incentive, you could be talked into being that kind of girl."

He could almost see her scowling at the phone as she sat behind her very tidy desk. "If you keep up with the sweet talk, my husband's going to hunt you down," she warned.

Her husband, a skinny, balding postal worker, wasn't much of a threat and they both knew it. Unless the guy attempted to whack Dean upside the head with his mailbag. "For you, I'd risk it."

"Uh-huh." She made a soft slurping sound—probably sipping her ever-present coffee—before saying, "So, you called me two hours before quitting time on a Friday afternoon in another pathetic attempt to sweep me off my feet?"

"Well, that wasn't the only reason." Dean bit into his pizza, chewed and swallowed before wiping his hand on his jeans. He slid his notebook toward him and flipped it open. "I need everything you can give me about a Terri—*T-e-r-r-i*—Long." He gave her Terri's social security number, date of birth and last known address. "I need everything you can find, the more personal the better."

"And you think I'm going to help you why?"

Dean took another bite of pizza and popped the top of a can of soda. "Because it'd take me at least three days to find out even a quarter of what you could discover in a few hours?"

"Yeah. That'd be why." She repeated back to him the information he'd given her. "Who's Terri Long?"

He finished his pizza. "At the moment she's my competition for a bartending job I'm interested in."

"Do I even want to know why you want a bartending job?"

"Probably not."

"Uh-huh." He heard the distinct sound of Katherine tapping at her keyboard. "You're not doing anything illegal, are you, Dean?"

"Not at the moment."

Silence filled the line. "What did you do?"

"Nothing." He switched the phone to his other ear. "Nothing you need to know about, anyway."

Like how he'd broken into The Summit last night and gone through Allison Martin's office until he'd discovered the name of the person she'd given his job to.

Technically, yes, breaking and entering was illegal. But he hadn't stolen anything.

Other than information, that is.

And most importantly, he hadn't been caught. In Dean's book, that meant he hadn't done anything wrong.

"If you get hauled off to jail again," Katherine warned him quietly, "don't even think about calling me. Especially if you're more than one hundred miles away from Manhattan."

"Now, you know how much I appreciated you flying down to Atlanta to bail me out. Didn't you get the gift basket I sent you?"

Katherine grunted. He would've been worried if he hadn't still heard her typing. "Next time you send me fancy chocolates, send them to the station. By the time

I got home, Mickey and the kids had already eaten half the box."

"You got it." He lifted his hips, pulled his wallet from his back pocket and took out his credit card. As soon as he got off the phone with Katherine, he'd call the chocolate shop.

"Want me to email you what I find?"

"That'll do. And thanks. I owe you one."

"You owe me at least a dozen. But who's counting?" Katherine asked with a sigh. "Just promise you'll be careful."

"Always."

He disconnected the phone and tossed it aside. Allison Martin needed his help to realize she'd hired the wrong person. Now all he had to do was sit back and wait for Katherine to work her magic. Then he'd make his next move.

He shot his crumbled paper towel into the garbage can in the corner. Once he had the job, once he had her trust, it was simply a matter of time before everything else fell into place for him.

He'd make damn sure of it.

BEING SURROUNDED BY barely dressed coeds sure made a woman feel every single one of her almost thirty-two years.

Allie drew a beer and handed it to her customer, a fully dressed, beefy kid of twenty-two. "Here ya go," she told him with a grin.

Hey, she could flirt with younger guys just as easily

as men her own age. And if she gave some kid a thrill by smiling at him, who was she hurting? In the dim light of the bar she noticed him blush all the way to the dark blond roots of his crew cut. He stammered a thank-you as he hurried off.

See? She was just doing her best to spread a bit of sunshine wherever she went.

Allie turned her attention back to her lineup of thirsty customers. A brunette in a bright pink tube top sauntered to the horseshoe-shaped bar in her three-inch sandals.

Someone needed to tell these kids that it may be called spring break, but that didn't mean they should dress as if they were in Florida. For God's sake, it was ten degrees outside.

Dear Lord, she'd sounded like her mother. And had called her customers—most of whom were barely ten years younger than her—kids.

She might as well start wearing support hose and let her hair go gray.

"Two cosmos and a strawberry margarita," the brunette said over the blaring jukebox and loud voices.

"Coming up." Allie poured the margarita ingredients into a clean blender and added a scoop of ice. With the machine whirring, she then worked on the cosmos. After making at least a dozen tonight, she didn't even have to consult the cocktail book Kelsey had given her.

Go her. If she didn't have another, oh, twenty or so people wanting drinks, Allie would take the time to pat herself on the back.

Too bad memorizing the ingredients in a few select

drinks was about the only thing that had gone right to-night. After a small Saturday night dinner crowd, The Summit had been inundated with college kids ready to party. The sight of her bar packed wall to wall with cus-tomers had made Allison's heart go pitter-pat.

Until Terri Long called five minutes before her shift was to start to say she wouldn't be coming to work for Allie, after all. Seemed she had a shot at the big time—whatever that meant—and wasn't even in Serenity Springs anymore.

Allie viciously shook her cosmo ingredients and filled two glasses. She hoped there was a special place in hell for people who blew off work.

That was the last time she'd ever hire someone with-out checking references.

She tossed straws into the cosmos and poured the margarita into a glass. She sent tube-top girl on her way and began filling the next order as the too-familiar open-ing chords of "Hotel California" came on the jukebox. Allie gritted her teeth. No doubt about it. This was not her night.

She finished the drinks and recorded the sale on the register. At least her male customers were easy to please. A smile or flip of her hair and they were falling all over themselves to charm her. Even after waiting in line for a solid fifteen to twenty minutes to get a beer. She just thanked God all they wanted to drink was either beer, shots or the occasional rum and coke.

Noreen, her very grumpy middle-aged waitress, was

keeping beer pitchers full and the rowdiest customers in line.

Allie glanced at the door, where Luke Ericson was perched on a stool, a grin on his too-handsome face as one of the three girls surrounding him whispered in his ear. When he'd walked in an hour ago, Allie had given him free drinks for the night in exchange for him checking IDs at the door.

None of that made up for the fact that her feet were killing her, she had a huge cranberry juice stain on the front of her favorite jeans and she was starting to wonder if she was breaking a fire code with so many people in the place.

She stepped back toward the line of customers, but stopped when something at the far end of the bar caught her eye.

Her heart thumped heavily in her chest—once, twice, before it found a quick rhythm. Well. Her night might be getting better, after all.

"You must've found something in town to keep your interest," she called over to Dean.

"How do you figure?"

She crossed to him. "You're still here."

"I'm heading out tomorrow. Got a job in Saranac Lake."

She kept her smile firmly in place. Well, that's what she got for not hiring him when she'd had the chance. "Congratulations. How about a drink to celebrate?"

"Whatever you have on tap is fine."

She got his beer and took it over to him. When he pulled out his wallet she waved him off. "On the house."

He studied her for a moment before putting his wallet away. "Appreciate it."

For the next half hour, she poured drinks, all the while aware of a pair of aquamarine eyes following her every move. She set a fresh beer in front of Dean—who seemed oblivious to the fact that the three giggling, just-this-side-of-legal girls next to him were vying for his attention.

Sometimes men could be so clueless.

"What can I get you?" Allie asked the girl with the cute pixie haircut.

She slid a look at Dean. "Sex on the Brain."

"Sweetie, sitting next to this guy—" Allie motioned to him "—would give my ninety-two-year-old grandmother sex on the brain. What drink do you want?"

The girl giggled and leaned on the bar, the better for Dean to have a clear view down her low-cut top. "Sex on the Brain *is* a drink."

Allie glanced at Dean, arching an eyebrow. He nodded. She sighed and brushed her hair back. Well, that figured.

"Could I speak with you for a moment?" Before Dean could answer, she walked around the end of the bar, took him by the arm and pulled him off his stool. "Don't worry, ladies. I'll bring him right back."

He didn't fight her and she easily hustled him behind the bar. "Quick. What's in a Sex on the Brain?"

He scratched his cheek. "Couple of things."

"Okay," she said to no one in particular, "that's it." She wrapped both hands around the lapels of his jacket and yanked him forward. Noted how his eyes widened slightly. "I'm not in the mood for games, so you can drop the laconic cowboy act."

He kept his hands at his sides. Just tilted his head to the side. "What act?"

She growled. "Listen, I'm tired, I have an endless supply of people waiting for drinks and I'm surrounded by about a million overly perky, faux-tanned coeds." Allie inhaled, then rushed on when he opened his mouth. "I've had to pull the same girl—intent on showing everyone her coyote-ugly act—off the bar not once, but three times, and I've been hit on by just about every guy in here. But the worst thing is I don't know what I'm doing. And I can't call my sister-in-law to come and show me because she caught some nasty stomach bug from my niece. Suffice it to say I'm not in the best of moods." Allie tightened her hold on his jacket and stood on her toes so that her forehead bumped his chin. "So, do not even think about messing with me."

"I wouldn't dream of messing with you," he said, his voice husky and somehow intimate.

Oh. She blinked. Pried her fingers open and stepped back. "Well then." She swallowed. "How do I make a Sex on the Brain?"

"I'll show you." He took off his jacket, and she could've sworn every female in the room sighed. His black T-shirt hugged the smooth planes of his chest and molded to his biceps. The man was beautiful.

Now if only he'd left his hat on, the moment would've been perfect. Allie knew she was going to have some erotic dreams about that hat.

Dean tossed his jacket on a shelf under the bar. "Fill a tall glass with ice."

She set the glass of ice in front of him. He stuck a straw in it and added a shot each of peach schnapps, vodka and Midori melon liqueur. He then laid an upside-down spoon against the glass and slowly poured in pine-apple juice, followed by orange juice and then sloe gin, resulting in a drink that resembled a stoplight: green on the bottom, yellow in the middle and red on top.

"You're a genius," Allie declared. "And my personal hero. I'll give you three hundred bucks to work the rest of the night."

She forced herself not to back up when he leaned toward her. "Darlin'," he purred into her ear, his warm breath causing her to shiver. "I thought you'd never ask."

CHAPTER THREE

ALLISON MARTIN DIDN'T know squat about tending bar.

But she sure knew how to work a crowd, Dean thought as he collected empty bottles and carried them to the recycling bin. She'd flirted, socialized and kept her customers happy while they waited for their drinks.

He glanced at her as she cleared tables. They'd had last call twenty minutes ago and after the final drink had been served, she'd turned on the lights and dived into the cleanup with the same get-it-done spirit she'd demonstrated behind the bar.

The owner wasn't afraid to get her hands dirty.

And she was easy on the eyes. Tonight she had on a pair of snug, dark jeans tucked into those same pointy-heeled boots she'd worn during his botched interview. Her shirt was the color of cranberries, with a wide, square neck and long, filmy sleeves that billowed out over her wrists.

Dean took the mixers apart to be washed. She'd had every poor sap in the place drooling over her, wishing that somehow, miracle of miracles, she'd end up with him tonight.

"Well, you sure proved me wrong," Allie said as she came behind the bar and set down her full tray.

She'd told him to call her Allie, although he wanted to continue to think of her as Allison. Or better yet, Ms. Martin. He needed to keep as much distance and formality between them as possible. But she didn't make it easy.

He stacked dirty dishes to the left of the three-bay sink. "How so?"

"I should've hired you in the first place." She gave him a pat on the arm, and damn if he didn't want to back up. Out of range. She moved away to empty the garnish tray. "You charmed every girl in here—heck, you even managed to get Noreen to smile, which, believe me, is an accomplishment."

"She was laughing at my suggestion that she stay to help clean up."

"Well, that makes more sense." Allie washed her hands and dried them on a clean towel. "I'm sure she told you cleanup's not part of her job."

He rubbed the back of his wrist over an itch on his forehead, then resettled his hat on his head. For some reason, Allie had asked him to wear it while he worked. "I couldn't repeat what she told me. At least not in mixed company."

Allie waved at a departing customer. "Noreen was one of the very few females in here tonight immune to your charms. And don't think I missed that brunette with the big—" he raised his eyebrows and she grinned "—*lungs* hand you a cocktail napkin. I'm guessing it had her name, phone number and even a hand-drawn heart on there, as well."

He kept his attention on the glasses he was washing. "It wasn't a cocktail napkin," he mumbled.

"I saw her give you something, and it wasn't very big." Allie swept her hair back and put it in a messy, sexy knot at the back of her head. "Please tell me she didn't write her number on toilet paper."

"Not toilet paper, either."

"Come on," she said, swatting him with the towel. "Don't be cruel. I'm too tired to play guessing games."

He pressed his lips together as he rinsed a glass, then cleared his throat. "It was her thong."

Silence filled the room. He glanced at Allie, just to make sure she was still breathing.

Her mouth popped open. "Oh, my God. You're a rock star." Chuckling, she shook her head. "Well, the poor girl was no match against you. You throw out some mighty strong pheromones."

To Dean's everlasting shame, heat climbed his neck. "She was just…friendly."

Allie laughed even harder. "I think it's safe to assume she wanted to show you how friendly she could be. Now I have to ask—did you keep it?"

"I thought it'd make a nice addition to my collection."

"No doubt about that." She poured herself a diet cola. "I hope you washed your hands after touching it."

"Washed them and then stuck them in the disinfectant just to be safe."

Allie picked up her tray. "You don't know how relieved I am to hear that."

He waited until she was out from behind the bar before saying, "And you were right." She stopped and looked at him. "Her name and number were on the thong," he said, "along with a little heart." Which had half amused, half horrified him.

Allie laughed again as she went to finish clearing tables.

Dean lifted his hat long enough to run a wet hand through his hair. He needed to watch himself. She was damn likable, but he couldn't let his guard down.

Allie came back and set her tray on the bar. "So, tell me about this job in Saranac Lake."

She stood on tiptoe and reached for her soda. He caught a brief, tantalizing glimpse of smooth cleavage and a lacy black bra.

He cleared his dry throat. "Tending bar at the Valley Brook Resort. Starts Monday."

"I'm impressed. The Valley Brook is pretty upscale. You must've wowed them with your interview."

"Like I didn't wow you?"

She tapped her fingertip against her glass. "Let's just say I'm used to more…vocal interviewees. You know, people who speak when spoken to."

"Good thing for me the people at Valley Brook didn't have the same problem." He dried his hands and grabbed a bottle of water from the cooler. "Besides, I'm not sure what you've heard, but it's important for bartenders to be good listeners. Not talkers."

She set her glass down with a soft clink. "Well, then you must be a great bartender."

He almost grinned. "I saved your ass tonight, didn't I?"

"That you did. Could you hand me a clean rag so I can wash off the tables?"

He handed her one, making sure he didn't touch her, then took a long drink before asking, "What happened to the bartender you did hire?"

"Not sure. She seemed excited to get the job, and was even apologetic when she called to tell me she wasn't coming in." Allie shrugged. "Guess she had a better offer."

Yeah. She had. He'd made sure of it. Katherine had found out that Terri Long's real ambition was the stage. She'd followed her boyfriend—a ski instructor—to Serenity Springs. Dean had pulled some strings and got Terri hired as an understudy in an off-, off-Broadway show, effectively ending Terri's desire to work at The Summit.

He wondered if it ended her desire for her boyfriend, as well.

"That's too bad," he said. "Hope you find someone else."

"OKAY, GUYS, NIGHT'S OVER," Allie told the last three men left in the bar. "Last call was forty-five minutes ago. Time for you to move on."

Two of them slid their chairs back, but the dark-haired one in the middle, the biggest one, didn't budge. "I'm not done with my drink," he slurred.

She sighed. Why were the biggest ones always so much trouble? "You've got five minutes to finish it and

get on your way. Or else I call the cops to come and escort you out."

"That won't be necessary," the taller, lankier one on
the left said, his Adam's apple bouncing as he swallowed. "Right, guys?"

The shorter one with the thick neck nodded, while
Big Guy glared at his beer.

"Five minutes," she repeated, walking away.

Since Dean had everything under control behind the
bar, she finished wiping off tables. She hated to think
about what her night would've been like if he hadn't
shown up. Even Noreen had said he wasn't half-bad.

And from Noreen, that was high praise indeed.

Allie scrubbed at a sticky spot on a corner table. She
had to admit Dean had impressed her. He'd not only
saved her ass—as he so eloquently put it—but he'd stuck
around to help clean up. Which meant she might get
home and in bed before the sun rose.

Yep, no doubt about it. Dean was her hero. She wiped
the table dry before setting the chairs on it. She just had
to figure out how she was going to persuade him to give
up his job in Saranac Lake and work for her instead.

She ran her hands down her jeans, picked up her rags
and headed behind the bar. "You have everything under
control back here?"

"So far," Dean said.

He was quite the man of understatement. But during
the past few hours she'd come to realize that although he
talked slowly and took his time, he was far from stupid
or lazy. He got the job done, kept the customers happy

and seemed at ease whether trying to sweet-talk Noreen into cleaning, or shutting down a young coed when they'd overimbided.

Hey, maybe there was something to being laid-back.

She'd have to give it a try sometime.

She refilled her glass, drinking from it and then nodding at the three young men getting to their feet. "I'm glad they're leaving. I was afraid I'd have to call Jack."

Dean tipped his hat back. "Jack? That your boyfriend?"

"No, my brother." She ran her finger through the condensation on her glass. "He's also the police chief."

"That's handy."

"It's great," she agreed. "I can always count on him to bail me out. And then lecture me until my eyes cross."

Was it any wonder she'd never told Jack what had happened a year ago, what she'd done, before she'd bought The Summit? Even after all these months she still had a hard time facing herself in the mirror. She didn't need to face her family's disappointment in her, as well.

She bent to tie a bag of garbage closed as the three kids passed the bar. Instead of moseying on out, though, the big one stopped. "I changed my mind." He hefted himself onto a stool and slammed his hand on the bar. "I want another beer before we go."

"Sorry, no can do," Allie said before Dean could respond. "We've already had last call."

"Come on, Harry," his tall buddy said, glancing warily at Dean. "Let's get back to the hotel. We've got a twelve-pack there, remember?"

Harry—did people still name their kids that?—stood and shoved his companion into the bar. "Back off. I want my beer here."

"I'm giving you ten seconds," Allie said, making her voice as cold as the weather outside despite the uneasiness in her stomach, "then I'm calling the cops."

Harry puffed up his chest, swaying with the effort. "I'll go when I'm ready to go."

Both of his friends began talking at once, trying to convince him. Before Allie could pick up the phone to call in the cavalry—namely Jack—Dean sighed and tossed down his cleaning rag. She grabbed his arm.

"What are you doing?" she asked.

He looked at her as if she'd been drinking the disinfectant solution. "I thought I'd convince young Harry and his followers to go home."

"But there are three of them."

He gently peeled her fingers off her arm. "I appreciate your concern, but I think I can handle the Three Stooges here."

Then he walked around the bar. She bent down and picked up the Louisville Slugger Dillon had made her promise to keep under the bar for protection. Her hands shook as she wrapped her fingers around the handle.

If she had to hit someone with this thing she was going to be mighty ticked off.

Dean, in no particular hurry that she could see, sort of…ambled…up to Harry and his friends. The kids flanking Harry took a step back. Must be Dean's sheer size. It couldn't be his fierce demeanor. From what she'd seen of him, the guy was so easygoing she was surprised he didn't slip into a coma.

"You're ready now," Dean said quietly.

Harry held on to the bar as if trying to remain upright. "What?"

"You said you'd go when you were ready. You're ready now."

"Says who?"

Allie blinked. Had she somehow been transported back to grade school? No, they weren't a couple of ten-year-olds calling each other names. They were two very large, fully grown men facing off in front of her.

Dean kept his hands loose at his sides. "Bar's closed."

"Back off." The guy punctuated his statement by shoving him in the chest.

Dean took a step back to keep his balance, and Allie tightened her grip on the bat, her pulse skittering. But instead of losing his temper, he looked at Harry's friends. "You'd better get your buddy out of here before he lands all of your asses in jail."

Harry sneered. "Why don't you go back to the range or wherever you came from?" He leaned forward and knocked Dean's hat right off his head.

Oh, Harry, that wasn't a smart move.

"Kid," Dean said with a quiet intensity that made her shiver, "you have a lot to learn. The first of which being don't ever touch another man's hat." He stepped forward. The two smarter ones backed up. "Now, you've got two seconds to get your butt out of this establishment—"

"Or what?" Harry asked, with more beer-induced bravado than brains.

Dean actually grinned. A dangerous and—okay, sexy—grin that said *please give me an excuse so I can smash your head in.*

Not that she blamed him. After all, Harry had knocked his hat off.

"Or else I escort you out personally," Dean said, making no doubt that it wasn't a statement, but a promise.

The two men stared each other down. Tension filled the room; the threat of violence permeated the still air.

Allie cleared her throat. "I hate to interrupt this testosterone battle, but do you want me to call the police?"

"That won't be necessary," Dean said, never taking his attention off the kid. "Will it, Harry?"

"No," Harry grumbled after a moment. His friends, sensing their chance, took hold of his arms and started pulling him backward. "This bar sucks, anyway."

She loosened her grasp on the bat. Crisis averted. Thank God.

Or it was until Harry wrenched free of his friends and swung wildly at Dean's head.

She gasped and raised the bat to her shoulder, but Dean didn't need her coming to his rescue. In one smooth move he stepped to the side, pulled his arm back and punched Harry. Allie grimaced at the crunching sound of bone hitting bone as Dean's fist connected with the drunk's nose.

Harry groaned and slid to the floor in a heap.

Allie's palms were so sweaty the bat slipped out of

her grip and hit the floor with a loud bang. But nobody seemed to notice. Harry's friends stared wide-eyed at Dean, and Harry…well, poor Harry wasn't doing anything except bleeding. While Dean stood there, big and imposing and a little scary, with his hands clenched.

He then raised an eyebrow at the two friends. They both shook their heads.

Holy cow. The man was like some Chuck Norris wannabe. No wonder he'd patted her on the head when she'd tried to talk him out of confronting Harry and his buddies. From what she'd just seen, she wouldn't be surprised to find out he could've taken all three of the younger men at the same time.

Her initial reaction to Dean had been right. There was way more to him than met the eye.

Dean snatched up his hat, sat it on his head and knelt next to Harry, who had come to enough to moan. "Another thing you need to learn," he told the kid cheerfully, "is not to start a fight you have no chance of winning."

WHY DID HE ALWAYS GET stuck working with the soft-hearted ones? In the past year he'd done jobs for both an inner city teacher whose students ran all over her, and a youth pastor in a small town who wanted to save the kids in his flock from the fires of hell. Too bad the kids were more concerned with having fun than being saved.

Dean shook his head and picked out two bottles of tequila from the supply closet. Once Harry had come around, Allie had hovered over the kid. She'd given him ice for his swelling and cut nose, asked if he needed some pain reliever. Then she'd spoken in depth to Harry's friends, making sure one of them was sober enough to drive. Luckily, the skinny kid was the designated driver or else she probably would've made Dean play chauffeur.

"Did you have to punch him so hard?" she asked as soon as he came back into the room.

"Next time someone takes a swing at me," he said as he added the tequila to the stock behind the bar, "I'll politely ask him to stop."

She crossed her arms. "I just hope he doesn't try and bring you up on charges of aggravated assault. You can claim self-defense, but he might counter that you used excessive—"

"I have a right to protect myself."

"Sounds like you know your law."

"I know my rights," he said, keeping his cool. "You're the one who's talking like a lawyer or something."

She blushed. "That's because I am a lawyer."

Even though he already knew about her past as a defense attorney, he played along. "You're a lawyer and a bar owner?"

"No." She picked up a rag and wiped off the already clean bar. "I…changed careers about a year ago."

He leaned against the counter. "Is your career change working out for you?"

She glanced up at him, a loose strand of hair curved over her cheek. "Oh, yeah. It's been great. Really, really, really great."

Uh-huh. All those *reallys* weren't fooling anyone.

"Were you any good?"

Her eyes grew sad for a moment. "Yeah. I was very good."

He watched her carefully. "Must've been hard to give it up."

The corners of her mouth turned up in a fake smile. "I needed a change."

And if that was the truth, the next time some drunk took a swing at him, Dean would let him connect. "What kind of law did you practice?"

"Criminal. So, I take it you excelled in the marines?"

After a moment's hesitation, he decided to go along with the change in subject. He knew when to let something drop and when to push. Besides, he had plenty of time to get to know Allie. To learn all of her secrets.

Using the broom she'd brought out, he swept behind the bar. "Why do you say that?"

"Uh, because of the way you flattened poor Harry. You must've gotten an A+ at hand-to-hand combat."

"Poor Harry?" Dean shook his head, kept sweeping. "First of all, subduing a drunk civilian doesn't take much skill. Secondly, weren't you the one who wanted poor Harry's butt hauled off to jail?"

She sprayed disinfectant onto the work areas behind the bar. "I wanted to scare him. I didn't realize you were going to go all Walker, Texas Ranger on him."

"I've worked in a lot of bars. Was a bouncer in a few of them and have dealt with plenty of drunken idiots." *True. Sort of.* "And believe me, after a man's been swung at enough times, he'd better be smart enough to learn how to duck. Or how to fight back."

She rolled her eyes. "Now you sound like Jack."

Jack Martin, the police chief brother. And, according to the information Dean had from the cute redhead who worked the desk at the motel, the first Martin sibling to run back to Serenity Springs from New York.

"Jack must be a smart man then," Dean said, picking up the dustpan.

"He is. He's great." She took the broom and swept the dirt into the dustpan he held. "But if he asks, I'll deny I ever said that. As a younger sister, it's my duty to bug, tease and annoy him mercilessly."

"I'll have to call my mother and thank her for not having any daughters."

"You don't know what you're missing."

He dumped the dirt into the trash can. "I have two younger brothers, Ryan and Sam."

"You're from Dallas, right? Is that where they live?"

"Yeah."

"You must miss them."

His fingers tightened on the dustpan's handle. He did miss his brothers. Missed his entire family. It'd been almost two years since he'd walked away from them. But he still couldn't forgive them. Not yet.

And he'd never be able to trust them again. Especially Ryan.

"Looks like we're about finished here." Hey, he could change the subject just as easily as she could. Yes, the best way to get someone to trust you was to pretend to open up to them yourself. But damn, he didn't want to have this particular conversation now.

Or ever.

Besides, the bar was too small, too intimate when they were the only people there, to talk about family. It was too easy to forget he was working.

"Oh. Right. Hold on." She opened the cash register, counted out some money and handed it to him. "I can't thank you enough for helping me."

"Something tells me you would've handled things on your own." He tucked the bills into his pocket.

She stepped closer to him. "What would it take to convince you to give up that job in Saranac Lake and work here instead?"

His heart picked up speed. He loved it when a plan came together.

"Why would I want to do that?"

"Saranac Lake is farther north. It's much colder up there than Serenity Springs." She laid her hand on his arm as she spoke, her fingers warm on his skin. He stood stock-still, his pulse drumming in his ears. His scheme was working almost too well. "Plus, I've been up to the Valley Brook. It's very fancy. You'd have to wear some dorky uniform."

"For what they're going to pay me, I'd wear a clown suit."

She inhaled sharply, as if bracing herself, and took her hand off his arm. "How much did they offer you?"

Since he really didn't have a job offer, he made up a figure he thought was reasonable. But when he told her, she winced. Then she swallowed and lifted her chin. "I'll match it. So, what do you say?" she asked hopefully.

When she smiled at him like that, his head buzzed. His hands itched to dive into her thick mass of hair.

Ah, hell. What he was going to do next could lead him into a whole mess of trouble.

It's for the job, he assured himself. To convince her he was just an easygoing cowboy with nothing more on his mind than his next paycheck.

Which was total crap, but he'd hold on to that justification for as long as possible. Because he wanted to touch her, to kiss her before they went any further.

Before there were too many secrets and lies between them.

"I'll accept the job," he said gruffly, "in approximately five minutes."

She laughed. "What? That makes no sense."

"It makes perfect sense." He edged closer to her. She took a step back. Then another, until she was pressed up against the bar. "You see, after I accept the job, you'll be my boss."

"You have a problem with me being your boss?"

"Not at all." He settled his hands on her waist. She tensed, her palms going to his chest. "But once you're my boss, certain…actions on my part would be inappropriate."

"They might be inappropriate even if I'm not your boss."

But she hadn't pushed him away—or hauled off and slapped him.

So, he was still in the game.

"They might be." He tugged her warm, lithe body

against his, crushing her hands between them. "I need those five minutes." He ignored how true that statement was—and how much it endangered his job—as he pressed his mouth against the rapidly beating pulse at her neck. She gasped. He rubbed his cheek against hers and leaned back so he could look into her eyes. His voice barely a whisper, his mouth hovering over hers, he asked, "What do you say?"

CHAPTER FOUR

ALLIE WANTED TO SET DEAN straight on how things worked at her bar. She was the boss and she didn't go around letting her employees put their hands on her. Or kiss her neck.

Her fingers curled into his chest. He was so warm. Solid.

He slowly lowered his head, but she pushed against him.

His eyes met hers. She blamed her lack of willpower on the intensity in his gaze. How could she worry about mistakes when he seemed so…sexy, yes…but more importantly, so steady?

She slid her palms up to his shoulders. "Okay," she breathed, linking her hands behind his neck and pressing against him.

Finally, his mouth brushed against hers, a featherlight kiss that drove a tingle of awareness and sharp, aching need through her body.

He pulled back and stared down at her. Okay, so curiosity had got the better of them.

No harm done.

She smiled up at him as she stroked the back of his neck, the silky ends of his just-this-side-of-too-long hair.

"We still have at least four minutes left. I think you can do much better than that."

Humor lit his eyes even as they darkened with desire.

And she knew that his desire was real—even while she suspected it was as unwanted for him as it was for her.

Then he kissed her again. He kissed like he'd done everything else so far this evening. Slow. Easy. And with great skill. As if he had all the time in the world to learn the texture of her lips, the taste of her, the way she fit against his body. His tongue swept across the seam of her lips. But not even the rasp of his tongue against hers could break the spell he'd put her under.

She groaned and pressed her breasts against the solid planes of his chest.

He wrapped one arm around her waist and lifted her so that her high heels came off the floor. He slid his other hand into the hair at the nape of her neck, his fingers loosening the knot she'd tied it in as he massaged her scalp, tilted her head and deepened the kiss.

Dear Lord, she hadn't realized one simple kiss could be so…dangerous. To her peace of mind. Her sense of what she could and could not control.

And most importantly, to her willpower.

Then, as if a switch had been flipped, the danger passed. Though he still held her flush against him, she had the sensation of him pulling away. While she would've sworn his earlier kisses had been driven by passion, the touch of his lips on hers now felt…deliberate. Practiced.

Contrived.

She pulled back, breathing hard—definitely harder than a fully clothed, vertical kiss warranted. Allie frowned.

Dean stepped away. His jaw was tight and his chest rose and fell with his own heavy breathing. And while she told herself she was being ridiculous, that like always, she was reading way too much into things, she couldn't help but think there had been something real and honest about what had happened between them when they'd first kissed.

She swallowed and tucked her trembling hands behind her back. "Well, I guess that's it for now."

He nodded. "We could always move our agreement back a few more minutes," he said, his tone serious.

Despite the fact that there was nothing funny about this situation, she laughed. At herself for being such a complete fool. Because even though her instincts were screaming at her not to trust this man, she was tempted to step back into his arms. "I think we'd better stick to our original agreement," she said.

"You're right." He put his jacket on. "When do you want me to start?"

"Tuesday. Your regular shift will start at seven, but I'd rather you come in around six so we can get all your paperwork filled out." She tossed the cleaning rags into the small laundry basket she kept stashed under the bar. "You'll get two fifteen-minute breaks and a half-hour lunch break. All employees get one meal on the house—"

"Free food?"

Funny how her male employees always perked up at that. "Yes, but there are two conditions. One, you eat what's on the menu for that night. There are no special orders."

He nodded solemnly. "Wouldn't want anyone to think this was a restaurant."

What a smart-ass. "It's a restaurant for paying customers, but even for them I have a limited menu. While I enjoy cooking and am glad we can offer lunch and dinners, The Summit is first and foremost a bar."

Or at least, that's what Kelsey kept reminding her.

"What's the second condition?" he asked.

"No complaining about the food. If you don't like my cooking, don't eat it. Bring a bagged lunch or go hungry. I don't care."

"I hadn't realized chefs were so sensitive."

Her face heated and she turned toward the stock in front of the large mirror. "I'm not sensitive," she muttered, rotating bottles so all the labels faced out. "But it's embarrassing to me—not to mention bad for my business—when an employee has pizza delivered, in front of the Friday night dinner crowd, because she thinks my beer-battered fried fish stinks."

He made a choking sound, as if trying to hold back a laugh, but when she glanced at him, his expression was neutral. "I never complain about a free meal. And speaking of meals, since The Summit's not open on Sunday, do you have any recommendations for a good place to eat in town?"

"You don't cook?"

"I can get by. But the motel I'm staying at doesn't even have a minifridge, so I'm limited to takeout until I can find a place to rent. I'll be glad for any opinions you have on the local real estate market, too."

"There are usually a few apartments listed in the *Gazette*," she said. Something kept her from mentioning the newly renovated two-bedroom apartment upstairs. "I'm sure you'll be able to find something decent before too long."

Kelsey had been after Allie for months to rent the space, but she didn't want the burden of being a landlord. And since The Summit's income was more than enough for her to live on, Kelsey didn't push the issue.

And who knew? If Dean stuck around long enough, they could always discuss his becoming her first tenant later.

"The Pineview has a terrific Sunday brunch," Allie continued, "but they close at three. If you're looking for a good lunch, you can't go wrong with Sweet Suggestions, the bakery on Main Street. Nina's food is great and reasonably priced. Other than that, I'm afraid your choices are limited to pizza or burgers." She didn't miss his quick grimace. "Is that a problem?"

"No. But eating pizza twice a day for three days in a row makes a man appreciate a home-cooked meal." He glanced at his watch. "If you're finished, I'll walk you to your car."

She blinked at the unexpected offer. "Oh. That would be great. Let me put the cash away and get my things."

She took the drawer out of the cash register and went

down the hall to her office. Tucking the money in her small safe, she locked it before slipping into her coat and picking up her gloves and purse. After checking to make sure the rear door was locked, she hurried back to the bar. Not that Dean seemed in any rush. He was leaning against the wall by the front door, one ankle crossed over the other, his hands in his pockets.

She grabbed her cell phone and stuck it in her coat pocket. "All set," she told him, zipping her coat.

He held the door open for her and they stepped outside into the cold night air. The wind blew her hair into her face as she locked the door. Shivering, she pulled on her gloves.

He flipped up the collar on his coat and hunched his shoulders. "You shouldn't park so far from the building," he said, nodding toward her red SUV at the other end of the snow-covered lot. "Especially since you leave work so late."

"You sound like Jack again." She carefully stepped off the sidewalk, not the least bit surprised when he took her arm so she wouldn't slip. One thing she did trust about Dean Garret—his manners were the real deal. "I usually do, but when I got to work, the guy who takes care of the parking lot for me was plowing, so I had to stay out of his way."

They kept their heads down as they slowly made their way. While her high-heeled boots were stylish, they weren't exactly practical. But Dean, God bless him, didn't comment or try to hurry her along. He just matched his pace to hers.

The wind blew swirls of snow, like little white tornadoes, around them. She stole a glance at Dean's strong profile. There was no doubt about it. He was one sexy cowboy. He was also, she reminded herself, new in town. He didn't have any friends and was staying in a half-rate motel that didn't even have a minifridge. And really, after the way he'd helped her out by pitching in behind the bar, the least she could do was make sure he had a hot meal.

Right?

A few feet from her SUV, she pressed the unlock button on her key ring. Her headlights flashed. He reached for the door and held it open for her.

"Thanks for all your help tonight," she said.

"No problem."

Her teeth chattered. "I guess I'll see you on Tuesday."

He raised his eyebrows. Maybe because her statement had sounded more like a question. Hey, when you go through seven bartenders in eight months, you start to feel a little insecure.

"I'll be there," he said.

"All right, then. Good night."

"'Night, boss."

She climbed into her vehicle and he shut the door behind her. She started the ignition, but instead of giving him a polite smile and driving away, she rolled down the window. "You should come over to dinner."

From the look on his face, she'd surprised him as much as she'd surprised herself. "Excuse me?"

"Tomorrow, Sunday dinner," she said, trying to make it sound less crazy than it was. It didn't work, but she wanted credit for trying. "At my parents' house."

"I wouldn't want to bust in on your family dinner."

"We always have room for one more."

He studied her, his expression unreadable in the dim parking lot. "If you're sure…"

"I am. And I'm not saying that because I'm not the one cooking. My mom's always thrilled to have guests."

Although Helen Martin usually preferred a bit of warning about aforementioned extra guests.

He nodded slowly. "I appreciate the invitation."

"Good." She gave him her parents' address. "It's easy to find. Take a right at the corner by the high school—do you know where the high school is?" Another nod, this one quick and jerky. "Go straight two blocks and then take a left onto Pleasant Street. Their house is the first one on the corner. Dinner's at six sharp."

Unable to stand the cold any longer, she rolled her window up, cutting off whatever he'd been about to say. She shifted into Drive and pulled out of the lot. It wasn't until she'd parked in her own driveway that she gave in to the urge to bounce her head off the steering wheel.

She should've kept her big mouth shut. Just because the man was new in town didn't mean she had to be a one-woman welcoming committee.

Besides, even though she'd hired him, even though he seemed like someone she could count on, she didn't trust him.

DEAN'S CELL PHONE RANG. He groaned and blindly reached along the table. His fingers brushed against his phone as it rang again. He flipped it open. "'Lo?"

"Well? Did you get it?"

He covered his eyes with his free arm, blocking out the sunlight filtering through the motel window. "What time is it?"

"Eight o'clock," Nolan Winchester said. "No, I guess it'd be nine for you. I figured you'd be up by now. And I don't know what the weather's like up there in the Arctic Circle, but here in Dallas it's a gorgeous and sunny sixty degrees already."

"When I get back," Dean muttered to the man who'd been his best friend since they'd met in basic training over ten years ago, "I'm going to kill you. And you can bet it will be painful."

Nolan laughed. Probably because Dean was too tired to put any real heat behind his threat. He'd been too keyed up to sleep when he got back to his motel room, having dozed off sometime after 5:00 a.m.

All because of Allison Martin.

"What do you want?" Dean asked.

"I haven't heard from you since Friday." The sound of kids shrieking made Dean wince and move the phone away from his ear. "Mitchell, put the butter back in the fridge before your sister eats it all."

"You running a circus down there?" Dean asked.

"Feels like it," Nolan said with his usual—and damned irritating—good cheer. "Cassie's sleeping in today and the kids wanted to surprise her with breakfast in bed." One of the three kids—the baby from the sound of it—started bawling. "What's the matter with Daddy's girl?" Nolan asked. The screaming grew louder, more than likely because Nolan had picked Grace up. "Cassie's going to love this delicious breakfast we're making, right, kids?"

Five-year-old Mitchell and three-year-old Ava gave hearty shouts of approval. Dean shook his head. His partner was one lucky guy. He and his high-school sweetheart had recently celebrated their tenth wedding anniversary.

Cassie was, in Dean's mind, about as close as a man could get to the perfect woman. She was a great mother, had a successful career as a real estate agent and hadn't balked when Nolan wanted to move from their home-town in northern Alabama to Dallas to start a business with Dean. Plus, when Nolan had been stationed over-seas, Cassie had remained strong and supportive and capable of living on her own.

And she could still fit into her high-school cheer-leading uniform. A fact Nolan had shared after a few too many beers at the Winchesters' Labor Day picnic.

"So, did you get the job?" Nolan asked.

"Yeah, I got it." Dean sat up and swung his bare feet over the edge of the bed, shivering.

"No kidding?"

"You sound surprised." He pulled the heavy bed-spread around his naked shoulders as he got to his feet and went to the heating unit on the wall. He squinted at the blurry numbers then flipped the tiny control as high as it would go. "You underestimating me?"

"Well, you said you'd have to use charm, and I've seen your charm. It's a wonder you ever get laid."

"Daddy," Dean heard Mitchell ask, "what's 'get laid'?"

Dean snorted as he used his teeth to rip open the single-serving bag of coffee.

"Hell," Nolan muttered, hopefully low enough that his kids didn't hear that, as well. "I said it's a wonder Uncle Dean even gets paid."

"No, you didn't," the boy told him.

"Why don't you get the eggs out for me?" Nolan asked.

"Can I crack some?" Dean knew from the kid's tone he was probably bouncing with excitement.

"Me, too!" Another voice, this one Ava's.

"Sure, sure. You can both crack some. But first I need you to watch your baby sister for a minute while I finish talking to Uncle Dean, okay?"

"Cassie's going to kick your sorry ass when she finds out what kind of language you've been using around her babies." Dean filled the coffeepot with water from the bathroom sink.

"Don't I know it." Nolan sounded decidedly less cheerful than when he'd first called. "No sense dwelling, though. Did you find out anything?"

He'd found out that Allison Martin was nothing like he'd expected. He'd also found out The Summit did a fair amount of business and, most surprising of all, people paid money to send their kids to this snow-ridden town to spend spring break—where spring was nowhere to be found.

"I just got the job," Dean pointed out as he poured the

water into the coffeemaker and turned it on. "I'm building trust. Playing the part of an easygoing good ole boy."

Sure. And that's what he'd been doing last night. Playing on Allie's trust. Playing his part. Which was the only reason he'd kissed her.

Just doing his job.

"Building trust?" Nolan asked. "You don't have time to build trust. Just find out what you need to know. Ask a few questions, knock a few heads together if you have to—"

"Right there is the reason I do most of the fieldwork while you stay behind and deal with the clients."

He and fellow PI Nolan had formed Leatherneck Investigations when Dean left the service. Though they were still small, their reputation for solving cases—especially missing persons cases—had garnered them plenty of business.

"No," Nolan said, "the reason you're there and I'm here is because you won't stay in Dallas more than a week at a time."

Leave it to his partner to get to the heart of the matter.

"Bashing heads won't help us solve this case," Dean said, watching the coffee slowly drip into the pot. "People in small towns think differently. They protect their own. Word gets around I'm asking questions about Allison Martin and any ties she has to a missing persons case, and I'll lose my advantage."

"I still think some well-placed intimidation—oh, hell. Mitchell! Ava! Freeze! Both of you...no...keep your hands where I can see them. Now set the eggs down. Carefully. Mitchell, I mean it. Don't even think about—"

The phone dropped with a loud clang.

Dean grinned. He poured coffee into a motel mug and took a sip as he crossed back to the bed. He set the cup and phone down and pulled a sweatshirt out of his duffel bag, tugging it over his head. Tucking the phone between his ear and his shoulder, he unplugged his laptop from the charger and turned the computer on.

"Sorry about that," Nolan said breathlessly.

"You're starting to show your age, old man," Dean said, even though he was two years older than his friend. "Back in the Corps you could run three miles—in full combat gear—in under twenty minutes. Now you're huffing and puffing over corralling your own kids in your kitchen?"

"They're faster than you think. You get that email I sent you? It had the financials you wanted me to check out."

"I'm booting up now." Dean leaned back and picked up the coffee. "Did you find anything?"

"Nothing new. The trail ends in Cincinnati. I still think you would've been better off staying there."

"No point. The lead was dead."

The New York cops had lost Lynne and Jon Addison's trail there, as well. And any interest in the case. According to the detective Dean had spoken with right before he'd headed up to Serenity Springs, the file on the disappearance of Lynne and Jon, the wife and young son of prominent businessman and philanthropist Miles Addison, was still open.

Still open but very much cold.

Now, almost a year later, Dean was trying to pick up the Addisons' trail.

He had very few leads. All he knew for certain was that on a sunny July morning a year and a half ago, Lynne Addison had kissed her husband goodbye before taking their son to the park six blocks away. They hadn't been seen since.

Dean accessed his email account and waited for his new messages to download before opening the attachment and scanning the documents Nolan had sent.

"Damn." He pressed the heels of his hands against his eyes. He'd been so sure he'd find a clue in Allison Martin's financial records.

"I know you think Allison Martin was involved—"

"She received a call at her office at Hanley, Barcroft, Blaisdell and Littleton from Lynne's cell phone shortly after Lynne and Jon left their residence the day they disappeared."

"Except the call lasted less than five seconds. Ms. Martin claimed there was no one on the other end, so she hung up. No other calls between the women turned up. I still think you're looking in the wrong area. Go back to Cincy, pick—"

"No." Dean closed his laptop and tossed it on the end of the bed. "There are too many coincidences here. First Allison Martin and Lynne Addison are seen having lunch together two weeks before Lynne and her son disappeared—"

"Allison had just saved Miles from a prison sentence," Nolan pointed out. "Lynne probably took her out to thank her."

Two years ago Miles Addison had been accused of sexually assaulting one of the young boys who attended his after-school program for underprivileged youths. Allison Martin had been lead defense counsel on the case, earning an acquittal for the businessman and a prime partnership offer for herself.

"If the meeting was a thank-you lunch, why were they overheard arguing? And according to their waiter, Lynne stormed out before the food was even served." Dean paced the length of the small room. "Add in the phone call the day Lynne and Jon disappeared, and the fact that Allison systematically cleaned out her personal bank account over a period of six months—starting the day before the Addisons disappeared. And considering she had to get a small business loan to purchase The Summit, where did the money go?"

"You're reaching. For all you know she may be an addict and the money was for her dealer."

Dean grabbed a large envelope from the side table and pulled out an eight-by-ten black-and-white photo of Allison. The picture had been taken during Addison's trial, but even dressed in a conservative suit with her hair pulled back there was no denying her sex appeal. He tossed the picture aside. Allison wouldn't be the first bright, driven, successful person to become an addict, but he couldn't picture her using. She had too much confidence and self-awareness to allow something like drugs to control her.

He'd check into it just the same.

"Wherever the money went," he said, "it doesn't explain why, six months after the Addisons disappeared, Allison quit her job and returned to Serenity Springs. I'm telling you, there's something here. I can feel it."

"I'll have to go with you on this one," Nolan said. "But it'd be a lot easier if you could tell Martin that Lynne's mother is looking for her, and ask her straight-out if she knows where Lynne and Jon are."

"When have we ever had a case that easy?"

"Never. But I can dream. Then I wouldn't have to deal with Robin Hawley calling twice a day, wondering if we've found anything yet."

Dean's fingers tightened around his phone. "If she'd believed her daughter about what a scumbag her son-in-law is, instead of testifying for the prick during his trial, maybe she'd still have her daughter in her life."

"You're projecting again. This isn't the same situation you went through with your family."

No, but in the end, both he and Lynne Addison had been betrayed by the people they trusted the most. "Next time Robin calls, tell her to be patient and let us do our job."

"You can't blame her. If what she told us is true, Miles Addison is dangerous. She's terrified he's going to find Lynne before we do. And given the guy's money and connections, she might be right."

Dean stood and stretched his free arm overhead. "Either way, her bugging you isn't going to help us find her daughter and grandson any sooner."

"*If* we find them."

"We will." He couldn't explain how or why he believed that, but he did. Just as he believed he was in the right place being in Serenity Springs. Dean tapped a finger on Allison's picture. "Martin is a solid lead and I'm betting she has information that will steer me right to Lynne and Jon Addison. And I'm not leaving Serenity Springs until I know for sure."

CHAPTER FIVE

"How's the new bartender working out?"

Allie squeaked as she jumped and spun around. She covered her racing heart with her hand for a second before hitting Jack in the arm with a red cloth napkin.

"You're thirty-three years old," she said. "When are you going to stop sneaking up on me?"

He grinned, his blue eyes—so like her own—lit with humor. "When it stops being fun." He set a stack of white dinner plates on the rectangular dining-room table. "Or when you stop jumping and squealing like a girl when I do it."

And therein lay the rub. Jack was surprisingly stealthy for a man his size. She figured it was the cop in him that made him such an expert sneak. Plus, he always managed to catch her daydreaming. Like now.

Just because he'd asked about her new bartender didn't mean he knew she'd been thinking about Dean. Questioning her decision to hire the cowboy. Wondering what he was hiding behind his sexy grin and guarded green eyes.

Her face heated and she ducked her head so that her hair fell forward, hiding the evidence of her blush as she folded napkins.

"Think this one will stick around for more than a few days?" Jack asked.

"'This one'?" Helen Martin asked as she came into the room, carrying a basket filled with silverware.

As usual, their mother looked flawless. She had on a loose tunic the color of a new penny over a pair of khaki corduroy pants. With her dark hair skimming her shoulders in soft waves and her face not really showing many lines, it was no wonder people often mistook her for Allie's older sister.

Jack began setting the plates on top of the red-and-white tablecloth. "Allie hired another bartender."

Helen frowned as she set the basket at the end of the table. "What happened to that girl you hired last week?"

"It didn't work out," Allie mumbled.

She didn't miss the loaded, wordless exchange that passed between her mother and brother. Allie squeezed a napkin in her hand, wrinkling the fabric. Seemed her entire family had that look down pat. It was part pity, part worry and part helplessness. As if they wanted to save her from herself but didn't know how.

Thankfully, her parents were big on allowing their kids to make their own decisions, and not interfering with their lives. Though she suspected it about killed family members not to ask her why she'd moved back to Serenity Springs.

Especially Jack.

But she couldn't tell her brother what happened, that a lapse in judgment had led her to make a huge mistake. Or what she'd done to rectify that mistake.

The oven timer buzzed. "There's the pie," Helen said, giving Allie's back a quick, brisk rub. She turned to leave, then sighed. "Oh, will you look at them?"

Allie followed her mom's gaze out the large picture window. "I thought you sent Dad out to get a load of firewood?"

"I did," she said, wrapping her arm around Allie's waist. "Emma insisted on helping him, and begged Kelsey to go out with them, as well."

Jack stood on Helen's other side and she linked her arm with his as they watched Larry Martin run through the knee-high snow pulling a giggling Emma on a red plastic sled. Duke, their large golden retriever, ran beside them, barking and trying to snatch Emma's hat. Kelsey, her hands stuffed into the pockets of her puffy coat, brought up the rear.

Helen shook her head and laughed softly. "I guarantee your father's going to regret that tomorrow." The oven timer was still buzzing and, after giving Allie a quick squeeze, she left.

Jack put down the last two plates. "Kelsey doesn't hold much hope this new bartender will work. Said her background was in theater and the only restaurant-bar experience she has is waiting tables."

"Actually," Allie said, placing a napkin to the left of each plate as she walked around the table, "that didn't work out, either."

Jack followed her, laying down silverware. "What do you mean?"

She acted casual as if she couldn't feel Jack's eyes

were on her. "Just what I said. She found a better offer. Didn't even work a day."

"Things must've been pretty slow on a Saturday night if you got by without a bartender."

"We were swamped." She placed the last napkin and went to her mother's antique cherry sideboard for glasses. "The spring breakers hit around nine and it didn't slow until closing."

"Why didn't you call Kelsey?"

"She wasn't feeling well. Speaking of which, she seems to have recovered."

Jack followed her nod toward the window, to find Kelsey engaged in a rigorous snowball fight against Emma and Larry. Duke ran back and forth between the three, trying to catch snowballs in his mouth.

"She thinks it was something she ate." He waved his hand in dismissal. "How did you manage without a bartender?"

"I had a bartender." Allie avoided his eyes as she carried over two crystal water goblets at a time. "I hired one last night."

"What? How?"

"I hired one of my earlier applicants."

He snagged her wrist, stopping her before she could evade him again. "Tell me you didn't."

She smiled up at him and even added a few quick bats of her eyelashes for good measure. "Didn't what?"

Jack, of course, didn't buy her innocent act. "Didn't hire the cowboy."

"How did you know about him?"

He raised one eyebrow. "How do you think?"

She glared at her sister-in-law through the window. "Your wife has a big mouth. What do you two do? Is my business pillow talk or something?"

He let go of her and crossed his arms over his chest. Sent her his most authoritative cop look. *Ha.* As if he could ever intimidate her.

"Kelsey said you didn't hire him because you didn't trust him."

"I changed my mind."

"Did you check his résumé? Follow up on his references?"

"Of course I read his résumé." She flipped her hair behind her shoulder. "I'm perfectly capable of hiring my own employees, you know."

"If you were so good at it, why have you gone through a dozen bartenders since the summer?"

"Seven. I've had seven bartenders since July." She crossed back to the sideboard for the rest of the glasses. "I'm not an idiot," she snapped. "I can handle my business."

"I realize you're not an idiot. You're one of the smartest people I know. But you also allow your emotions to get in the way of your sense sometimes." He took hold of her arms, turning her so she faced him. "You can't save the world, Allie."

Her throat constricted and she pulled away from him. "I have no interest in saving the world."

Not anymore. Not since she'd discovered that in the process, you sometimes save someone undeserving.

Too bad she hadn't remembered that before she'd saved Dean from another take-out meal by inviting him to dinner.

"You can't keep collecting strays. That kid you have working in the kitchen is a perfect example."

"So, I gave Richie a break."

"He needs more than a break. He needs an intervention. Or better yet, a few months in lockup so he can detox."

"How many times do I have to tell you he's not on drugs? Not anymore."

Jack stabbed a hand through his short, dark hair. "Just because an addict tells you he's not using doesn't make it true. No matter how much you want to believe it. And what about this new guy? What's his issue? What do you even know about him?"

"I knew enough to hire him…because he was the only candidate for the job left!" she said, not caring that she sounded like a bratty, rebellious teenager.

If Jack would knock off the bossy big brother act, she wouldn't have to get so defensive.

"Desperation is no excuse. Do you know his work experience? His previous places of employment?" Jack asked. God, he was like a pit bull once he sunk his teeth into something. "I bet you didn't even check his background."

She slammed a glass down so hard she was lucky the stem didn't break off. "I know Dean can mix drinks and keep the bar running smoothly." She also knew every female in the place had been half in lust with him. And that his kiss made her want to drop-kick her self-preservation instincts off a cliff. "He can also handle difficult situations—"

"Difficult situations? Like what? Running out of lemons?"

"No," she said coldly, surprised the word didn't come out in a little burst of frost. "Things like handling a large, belligerent drunk and two of his friends who refused to leave at closing time."

A muscle jumped in Jack's jaw. "What happened?"

She waved her hand in the air. "Nothing I couldn't handle. Well, nothing Dean and I couldn't handle. Which is just the point. I'm a grown woman completely capable of taking care of myself and my business."

"If someone was giving you a hard time, you should've called me—"

"No. I shouldn't have. I don't need rescuing, Jack, and even if I did, it wouldn't be your job. Besides," she continued before he could argue, "as much as I love that you want to protect me, what I need even more from you is some trust. In me. In my decisions."

"Trust?" he asked, so harshly she winced. He glanced at the doorway to the kitchen and pulled her to the far corner, lowering his voice. "You don't want us to trust you. What you want is for us to sit on our hands and smile while you run from whatever it was that happened in New York. Whatever sent you back to Serenity Springs."

She tucked her trembling hands behind her back. "I'm not run—"

"Bullshit."

She shoved a chair into the table with enough force to rattle the glassware. "I told you when I bought The Summit why I came back. I was burned out. Disillusioned." Both of which were more true than he'd ever know. "I was working over seventy hours a week. I had no social life and no time for myself. What I did have was an endless caseload and the beginnings of an ulcer."

"You knew you'd have to work hard," Jack pointed out, bless his pragmatic heart. "All you talked about since graduating from law school was making partner at a prestigious firm before you were thirty-five."

"Sometimes what we want and what's best for us are two different things." She edged past him and went to the head of the table. Flipped the knife over so the edge faced the plate. "That's what I realized when I was offered the partnership." She slid the spoon down so the bottom of it was flush with the bottom of the knife. "It was the moment I'd worked so hard for, but when it was within my grasp, I knew it was wrong for me."

"I understand you wanted a break, that you wanted to come home," he said as he sat in the chair to her left. "I felt the same way after Nicole died. But what I don't understand is why you gave up practicing law altogether. Why buy a bar? Why not start your own practice right here?"

"I didn't like what had become of my life. What I'd become." She told him the truth. As much of it as she could admit, anyway.

"See?" Jack leaned forward. "That's what I'm talking

about. What do you mean, you didn't like who you'd become?" When she remained silent he caught her hand, tugged on it until she lifted her head. "Talk to me. I want to help you."

She forced a laugh. Ignored how hollow it sounded. "I don't need any help. I'm fine. Better than fine." She pulled free of his hold. "I own my own home and my own business, which is growing and thriving. Deciding to step away from practicing law wasn't an easy decision—actually, it was one of the hardest decisions I've ever had to make—but I made the right choice. All I need now is for the people I love to believe that as well."

She held her breath as he took in what she'd said. "I do believe you coming home was for the best," he said. "Never doubt that."

She exhaled softly. *Thank God.* Maybe this time she'd finally gotten through to him. Her big brother was nothing if not incredibly stubborn.

"What I don't believe," he said, "are any of the reasons you gave me for why you came home. But I'm willing to let it drop. For now. When you're ready to tell me the whole truth, I'll be waiting."

She kept her shoulders back and pressed a hand against her churning stomach. As soon as Jack left the room, she slumped into a chair, but the nausea remained. How could she tell him what had really happened? What she'd done, why she'd returned to Serenity Springs? If he knew, he'd try to stop her.

She still had so much more to make up for. People

who depended on her to keep their secrets. To keep them safe.

And most importantly, to keep them hidden.

AT TEN TO SIX, Dean stepped up onto the Martins' porch. He shifted the bouquet of flowers from his right hand to his left and knocked on the door. A few moments later, it opened to reveal a tall, dark-haired man.

Dean had thoroughly researched everything there was to know about Allison Martin. Including the glowering man before him. Jack Martin. Serenity Springs's chief of police. Ex-NYPD detective. And Allison's older brother.

Dean took in Martin's dark expression, the suspicion in his eyes. It wasn't going to be so easy to fool the good chief here.

Dean loved a challenge.

"Something I can do for you?" Martin asked, his body blocking the doorway.

"I'm Dean Garret," he said, keeping his free hand loose at his side. He didn't doubt Martin would rather slap cuffs on his wrists sooner than shake his hand. "Allison invited me to dinner."

"She did, did she?" he asked in a low, dangerous tone.

"Your skills are slipping," Allie said to her brother as she sauntered up behind him. "After all, you helped set the table. Didn't you notice the extra place setting?"

"Guess I was too busy trying to figure out what in the hell you were doing with your life."

And Dean couldn't help but wonder what Jack meant. Did he have his own suspicions about his sister?

Allie nudged Jack with her hip, then brushed past him. She gestured to Dean. "Come on in."

He took off his hat and stepped into the narrow foyer as she shut the door. He could hear the faint sounds of voices and smell roast beef and a wood fire. After his parents' divorce, his mother couldn't afford the upkeep on the house, so they'd moved onto the ranch Dean's grandparents owned. His mother's favorite part about returning to her childhood home was having a fireplace again. During the holidays, she'd always insisted they light a fire even though there was rarely a need for one. She'd said it created ambience.

"Those are so beautiful," Allie said, taking the flowers from him. She pressed her nose against them and inhaled. "Thank you."

"They're not for you. They're for your mother."

"You are one smart man. She's going to love them. Here, let me take your coat."

Dean shrugged out of it as Jack cleared his throat.

"Oh, right. Dean," Allie said as she jerked a thumb behind her, "this is my overprotective, overbearing, slightly anal brother, Jack."

Jack didn't so much as blink. "Actually, it's Police Chief Jack Martin."

"For the love of God," Allie muttered. "Yes, my brother is not only very scary with that glower he's got going on, but he's also really intimidating. And since you now know he's the—" she held up the flowers and made quotation marks in the air "—chief of police, I'm sure we can trust you not to steal the silverware."

"And I was hoping to add another spoon to my collection," Dean said.

Allie pursed her lips. "I thought you collected panties?"

"Do I even want to know how you'd know that?" Jack asked.

She patted his chest. "Probably not."

"I should've traded you for Melinda Hatchett's puppy when you were three, but Mom and Dad wouldn't let me," the chief said in an easy tone that didn't hide his frustration.

"Oh, ha ha." Allie cuffed his arm. "I'll remember that this Mother's Day when you come crying to me to help you pick out the perfect gift. And this year you have two mothers to buy for."

Jack winced. "Have I ever told you you're my favorite sister?"

"It's too late to suck up now." But Dean noticed she squeezed Jack's arm. "Of course, bribes are always welcome. And don't think Rachel didn't tell me you said *she* was your favorite at the wedding."

Rachel, Dean knew, was the youngest Martin sibling, a doctor who lived in New York City. Dean stood there, hat in hand, and watched the byplay between this brother and sister. He hadn't been sure what to expect. With Jack being a cop and Allie a defense attorney, he'd wondered if there would be friction between her and her family.

He had his answer.

But were they so close that Jack would do anything for her? Would he break the law? Bend it a little and use his love for his sister as justification? Would he help hide a woman and child?

Dean couldn't fault Allie for helping Lynne Addison keep her son away from a possible pedophile. Even if he did wonder how she could represent the man in court in the first place. But when Lynne took Jon with no custodial agreement, she'd broken the law.

The same law Jack Martin had taken an oath to uphold.

Allie tossed Dean's coat at Jack and then gestured for Dean to follow her. He made a mental note to dig into the police chief's past. There was right and there was wrong. And wearing a uniform and a badge didn't absolve a man from those two basic facts. Facts that Dean based his career on. Based his life on.

He followed Allie into the kitchen. The room was a mixture of dark and light—cream walls, white cabinets, granite countertops and a rich, wide-board cherrywood floor.

"Dean, these are my parents, Larry and Helen Martin," Allie said. "Mom, Dad, this is Dean Garret. My new bartender."

"Nice to meet you, sir," Dean said, shaking Mr. Martin's hand. He knew Larry Martin had also been a cop, retiring a few years back from the position his son now held. Allie's dad was a few inches shorter than his son, with more gray than black in his short hair. Dean turned to Allie's mother. "I appreciate you having me for dinner."

"You're more than welcome," Mrs. Martin said.

"We're used to Allie bringing home strays," Jack said drily.

"Shut it," Allie told her brother in a singsong voice. "Dean brought you these flowers, Mom."

"How lovely." She took the bouquet and smiled as she trailed her fingertips over the petals. "Thank you, Dean."

He nodded, feeling an odd, fluttering sensation in his stomach. If he didn't know better, he would've sworn it was guilt trying to worm its way past his defenses. Which was nuts. He didn't feel guilty about working this case.

Of course, he'd never been invited to share Sunday dinner with someone he was investigating.

"You've met Kelsey," Allie said.

"Nice to see you again," he told the redhead.

Kelsey smirked at Allie, then wiggled her eyebrows. Allie coughed as if covering a laugh. "And this," she continued quickly as a little girl scampered into the room, her dark blond hair in two high pigtails on top of her head, "is my niece, Emma."

Dean liked kids. Really. But they never failed to remind him of what he'd lost. Even his former partner's three children. If he was still on speaking terms with his family, he'd have more experience around kids, since his brother Ryan and his new wife had a one-year-old daughter. A niece Dean had never met.

If only Ryan's new wife hadn't, at one time, been Dean's old wife.

If only Ryan didn't have what Dean had thought he'd never wanted—and would probably never have.

He crouched so he and Emma were eye to eye. "Nice to meet you."

She pressed her small, warm hand into his. He gently closed his fingers around it, hyperaware of her delicate bones.

Allie playfully tugged one of Emma's pigtails. "Aren't you going to say hello?"

The child's grin widened, revealing a missing tooth on the bottom. She waved.

Allie laughed. "What's gotten into you? Cat got your tongue?"

Emma shook her head so hard her hair almost hit Dean in the face. He straightened. When she stopped shaking like a wet dog, she stuck her tongue out at Allie.

"Emma…" Jack said sternly.

"Relax," Kelsey said, moving to stand next to him. He slid his arm around her waist. "She's showing Allie that she still has her tongue."

Emma nodded.

Helen walked by, carrying a bowl of mashed potatoes. "She hasn't said a word since she came inside."

"That's because she's not talking," Kelsey said. "At least not until dessert. Right, Emma?"

Again, the blonde pixie nodded. She sure was a cute little thing.

Allie picked up the bowl of rolls; from the slight rise of steam Dean figured they were still warm. "I thought it was physically impossible for Emma not to speak. What's going on?" she asked.

"You'll see," Kelsey said with a sly grin.

"Ooh…a secret, huh?" Allie handed the rolls to Jack. "I bet some tickling could get her to spill the beans."

This obviously wasn't the first time Allie and her niece had played this game. No sooner had Allie said the word *tickling* than Emma gave a high-pitched shriek and bolted, Allie hot on her heels. Larry lifted the platter of sliced roast and sidestepped the pair as they raced out of the kitchen.

"Everyone take your seat," Helen said. She opened a drawer and pulled out a corkscrew. "Jack, please tell your sister to stop chasing Emma so we can all sit down."

The pair in question burst back into the kitchen, Emma still giggling. Before Dean could evade her, she clutched his leg and swung herself around behind him.

Allie skid to a stop. "No fair."

Emma giggled again.

"Come on, squirt," Jack said, picking up his daughter. "The sooner we eat dinner, the sooner we'll get dessert."

At the table, Dean held out Allie's chair for her, ignoring the chief's scowl. He took his own seat and forced his mind to clear. To stop thinking about how all of this— the house, the food, the closeness of these people—reminded him of his own family.

Of how they used to be.

And he couldn't believe he was going to admit this, even to himself, but he really did feel guilty, after all. That guilt made him even more uncomfortable when Larry Martin said grace and everyone bowed their heads.

So what if they'd welcomed Dean into their home? Allowed him to share a meal with them? He had to keep his focus. Just because the Martins seemed like a nice family—hell, they probably *were* a nice family—that didn't make a difference to him or what he had to do.

Without lifting his head, he glanced over to find Jack watching him, mistrust clear in his cold gaze. Dean also had to remember he wasn't dealing with regular civilians here. Not that some small town chief of police worried Dean. By the time Jack figured out what he was really doing in Serenity Springs—*if* he figured it out—Dean would be long gone.

And he'd have the one thing he'd come here to collect.

A missing woman and her child.

CHAPTER SIX

DINNER PASSED WITHOUT INCIDENT. Thank God. But Allie wasn't taking any chances. She turned on the coffeepot and took down the good cups and saucers from the upper cabinet. During a delicious meal of tender roast beef and all the trimmings, the conversation had been steered toward neutral subjects.

Mainly because Allie had rarely allowed Jack or her father to get a word in edgewise.

Or to ask Dean too many personal questions.

Sure, she was curious about Dean herself, but wanted him to open up on his own. Not because he was being interrogated.

After Allie convinced her mom she deserved to relax after doing most of the cooking, Helen, along with her husband, Kelsey and Emma, went into the living room. Jack and Dean stayed behind to help Allie clear the table.

Her best bet would be to keep her brother and Dean as far away from each other as possible. Easier said than done, since Jack seemed more interested in loading the dishwasher than joining his wife and daughter in the other room.

Dean came into the kitchen and set a stack of dirty plates on the counter. "Anything I can do to help?"

"You wash," she said, tossing a towel over her shoulder before handing him a bottle of liquid soap, "and I'll dry."

He unbuttoned his sleeves at the wrist and rolled them to his elbows before squirting in soap and filling the sink with hot water.

"We've got this under control," she told Jack, who'd just added detergent to the dishwasher. "Why don't you join everyone else?"

"No sense you two doing all the work." He snatched the towel off her shoulder. "Besides, this is a great opportunity for me to get to know your new employee."

Oh, she didn't like that glint in her brother's eyes.

"Allie says you're new in town," Jack said to Dean. He held the towel out of Allie's reach when she tried to grab it.

"I got in on Wednesday."

"What made you come to Serenity Springs?"

Dean washed and rinsed the gravy boat. Handed it to Jack. "I heard about the job opening. Thought I'd check it out."

"Not very many people outside of town have heard about The Summit." Jack handed the dry dish to Allie to put away. "Or that it had an opening for a bartender."

"That was so subtle," Allie said. "Don't tell me, when you were in New York, you always got to play the bad cop?"

"Only on even days." He dried a bowl. "I'm trying to get to know our guest. Unless—" he glanced at Dean "—you have something to hide?"

"He doesn't." She snatched the bowl from him. "But that doesn't mean you have the right to interrogate him, either."

"I spent the last few months in Syracuse," Dean said mildly, "and I saw the ad for the job opening online."

"Syracuse?" Jack asked. "That's a long way from... where is it you said you were from? Denver?"

Dean kept his head down as he scrubbed the roasting pan. Why were men who were up to their elbows in dish suds so damn sexy? "Dallas."

"How'd you end up in Syracuse?"

Allie managed to snatch the towel out of Jack's hands. She stood between the men and glared at her brother, her hands fisted on her hips. "What is up with the interrogation?"

She'd hate for Dean to be scared away by Jack's tough cop routine. Plus, it was humiliating to have Jack acting like they were teenagers again and she'd brought home a boy for the first time.

"It's all right." Dean skimmed his wet fingers over her arm, giving her goose bumps. "A buddy of mine from the Corps lives in Syracuse. He got me a job at a hotel his sister managed there."

"Since you're here, I take it that didn't work out. Did you get fired?"

She squeezed the towel between her hands and pretended it was her brother's fat neck. "Jack, I swear—"

"My full name is Dean William Garret," he said, shifting so that he stood beside her, facing Jack. Though his voice was still low, she detected a thread of impatience. "Allison has my social security number and birth date from my job application. I was born and raised outside of Dallas, joined up when I was twenty-one and spent the next nine years in the service."

"You don't have to tell him any of this," Allie said.

Dean dried his hands on the towel she still held. "As you said, I have nothing to hide."

She bit her lower lip. She believed that. Didn't she?

"I'm divorced," he continued. "No kids. I served in both Afghanistan and Iraq. After my discharge—"

"Honorable?" Jack asked.

Allie tossed the towel at him, but he caught it before it hit his face. "You are going to pay for this," she promised.

Jack slung the towel around his neck, held on to the ends. "You'll thank me if he's AWOL and they have a warrant out for him."

This whole thing was surreal. Jack had always been overprotective, but he was going overboard. Just because she'd been taken advantage of by a few of her previous employees… It was as if she was seeing her brother as a cop, for the first time.

She couldn't say she much cared for it.

And honestly, witnessing these two facing off was getting on her nerves. Jack was cool and in control, while Dean stood unflinching, his attitude laid-back. But his body was tense, as if gearing up for a fight.

And wouldn't that be a lovely way to end the evening?

"I'm not AWOL," Dean said. "I served my country and was honorably discharged."

"And haven't had a steady job since?" Jack pressed.

"That's it," Allie snapped as she seized Jack's arm and hauled him toward the door. "Go into the living room and cool your jets," she told him, "and maybe I'll speak to you again in five years."

"I was trying—"

"Yeah, yeah. You were trying to help. Trying to protect me. I get it." She shook her head, unable to keep the anger and disappointment out of her voice as she said, "But you overstepped, Jack."

He stared at Dean for two long heartbeats before nodding.

Her shoulders slumped as she watched Jack disappear into the living room.

"You all right?" Dean asked.

She straightened and faced him. "Fine." She crossed back to the counter and picked up a large serving tray. Yanking open the silverware drawer, she scooped up a handful of dessert forks. "I'd apologize for my brother, but really, what's the point?"

Dean let the water out of the sink. "He's just doing his job."

She slammed the drawer shut. "Even cops have days off."

"Not that job." He dried his hands. "The job of watching out for you. That's what older brothers are for."

"Is that what you do for your brothers?"

His hesitation was brief but noticeable. "I think it's different with sisters."

She tossed the forks onto the tray with a loud clang. "Why do you do that?"

"Do what?"

"Give me a nonanswer when I ask you something? If it's too personal, just say so."

"It's too personal."

"See?" she asked irritably. "That wasn't so hard." She turned her back on him, set dessert plates on the tray before spinning around again. "It's not like I expect you to share all your secrets with me just because I hired you—despite your less than stellar résumé."

His brow furrowed. "You hired me because you were desperate."

She waved that distinction away. "I'm giving you a chance."

"And I appreciate it."

"I don't want your gratitude," she almost growled.

"What do you want then?"

A straight answer. To stop feeling like she'd been wrong to hire him. To trust him.

She wanted him to do or say something that would put her mind at ease about him.

"Nothing." She went to the refrigerator for the milk. "I'm sorry. I'm mad at Jack and taking it out on you." She poured milk into a ceramic creamer. "It's not like we're friends, right? And it's obvious you want to keep it that way—"

"You're my boss," he pointed out.

She flashed him a forced smile as she put the milk away, opened the freezer and took out a gallon of vanilla ice cream. She set it on the counter. "That I am. And even though I have friendships with several of my employees—and am related to my manager—you and I will keep our relationship strictly business from here on out."

Despite the fact that she'd invited him to Sunday dinner. And that he'd accepted.

Or that he'd kissed her last night.

He shoved a hand through his hair. "I doubt someone like you needs any more friends. You probably have more than you know what to do with."

"True." She put the coffeepot on the tray along with the sugar bowl. "I just thought…"

"What?"

"I thought maybe you could use one."

He looked shocked and, to her surprise, insulted. "I'm an island."

She grinned. "Like I said, I'll leave you alone. Can you get the tray for me, please?"

She picked up the apple pie and ice cream and headed to the door. She'd made it to the threshold when he said, "It's nothing personal."

"You don't have to ex—"

"I had a…falling-out with my family," he said, unrolling his sleeves, "and we haven't spoken for a while."

"I'm sorry." Even as mad as she was with Jack, she couldn't imagine not seeing him, talking with him— or anyone else in her family. "I shouldn't have pressed. Let's forget I said anything."

"I hate spiders."

She frowned. Maybe all of this talk about opening up had pushed the poor guy over the edge. "Excuse me?"

"Spiders." He shoved his hands into his pockets. "I hate them."

She adjusted her grip so that the pie pressed against her rib cage, taking some of the weight off her wrist. Dean seemed at ease in her mother's kitchen. He leaned back against the counter, his shoulders relaxed, his long legs stretched out in front of him.

But there was a challenge in his eyes. As if he was daring her to say something about what he'd admitted. And that's when she realized he didn't just hate spiders. He was afraid of them.

He'd shared one of his secrets with her.

"I won't tell a soul," she promised, shifting the ice cream so she could make an X across her heart.

"I appreciate that." But despite the slight upward curve of his mouth, he didn't really seem amused. If anything, he seemed…triumphant. Almost predatory. She could only stare as he closed the distance between them. "What about you?" he asked, reaching out as if to touch her cheek. But then he fisted his hand and dropped his arm back to his side. "Any secrets you'd like to share?"

She swallowed in an attempt to work moisture back into her mouth. "Nothing quite as dark as arachnophobia."

"You sure?" His eyes were steady. Intense. "Because you know what they say about confession being good for the soul."

Except she didn't need confession. Not when she'd already taken care of her penance on her own.

"I'm positive."

"Everyone has secrets, Allison. And I'm guessing yours are more interesting than most." He leaned forward and she slanted back, kept the ice cream and pie between them. "Guess I have my work cut out for me," he murmured.

Fear, irrational and unsettling, filled her. "What work is that?"

One side of his mouth lifted. "Finding out what your secrets are."

ALLISON'S FACE DRAINED OF color and she took a hasty step back. "I...they're waiting for us...."

Then she raced out of the room.

Dean scratched the side of his neck. *Smooth move, Garret. Scare the hell out of her. Good plan. That'll make it easier to find out where Lynne and Jon are.*

He made it to the hallway before remembering the tray in the kitchen. With a mild curse, he headed back the way he'd come.

He could do this. He'd fought in the mountains of Afghanistan and the streets of Baghdad. All he had to do was get through coffee and dessert, make more inane small talk. Ignore Chief Martin's suspicious glare and leading questions.

Dean would rather be on a recon mission searching for suspected terrorists.

He picked up the tray and walked out of the kitchen.

He'd accepted Allie's dinner invitation so he'd be able to subtly pump her family for information about her. Or better yet, get her to open up—or in this case, slip up—and give him a clue he was searching in the right direction.

He hadn't counted on her brother being as anxious for information about him as he was about Allie.

Dean went into the living room. A sofa faced two plump armchairs in front of the fireplace, a glass-topped coffee table between them. Kelsey sat in one chair, Emma wiggling—either in excitement or because she had to go to the bathroom—on her lap. Jack sat at his wife's feet.

Helen and Larry were on the sofa. Dean raised his eyebrows when he noted their linked hands. Maybe Nolan and Cassie weren't the only happily married couple in the world.

Just one of the few.

Allie, perched on the second armchair, didn't so much as glance up when he entered the room.

"Thank you, Dean," Helen said as she rose. "You can set it on the coffee table."

"Great. As soon as everyone has their dessert, Emma can share her secret," Kelsey said. "She's had enough of being silent. Poor kid's about to bust."

Allie slid a slice of pie onto a plate, then handed it to Jack, who added a scoop of ice cream. "I think it's cruel you made her stay silent for so long."

Kelsey set Emma down and accepted the plate from Jack. "Hey, it was her idea. She wanted to make a big production out of this secret, not me. And she thought the safest way not to spill the beans early was if she didn't speak at all."

"Dean, please sit down," Helen said, indicating the end of the sofa across from Allie. "Coffee?"

He nodded and sat as Helen served it and Allie dished up the pie. He accepted his piece and took a bite, almost groaning in pleasure. Sweet, warm apple filling wrapped in a crust as flaky as his mother's. What could be better? He refused to feel ashamed about accepting their hospitality—and their damned good pie—under false pretenses. And while he knew better than to like the people he was investigating, it was easy to like the Martins.

He flicked a glance at Jack. Well, most of the Martins.

But liking them was okay. As long as it didn't interfere with the job.

Reaching for a napkin, Allie leaned forward, giving Dean a peek at her cleavage and the lacy edge of her cream-colored bra. He choked on a mouthful of cinnamon-laced apples.

And found Jack staring at him.

"You all right?" Allie asked, her elbows on her knees.

She was torturing him. He stole another look at Jack. Or else she was trying to get him killed.

"I'm fine," he wheezed. He took a large sip of his coffee and cleared his throat. "Sorry."

"Well, kiddo, it's time," Kelsey said, pulling a piece of glossy white paper out of her back pocket. She handed it to Emma, who pressed it against her chest. "You ready to share your news?"

The child skipped to the center of the room, her grin huge and excited. "Look," Emma ordered, shoving the paper in Allie's face.

Allie leaned back as if to better focus on the picture, then her expression softened. "Oh…" she breathed in that awed tone women used when they came across puppies, babies or a man who brought them flowers for no reason "…it's an ultrasound."

Larry leaped up with a whoop, practically hurdled the table and enfolded Jack in a bear hug. Helen, a bit slower to her feet but just as enthusiastic, hurried over to Kelsey, tears in her eyes as she hugged her daughter-in-law. Allie picked up Emma and joined her mother and sister-in-law in one of those group hugs women liked.

Everyone started talking at once. Questions and answers about due dates and morning sickness, baby names and cravings flew around the room. Jack clarified it was too early to tell if the baby was a boy or girl, but Emma, obviously hoping for that brother, told him in no uncertain terms it was a boy. She was sure of it. Allie asked if Kelsey wanted to cut back her hours. Helen talked about getting the old crib out of the attic, and Larry went to get a bottle of wine—and ginger ale for Kelsey and Emma—so they could share a toast.

And Dean sat there, his blood cold as he took it all in.

His hands were unsteady as he set his cup and plate on the table. He'd been here before. Except the last time he'd been to a family function where someone announced a pregnancy, it'd been his brother Ryan announcing the woman he loved was pregnant with his child.

And then Dean had lost control and broken Ryan's nose.

He forced himself to get to his feet and calmly walk over to Allie.

She was now hugging Jack, so Dean waited until she'd let go of her brother before touching her elbow. "I'm going to head out."

She was so happy, it was almost painful to witness. "What? But why?"

"This should be a private celebration," he said. He then thanked Helen for her hospitality and congratulated Kelsey and Jack.

"Let me get your coat," Allie said, following him out into the hallway.

Larry came down the hall carrying wineglasses by their stems in one hand, a bottle of wine in the other. "Allie, can you get the ginger ale?"

"Sure, Dad. I'm going to walk Dean out first."

"I appreciate you having me in your home," Dean said.

"You're more than welcome, son," Larry said. "We're always happy to meet Allie's friends."

Sweet God but some people were gullible. Thankfully, Dean wasn't the type of man to succumb to guilt.

Allie opened the closet door and reached up to the shelf for his hat. "Damn you, Jack," she muttered, her fingers barely grazing the brim.

His Stetson was at the back of the shelf—right where

Chief Martin must've tossed it. Dean also noticed Allie's jacket, the red leather one she'd worn the other day, hanging to the left.

"Let me help you," Dean said, coming up behind her.

He reached for the hat, trapping her between the coats and his body. His arm brushed her shoulder and she twitched. With his fingers curled around the brim of his hat, he stepped back out into the hall.

Where he could breathe.

She handed him his coat without meeting his eyes. Laughter broke out in the other room and she glanced over her shoulder.

"I can see myself out," he said.

"Are you sure?"

He nodded, kept his expression blank. "I'd hate for you to miss any of the celebration. Go back to your family." He put his hat on. "I'll see you Tuesday."

She looked at the front door and, obviously feeling he'd be able to handle leaving on his own, said, "Okay, then. Good night, Dean."

Instead of watching the sway of her hips as she walked down the hall, he stared into the closet at Allie's red leather jacket. Shrugged his coat on as he remembered her putting her cell phone in her pocket last night.

After making sure the hallway was empty, he wrapped a scarf around his hand, reached into Allie's right coat pocket and picked up her phone. He then dropped it into his own pocket and put the scarf back.

He kept his strides unhurried as he left the house. Standing under the porch light, he buttoned his coat. Despite the cold, the sky was clear and there were almost as many stars visible as there were back home.

Best of all, his evening hadn't been a total waste.

He patted the pocket with Allie's phone as he made his way down the steps. The snow beneath his feet crunched and the cold air stung his lungs. He couldn't wait to get back to Texas.

He'd discovered a few useful things tonight. Such as there was no sense trying to gain information about Allie from her family. The way Chief Martin had acted, Dean knew it would be in his best interest to keep as low a profile as possible during his remaining time in town.

He unlocked his truck, slid inside and started the engine before he even shut the door. He'd also learned that Allie truly was one of those people who lived to help others, which played into his theory that she'd helped the Addisons run away from a pedophile.

And though Dean had taken a misstep in the kitchen by admitting he wanted to discover her secrets, Allie's reaction had confirmed what he'd already suspected.

She was hiding something.

He pulled away from the curb and turned the radio up when Brad Paisley's latest came on.

But he still couldn't figure out why Allie had represented Miles Addison in the first place. Of course, even Lynne's mother had admitted to being tricked into believing Miles was innocent. Maybe Allie had been, too?

Not that it mattered; he didn't need to figure out Allison Martin and her motives. All he needed to do was find Lynne and Jon. Whether they wanted to be reunited with Robin—or even wanted to be found—wasn't his concern.

All he cared about was completing this job.

And moving on to the next one.

"Hey, Richie," Allie said late Monday morning as she walked into The Summit's kitchen.

She was running late after spending almost an hour with her cell phone provider, reporting her lost phone. She'd discovered it missing last night when she got home. When her mom couldn't find it either, Allie had canceled her service.

Only to find her phone wedged in back of the driver's seat not twenty minutes later. She'd missed it last night—which was what she got for searching her car in the dark—and would've missed it today if she hadn't spilled the large coffee she'd bought at Sweet Suggestions.

She really hated Mondays.

She unwound the scarf from her neck and narrowed her eyes at her assistant—or, as he liked to think of himself, her sous-chef. Richie's brown hair was covered with a baseball cap, his stubby ponytail pulled through the hole in the back, his thin face was pale, his brown eyes watery.

"You feeling all right?" she asked him.

"Yeah, I'm good." He stopped chopping onions long enough to take a long drink from his water bottle. "I think I'm coming down with a cold, that's all."

"You sure you're up for working today?" She slipped

off her coat and laid it over the back of a chair before going to him at the counter. "You know how slow Mondays are. I'm sure I could manage without you."

"I'll be okay."

"If you say so. But let me know if you feel worse. I talked to Ellen earlier and both she and Bobby have head colds, so it's definitely going around." Ellen Jensen, Allie's hairdresser, had called to change Allie's appointment to Wednesday, hoping her son would be back in school by then.

Allie dug a notepad and pen out of a drawer. "Why don't I make tortilla soup tonight? Sort of my Mexican version of chicken noodle soup, minus the noodles." She wrote a list of the ingredients she'd need. "Can you run to the store for me? And it'd be better if I handled the food prep tonight. We don't want any contamination."

Richie took the list, shoved it into the pocket of his baggy jeans. "It's not like I spit in the food," he muttered. "I wash my hands after using the bathroom and everything."

She raised her eyebrows at his tone. "You sure you're all right?"

He dropped his eyes and shrugged his bony shoulders, looking more like a teenager than a man of twenty-three. "Sorry. Guess I'm not feeling as well as I thought."

"Why don't you forget the groceries? I'm sure I'll have time later—"

"Nah. I've got it." He took his coat from one of the hooks on the wall. "I'll get the groceries, drop them off and then maybe head home for a quick nap. Some sleep will make me feel better. Besides, I don't want to leave you hanging. Mondays might not be the busiest but they're usually pretty steady."

Wasn't he sweet? She'd definitely made the right decision to hire him, no matter what Jack said. Yes, Richie had previously had a problem with drugs, but he did his best each day to fight it. To make a better life for himself.

And she was helping him do it.

"All right," Allie said, taking her wallet out of her purse. She handed him a fifty and a couple of twenties. "If the avocados are decent, get a few extra and I'll make guacamole, too. And you'd better see if Kelsey needs anything for the bar."

He put on his coat and pocketed the money before pulling on his knit hat and picking up his water bottle. "I should be back in a couple of hours," he said, then pushed through the door to the dining room.

Allie washed her hands and finished chopping onions. Scooping them into a large bowl, she covered it and stuck it in the refrigerator.

"Can you call Noreen for me?" she asked Kelsey, who was mopping the floor in the barroom. "See if she can come in and help me prep dinner?"

"Hello. I'm great, thanks for asking." Kelsey stuck the mop into the industrial bucket. "Second day in a row I haven't thrown up my breakfast. Although I almost did when I walked into the kitchen and smelled those onions Richie was cutting."

Allie wrinkled her nose and went behind the bar. "I

think I liked our relationship better when you didn't share quite so much information."

"Just doing my best to keep you abreast of all of this pregnancy stuff. You know, so you're not shocked when it happens to you."

Allie clenched her hands, her fingernails digging into her palms. It'd been a long time since she'd considered a family of her own. "I don't think we have to worry about that happening anytime soon, seeing as I haven't even been on a date in more than five months."

Kelsey dunked the mop in the soapy water a few times and then set it in the wringer. "You brought a guy to Sunday dinner at your parents' house."

"That wasn't a date. I felt bad for Dean being alone in town."

Kelsey mopped under a table. "Uh-huh."

"I did," she insisted, stopping shy of adding a foot stomp for good measure. She filled a glass with ice and took a bottle of cranberry juice from the minifridge. "And I honestly don't see why Jack had to be so overprotective. I've invited both Richie and Noreen for dinner before, too."

"Yeah, but to my knowledge, neither Richie nor Noreen ever stared at you as if you were a Dallas Cowboy cheerleader—complete with hot pants."

Allie poured juice into her glass and shook her head. "Where do you come up with this stuff?"

"Hey, I'm calling it like I see it, that's all." Finished mopping, she took a chair off the table and set it down. "Although Dillon often asks me that same question."

"It doesn't matter." Allie added lemon-lime soda to her juice and gave it a quick stir with a straw. "Even if Dean did look at me in that way, I'm not going there."

She sipped her drink. Their kiss the other night had been an acknowledgment of the attraction between them. A way of diffusing that attraction, and the curiosity that went along with it, before it became an issue.

One they'd have to act on.

But she couldn't chance a relationship with someone she didn't trust completely. She couldn't risk getting too close to anyone and having her secret come out.

"I'm glad to hear it," Kelsey said, dragging the bucket toward the pool table.

"That's a switch. Usually you're telling me to loosen up." She put the juice back and shut the door with her foot before coming to stand on the other side of the bar. "Last month you thought I should hook up with that ski instructor."

"I wasn't trying to pimp you out. I thought you could have fun with the guy. Enjoy life a bit."

"Hey, I do enjoy life."

"You don't have a life," Kelsey said, sitting on a stool next to Allie. "You spend most of your time here, and the only people you hang out with are your family, Dillon and Nina, and once in a while Ellen and her kid."

"I like being here," Allie muttered. "And so what if I hang out with my family and a few close friends? I love you all."

"God." Kelsey's eyes welled with tears. "No fair getting sappy around the pregnant lady." She pressed the heels of her hands against her eyes. "Stupid hormones."

Allie patted Kelsey's knee. "Aww…you're nothing but a big softie."

"Be that as it may, I do love you," Kelsey said, surprising Allie by squeezing her hand. "You're the best friend I've ever had."

"Now you're going to get me started," Allie complained, blinking furiously. "Are hormonal fluctuations catching?"

"No, and you can't use my pregnancy as an excuse for your weepiness, so suck it up and focus." Her mouth thinned. "I'm not so sure hiring Dean was the best idea."

"Weren't you the one who wanted me to hire him to begin with?"

"Hey, I'm allowed to change my mind. Which I did after witnessing you two last night. But, since you hired him, I think you should be careful. When a man looks at a woman like Dean Garret looks at you, he wants something. Something more than getting you into bed."

Allie twirled her straw between her fingers. "I think Jack is rubbing off on you. And not in a good way."

What else could she say? That she'd had the same concerns about Dean last night when he'd made that comment about discovering her secrets? About having his work cut out for him? Why should both of them worry she'd messed up?

Besides, she'd already decided to watch herself around Dean. Maybe his comment had been harmless. After all, she'd started that conversation as a way to get him to open up, to somehow forge a friendship between them. Maybe that had been his way of responding in kind.

But in case it wasn't, Allie would be sure to keep her guard up around him, and keep her secrets to herself.

CHAPTER SEVEN

"WE HAVE A PROBLEM," Dean said at work Wednesday night as Allie walked by him on her way to clear tables.

She brushed her hair from her face. "If it's another drunk who's being unreasonable, you are not to punch him. Not under any circumstances."

He motioned for her to follow him to the back of the bar, where they could talk in private and he could still keep an eye on everything. Tonight was even slower than Tuesday had been—which was saying something—but there were two couples who'd stuck around after dinner, and a group of college kids playing darts.

Of course, it wasn't even eleven. Still early. And on Tuesday, they'd had a decent-sized crowd by midnight.

"I don't go around punching every drunk who annoys me," he said. What did she think he was? Some newbie recruit on his first mission? "Just the ones who deserve it."

"There's nothing I like more than a man with his own warped code of honor," she said drily. "So, what's this problem we have?"

"I guess I shouldn't have said *we*," he clarified, curling his fingers into his palm. "More like you have a problem. Or at least, that guy you have doing dishes has a problem."

One of the college kids came up to the bar and Dean went to take his order, gesturing for Allie to follow. After getting the student a beer, he rang up the order on the cash register.

"Your assistant's using," he told her quietly.

"Who? Richie?" She looked over her shoulder. "That's ridiculous. He's been clean for more than nine months now."

Dean raised his eyebrows. So, she knew the guy was an addict, but had hired him anyway?

"Then he's using again. Have you seen him today? He's on something."

Her hand shook as she picked up the rag and wiped the bar. "He's sick," she insisted, "not stoned. He's probably just loopy from the cold meds he's taking."

Was she for real? While Dean appreciated her trusting nature—it made his own job that much easier—he sure didn't like the idea of anyone else taking advantage of her.

He shoved his sleeves up and washed a glass, scrubbing harder than necessary. Not that he was taking advantage of her. He was doing his job. He wasn't using her. And after he found out for sure whether or not she knew where Lynne and Jon were, he'd be on his way.

But it wouldn't affect Allie. She wouldn't get hurt.

That Richie guy was another story.

She was watching Dean expectantly, as if waiting for him to agree with her. "I'm sure his pupils are dilated because of his cold," he said sarcastically. "And he's probably picking at his arms because of his medicine's side effects."

"You're wrong." She seized hold of the bottle of spray disinfectant and, even though they had three hours until closing, squirted cleaner. "I know Richie." She vigorously wiped the bar. "You don't."

"True." Dean stepped back when she started spraying again, saving himself from asphyxiation by taking the bottle out of her hand. "But just to be certain, when you go back in the kitchen, why don't you take a good look at him? His hands are trembling and he can't meet anyone's eyes."

"Maybe you intimidate him."

"Me?" Dean laid his free hand on his chest. "Darlin', I'm harmless."

"That's not quite the word I'd use to describe you."

"Check it out. The guy's got all the signs."

The glare she sent him told him she wasn't too happy with his pressuring her about this. Or about the possibility of him being right.

Good thing he didn't care if she was happy with him or not.

"I'm not going to accuse a trusted employee—and someone I consider a friend—of doing drugs," she said coldly. "Especially when I don't have proof. And I'd appreciate it if, in the future, you keep your baseless accusations to yourself."

He ground his teeth together to keep from blasting

her. She didn't want his help? Fine. He had better things to do.

"Yes, ma'am." He handed her the cleaner. "I'll be sure to mind my own business from here on out."

With all the disdain and superiority of a queen to a peasant, she snatched the bottle from him and stalked off.

Guess she hadn't liked his conciliatory tone.

A woman who'd entered the bar while he and Allie were talking requested a glass of white wine. Dean filled the order and fought his growing irritation. So what if Allie had an addict working for her. She was an intelligent and capable woman. Sooner or later she'd figure out that she needed to get rid of Richie.

If she didn't, Dean was sure her brother would protect her.

He glanced over to where Allie was wiping off a table. Today she had on a deep green top, snug dark jeans and black heels. The college kids were having a great time checking out her ass. But she either didn't know she was fueling their fantasies or didn't care.

More than likely she was too ticked off at him to notice.

Not that she had any reason to be angry. He'd only been trying to help. It'd taken him two days to say anything about his suspicions in the first place.

After his slipup Sunday at her parents' house, he'd taken a step back. Hadn't wanted to give Allie any reason to think he was more than what he seemed. Especially after he'd taken her cell phone, noted all outgoing and incoming calls, and gotten enough information for Nolan to hack into her personal account. Dean had then slipped over to her house late that night, broken into her vehicle and planted the phone where it would look as if she'd dropped it.

The way this case was going, though, he shouldn't worry about having his true motives revealed. He wasn't any closer to proving Allie knew where Lynn and Jon were hiding. Maybe he should just confront her.

Nolan had discovered two phone numbers Allie had called frequently over the past year. Both were to cell phones and when he and Dean had learned the first belonged to a Sheila Garey in Salem, Oregon, they thought they'd caught their first real break.

Sheila, it turned out, wasn't an alias for Lynne Addison, but a friend of Allie's from law school.

The second number was from a prepaid cell phone account. Since the phone, and the card to add minutes, had been purchased at a discount store, there was no way to trace it. The number had a Cincinnati area code—where Lynne and Jon were last spotted—but when Dean tried to call it, it was no longer in service.

In his pocket, his cell phone vibrated. He pulled it out and checked the number before flipping it open. "Hey there, darlin'," he said into the phone. "I was hoping you'd call."

"I have that information you asked for," Katherine said, as usual, getting right to the point. "Is this a bad time?"

"I need two minutes to get somewhere less crowded."

He covered the mouthpiece as Allie set her tray of dirty glasses on the bar. "Mind if I take my break now?"

She shrugged, which he took as a yes. He rounded the bar and went outside, the cold hitting him like a right jab.

"Sorry 'bout that," he told Katherine as he hurried to his truck. "What did you find out?"

He climbed inside and started the ignition. He'd dug into Allie's past and kept her under surveillance the past three days, but hadn't discovered anything new except that she speed-walked four miles every morning—no matter how cold—and if her stopping by the local bakery afterward was any indication, had a serious sweet tooth. Neither of which led him to Lynne and Jon Addison.

"Allison Martin worked for the public defender's office a year before being offered a job at Hanley, Barcroft, Blaisdell and Littleton," Katherine said.

"I knew that. Guess the bigwigs there had been impressed with the number of cases she'd won." Dean sure had been.

Katherine grunted. "Every case she won was a check mark in the loss column for the good guys—you know that, right?"

The good guys in this case being the NYPD. "Now don't take it personally. Besides, you have to admit, she was an excellent attorney. She'd been on the fast track for a partnership even before she took on Miles Addison as her client."

"I don't have to admit any such thing," Katherine said. "And if you know so much, why'd you ask me to check her background?"

"Because that's all I could find out—*her* background—when what I need to know is about the Miles Addison case."

"Not much to find out. From what I can tell, Allison Martin may have been right to take his case."

"Wasn't he accused of molesting a young boy?"

"Yeah, but it was a tough one to prosecute. For one thing, Addison had public sentiment on his side. He's successful, wealthy, handsome and intelligent. He's also a well-known name in New York. He serves on the boards of numerous charitable organizations, donating millions of dollars to those in need each year."

"Sounds like a real prince. So, his popularity kept him from going to prison? Or was he really innocent?"

"You think I have a crystal ball or something? All I know is that there was no physical evidence, just the kid's word against Addison's. Addison claimed the boy's mother had been blackmailing him for the past six months, that she'd threatened to bring him on up these charges if he didn't pay her."

"He go to the cops?"

Katherine snorted. "Nah. Turns out at the time all of this happened he was debating a run for public office. He figured if he didn't pay her, she'd force her son to lie and he didn't want anything to derail his ambitions. Phone records indicated the mother called Addison at his office twice a month for the preceding six months, which supported his claim. He also had bank slips showing large withdrawals on the same dates as the phone calls. He maintained that after she called, he'd get the money—in cash as per her orders—and meet her at a bar in Brooklyn. The defense team even got one of the bartenders who worked there to testify he saw Addison and the mother together at least twice."

"If he was paying her, how'd he end up in court?"

"I guess she asked for more than he was willing to give. When he balked, she threatened to tell not only his wife what he'd allegedly done but also the newspapers. He realized how much power he'd given her. He told her he wasn't giving her another cent and he just had to have faith that the truth would win out. The next day, the charges were filed."

"Sounds like Allie had more than enough evidence to prove there was reasonable doubt at the trial."

His comment was met with silence. "'Allie'?" Katherine finally asked. "You're not getting too friendly with this girl, are you, Dean?"

He tugged on his left ear. "You know me. I'm playing my part."

"I hope so," she muttered. "But you're right about *Ms. Martin* proving reasonable doubt. After she cross-examined the mother on the stand, it looked as if the woman had set Addison up. If you ask me, the prosecution rushed the case to trial. They had no physical evidence so it came down to the kid's word against Addison's. It took them three hours of deliberation before acquitting him."

He drummed his fingers on the steering wheel. "Do you think Addison really *was* innocent?"

"Anything's possible," Katherine said. "And it's equally possible he was guilty."

That was why Dean had wanted more information about the case. He needed to know what Miles Addison was capable of. Robin had told Nolan her son-in-law was dangerous, and if that was true, Dean had to find out how many resources Addison had. How far he'd go to get his wife and son back.

He needed to keep Lynne and Jon safe once he found them.

He thanked Katherine for her help, promised he'd be careful, and then shut the ignition off and got out. So, now he knew how the case against Addison had gone down. Too bad it didn't prove anything. He shoved his hands into his pockets and ducked his head against the wind. He still didn't know why Allie had defended the man—because she'd believed him innocent? Because she'd wanted a tough case to prove her worth? And it sure didn't give her motive for hiding Lynne and Jon.

Unless there was more to the story.

He pushed open the door to The Summit with enough force for it to bang against the inside wall. Several heads turned his way but he ignored the patrons.

Worse than being wrong or not solving the case was the idea of walking out on Allie. Leaving her alone with her denial about Richie and her savior tendencies left a bitter taste in his mouth.

He needed to remember the number one lesson of undercover work: don't get involved.

"IF YOU DON'T WANT TO believe what's happening under your nose," Dean told Allie over an hour later, "that's your business. But I think you should be careful."

"Are we still talking about Richie?" He nodded as she unloaded empty beer bottles and a dirty wineglass off her tray. "You're the second person to give me that excellent advice this week."

"What do you mean?"

She tucked her hair behind her ear. "Kelsey. She's… concerned about my hiring you."

He kept his expression carefully blank. "Her husband doesn't trust me—"

"That has nothing to do with it. Kelsey's not swayed by Jack. Or at least, not much. She's the most independent person I know. *She* doesn't trust you." Allie met his eyes. "And she doesn't think I should trust you, either."

Shit. "What about you? Do you trust me?"

"I'm not sure," she admitted. "I trust you to do your job. So far you've been nothing but an asset to my business."

He almost smiled at her thinking of The Summit's bottom line. He put the empty beer bottles in the recycling bin. "I've only worked for you two days."

"Three if we include Saturday, which is already one day longer than either of the previous two bartenders I hired."

"I'm not going to leave you hanging," he said even though that's exactly what was going to happen. He already had a replacement bartender lined up for when the job was over.

Someone Allie really could count on.

She crumpled up a few paper napkins. "That's still to be decided, isn't it?"

Damn, why couldn't she accept him for who he said he was?

What the hell was he doing wrong?

At the end of the bar, the same gray-haired man who'd been sitting there last week when Dean first walked into The Summit, raised his empty glass. Dean pulled a beer and took it down to him as Allie threw away napkins behind the bar.

He needed to figure out how to play this. How to work this to his advantage.

"I thought we were friends," he said when he came back. "Wasn't that what you wanted? For us to be friends?"

She jerked one shoulder. "I was wrong."

"So, you'll trust Richie, the drug addict—"

"Recovering drug addict."

"—but not me?"

It bugged him only because it compromised his cover.

She studied him. He waited for her to smile. To tell him of course she trusted him.

But she just picked up the tray and walked away.

Well, Allie didn't have to trust him, to like him, for him to get the information he needed.

But it would make his job a lot easier.

One of the braver college kids approached Allie as she cleaned off the table the couple had vacated. He said something to her and she laughed, tossing her hair over her shoulder. Dean's eyes narrowed.

The kid she'd turned on the charm for looked as hopeful as a tyke on Christmas Eve. Like if Allie stuck a bow on her head, his holiday would be complete.

Poor sap didn't have a clue. Dean would have to save him.

He tossed the rag down and strode over to them as the kid was saying "—done, we could maybe get together?"

"You're out of your league," Dean said before Allie could respond to the bumbling come-on. "Head on back to your friends before you humiliate yourself any further."

The kid swallowed, his Adam's apple bobbing. "I…I just thought—"

"No one blames you for dreaming big," Dean said as he put his arm around the youth's shoulders and steered him away from Allie. "How about a round on the house for you and your buddies, to take away the sting?"

He slapped the kid's shoulder hard enough to make him stumble forward. The student took the hint and kept walking back to his buddies at the pool table.

Allie stood, her mouth open, her eyes wide. What do you know? Dean had managed to surprise her. Maybe he hadn't lost his touch completely.

He winked and went back to the bar.

ALLIE'S HAND SHOOK so hard the glasses on the tray she held clinked together. She set it down before she could give in to the urge to throw it at Dean's smug head.

She slowly approached the bar. "What in the hell do you think you're doing?"

He filled a pitcher with beer. "Getting a round for lover boy and his friends."

She held her hair back with both hands. "Do I look like someone who can't take care of herself?"

He appraised her. She let go of her hair and crossed her arms. "From what I've seen," he said, flipping the dispenser off, "you take care of yourself just fine."

Warmth suffused her, but she wasn't about to be swayed by what had sounded like a sincere compliment. "Exactly. So, why would you take it upon yourself to scare the crap out of some poor guy just for talking to me?"

He held up the pitcher. A moment later, one of the college kids came over and took the beer without making eye contact with either one of them.

"Listen," Dean said, wiping up a few drops of beer, "it would've been cruel of me to stand back and let the kid get his hopes up."

She slapped her hands on the bar and leaned forward. "I have plenty of practice deflecting unwanted advances. I didn't need your help. And didn't you promise me not ten minutes ago that you were going to mind your own business?"

The door opened and six more college kids walked in. While she appreciated the business the spring breakers brought in, she wished the bar was empty tonight so she could close up and go home.

Instead of having to deal with Dean. Or the possibility that he might be right about Richie.

"I wasn't butting into your business and I didn't set out to help you," Dean said, nodding at the newcomers. "I was helping the kid."

She blinked. "What?"

"Someone had to get him out of there before he decided he had a chance with you. Although you lay it on thick, we both know the only way you'd give a kid like him the time of day is if he needed to be saved." Dean grinned. "Or maybe adopted."

She didn't return his smile. Couldn't. Not when anger made her see red.

"So, not only am I stupid for not seeing supposed drug use by one of my employees, but I'm also what? A tease? Oh, I know. Maybe I'm a man-eater. Well, thank God you stopped me before I got my claws into that unsuspecting boy."

His grin slid away and he reached out as if to touch her. "Hey, I didn't mean—"

"Never mind," she said, stepping back. "This isn't the time or place for this, anyway." Her movements were jerky as she gestured toward the two guys standing at the other end of the bar. "You have work to do and so do I."

She crossed the room for her abandoned tray and carried it into the kitchen. No sooner had the door swung shut behind her than she went to the table, set the tray down with a clang and sank into a chair.

"You okay?" Richie asked. He stood at the sink, finishing up the dishes from dinner.

She sighed. "I'm fine. Just tired." She even tossed in an insincere smile.

At least she should get points for effort.

But Richie didn't seem to notice anything was off with her. He nodded, his eyes...vacant.

She linked her hands together in her lap. Damn Dean for making her question Richie. When he'd returned from the grocery store Monday with no receipt and no change—even though she knew he couldn't have spent all the money—she'd told herself not to be paranoid. But now she wasn't so sure. And he kept sniffing and twitching. His hands trembled as he set a cast-iron pan aside.

If Richie had started using again, she needed to find out now. Before he got in too deep.

Before she couldn't help him.

She stood and cleared her throat. "I know it's late notice, but do you think you could stick around tonight and mix up meatballs for tomorrow's menu?"

"Sure." He glanced at her over his shoulder. "But this time we use my grandma's recipe."

"What's wrong with my recipe?"

"Nothing." He pulled the plug from the sink and dried his hands before folding the towel. "Except for that one batch when you tossed in too much sea salt."

"Now you can't hold that against me. It's not like I served them to paying customers."

"You're going to love Grandma's meatballs." He unfolded the towel, then folded it again. "Trust me."

Her breath hitched. She wanted to trust him. About way more than meatballs. "Sounds good. Let me check to make sure Dean has everything under control in the bar and we'll get started."

Since she needed her tray—and because she hadn't meant to bring it into the kitchen in the first place—she picked it up. Pushed through the door.

Was she crazy to think Richie would jeopardize the life he'd built for himself? After all, he was more than happy to work late, and his job meant so much that he became personally invested in meatballs, for God's sake. They'd even been discussing the possibility of him taking over the cooking twice a week to give Allie a break. And he'd told her that one day, when he'd saved up enough, he'd like to attend culinary school. Maybe open a restaurant.

Her fingers tightened on the tray. Richie wouldn't risk his future, everything he'd worked so hard to achieve these past few months of staying clean. She'd bet on it.

She went back into the kitchen to tell him to go home, that they'd make the meatballs tomorrow morning, but the room was empty. And his coat was gone.

She frowned. Maybe he'd gone outside for…for what? It was fifteen degrees out. And if he'd had to use the restroom, why take his coat?

Unless there was something in his coat he needed.

Her throat clogged. She was going to have to confront Richie whether she wanted to or not.

CHAPTER EIGHT

THOUGH SHE FELT DEAN'S intense gaze on her, Allie managed to ignore him for the rest of the night. Not an easy task, since Noreen only worked until they stopped serving food at ten on weeknights and Allie had the combined jobs of waitress and busboy, forcing her to work in the bar instead of hiding in the kitchen until closing time. Luckily, both she and Dean were kept busy when the crowd grew to a decent size.

Other than Dean trying to catch her eye, and her stomach twisting with nerves about talking to Richie later, the evening went smoothly. There were no fights, no one had to be cut off, and best of all, "Hotel California"—a song she'd heard way too many times since buying the bar—wasn't played even once on the jukebox.

After last call, the bar slowly emptied. Carla Owens, a pretty nurse who sometimes met a group of friends there after her shift at the hospital ended, was last to leave. Alone.

That was surprising because Carla had spent the past two hours flirting with Dean.

It hadn't seemed to bother the cowboy. Guess it only bugged him when Allie flirted.

He was such a hypocrite.

While Dean locked up after the last customer, Allie took off for the kitchen.

"You running away from me, Allie?" he asked, stopping her in her tracks. She shivered at the low timbre of his voice. But it was the amusement in it, the challenge, that made her turn.

"No. Richie's waiting for me."

"Really?" Dean walked toward her, his strides unhurried, his expression blank. "And why is that?"

She stepped to the side and set a chair on top of a table. Just to give her hands something to do. "I'm going to talk to him about what you...your concerns about him."

He took the next chair from her and set it on the table. "You believe me?"

She concentrated on brushing a piece of lint off her sleeve. "I want to ask him a few questions. To ease my own mind."

"And you were going to confront him alone?"

Her shoulders stiffened. Even though Dean sounded calm, she could tell he thought that was a stupid idea. Well, it was *his* idea, damn it, so he could can it.

"I'm not confronting him. I'm just going to talk to him."

"I'll go with you."

"That's not necessary. I can handle this on my own."

"See now, here's the thing. I know you can handle it. But if I'm right and Richie is using, you can't be sure how he'll react to you...easing your mind about him."

"Richie would never hurt me. He'd never hurt any-one."

Dean studied her as if wondering whether she really was as naive as she sounded.

But her naïveté was all in the past. And while she'd willingly give Richie the benefit of the doubt, she wasn't about to let him take advantage of her.

"I'm sure Richie's a regular old pussycat when he's sober," Dean said. "But if I'm right and he is high, I'd feel better knowing you weren't questioning him alone. Besides, you're confronting him because of what I told you. I have no problem standing up and letting him know I'm the one behind the accusation."

"Definitely not. I don't want him to feel accused, or worse, cornered."

Dean shifted and hooked his thumbs in his belt loops. "What if I apologized?"

"To Richie?"

"To you."

"For what, exactly?" Yeah, she was messing with him. But no more than he deserved. She thought he'd blow it off or say he was sorry for making her mad. Most men, in her experience, never knew what they were apologiz-ing for half the time.

He bowed his head for a moment, but when he raised it again, didn't look angry. Just...sheepish. "For stick-ing my nose where it didn't belong. For acting as if you needed help with Richie and that college Romeo. And for making it seem as if you were some sort of cheap flirt."

"Well." She cleared her throat. Holy cow, he was

good. When she met those intense green eyes of his, she wanted to believe he meant every word. "I guess I'd accept your apology. *If* you meant it."

"Fair enough." He rubbed his chin and then let his hand drop. "To be honest, I'm not sorry I told you my suspicions about Richie. But I am sorry you have to do what you're about to. I'm sorry you've been let down by someone you care for."

"And the thing about my flirting?"

A muscle jumped in his jaw. "Do you really want to know why I sent that drooling kid on his way?" he asked quietly. "How I felt to see you smiling at him? Or when he put his hand on you?"

Her throat went dry. The last thing she wanted was to admit the attraction between them was real. She needed to ignore it for as long as possible. Maybe even forever.

"Apology accepted," she said.

He seemed almost as relieved as she was.

"I'd like to sit in while you talk to Richie."

Although he'd made it a statement, she knew what it really was. A question. And she couldn't help but appreciate that he was asking.

"Fine. But let me do the talking."

"Sure thing, boss."

She inhaled and put her hand on the door, but couldn't push it open. What if she was wrong? What if there was some reasonable explanation for Richie's odd behavior?

She sighed. And what if she didn't confront him? What if she pretended not to see what was in front of her?

Like with the Addison case.

She couldn't let that happen. Not again. She'd already paid too high a price for believing in Miles Addison. She wouldn't make the same mistake twice.

Dean placed his hand on the small of her back, the warmth of his fingers seeping into her skin. "It's okay," he said into her ear, his breath warm as it caressed her cheek. "I'm right behind you."

And why that meant as much to her as it did, she'd never know.

She pulled her shoulders back and entered the kitchen. Richie was taking a pan of meatballs from the oven.

"Richie, what—"

He spun around, losing his grip on the large pan in the process. It crashed to the floor. Grease splattered and meatballs rolled everywhere, some crushed under the heavy container.

"I'm sorry, Allie." Richie tossed the pot holders onto the counter and dropped to his knees in the midst of the mess. "I'll clean it," he said, sweeping meatballs into a pile with his forearm. "It'll only take a minute."

"Those are still hot," she said, avoiding as much of the grease as possible as she crossed to him. "Why don't we let them cool first, then I'll help you? After all, you wouldn't have dropped them if I hadn't startled you."

Richie blinked up at her. "Yeah, yeah. Good idea."

She helped him to his feet and tugged him away from the chaos. "I thought you were mixing the meatballs tonight. Not cooking them."

"I wanted you to taste one." His quick grin made him

look five years younger. "So, you'd know Grandma's were the best."

"I'm sure they're great," she said as he wiped his hands down the front of his jeans. Even though the kitchen was a comfortable temperature, sweat beaded his upper lip. "Richie, I was hoping I could talk to you before you head home."

"Sure, sure. No problem." His eyes widened and Allie turned to see what had spooked him.

She ground her back teeth together. Dean had so far kept his word by not speaking, but his body language said plenty. He stood by the door, his large arms crossed, his hat partially shading his hooded eyes.

"Dean, why don't you get yourself something to drink?" she asked, although from the way he raised his eyebrows, he understood it wasn't a suggestion. "And there are plenty of leftovers in the fridge if you want to heat up a late dinner for yourself."

Their eyes locked as they silently battled. She didn't so much as blink. After all, facing down hostile witnesses, egomaniac judges and jurors had all been a day's work for her not too long ago. No way was some smooth-talking, stubborn cowboy going to get her to back down.

He took his sweet time pushing away from the wall and moseying on over to the fridge. If she hadn't seen him punch Harry the other night, she would've sworn the man only had one speed: slow-enough-to-drive-a-person-insane.

"Is everything okay, Allie?" Richie asked. "Am I in trouble?"

"Everything's fine." She even added a smile, but figured it came across more like a grimace. Not that Richie seemed to notice. He was too busy sending nervous glances Dean's way.

She sat down. "Richie," she said, when he remained standing, staring as Dean straightened from the refrigerator, a can of soda in his hand. "Richie." This time louder. "Please sit down."

His body twitched as if someone had shot electricity through him, but he finally sat opposite her. "What's up?"

Her throat tightened. Dean had been right—Richie was using again. His pupils were dilated and he kept fidgeting. Picking at a small ding in the tabletop. Tossing his head to get the hair out of his eyes. And he'd hooked his foot around the leg of the chair next to him and kept pushing it away and pulling it back again.

She clasped her hands in her lap so she wouldn't reach over and shake the living hell out of him. How long had he been using? How could he do this to himself? What had happened to send him back to the drugs?

And the biggest, scariest question of all: Why hadn't she noticed before?

"I need to ask you something," she told him, trying to hold his gaze. "And all I want is for you to be honest. Whatever your answer, I hope it's the truth."

"Yeah, yeah. Okay." He scratched his arm, his eyes flicking to Dean, then to her again. "What is it?"

She linked her hands on top of the table. "Are you using again?"

He reared back. "No." But his voice shook. "I'm clean. You know that."

"You've been acting strange," she said with a calmness she didn't feel. "You've been late for work several times in the past few weeks—"

"I told you, I had a flat tire that one day." He ran a trembling hand over his face. "And that other time, my alarm didn't go off."

And she was such a fool, she'd believed him both times. "Plus," she continued, "you look terrible. You're pale and sweating and—"

"I've been sick," he cried, slamming his hands on the table. "You know I've been sick. But I'm feeling better. I'm sure tomorrow I'll be fine. And I won't be late again, I swear."

"I saw you using," Dean said. Though the words were spoken softly, they seemed to fill the room.

Richie jumped to his feet, knocking his chair backward. "You're a damn liar."

Dean set his soda can on the table. "Sit down."

"He's lying," Richie repeated, this time looking at Allie as if willing her to believe him. Begging her to. "I'm clean. I swear it." He looked ready to cry.

She could relate.

Allie stood, ignoring how unsteady her legs were. "Let me help you. Sit down so we can discuss—"

Richie kicked the chair. It skidded through the meatballs and banged into the counter. "You either believe him or me."

Her heart pounded heavily. She stepped toward Richie, stopping when Dean took hold of her arm. She tried to shake him off but he tightened his grip.

"We'll get you back in rehab," she told Richie. He looked at her with such anger and contempt, she shivered. "Your job is still secure. And once you come back, you—"

"Forget it," he snarled. He crossed the room and snatched his coat off the hook on the wall. "I'm not going to rehab and I don't need your help." He opened the door. "I thought you were different," he whispered roughly. "I thought I could trust you."

And then he walked out and slammed the door.

She jerked out of Dean's hold and, willing her tears away, walked to the closet for the broom and dustpan. Feeling Dean's gaze on her, she leaned the broom against the counter, picked up the baking dish and set it on the counter before sweeping meatballs into the dustpan.

She emptied them into the trash, biting her trembling lower lip when Dean touched her shoulder. "Hey, you—"

"Don't," she muttered, shrugging his hand off. She bowed her head and struggled to swallow past the lump in her throat. "Don't…please…don't ask me if I'm okay. Or tell me I did the right thing."

"All right," he said. Then he took the broom and walked over to the mess.

She frowned. "What are you doing?"

He swept some of the meatballs into a pile. "You spend a lot of time cleaning up other people's messes. Tonight, you don't have to do it alone."

THE NEXT MORNING, Dean spent close to five minutes staring at the pink, heart-shaped wreath on Allie's door while he waited for her to let him in. He'd rung the bell for the seventh time when the door opened.

He'd obviously woken her. She wore a pair of baggy gray sweatpants, a faded Columbia University sweatshirt and a pair of fuzzy red socks. Her hair was a mess.

And she was still the most beautiful thing he'd ever seen.

His fingers tightened on the two plastic grocery bags he held. "Morning," he said, working to keep his voice even. Not an easy task when she looked all warm and sleepy, as if the only thing she wanted was to crawl back into bed.

Which, when he thought about it, didn't sound like a bad idea.

She yawned. "Hi. Everything okay?"

"Fine. A bit cold…" Yeah, just a bit. He'd lost feeling in his fingers three minutes ago.

She blinked slowly. "Sorry. Come on in."

He took his hat off as he stepped inside, careful not to brush against her. She closed the door and then leaned against it. A black, long-haired cat meowed and wound around his legs.

Dean set his bags down and scratched behind the cat's ears. She purred, lifting her head and closing her eyes. "What's her name?" he asked.

"Hmm?"

He bit back a grin. He'd come here hoping to get more

information about Allie, and he'd already learned something new. She was not a morning person.

Not that he thought that insight would help him finish his job, but it didn't hurt to know she wasn't always at the top of her game. And part of the reason he was there was to try and catch her off guard, find out who the number from her cell phone he and Nolan hadn't been able to trace belonged to. A friend? An ex-lover?

Or Lynne Addison?

"Your cat's name," he said. "I'm assuming she has one."

"Of course. It's Persephone." Allie yawned again. "I don't mean to be rude, but what are you doing here?"

He picked up the bags and straightened. Held them up as Persephone meowed again and nudged his leg with her head. "I'm making you breakfast."

"What? Why?"

"You've fed me for almost a week. I thought I should return the favor."

She frowned, looking adorably confused. "But… that's a perk of your job."

"Dinner Sunday night wasn't."

"Still, you don't need—"

"I want to." He stepped forward so that only a foot separated them. Wariness entered her expression. "Besides, I thought maybe you could…use a friend. After what happened last night."

Her mouth popped open and she acted as if he'd thrust the bags at her and demanded she make *him* breakfast.

"I really need coffee," she muttered.

She shuffled away and around a corner, Persephone giving chase. Still holding his hat, Dean rubbed his chin with the back of his hand, noticing a wooden bench, like an old church pew, against the wall behind him. He tossed his hat on the glossy, dark wood, then sat. After taking off his boots and setting them on a heavy mat under the bench, he stood and laid his coat down. With the bags in hand, he went in search of his unwilling host.

And if he felt like the biggest jerk for using her innate goodness and her worry about Richie to worm his way not only inside her home, but inside her head as well, he'd get over it.

The end always justified the means.

When he found her in the small kitchen, he pursed his lips. Bent at the waist, her ass in the air, her head resting in her folded arms on the counter, she was muttering at the coffeepot to hurry up. Beside her were two mugs and a container of some sort of flavored creamer. Persephone, sitting at Allie's feet, purred loudly.

He cleared his throat. "Does talking to the pot like that make it work faster?"

"I hope so."

He set his bags on the table and started unloading them. "I hope you like pancakes. I make my mother's secret recipe."

She grunted. Allison Martin—classy, stylish, always put together, always one step ahead of everyone—just grunted at him.

Was it any wonder he got such a big kick out of her?

"Hallelujah," she breathed at last. She poured coffee into one of the mugs, then added at least as much creamer. He grimaced. Why ruin a perfectly good cup of coffee by making it taste like sugar cookies or some other crap?

She wrapped both hands around her mug, lifted it to her face and inhaled.

"Are you sniffing your coffee?" he asked.

"Please. I'm having a moment here." She sipped, her eyelids drifting shut in apparent ecstasy.

And damn if he didn't want to see if *he* could put that look on her face. Even if he couldn't, he bet they'd have a lot of fun trying.

After a few more sips, she poured him a cup. "Do you want anything in yours?"

"Black's fine." When she handed it to him, he purposely allowed his fingers to linger over hers. As a test. For both of them. "Thanks," he said.

She swallowed and he noticed she curled her fingers into her palm. She nodded at the groceries on the table. "I'm fine, you know. You don't have to do this."

"I want to."

Last night she'd been so upset, she hadn't said a word after Dean told her he'd stick around and help her clean up. But it wasn't her silence that had bothered him. That had him wanting to take her in his arms and tell her that no matter what happened, everything would work out. That made him want to protect her.

It was because she'd seemed so vulnerable. So crushed.

She opened a can of cat food and dumped it into

Persephone's dish, then filled the other dish with fresh water and washed her hands. "Well, since you're sort of insisting and all," she said, drying them on a tea towel, "what can I do to help?"

"I need half of these chopped." He tossed her a small bag of pecans, impressed by her one-handed catch. "Where are your mixing bowls?"

She picked up a cutting board and knife and gestured to her left. "Bottom cupboard."

By the time he found the bowls, she'd set out measuring cups and spoons.

"How are you holding up?" he asked.

She poured the pecans into a large glass measuring cup before scooping out exactly half onto the cutting board. "I'm fine."

He crumpled the plastic bags and set them on a chair. "You seemed pretty upset last night."

"I just…I don't want to talk about it."

"No talking." He saluted her with a banana. "No problem."

She set to work chopping pecans, one nut at a time, into tiny, even pieces.

"They don't have to be quite that…perfect," he said.

"Is it hurting anything if I do it this way?" Her chilly tone told him that was a trick question that had no right answer.

"No?"

"Then I guess I'll keep doing it the way I want."

And if he'd said yes, she would've challenged him on

why the pecans had to be chopped a certain way. See? No right answer.

He poured buttermilk into the large bowl and added three eggs and some vanilla before whisking them together with a fork. Patience was all a part of the game, of his job.

Not that he'd have to wait long. He'd been around Allie enough to know that she didn't stay quiet for long. At least not once she had her morning coffee. She always seemed to be engaged in conversation, be it with a customer, an employee or the guy who delivered the beer. She also had a bad habit of saying whatever was on her mind.

It was only a matter of time before she cracked. After all, he hadn't come here just to make pancakes.

He stirred the dry ingredients together in the small bowl. Dumped the rest of the pecans back into the bag so he could melt butter in the glass measuring cup in the microwave.

"I feel so stupid," Allie blurted.

Damn, he loved being right.

He took the butter from the microwave and set it on the table before adding the dry ingredients to the larger bowl. "One thing you're not is stupid."

Finished with the pecans, she brushed her hands together. "I didn't know Richie had started using again."

Dean mixed the ingredients together and added the butter and chopped pecans. "It's hard to see things we don't want to see."

That he knew from firsthand experience.

"You saw it," Allie groused, making it sound like an accusation.

"I'm not emotionally invested in what happens to Richie. Sometimes you have to step away from a situation to be able to see it clearly." He handed her three bananas. "Want to slice these for me?"

"Bananas in pancakes?"

"You'll love them. Trust me."

While she worked on the bananas, he found a large skillet and set it on the stove, turned the flame on underneath it.

"So, your theory on stepping back…is that your educated opinion? Or are you speaking from experience?"

He added butter to the pan, listening to it sizzle as it melted. "Experience. Definitely experience."

"I was married," Dean said, his back still to her.

"I know," Allie replied. He glanced at her over his shoulder. "Remember? Sunday when Jack was interrogating you, you told him you were divorced."

Dean nodded and turned back to the stove. She sipped her coffee. It was lukewarm, so she got up and refilled both their cups. The scent of melted butter filled her kitchen. Dean poured batter into the hot pan and then picked up the cutting board with the sliced bananas.

This entire…thing…was too weird. And growing weirder by the moment. The last person she'd ever expected to see on her doorstep was Dean Garret. And yet there he stood, in her kitchen, big as life. It was surreal. To be honest, she should be freaked out. She hadn't brushed her hair or her teeth yet, for God's sake.

But she couldn't muster the energy to care.

She took down two plates and set them by the stove, then added cream to her coffee. "Divorce is never easy," she said, a not-so-subtle nudge to get him talking again.

He pressed some banana slices into the pancakes. "You divorced?"

"Well, no—"

"And your parents have been together how long?"

"Thirty-five years," she admitted, leaning back against the counter, her feet crossed. Persephone curled up next to her. "But half of all marriages end in divorce, and I have friends who've been through it."

He smirked. "Darlin', having friends who get divorced isn't quite the same as going through it…or your parents splitting up." He expertly flipped the pancakes.

She kept her hands wrapped around her mug. She knew if she touched him like she wanted to, he'd shrug her off. "That must've been rough."

He slid the cooked pancakes onto a plate before adding more batter to the pan. "My mom made these pancakes on special occasions, like our birthdays or Christmas. And the last day of school. She always said the last day was more cause to celebrate than the first day."

"Smart mom."

"She is at that." He added the bananas and then went to the table and poured maple syrup into the measuring cup, placing it in the microwave to warm. "The only other time she made them was the morning she told us

Dad had moved out. There was no warning, just…Dad's gone and he won't be coming back."

"You had no idea they were having problems?"

"If they were—and the fact they started divorce proceedings the next day tells me they were—we didn't know it."

"How old were you?"

"Eleven." He finished the pancakes. Handed her both plates to carry to the table while he grabbed the syrup. "Ryan was nine and Sammy was six."

She set the plates down, wondering what he'd been like at that age. Had he ever really been young and carefree? Or was he always serious and contained? Did his parents' divorce force him to take on that protective outer shell? And if so, what did he think he needed protection from now?

"How did you deal with it?" she asked, placing glasses, forks and napkins on the table before getting a carton of orange juice out of the fridge.

He snorted. "We had no clue what she was telling us. What she meant by they weren't in love anymore. That Dad had decided to take a job in Austin, but we could still visit him. Maybe stay at his new house for a week or two during the summer." He added whole pecans to the syrup and pulled her chair out for her, waiting for her to sit before he did the same. "It wasn't until about a year later that I realized all the signs were there." He tapped his fist against the table. "I'd just been blind to them."

His voice was flat, his face expressionless. She knew discussing this was hard on him. And even though he probably didn't want her sympathy, she couldn't help but offer it in some small way.

She covered his clenched hand with her own. "Give yourself a break. You were just a kid."

He slid his hand out from under hers and poured syrup over his stack of pancakes before passing it to Allie. "It happened again when I was older. In my own marriage."

"I don't understand. What happened again?"

He picked up his fork and cut into his pancakes, but didn't eat. "My not noticing what was right in front of my face. Not wanting to see how unhappy my wife was, so I could pretend that everything was all right."

After a long silence, Allie turned to her plate of pancakes and began to eat for lack of anything helpful to say. They were light and fluffy, and the bananas added a touch of sweetness while the pecans added crunch. She hesitated and then finally said, "I hope you don't mind me saying this, but I can't believe your ex-wife wouldn't stay married to you just for these pancakes."

One side of his mouth quirked in that half grin she found so appealing. Some of the knots in her stomach loosened. She didn't want to see him morose. She had that emotion covered, thank you very much.

"Actually, I don't think I ever cooked for her. Something else I screwed up."

Allie took a sip of juice. "Wow. I'm impressed."

"Don't try and sweet-talk me. My mother would skin me if I gave out her secret recipe."

"Not with the pancakes." Although she did wish she'd been awake enough to pay attention while he'd mixed up the batter, so she could make them herself. "With the amazing breadth of your shoulders. How do you manage to stay upright carrying around all that guilt and responsibility?"

He narrowed his eyes. "Guilt has nothing to do with it. I take accountability for my actions. That's all."

"Doesn't your ex-wife get to be accountable? After all, you didn't marry yourself."

"Marrying her wasn't my first mistake. Getting her pregnant was."

CHAPTER NINE

ALLIE CHOKED ON HER COFFEE. "You have a child?" she sputtered.

Pain he thought he'd blocked years ago resurfaced, threatening to bring him to his knees. "No. He was still-born."

"He?"

His mouth tightened. "Robert James. He would've turned nine this past summer."

"Dean," she said, laying her hand on his again, "I'm so sorry."

He pulled back and picked up his fork. Ate a bite of pancake even though it now tasted like sawdust. "My marriage never should've happened. Jolene and I dated casually for a few months. I wasn't looking for anything serious and, at the time, didn't think she was, either." He stared at the kitchen wall above Allie's head. "Two months after we stopped seeing each other, I enlisted. When she told me she was pregnant, I was so shocked, all I could think about was myself."

"That seems pretty normal for a young man."

He forced himself to finish his breakfast and drink his juice. Anything to keep from looking at Allie as he admitted his greatest failure.

"Even through the shock, I knew what the right thing to do was." He stood and carried his dishes to the sink. "I'd never met Jo's parents, didn't know when her birthday was or her favorite ice cream. And I didn't love her. But none of that mattered. So, I said, 'Well, I guess we'd better get married.'" He'd been such an idiot. "At the time, I thought she was disappointed because I didn't have a ring for her. I recently figured out it was my piss-poor proposal that did it."

"There's no right or way wrong to act when something like that is dropped in your lap."

Allie's kind words set his teeth on edge. The last thing he wanted was her sympathy. Or her understanding. Not when he didn't deserve either.

Not when he was opening up to her in an attempt to get her to do the same.

"Maybe not," he agreed. "But even though I was young, I could've handled it better. I *should've* handled it better." He tapped his fist against his thigh. "We got married and she came with me to San Diego for boot camp two weeks later. We were there three months, and when I got my orders to go to Afghanistan, I started thinking we'd be okay."

He'd been desperate to make his marriage work. Because somehow he'd come to love his unborn child more than anything.

"The shock had worn off by then," he continued, "and I was excited to prove I could do a better job of parenting than my old man. I swore I wasn't going to shuffle my kid from house to house. Or worse, forget I had a child if the marriage failed—like my dad. Once he re-married and became a stepfather to his new wife's kids, his own three sons no longer existed." Dean shrugged. "Jolene and I had decided she should move back in with her parents while I was overseas. I was on a recon mission when she went to the hospital. She hadn't felt the baby move all day." He exhaled heavily. "They induced labor. Jolene had to go through childbirth knowing our son was already dead. And I wasn't with her."

She covered his hand with hers. "Even if you'd been there," Allie said gently, "there wasn't anything you could have done."

He sat back, pulling away from her touch. "I could've seen my son. Held him at least once. Jo was so crushed, she had the funeral two days later. I didn't get home until that night."

And that was a betrayal he'd never be able to forgive.

"I'm so sorry, Dean," Allie whispered.

"The baby was the only thing that held us together. But for some reason—stubbornness or pride—we stuck it out for five years." He rotated his coffee cup and sighed. "Jolene wanted another baby but I...I couldn't do that. When she asked for a divorce, I was relieved. I told myself she was too needy. But all she wanted was a real marriage and a family. Neither of which I was willing to give her."

"Maybe..." Allie stared at the remains of her breakfast, a frown on her face as if she was searching for the right words. "Maybe you weren't *able* to give her either of those." She raised her head. "You made a mistake, but you can't keep punishing yourself for it."

He forced a smile. "It all worked out for the best. Jolene remarried. She even has a one-year-old daughter."

"So, you and Jolene still keep in touch?"

He shoved his cup away. "Not really."

"Then how did you know…"

"The man she married, the father of her child, is my brother."

SHOCKED, ALLIE SAT BACK. "I'm not sure what to say…. Those first few family get-togethers must've been weird."

"I wouldn't know," Dean said, picking up an empty grocery bag and shaking it in front of Persephone. The cat leaped back, then crouched, ready to make her move when he shook it again. "The last time I saw my family was two Christmases ago."

"What does that mean? You all haven't been together since then?"

Persephone pounced on the bag and Dean swept it— and the cat—from side to side. "I'm sure they've gotten together. They just haven't invited me."

Uh-oh. "What did you do?"

"What makes you think I did something?"

"Because you were upset. And often times when people are hurt, they lash out."

He straightened and laid his hands flat on the table, his expression etched with anger and regret. "How the hell did they think I was going to react? I'd just been discharged from the marines and was looking forward to spending Christmas with my family for the first time in five years. Except, when I get to my mother's house, I find out my brother's not only been seeing my ex-wife for the past seven months, but my entire family knew and no one bothered to tell me."

Oh, poor Dean. First he lost his son and then his family kept something like that from him? No wonder he had trust issues and moved from town to town. He couldn't go home. "Why the secrecy?"

"Guess they were worried about my reaction." He leaned back and crossed his arms. "So, instead, they thought it'd be safer to spring it on me as I walked through the door. And then Ryan tells us all that Jolene's pregnant."

Allie winced. "They just dropped one bomb after another on you, didn't they?"

Dean laughed but the sound was hollow. "You could say that. I was furious. I said some things I shouldn't have said, which set Ryan off, and the next thing I knew, I broke his nose and he split my lip." He opened and clenched his fist as if he'd punched his brother minutes ago instead of years. "We haven't spoken since."

She rested her elbows on the table. "Because you don't want to? Or because neither one of you knows how to make the first move?"

He shrugged. "At first I was too angry, but as time went by it became…easier…to avoid my family. Especially after Jolene had the baby."

"You've never even seen your niece?" Allie asked.

The idea of not being with her own family for that long made her heartsick.

He gave his head a quick, jerky shake. "Sam emailed me a picture but I...I couldn't make myself open it."

Yes, he'd acted like an idiot with his brother and family, but she understood why. And it wasn't because his brother had fallen in love with Dean's ex-wife.

It was because Ryan and Jolene had what Dean and Jolene lost.

A child.

"It sounds to me as if you're punishing yourself," she said, ignoring the look he shot her. "By keeping away from your family, you're not just hurting them, you're hurting yourself."

"I'm not trying to hurt anyone."

"But...don't you miss them? Don't you want to meet your niece?"

She didn't think he was going to answer, but then he said, "I used to wonder if things might've worked out differently if I hadn't joined up. If I'd been with Jolene at the time..."

"What could you have done? It was out of your hands." Allie softened her tone as she added, "Do you honestly think if you'd still been in Texas your baby would've lived?"

He stabbed a hand through his hair. "No," he admitted helplessly, "but I can't help feeling responsible for the failure of my marriage. For not being able to give Jolene what she wanted most." He straightened his legs.

"You and I are a pair, huh? Both trying to fix things that are out of our control."

She raised her eyebrows. "I'm out of the fixing-people game. I tried that once and it didn't work out so well for me."

"Really? Then why were you so upset about Richie?"

"I just…wish I'd recognized earlier that he needed help."

"So, you're not trying to save him?"

"Absolutely not." Even if the little voice inside her head called her a liar.

"Good. You should be focusing on yourself, on your own life. You should be going after what you want, not worrying about everyone else."

"The last time I went after what I wanted I—" She clamped her lips together and pushed her plate away, her throat burning with unshed tears. "Never mind."

"No." He caught her by the wrist as she shoved her chair back. "Don't run. What happened? Why can't you put yourself first?"

She tried to pull away from him, but he wouldn't let go. "Because the last time I did," she said hoarsely, "I helped a pedophile go free."

HE WASN'T GOING TO FEEL bad about doing his job. About digging to find out what Allie was hiding. Not after he'd laid himself bare to her.

"I don't understand," Dean said. "What do you mean, you helped a pedophile?"

She tugged on her arm and he released her. She took

her empty dishes to the sink. Kept her back to him. "Do you know why I chose to become a defense attorney?"

He stood and put the juice and butter in the fridge. "Too many episodes of *Matlock?*"

"No." She turned around, but her smile was sad. "Although I did admire how he went all out for his clients." She turned on the water and rinsed plates before putting them in the dishwasher. "It was because of my dad."

"Wait, didn't I hear your dad was the ex-police chief?" She nodded. "I would've thought he'd sway you to become a district attorney or something."

"He's pretty liberal minded, for a cop. He told me that while our legal system is one of the best out there, it's still far from perfect. But it couldn't work at all if both sides weren't represented." She closed the dishwasher and began filling the sink with water, adding a squirt of soap. "He says the concept of innocent until proven guilty couldn't be possible without lawyers—defense attorneys in particular. That lawyers are advocates, while justice is the responsibility of the judge and jury."

"And you believed defending the accused was the most important part of the system."

"I thought I could help more people as a defense attorney." She scrubbed the skillet, her mouth a thin line. "I started off so idealistic. And naive. As cliché as it sounds, I thought I could change the world."

He dried the skillet and set it on the counter. "That's a big order for one person, no matter how good the intent."

She drained the water and wrung out the dishcloth. "No kidding."

He poured the rest of the coffee into their mugs, adding cream to hers and handing it to her. "What happened?"

She tossed the dishrag into the sink, took the coffee in one hand and scooped up Persephone with the other. Allie sank into her seat, sitting sideways, her gaze on the floor as the cat curled up in her lap. "Winning became very important to me. Too important."

"There's nothing wrong with wanting to do your best."

She looked up, her expression bleak. "There is if winning cases becomes more important than helping your clients."

He pulled out the chair next to her and moved it so he sat with his knees touching hers. "I can't see you ever allowing that to happen."

"I couldn't, either." She set her cup down and stroked Persephone. He had no doubt it helped soothe Allie, too. "At first, I talked myself into believing working for the big firm would be the same as what I'd been doing. Except the pay was three times what I was making at the public defender's office."

"Sounds like a win-win situation."

"I thought so. And I was willing to do whatever it took to prove their faith in me wasn't wasted. After two years I was moved from associate to lead attorney. My goal was to make junior partner before I was thirty-five." She sat back, her expression one of self-disgust. "I started out wanting to work for the greater good, and ended up throwing it all away because of my ambition for a corner office."

"But you gave it up," he pointed out. "You realized you were no longer happy."

"I realized I was a fraud."

He didn't want to spook her by seeming too eager to hear what she had to say. And…well…he hoped she'd *want* to tell him.

"I won the biggest case of my career," she admitted.

He raised his eyebrows. "And that's a bad thing?"

"I didn't think so at first, even though I was representing a man accused of sexually abusing a child. I was…" She closed her eyes and swallowed. "God, I was excited by the challenge of it. He was a pillar of the community, a happily married man. And I believed he was innocent."

"You couldn't be a defense attorney—at least, not a successful one—if you only represented people you felt were innocent."

She nodded. "You're right. But I was morally opposed to representing people accused of sex crimes." She set the cat on the floor and got up to pace the short length of the room. "Until this case." The remorse in her voice made his chest hurt.

"But my client was guilty," she exclaimed, "and thanks to me, to my expert defense, he was allowed to go free. Dean," she said raggedly, "he hurt a little boy and I helped him get away with it."

"Hey, now…" Dean crossed to her, wrapped his arms around her because there was no way he could keep from touching her, comforting her. "You're not to blame for his crimes. You were doing your job—"

"That's just it. All I cared about was doing my job." She clutched him, her arms around his waist, her head on his chest. "I didn't care about finding out the truth, didn't even consider the possibility he could've been guilty."

Dean held her away from him. He hated that she was upset. Hated even more that he'd manipulated her into sharing what was obviously a source of great guilt and pain.

"Stop it," he said quietly. "You weren't the only one to believe him. He had everyone fooled, even his wife."

Allie pushed him back a step. "How do you know his wife was fooled?"

CHAPTER TEN

DEAN'S EYEBROWS DREW together as if he was trying to figure out what she was talking about. "You mentioned he was married. I just assumed his wife stood by him during the trial."

Her shoulders slumped. "You're right. She did."

He rubbed his hands up and down her arms. "You had evidence the guy was innocent, and a jury agreed. What makes you so sure he really was guilty?"

"The day after the trial ended," she said slowly, "the boy ended up in the hospital. He…he tried to kill himself."

Sympathy softened Dean's features. "That's not your fault," he said, cupping her face in his large hand. "You couldn't have known."

She pulled away from his touch. "That doesn't make it easier. That kid had no one to protect him. He's the one who needed help, not Miles. But it was my job to see only what I needed to see." She hugged her arms around herself. "And I was very good at my job."

"That boy could've had a number of reasons to hurt himself," Dean pointed out. "You can't be sure it's because your client abused him."

She began pacing again. She couldn't stand to be so

close to Dean, not when she felt so weak. Not when all she wanted was to wrap herself around him and never let go.

"You're right, but it was enough to make me wonder if Miles *had* been abusing him. To start to question my part in what happened." She put her chair back, straightened his and pushed it in as well. "A few days later, Miles hosted a party at his home. At the end of the night, as I was leaving, Lynne—Miles's wife—stopped me. She'd had too much to drink, so when she started babbling about how I was to blame, I figured she was drunk."

Allie shivered, remembering Lynne's despondence, hearing the anger and desperation in her voice. "But then she…she broke down. Started crying. She told me she'd never be able to get her son away from him now. That Jon would never be safe."

"You didn't mention this guy had a kid."

She crossed to the refrigerator and traced the heart in a drawing Emma had given her. "Jon was six."

Dean straightened, his expression hard. "You think his wife was trying to tell you he was abusing his own son?"

Tears formed in her eyes but she refused to let them fall. "I don't know. I was too shocked to even move. When Miles joined us, he joked about his wife not being able to hold her alcohol. I was ready to shrug the whole thing off—I wanted to shrug it off," she said shakily, remembering the moment. "But when I got home, I couldn't stop thinking about what Lynne had said." Allie walked to the sink, stared at the softly falling snow out the window. "And since I couldn't let my doubts go, I asked a friend of mine, a detective, to do a bit of digging."

Dean watched her steadily. Patiently. Warmth suffused her, settled in her stomach. Her response to him was so elemental, and undeniable. But was that enough to warrant her desire to open up to him? To trust him when she hadn't been able to trust her family?

She cleared her throat. "He discovered some things... things that made me realize how wrong I'd been—"

"How wrong *you'd* been? Jeez, Allie, give yourself a break."

"How can I?" she cried. "All I could think about was that boy Miles had molested, and if his own son was suffering the same abuse. I had to make things right."

Dean frowned, his gaze intense. "Make things right? How?"

She stared down into the sink. "Worrying about making another mistake wouldn't help me or my clients, so I quit my job. The rest you know."

"What happened to them?"

"Who?"

"The wife and kid?"

The nape of her neck prickled. His question seemed innocent, so why did she feel as if he was digging for something? Didn't he realize she'd already told him all her secrets?

Or at least the ones that were hers to share.

"I have no idea. I never saw Lynne Addison again."

SHE WAS LYING TO HIM.

During his years as a PI, plenty of people had lied to him. So, why did it make him so mad that she was doing it?

Dean fisted his hand. He wanted her to tell him the truth. He wanted to forget the job and stop all the games between them.

He wanted her to trust him.

He couldn't ask her about the phone call Lynne had made to her office the day she and Jon disappeared. He had to tread carefully. He'd almost slipped up once by mentioning how Addison's wife had stood by him, and Dean couldn't blow it now. Not when he was finally getting somewhere.

He'd gotten the confirmation he needed to prove he'd been right all along. Allie did know what happened to Lynne and Jon. He'd bet his reputation on it.

She may have given up on saving the world, but something told him she hadn't given up on saving the Addisons.

In his front pocket, his cell phone vibrated, but he ignored it. "You're not to blame," he told her as he walked over and stood next to her. He gently gripped her chin and lifted her face, forcing her to meet his eyes. "You're not to blame," he repeated, because she was too stubborn to see it herself. "Not for what he did to that boy and not for any abuse his kid might have suffered."

"It's just that…all I've ever wanted to do was help. But like with Richie, wanting to help wasn't enough." She rolled her eyes. "God, I hate whiners."

Dean dropped his hand. "You sound like someone who wants to make a difference. There's nothing wrong with that."

"It's hard to make a difference when you don't trust yourself to make the right decisions." She glanced at him. "When you've lost your ability to trust in others."

Before he could analyze the movement, he swept her hair back. Once his fingers were intertwined with the silky strands, once he was close enough to feel the brush of her thighs against his, feel warmth, he couldn't back away. He curled his fingers in the hair at her neck.

"I don't think you've lost that ability," he said softly. "You trusted me."

When he would have removed his hand, she tilted her head so that he cupped her cheek. "I guess I'll have to wait to see if that was a smart move."

"Not trusting yourself because of an error in judgment isn't so smart. Seems to me you gave up a lot more than just your job because of that guy. You said I was punishing myself by staying away from my family, but what about you? When are you going to stop letting your mistake rule your actions?"

She reached up and squeezed his hand. "That cowboy insight of yours is right on target."

"I'm not sure about that." He linked his fingers with hers. "But a person's character shows up best when tested. And yours showed up big-time."

She laughed softly, her warm breath caressing his cheek. His body tensed. In her eyes he saw the same desire he felt coursing through his veins.

He traced her jaw with the tip of his finger. Then he raked his fingers through her hair, combing the length of it before massaging her scalp. She made a mewling sound and her eyes drifted shut.

Every day for the past week he'd fought his attraction to her. But now, standing in her tiny kitchen—with her wearing ugly, shapeless sweats and no makeup—he wanted her more than ever.

Damn it all to hell.

She wrapped her free hand around his forearm, her other hand still gripping his. Sexy. And beautiful. She looked unsure and at the same time so hopeful. He'd be a first-class idiot if he walked away.

And a first-class asshole if he didn't.

Slowly—so slowly he had plenty of time to evade her—she closed the distance between them. Her breasts pressed against his chest and he flinched, unsure how long he'd be able to maintain control.

Unsure if he even wanted to control himself any longer. Not when giving in meant he might get the chance to kiss her again. To keep touching her.

"Remember when you said I need to start putting myself first?" She slid her hand up his arm, under the sleeve of his T-shirt, to wrap around his biceps. "Is that what you really think?"

"Yeah," he croaked. He shut his eyes and cleared his throat. She turned him inside out. "Yeah. I do."

She glanced up at him from under her lashes. "So, that means if I…want something…I should go after it?"

No. No, no, no. no. Hell no. "You should. Definitely."

"Good." She lowered their linked hands and, watching his face, pressed his open palm to her breast. "Because what I want," she whispered, "is for you to touch me."

He glanced at his hand on her. Jerked his gaze up so that he was looking over her head.

"Dean," she asked uncertainly, "do you want me?"

He pressed his free hand to the small of her back and rocked his hips against hers. Her eyes darkened at the unmistakable feel of his arousal.

How could he not want her? But he'd promised himself he wouldn't touch her. Wouldn't cross that line, not when so many lies were between them.

She slid her hands into his hair and totally blew what little control he had out of the water. "I want you, too."

ALLIE KISSED DEAN BEFORE she could change her mind.

His body stiffened and his mouth was unyielding under hers. The only way it could've been worse was if he'd turned his head at the last minute so she'd ended up kissing his cheek.

A tactic she'd used many times herself.

She fell back to her heels, her face on fire. She wished something would happen to distract him from this moment. A meteor shower right about now should do the trick.

She smiled ruefully. "Well, that was humiliating."

And the way he stared at her, his fierce expression, was unnerving. She dropped her hands to his shoulders and started to step back, but he tightened his hold. She frowned. "Wha—"

"I'm sorry."

She winced. She'd been wrong. Him apologizing for not wanting to kiss her was even worse than an evasive do-not-kiss-me maneuver.

Still, she did her best to salvage some pride. "You don't have anything to apologize for."

"Not yet," he said, cupping her breast through her sweatshirt. His thumb brushed against her nipple and she caught her breath. "But I'm about to."

His mouth crushed hers, his tongue sweeping into her mouth. She moaned and wrapped her arms around his neck, pressing against him. He gently kneaded her breast. Her nipples tightened, rubbed against the material of her sweatshirt.

He kissed along her neck, and she dropped her head back to grant him better access. Her mind whirled when he scraped his teeth across the sensitive skin below her ear.

He kissed his way back up to her mouth, shoved his fingers into her hair and held her head still. She smoothed her own hands over his broad shoulders, down his arms and back up again. Frantic to touch him, to feel his skin, she tugged the hem of his shirt up and caressed his lower back.

He twitched and jumped, so that her fingers brushed his sides. She took the opportunity to skim her hands over his rib cage, trailing her nails down the flat panes of his stomach. He growled and yanked her to him, trapping her hands between them as he spun them so that he leaned against the counter.

She stood between his legs, his hands gripping her butt. He rolled her hips forward and she arched against him.

He spun them again. With Dean's mouth on hers, his body pressed against hers, she didn't care that the hard edge of the counter dug into her spine or that she was pawing at him as if she'd go insane.

All she cared about was him. She wanted more.

She brushed her palm down the length of him. He swore gutturally, gripping her upper arms as if to hold her still.

That was such a crazy thought, she couldn't help but smile. "It's okay," she told him, "I won't hurt you."

But he didn't return her smile. If anything, his expression darkened. "I don't want to hurt you, either."

She wasn't sure if she'd heard him right, but then he kissed her again, and in one smooth move, he'd stripped her sweatshirt over her head and tossed it aside. The cool air in the kitchen washed over her heated skin.

She raised her arms to cover herself but he just looked at her. Her heart hammering, she slowly lowered her arms.

Dean's breathing was uneven as he skimmed the tip of one finger down her left breast. She shivered.

"You are the most beautiful woman I've ever seen." He cupped her breasts in his hands, rubbed the rough pads of his thumbs over her skin. "And that's the honest truth."

He bent his head, took one nipple in his mouth and sucked. Allie's hips bucked. She shoved her hands in his hair as he rubbed his tongue against her before moving to her other breast. The rasp of his tongue, the gentle abrasion of his teeth against her sensitized flesh made her knees wobbly. Her thigh muscles quivered.

He raised his head and, watching her face, skimmed his fingers along the elastic at her waist. She involuntarily sucked in her stomach. Gooseflesh prickled her skin. Inch by inch, he pushed her sweatpants past her hips. Down her legs. When her pants were pooled at her feet, he glanced downward.

He exhaled heavily and hooked one finger under the leg of her red, silky panties. His knuckles rubbed against her skin as he slid his hand up to her hip bone, then down. He brushed at the curls between her legs, and her pelvis jerked.

He reached behind her, shoved aside the skillet he'd put there earlier, and lifted her. She gasped, both from the feel of the cold countertop against her bare thighs and the ease at which he'd set her up there. When she reached for him, he forced her arms back to her sides.

"Hold on to this." His voice was ragged as he pressed her hands against the counter edge. He must've seen her confusion because he shook his head. "I lose control when you touch me."

His admission made her feel sexy. And powerful. "I don't want you to be in control."

"Yes. You do. And so do I," he said, so solemnly, she wrapped her fingers around the counter's edge.

He smiled and her heart picked up speed. He leaned forward and kissed her, kept kissing her while he caressed her breasts. Her body grew warm and relaxed. Still kissing her, he skimmed his hands down her rib cage, over her hips and settled them on her thighs. He pulled back and searched her face as he trailed his fingers across her collarbones, over her shoulders and down her arms.

Her own fingers tightened their grip on the counter. Dean lightly stroked her legs, over her knee to her ankle and back up. He placed one hand on each thigh and nudged them apart.

When she tensed and tried to draw her knees together, he lifted his head. "Trust me," he whispered.

She swallowed. That was the problem. She liked him. He was steady and solid and one of those guys who loved to ride to the rescue. And she wanted him. Wanted him so much it scared her.

But trust him? How could she when she was too afraid to trust anyone ever again?

None of that mattered now. She needed to forget, just for a little while. To stop worrying. Stop thinking.

All she wanted was to feel.

And Dean seemed more than willing to help with that.

She let her legs fall open. He stepped between them and kissed her once, stroking her hair. He touched her everywhere, his hands caressing her as if he wanted to memorize the shape of her. The feel. From her breasts to her thighs and calves and back again, leaving tingles of sensation in his wake…

Her head fell back against the cabinet as he repeated the process. He took her breast in his mouth again and she squirmed. He pulled her closer so that she sat at the edge of the counter, and then he skimmed his fingers over her panties, between her thighs.

It felt so good. But it wasn't enough.

Dean continued those feathery strokes as he moved to her other breast, his free palm rubbing against the nipple he'd just released. Her mouth opened as she dug her heels into the counter below and thrust against his hand.

But instead of heeding her silent command for him to touch her harder, faster—to tear away her panties and touch her, skin to skin—he continued his slow torture.

He released her breasts and dropped to his knees. "Watch me touch you," he commanded softly.

And he pressed his mouth to her and exhaled, his hot breath washing over her. The world spun, pressure building slowly, and when he scraped his teeth against her, she cried out as waves of pleasure spiraled through her.

Breathing hard, her entire body a quivering mass, she slid to her feet. But Dean was there to hold her up, his face pressed against her neck, his body taut against hers.

She finally managed to lift her head and brush her hair back. "I'm going to need a quick moment to recover the use of my legs. Or else," she said huskily as she kissed his neck, "you could always carry me up to the bedroom."

He reacted as if she'd taken a big old bite out of him.

She blinked. "You okay?"

He nodded, but didn't look okay. His mouth was tight, his hands clenched at his sides.

She was more than ready to finish what he'd started. But when she reached for him, panic crossed his face.

"I have to go," he blurted.

Her eyes widened. "What? But…why?"

He took two quick steps back. "I just…have to."

Goose bumps covered Allie's skin and she pulled up her pants. Picking up her sweatshirt, she held it in front of her. "Dean, what's going on?"

"Nothing." But he wouldn't look at her. "I'll see you tonight."

Then he left. As fast as he could go.

Persephone padded into the kitchen, sat and tilted her head at Allie.

"Don't look at me," she said, slumping back against the counter. "I'm as surprised as you are."

And while she usually liked surprises, this one just plain sucked. If she hadn't been on the receiving end of his very clear interest, if she hadn't felt his arousal, she'd be having a major case of performance anxiety about now.

She straightened and roughly pulled her shirt on. After a few calming breaths, she picked up her cat. There was definitely more to Dean's quick escape than second thoughts. Something important.

"I have no idea what happened," she said as she scratched behind Persephone's ears. "But you can bet I'm going to find out."

CHAPTER ELEVEN

DEAN DROVE WITH BOTH windows down and the heater off. He pulled into the motel's driveway before his blood cooled off enough for him to think straight. Parking in front of his room, he rolled the windows up.

He slammed his fist against the steering wheel. What was wrong with him? Why hadn't he gotten out of there when she'd lied to him about not seeing Lynne Addison again? He should've hightailed it back to his room, called Nolan and gotten to work trying to link Allie to Lynne and Jon's disappearance.

Instead, he'd given in to his need to comfort her.

And then he'd just given in to his need for her.

There had been nothing contrived or planned in his actions. Hell, he'd even managed to maintain control when she'd kissed him. But then she'd looked up at him, a self-deprecating smile on her beautiful face, and he couldn't stop himself.

He hit the steering wheel again. He *should've* stopped himself.

Who was he kidding? He'd crossed a line. There was right and there was wrong.

The worst part was, he couldn't even regret it. He'd just have to make damn sure it never happened again.

He climbed out of the truck and unlocked the door to his room. After tossing his motel key card and truck keys on the table, he fell face-first onto the bed. And tried not to think about what he was missing by not carrying Allie up to her bedroom.

His cell phone buzzed and he shifted, digging it out of his front pocket. Caller ID showed Nolan's number. Dean flipped his phone open. "Hey. What's up?"

"I've been trying to reach you for the past hour," his partner groused. "What's the use of having a cell phone if you're not going to answer it?"

"I didn't hear it ring," Dean lied, remembering when it had vibrated back at Allie's house. "You need something?"

"I may have found that connection." His excitement meant he believed they were close to a breakthrough. "The one that proves your hunch about Allison Martin is on target."

Dean rolled over and sat up. "What?"

"Lynne and her son were last seen in that high-priced bookstore-café, Montgomery's, right?"

"Right. Lynne bought a couple of books for the kid and paid with her credit card. It was the last credit card transaction she made."

"Remember how we thought it was weird she'd gone to that particular bookstore, since it was six blocks from the park she was taking Jon to? Six blocks in the opposite direction? And that there are no records indicating she'd ever stepped inside Montgomery's before? No receipts. And none of the employees had ever seen her before that day."

"And this proves my theory how?"

"It seems the only clerk working at the time Lynne and Jon were in Montgomery's was Sarah Lambert, a twenty-five-year-old, part-time college student. Now here's where things get interesting." Dean could hear papers rustling as Nolan searched through his notes. "It seems that when Miss Lambert was nineteen, she was charged with voluntary manslaughter for the shooting death of her junkie boyfriend. At the time, Sarah was also an addict, and couldn't afford legal representation, so an up-and-coming attorney in the public defender's office took the case."

Dean stood, his fingers tightening on his phone. "Allison?"

"Bingo. She argued Sarah acted in self-defense, as the boyfriend had a history of abuse. Halfway through the trial, the D.A. offered a deal. Sarah spent a few years in medium-security lockup, got clean and earned her high-school diploma. I wasn't sure you were right about this," Nolan admitted. "But if we can find a reasonable motive as to why Allison Martin would defend Addison, only to turn around and help his wife and kid run off, we might be able to blow this thing wide open."

Dean viciously kicked his duffel bag across the room. Why did he have to be right? Why couldn't Allie have been clueless about Lynne and Jon's whereabouts?

I had to make things right. That's what Allie had said after she'd told him she'd realized Addison had been guilty. Helping his wife escape was obviously her way of making things right.

But did she know where they were now? Or had she given them enough money to get by, and then left them to their own devices?

He tipped his head back and blew out a breath. He could tell Nolan he hadn't found a motive or a connection that proved Allie had helped Lynne. He might even be able to convince his partner that the information he'd discovered about Sarah Lambert was a coincidence. If Dean kept what he knew to himself, he could leave. Pack up and be gone before he got even more involved with Allie. He could put something else before the job and just…walk away.

After all, from what Allie had told him and from the information they had from Robin, who's to say Allie hadn't been right to help Lynne get away from her husband?

"Hey, you still there?" Nolan asked.

Dean sighed. "Yeah. Sorry. I think we lost the signal for a minute."

Nolan grunted. "I'll be glad when this case is over. I can appreciate Robin wanting to see her daughter and grandson again, but the way she keeps breathing down my neck, it's like she's inside my shirt. Lucky for me, you're the one who's going to have to give her an update Saturday."

"What?"

"She wants to meet with you face-to-face, and since

we told her you were following leads in Cincy, you get a chance to play coddle the client."

"Damn it, I don't have time for this, Nolan. Not when I'm finally getting somewhere."

"You're getting somewhere?"

"I found Allie's motive," Dean said slowly. He filled Nolan in on what she had told him. "Her empty bank accounts and the fact that she had to get a loan to buy The Summit make sense now. I'm guessing she gave money to the Addisons, since they had no way of getting cash on their own."

"I'm on the red-eye to New York tonight," Nolan said. "I'll talk to Sarah, play up how she could be busted for lying to the cops, interfering with an investigation… the works."

Dean's stomach tightened. "Yeah, that's what I'd do, too. If she played a part in helping them disappear, she might get nervous."

"Exactly. And people who are nervous often screw up. Who knows? She might lead us right to Lynne and Jon."

"At the very least, maybe she'll contact Allie. Either way, I'm going to stick close to Allison." He clenched his hand as he remembered just how close he'd been to her not twenty minutes ago.

SATURDAY, DEAN PAID the cabbie and stepped out into the brisk wind. His brain was turning after a sleepless night and an early morning drive into Syracuse so he could catch the flight to Cincinnati for his 10:00 a.m. meeting with Robin Hawley. And the information he'd discovered about Miles Addison.

Mainly that there had been rumors of Addison abusing boys in both Boston, where he'd lived before moving to New York, and his hometown of Chicago. The cops who investigated told Dean they'd found evidence money had exchanged hands between Miles and the victims' family, but no formal charges were ever filed.

Seemed the prick really had a system down. From what Dean gathered, Addison targeted underprivileged boys without strong father figures. He earned their trust simply by paying attention to them, taking them places and buying them things.

The detectives Dean spoke with who'd investigated Addison in Boston and Chicago had wanted to take the case to trial. Unfortunately, without the victims' testimony, they didn't have a shot of getting a conviction.

Too bad. If there was someone who deserved to be behind bars, it was Miles Addison.

Dean entered the crowded coffee shop. He couldn't believe he'd let Nolan talk him into meeting Robin Hawley, but as his partner had pointed out, if Dean didn't meet with her, she might call the investigation off.

Dean spotted her at a corner table in the back of the large, noisy room. She looked the same as the day she'd come to their office in Dallas to hire them, tidy as a preacher's wife at Sunday services. Her silver hair was shorter than Dean's, but instead of looking mannish, the style complemented Robin's softly lined features.

She lifted a hand in greeting as he approached, the

sleeve of her subdued pink blouse sliding back to reveal a slim, expensive-looking silver watch.

"Thank you for meeting with me," Robin said when Dean reached the table. She gestured to the empty seat across from her. "Can I get you something? Coffee?"

"No, thank you, ma'am," he said as he sat down. "I'm afraid I don't have much time."

"I understand, and I appreciate how dedicated you and Mr. Winchester are to your job."

Her eyes welled with tears and Dean shifted uncomfortably. *Please don't let her start crying.* That was the last thing he needed. This was Nolan's job, not his. Dean was the one who infiltrated people's lives, tracked down leads and sifted through the lies until he found the truth.

He wasn't cut out for customer care.

Robin shook her head. "I'm sorry. I just miss them both so much." She opened her purse and took out some photos, handing them to Dean. "I wasn't sure if you needed more pictures. That one," she said, pointing to the top picture, "was taken a few months before the trial."

Dean glanced down at the picture of Robin and Lynne dressed up in front of some sort of fancy fountain. Both women were holding champagne glasses and smiling.

Dean flipped to the next photo, in which Robin knelt next to Jon, her arm around his shoulders. The boy wearing a backpack that was at least as big as he was, didn't look as thrilled as she did.

"That was Jonny's first day of kindergarten," Robin said, her voice thick with emotion. "I'm not sure who was more nervous, him or Lynne. Once he got to his classroom, he was fine—he's such an easygoing, friendly boy." She laughed sadly. "But poor Lynne was such a wreck. She stood in the hallway for two hours just to make sure he was really all right."

"We're doing everything possible to find your daughter and grandson, Mrs. Hawley," Dean said, tapping the edge of the photos against the table.

She sipped her coffee. "Mr. Winchester said you might have a new lead?"

"We're following up on several possibilities," he told her, trying to make it sound as if he wasn't hedging. He and Nolan had learned early on that while it was important to keep clients informed, too much information in the wrong hands could shoot a case all to hell. "We're positive Lynne and Jon lived right here in Cincinnati until a few months ago."

He then filled her in as much as he could while keeping Allie's possible connection—and his work in Serenity Springs—to himself.

"You've gotten much further than the other three firms I tried," she said, sounding hopeful. "Maybe this time I'll really find them."

"Like I said, we'll do our best."

She sat up straighter in her chair. "That's all I can ask, isn't it? I know you're in a hurry, so I won't keep you any longer, but I just want to reiterate the condition that if you find Lynne, you don't mention my involvement." She tore at her paper napkin. "I need to face her myself and if she finds out I'm looking for her, she may run away again before I apologize. I was so wrong to testify at the trial, but at the time, I honestly thought I was doing the right thing. What Lynne wanted."

"You believed your son-in-law was innocent?"

"Of course. Everyone did, even Lynne."

"What changed your mind?"

Her lips thinned. "Actually, I'm not convinced he was guilty. All I know is that Lynne left him for a reason and didn't feel she could come to me for help. Whether Miles is guilty or not, the end result is the same. My daughter and grandson are out there somewhere and I may never see them again." She swallowed. "I may never get the chance to apologize." Her eyes beseeched him. "All I want is my family back."

He nodded. Yeah, he could relate. He stood and tucked the pictures in his pocket. "I appreciate the photos. We'll be in touch, but if you have any questions, just call Nolan. He's easier to get ahold of than I am," he lied, having no qualms about throwing his best friend under the bus.

Dean made his way back to the door, thinking about the similarities between what had happened with him and his family and Robin and her daughter. Once outside, he went to the curb to hail a cab back to the airport. His family crap wasn't important. What mattered was getting this job done. If they didn't, Robin would hire someone else, that much was a given. And if she did, that other PI might discover Allie's involvement with the case. She could be accused of aiding and abetting a child abduction

No. This was Dean's job. He'd find Lynne, reunite her

with her mother and help Allie get rid of the guilt she'd been carrying around these past two years.

He'd help her get on with her life.

Once she realizes I'm not going to force Lynne to go back to her bastard of a husband, Allie might even be grateful to have my help.

If she ever forgave him for lying to her.

ALLIE HAD NEVER HAD A MAN ignore her for three days before.

Actually, she'd never had a man ignore her for as much as three minutes. She couldn't say she liked it.

She smiled distractedly at the two couples she'd just taken drink orders from, and lifted her full tray. She wove her way back through the crowd. Kelsey's Speed Date Your Way Through Valentine's Day was a hit. The Summit had been packed since the event started at eight, and though there were only two ten-minute sessions left, it didn't look as if the event was losing any steam.

She went behind the bar and set the tray down. Noreen was picking up empty glasses and bottles by the pool table, while Kelsey worked the right side. Since this was Kelsey's baby, Allie had left her in charge of all the setup logistics, keeping time for the dates and planning the mix-and-mingle periods.

She glanced at Dean, who was filling drink orders at the other end of the bar.

She just didn't get it. Ever since he'd left her house Thursday morning, he'd managed to pretend she didn't exist. She tossed an empty into the recycling bin with a loud clang. He'd speak to her if she asked him a direct question, but he didn't meet her eye. And as soon as he'd answered her, he'd find some task that needed his immediate attention.

The way he was acting, you'd think he'd been the one left standing practically naked in the kitchen.

"Would you stop?" Kelsey asked as she came up beside her.

Allie looked away from Dean's strong profile and frowned. "Stop what?"

Her sister-in-law added a shot of rum to a glass and then topped it off with cola. "Stop mooning over your bartender. It's pathetic, so knock it off."

Allie's jaw dropped. "Excuse me," she said haughtily, "but I've never mooned over a man in my life."

"You've never *had* to moon over a man before." Kelsey stuck a stir straw in the glass and gave Allie a knowing look. "Most guys go gaga over you and generally make asses of themselves trying to get you to notice them. So, even though I wish you'd set your sights somewhere else, I'm glad he's smart enough not to give you the time of day."

Allie narrowed her eyes as Kelsey handed the drink to a customer. When she came back from ringing up the sale and taking another order, Allie said, "You're supposed to be on my side. And I haven't set my sights on Dean." She lowered her voice. "We had a…moment the other day—"

"Crap," Kelsey said, opening a bottle of beer and setting it on the bar. "You slept with him."

The guy waiting for his drinks grinned. Allie's face heated.

"I did not sleep with him," she hissed, turning her back to the bar. "I'm just wondering what's going on with him."

Kelsey opened another beer and, after the customer left, pulled Allie to the back of the bar. "You want to know why he's ignoring you after your shared moment—in which no sex was involved. Is that about right?"

"I want to make sure he's okay, that's all. He's been acting strangely and—"

"You only met the guy a week ago," Kelsey said. "How do you know if he's acting strangely or not?"

"I just know."

"Why must I do everything?" Kelsey muttered to no one in particular. Then she strode toward Dean. Not liking the look in her eyes, Allie followed. When Kelsey glanced back at her, she turned and stuck her hands in the sink, as if her intention all along had been to wash dishes.

"How's it going?" Kelsey asked him.

He didn't even look up from the beer he was pouring. "Other than that damn air horn blasting every ten minutes and a line five deep because you chat more than you pour drinks, it's going great."

"Hey, that air horn is the cue for people to move on to the next date. And there are only two left, so you'll just have to deal. And I wouldn't have to stop and chat if you hadn't had a *moment* with your boss the other day and are now determined to ignore her."

He gaped at Allie, his hand still on the beer tap. "You told her?"

She clenched her teeth. What did he think, that she'd told Kelsey he'd given her a mind-blowing orgasm in the middle of her kitchen?

"I didn't tell her anything because there was nothing to tell," Allie stated. She nodded at the overflowing glass in his hand. "And you're wasting beer."

He looked down and cursed. Turning off the tap, he carried the beer to his waiting customer.

"And just for the record," she said to her sister-in-law, rinsing a glass, "I don't appreciate you sticking your nose where it doesn't belong."

"I was only trying to help." Kelsey tried but failed to pull off an innocent expression. "I butt in because I care."

Allie knew that. But it didn't make her any less angry. "Well, I'll handle things from here." She pointed a wet finger to the lineup of thirsty people. "Now would you please get back to work before you force me to fire your skinny ass?"

"Killjoy." Kelsey pouted.

Within fifteen minutes, another ten-minute dating session had started and the line had died down enough for Allie to have cleaned most of the glasses. She'd had enough time to think a few things through. The other day Dean had asked her when she was going to stop allowing her fear of making another mistake rule her actions. She hadn't realized until this moment exactly how much she'd changed. If a man had run off on her two years ago, she would've tracked him down and demanded an explanation. But now, all she did was wait around like some timid schoolgirl with her first crush.

Somewhere along the line, she'd lost her faith in herself. And she wanted it back.

She waited until Dean had a break, then told Kelsey to cover the bar before following him into the kitchen. "You've been avoiding me," she said, as she entered the room.

"I haven't been—"

"Bull. I know why you're doing it, just as I know why you walked away from me the other day."

He seemed leery, as if she'd guessed some big, dark secret. "You do?"

She nodded. "You didn't want to take advantage of me. Which is sweet—" His laughter cut her off. She frowned. "What?"

"Oh, I wanted to take advantage," he said with a sexy grin. "Believe me."

She cleared her throat. "Well, be that as it may, you didn't. Uh, take advantage of my…weak moment. And I want you to know, since I wasn't thinking clearly at the time, I appreciate your restraint and good judgment."

He turned the water bottle in his hands. "So, you're glad we didn't go any further?"

Hell, no. "Yes. I am. Just because we're…attracted… to each other doesn't mean we can't control our baser instincts. We're not animals."

"Speak for yourself," he mumbled.

"Excuse me?"

"Nothing."

"So, we're both in agreement that nothing…irreversible happened between us. There's no reason for you to avoid me. We can get back to being what we were before…"

"You mean, boss and employer?"

"Yes, but I think we can be more than that. Friends."

He seemed less than thrilled by the idea. "Don't you have enough of those?"

"There's always room for one more," she told him with a wink. Then she walked away. And for the first time since she'd moved back to Serenity Springs, she felt like her old self.

CHAPTER TWELVE

HALF AN HOUR LATER the speed dating thing had ended—
and Dean had tossed the air horn in the Dumpster out
back. He mixed what had to be his sixtieth cosmopoli-
tan of the night and wondered about the allure of pink
drinks. The ladies in The Summit sure couldn't get
enough of them.

Probably because Allie had made all red and pink
drinks half price in honor of Valentine's Day.

After finishing the order, he dunked a fresh cloth in
cleaning solution. He heard the unmistakable sound of
Allie's laughter, which was crazy seeing as the noise
level in the room was off the charts. Wringing out the
cloth, he raised his head as he searched the crowd for her.

He slapped the cloth onto the counter when he found
her holding court by the pool table with a half dozen
males of various shape, size and age. The only thing they
had in common was their open appreciation of Allie.

Or at least, their appreciation of how well she filled
out that damn red sweater of hers.

Dean scrubbed at the counter. He hadn't been able to
stop thinking about what happened in her kitchen the
other day. How she'd felt under his hands and mouth.
How she'd trembled.

"I take it you're not into competition?" Kelsey sidled up next to him, a smirk on her face.

"Why?" he asked. "You want to challenge me to an arm wrestling match?"

"If I thought I could win, you bet." She nodded toward the small jungle of flowers by the cash register. "How many bouquets do you think Allie got today? Five? Six?"

"Eight," he said before he could stop himself.

She pursed her lips. "Right. Eight. Plus three boxes of candy and one very ugly red teddy bear. What does that tell you?"

"That the florists and gift shops in Serenity Springs praise the day she moved back to town?"

Kelsey opened a bottle of water and took a long drink, watching him steadily over the rim. "You know, despite my initial doubts, I think I could learn to like you."

"I'm a very likable guy." He gave her his most charming grin.

She twisted the cap back on the bottle. Untwisted it. "Be that as it may, I can't help but wonder if you're pulling the deep freeze on Allie because of all the attention she gets from the opposite sex." She gave his hand a pat. "What's the matter? Feeling insecure?"

"I'm not freezing her out and I'm not threatened by the attention she gets from, or gives to, the opposite sex. Allie and I have a business relationship. Period."

"For your sake, I hope you're telling the truth. Because if you do anything to hurt her," Kelsey said, pointing her bottle at him like a weapon, "I will come after you like the wrath of God."

He'd been warned off by a redhead who probably weighed one hundred and ten pounds soaking wet. And yet he was just the slightest bit scared of her.

One thing was for sure. This job hadn't been boring.

He watched Allie lead a middle-aged man in a dark suit over to a back table. "You don't think she can take care of herself?"

"Please. Allie can take care of herself, this bar and half the population of Serenity Springs without breaking one perfectly manicured nail."

"Exactly." Dean gestured to a chubby brunette, one of the many women who'd come for the speed dating, that he'd be with her in a moment. He turned back to Kelsey. "Allie's one of the smartest, savviest, most capable people I've ever met. But if it'll set your mind at ease—and get you off my back—I promise I'll do everything in my power not to hurt her."

He left Kelsey with a thoughtful frown on her face.

"Evening," he said to the brunette. "What can I get you?"

Behind her black, rectangular glasses, she blinked her muddy-brown eyes. "Uh…white wine?"

He grinned. "You asking or ordering?"

She brushed her heavy, brow skimming bangs to the side. "Sorry. I'd like a glass of white wine. Chardonnay, please."

She took off her gray coat and then dug through her purse as he poured. While he knew she hadn't been in The Summit before, he must've seen her around town because she seemed vaguely familiar. Then again, dur-

ing the course of the evening he'd recognized several Serenity Springs's singles taking part in the speed dating,
including a bubbly redhead who worked at the bakery,
a local cop who looked more like a linebacker, and the
guy who delivered mail to the bar.

The woman pulled out her cell phone and a twenty
and set her bag aside. Twisting a chunk of drab brown,
shoulder-length hair around her finger as she opened
her phone, she checked something, then closed it again.

"Here you go." He set her drink in front of her.

"Thank you." She handed him the twenty but knocked
her glass over. "Oh!" She grabbed her phone with one
hand, righted the now empty glass with the other. "I'm
so sorry. I'm such a klutz."

"No problem." Dean wiped up the mess and took the
glass from her. "Let me get you another one. On the
house."

She blushed and shook her head. "Thank you, but I'd
rather pay for both."

"It's really not—"

"I insist."

He raised his eyebrows. Who knew a stubborn streak
could be hidden under such a plain exterior? Guess that
proved what his mother always said about not judging
by appearances. Was his mom ever wrong?

He refilled the customer's glass. "Can I get you anything else?"

She smiled shyly at him. "No, thanks."

He rang up her wine—both glasses—and handed her
the change. "You here for the dating extravaganza?" he

asked, even though he'd seen her switching dates a few times this evening.

She sipped her wine. "My boss asked me to come with her, and I've always had a hard time saying no to the person signing my paycheck."

He nodded at the college kid who held up his empty glass. Mixing another rum and coke, Dean realized where he'd seen her before. She worked at that beauty parlor next to the pizza place on Union Street. He'd followed Allie there on Wednesday and seen the brunette through the window.

He gave the rum and coke to his customer as Allie joined them. "Ellen," she said as she hugged the brunette. "I didn't know you were coming tonight."

"Georgie talked me into it. She didn't want to come alone so…"

"So, you got stuck playing her wing-woman?"

Ellen smiled. "She's been so good to me, I didn't see the harm."

"So, how was it?" Allie asked. "Did you meet anyone special? Make plans to get together again?"

Ellen looked as horrified as if Allie had just attempted to pimp her out to the highest bidder. "No. I mean… I wasn't serious. It was more to pass the time."

"Well, that's too bad," Allie said. "I saw you sitting with Jared during that last round and he's so nice—cute and smart *and* funny. The kids he teaches at the high school love him. If you want I could—"

"Hey, Yentl," Dean said to Allie when he noticed Ellen's pale face and the death grip she had on her purse, "ease up on the hard sell."

Allie glared at him before she saw how freaked out Ellen was. "Sorry. I guess I…got carried away by the spirit of the evening."

"I appreciate the offer but really, I'm not interested."

"No problem. If you change your mind, though, Jared is a very nice man."

Dean winced. Sweet God, if a woman as sexy as Allie ever described him as a very nice man in any context whatsoever, he hoped someone would shoot him and end his misery.

He waited on another customer while Allie and Ellen chatted. When he returned, the brunette was gone.

"What happened?" he asked Allie. "Did you scare her off?"

"Hardly." She scooped ice into a glass and poured cranberry juice over it. "Her son's recovering from a bad cold so she went home."

"More than likely she got out of here before you brought up nice-guy Jared again."

"It's not like I dragged the man over here," she said, waving the bar's soda gun around. "I was simply pointing out that if she was in the market for a date, so to speak, she could do a lot worse than Jared." Allie stabbed a straw into her glass. "I didn't sell her into matrimony."

"I thought after what happened with Richie you were going to stop saving the world and put yourself first?"

She met his eyes. "I tried that the other day. It didn't quite work out, remember?"

His phone vibrated, but even though he was waiting for a call from Nolan, Dean ignored it. He edged closer. He was so tired of keeping his distance, of fighting his feelings for Allie. She stood her ground.

"Seems to me things worked out just fine for you that morning," he said huskily. He slid a finger over the back of her hand. "And I sure don't have any complaints."

Instead of backing up as he expected her to do, she took a step forward so that their thighs brushed. "If you hadn't run off, you wouldn't have had any complaints about what happened next, either."

His mind blanked and then filled with images of them together. "You might not understand this," he told her, "but I'm trying to do the right thing here."

Her smile was slow and sensual. "Who's stopping you? Now, you might want to answer your phone or turn it off. Or else people are going to think that vibrating bulge in your pocket is something else entirely."

"Hello?" Luckily, the voice on the other end wasn't Nolan's, or else in Dean's state, he'd probably blow his cover wide open.

"Hello, sugar! Happy Valentine's Day."

Even though it'd been this past Christmas since he'd last heard that voice, he had no trouble placing it. "Mama?" He noticed Allie watching him curiously. "Is everything all right?"

"Everything's just fine, thanks in part to the gorgeous dozen roses you sent. But a visit from you in person would've been even better."

There was no way he could fend off his mother's reproach while under his boss's watchful eyes. "Could you hold on a minute?" He covered the mouthpiece. "Do you mind if I take a quick break?" he asked Allie.

"By all means," she said, shooing him away. "I'll handle your end of the bar."

He nodded and brought the phone back up to his ear, holding his free hand over his other ear to block out some of the noise. One good thing about talking to his mother, hearing her voice killed any sexual thoughts he might have been having about Allie.

He might have to send her another dozen roses just for that.

ALLIE PULLED TWO DRAFTS and had Kelsey mix up a raspberry lemon drop, which she gave the customer for half price as part of her Valentine's Day red drink promotion. Allie was pouring three shots of Jack Daniel's for a trio of twentysomething guys in jeans and polos when Dean returned.

"Thanks," he said, filling the next order for an imported beer. "I'll take it from here."

"This the no-good, untrustworthy, womanizing cowboy I've been hearing way too much about?"

Next to her, Dean bristled. Allie sighed. "Did Kelsey really call him a womanizer or did you make that part up?" she asked Dillon Ward, who stood at the bar, his arm around Nina Carlson's waist.

Dillon ran his free hand through his auburn hair. Even though she could tell he'd recently had a trim, the ends still reached his collar. "You think I would use the word *womanizer* on my own?"

"Well, in that case, yes, this is him," Allie said. "Dean, these are dear friends of mine, Dillon Ward and Nina Carlson. Dillon is Kelsey's brother."

"That would explain it," Dean said.

"Nice to meet you." Nina's dimple flashed as she smiled. She turned to Dillon. "While you two do your manly, sizing each other up thing, I'm going to go over and say hi to Kelsey." She kissed his cheek, rolled her eyes at Allie and walked away.

"I have customers waiting," Dean said. "I think I'll skip the sizing up portion of the evening."

Watching Dean move down to serve the next person, Allie leaned her elbows on the bar. "Good to see you still know how to clear a room with your sparkling personality, Dillon."

"Room's still full. I want to talk to you."

"If you're here to discuss Dean—"

"The cowboy?" He laughed. "I'm not. We both know that if you wanted, you could have him wrapped around your little finger. My sister's time would be better spent worrying about how that poor bastard's going to survive *you*."

"It's not like that between me and—oh, sit down." She opened a bottle of his favorite beer and gestured toward an empty stool.

He shoved his hands into his coat pockets. "Can we go into the kitchen? I need to ask you something."

"Sure." She took his beer and her drink, told Kelsey

she'd be right back, and followed him out of the room. "What's up?" she asked as she sat at the table. "Is everything okay with Nina and the kids?"

"Yeah, they're all fine." But he wouldn't look at her and he kept pacing.

"Trey didn't get his visitation rights back, did he?"

A few months ago, Nina had petitioned family court to grant her full custody of her two young children. She had needed to get them away from her ex-husband's physical and emotional abuse.

"No, he still only has supervised visits twice a week for a few hours."

She wiped her damp palms down the legs of her jeans. "Well, what is it then?"

Dillon dug into his pocket, pulled out a silver jeweler's box and slammed it onto the table. "Open it."

Her heart racing, Allie set her drink aside before lifting the lid. "Oh," she breathed, "it's beautiful." She held the box up so the solitary princess diamond caught the light. She glanced at him. "But shouldn't you be kneeling? If a guy's going to propose to me, he'd better want me badly enough to get on his knee."

"Then it's lucky for me I'm not proposing to you, isn't it?"

"That's a shame, because to get my hands on this ring—or should I say, to get this ring on my hand—I might have said yes."

He snatched the box from her, scowling. "Do you think Nina will like it?"

Allie stood and squeezed his arm. "If she doesn't, she's not the woman I think she is."

He snapped the lid shut. "It's not much. The ring Trey gave her was probably bigger. Flashier."

"Are you kidding?" Allie's heart was so full of love for him, she thought it would burst. "That sucker was huge. It was like she had a small boulder on her finger."

He gave her one of his I'm-a-big-bad-ex-convict-and-you'd-better-not-mess-with-me looks. The one that had sent more than one person in town running.

"Don't be an idiot. This ring is perfect. Besides, do you really think Nina's going to care about what size diamond you give her? Or worse, compare you to Trey?"

He tapped the box against his thigh. "You're right. It's just that… I'm so nervous. I haven't been this afraid since my first day in prison," he admitted quietly.

"Any time a man asks a woman to marry him, he should be nervous." Allie rubbed his back. "But Nina's crazy about you. And so are her kids."

He stuck the box back in his pocket. "The feeling's mutual." He took a long drink from his beer, leaning against the table, then he picked at the label on the bottle. "I even got Hayley a necklace with a diamond that matches the ring. I wasn't sure what to give Marcus so I wrote him a letter, telling him how proud I am of him and how I'll always be there for him no matter what."

Her eyes welled. How could such a strong man seem so unsure of himself because he wanted to make the people he loved happy? Because he wanted to do right by them?

"The necklace and the letter are both wonderful, thoughtful gifts," she said. "Nina and the kids are so lucky to have you in their lives."

"Hey," he said, straightening quickly and setting down his beer, "turn off the waterworks. You'd think someone died or something."

She sniffed but couldn't stop the tears from running down her face. "I'm so happy for you. Less than a year ago you were pathetic and alone—"

"Pathetic?" He looked to the ceiling. "Why me?"

"I was your only friend—"

"What you were was a pain in the ass who wouldn't let me live in peace."

"No one would hire you. Half the town was afraid of you." She crossed to the counter for a paper towel. Wiped her nose. "And you spent most of your time cultivating your dangerous reputation so people wouldn't find out that underneath that tough-guy exterior is nothing but a big old mushy teddy bear."

He pinched the bridge of his nose. "If you don't knock it off, I might start bawling, too."

"And now you have a relationship with your sister again and you're in love with a wonderful woman—a woman who loves you right back and whose kids are nuts over you," Allie said, her voice breaking. "I'm ju-just…so ec-ecstat…happy for you!" She jumped into his arms, sobbing into his neck. "You deserve a family of your own." She leaned back and grinned, her face still wet with tears. "I love you, you know that?"

He rolled his eyes. "Yeah. I know." Then he shocked

her by squeezing her tight, which only succeeded in making her cry again in earnest. "I love you, too." He set her on her feet and tapped the end of her nose. "But you're still a pain in the ass."

SHE WAS DRIVING HIM CRAZY.

Dean gritted his teeth and slammed a chair onto a table. He could ignore Allie playing the radio, filling the empty bar with the latest pop tunes instead of the classic rock on the jukebox. He could even deal with her singing along to aforementioned pop songs, mostly because, as he'd noticed when he'd walked into the kitchen for his interview last week, she didn't sound half-bad.

But he couldn't handle how she shimmied and otherwise shook her ass to each and every song. Or worse, the stab of jealousy he'd felt earlier when she'd walked out of the kitchen with Dillon Ward, her arm linked with his, her head on his shoulder. Tears in her eyes.

Wondering what she'd been crying about—and why she'd chosen some other man to comfort her instead of him—about killed Dean.

The song slowed and Allie, cloth in hand, straightened from the table she was washing. She closed her eyes and lifted her arms over her head and swayed to the music. He caught his breath, his body tense.

He was too old for this kind of torture. He slammed another chair down.

Her eyes flew open and she frowned, but at least she stopped moving. "You okay?"

"Dandy," he muttered.

"You sure?" She flipped off the radio. "You've been quiet ever since we closed."

"I'm trying to get this done," he said pointedly, "so we can get to bed." Not what he'd meant to say. "So we can get *home*," he amended. "It's been a long day."

Made even longer thanks to Nolan's text message a few hours ago. He hadn't had any luck tracking down Sarah Lambert yet.

"Is everything okay with your mom?" Allie asked.

"What?"

"I couldn't help but overhear you talking with her," she said. "It was kind of late for her to be calling, and you've been so grumpy—"

"I am not grumpy," he snapped. She made him sound like a cartoon bear or something.

"I thought...maybe something had happened."

"I said everything's fine."

"Sorry I asked," Allie said going back to wiping off tables, her movements jerky.

Dean sighed. He'd hoped Nolan would have found Sarah by now and gotten the evidence they required to confront Allie about helping Lynne and Jon escape Miles Addison. Dean needed a way to back her into a corner so she'd be forced to tell him the truth. He needed proof.

Without it, he'd be revealing his hand too soon. And he'd lose any headway he'd made in getting Allie to trust him, without anything to show for it.

Dean finished setting the chairs up and went to get the broom.

"Let's leave the floor until tomorrow," Allie said as she stepped behind the bar and washed her hands.

"You sure?"

"You're right, it's been a long day." She opened a heart-shaped box of chocolates, nibbling her lower lip as she chose one. She bit into it, her eyes closing in pleasure.

This job couldn't be over soon enough.

"Want some?" she asked, and damn if her voice didn't sound husky and alluring.

"No, thanks." When she shrugged and chose another chocolate, a growl rose in his throat. "You about ready to go?"

She looked up, no doubt startled at his gruff tone. "Uh...sure." She put the lid back on the chocolates and stacked it with the other two boxes before picking up a pen. "Let me get the cards off of these flowers first."

"You're not going to take them home?"

"Just the ones from my dad," she said, pointing to a bouquet of yellow roses. She wrote something on the card from one of the three vases of long-stemmed red roses. "The other ones I'll drop off at the hospital tomorrow."

"So, all those poor saps who sent you flowers wasted their time and money?"

She narrowed her eyes. "Well, I was going to sleep with them all—one at a time, of course—as a thank-you for them breaking out their credit cards," she said coolly. "Considering I've met most of them only once or twice, that seems beyond generous on my part. But since that would take up my next two months of Saturdays, I decided to draw a name to see which lucky guy got me."

"I didn't mean—"

"On second thought," she said, "I think I'll stay a little while longer. Don't wait for me. I can find my car by myself."

And with that, she lowered her head and gave all her attention to a second florist card.

In the kitchen, he got his coat and carried it back out. She didn't look up when he stood in front of her, separated by the bar.

"I didn't get you flowers," he said, as if challenging her to make a big deal of it.

She slowly lifted her head and tucked her hair behind her ear. "I didn't expect you to."

He reached into his pocket and tossed a plastic grocery bag on top of the card she was writing on. "That's for you."

She nudged the bag with the tip of her pen. "What is it?"

"Just open it."

She unfolded the bag and attempted to smooth out the wrinkles before she gingerly complied. It took all he had not to rip it away from her and dump out the contents. She probably took forever to unwrap her Christmas gifts, too.

She pulled out a small blue bag of trail mix and stared at him.

He scratched the back of his neck. "It has dried cranberries in it, and since you're always drinking cranberry juice, I thought you'd like it."

"I...I do. Thank you."

Then she took out the pink, heart-shaped stuffed mouse.

He twisted his coat in his hands. "I thought maybe Persephone might like it," he said defiantly.

He felt like a fool standing there, a blush heating his neck even as he hoped she liked a bunch of stupid things he'd picked up at the convenience store.

"Dean," she asked, running a finger over the mouse's ears, "what are these? Why are you giving them to me?" Her lips twitched. "Are these valentine gifts?"

"It's not Valentine's Day anymore."

"So, you don't want me to be your valentine?"

He shoved a hand through his hair. "What are we, ten years old?"

"Well, in that case, thank you for the gifts—which you gave me for no particular reason." She put them back in the plastic bag and came around the bar. "But for the record, if you had sent flowers, I'd have taken them home with me."

He cleared his throat. "Give me your keys. I'll warm your car while you finish up."

"Thank you."

"I'm going out to start my truck anyway—"

"No. Thank you for the gifts." She left the room and came back almost immediately with her keys, but instead of handing them over, she clasped them in her hand. "Dean, why did your mother call you tonight?"

"Does she need a reason to call me?"

"So, she called to wish you a Happy Valentine's Day?" Too bad his evasive maneuvers didn't fool Allie.

He met her eyes and knew she suspected the real reason for that phone call. How could she know him so well? And why did the thought scare him so much?

"She called to thank me for the flowers I sent her. And," he admitted, "to tell me that Rene loved the carnations and balloons I sent her."

"Rene?"

"My niece."

Allie smiled. "You sent your niece flowers?" she asked, as if he'd single-handedly stopped global warming. "Did you talk to your brother? If you want to go down to Dallas, I'm sure we could figure a way to give you a couple of days off."

"I didn't talk to Ryan or Jolene, and I don't think any of us are ready for me to pop up on their doorstep." Allie looked so disappointed Dean almost grinned. She sure was a sweetheart. "I'm taking things one step at a time."

Steps he should've taken years ago, he knew. Steps he hadn't been able to take until he'd opened up to Allie about the loss of his son. That, combined with witnessing Robin Hawley's need for forgiveness from her daughter, made Dean realize he had to stop being a coward and make amends.

She nodded. "I know it wasn't easy—"

"All I did was call up a florist and order some flowers. Don't make more of this than it is."

"I'll make more of it if I want to. Just like I'll tell you

I'm proud of you if I want to." Before he could evade her, she closed the distance between them, stretched up on her toes and kissed him, a soft, warm press of her lips against his. "You're one of the good guys, Dean."

She couldn't be more wrong.

"Your keys?" he asked.

"Oh. Sure. Sorry." She dropped them into his open palm, confusion on her face. "I'll just be a few more minutes."

He nodded and slipped on his coat. Once outside, he tilted his head back and inhaled deeply, the cold air burning his lungs. He needed to stop straddling the fence with Allie. He needed to tell her what he was really doing there.

He just hoped like hell she'd forgive him.

Maybe she'd understand. After all, he wanted to reunite Lynne and Jon Addison with Robin, not hurt anyone.

Not that it mattered. He couldn't keep this up. He couldn't keep lying to her.

He turned back to the door, but the sound of crunching snow to his left made him stop. He listened, the hair on the back of his neck standing on end. One heartbeat. Two. When he didn't hear anything else, he began to push the door open. Out of the corner of his eye, he saw a shadow. He turned, but it was too late. Pain exploded in the side of his head and he fell face-first into the snow.

CHAPTER THIRTEEN

ALLIE TUCKED THE florist cards in her purse. Even though she didn't want the flowers—or any of the guys who'd sent them—she'd still acknowledge the gifts from the men she personally knew. Of course, she'd already thanked the two guys who'd delivered their own gifts. And let them know, as politely as possible, she wasn't interested. Despite what Dean thought about her flirting, she had a strict policy about not leading men on.

She'd keep the three boxes of chocolates, though.

She put her coat on and pulled her hair out from under the collar before picking up the flowers from her dad.

She heard the door open. "Just in time." She turned and almost dropped her flowers. "Richie? What are you—"

"You weren't supposed to be here." Her former assistant slammed the door shut.

Her stomach pitched. His hair was greasy, his coat open to reveal he had on the same clothes he'd worn the last time she'd seen him. And from the wrinkles and stains, it was clear he hadn't washed them—or himself—since then.

"It's after four," he said, as if she had no right to be in her own bar. "Why are you still here?"

She smiled shakily, trying not to let him see how uneasy she felt. "Dillon and Nina stopped by," she explained slowly. "They'd taken the kids to a movie and then went out to dinner, so they didn't get here until late. We didn't start cleaning until almost three." She casually put the flowers down and walked out from behind the bar. "I'm so glad you came back...."

It wasn't until she was a few feet away from him that she noticed his dilated pupils. The sweat beaded on his upper lip. The rank scent of body odor.

And the gun held loosely at his side.

The blood drained from her face. "Wha-what are you doing with that?" Her eyes widened and nausea churned her stomach. She stepped toward the door. "Where's Dean?"

"Don't move!" Richie lifted the gun, pointing it at her chest, his hand shaking. "He wasn't supposed to be here, either."

She held her arms out at her sides. "I'm not going to hurt you."

Which was a really ridiculous thing to say, since she wasn't the one with the gun.

And the way he was waving it around didn't bode well for her. He might accidentally shoot her.... Because surely he wouldn't shoot her on purpose.

The Richie she knew, the Richie she'd shared the secret to her roux sauce with, who'd dressed up as Fred Flintstone to her Wilma last Halloween, would never hurt her.

But this wasn't that man, was it? This Richie was

strung out, highly agitated and worse, unpredictable. The old Richie was still in there, though. He had to be. All she had to do was get through to him.

"Where's Dean?" she asked again, keeping her voice even. She inched toward the door. "Is he all right?"

Richie wiped the back of his hand over his forehead. "I didn't want to hurt him. I didn't mean for anyone to get hurt."

Her lungs constricted with fear. *Oh, God. No.* "Where is he?"

"Outside. By the door."

Dean had to be all right. If Richie had fired his gun—had shot Dean—she would've heard the discharge. "I need to check on him."

"You can't leave," he said, pointing the gun at her head. "You can't go to the cops."

She swallowed, but the lump in her throat remained. "I'm not leaving. I promise. I'm just going to check on Dean. That's all. Please," she begged. "Let me open the door."

He nodded and slowly lowered the gun, but he didn't put it away. She took a deep breath and prayed she wouldn't find Dean's lifeless body in the parking lot.

Wiping her sweating palms down the front of her jeans, she opened the door. Light spilled out, illuminating Dean's crumpled figure on the sidewalk.

She gasped and raced outside, sliding in her high-heeled boots. Falling to her knees beside him, she frantically felt the side of his neck for a pulse. His skin was cold, his lips tinged blue, but his heartbeat was steady. *Thank you, God.*

"Is he…dead?" Richie asked from the doorway.

"He's breathing." She gently brushed his hair back. Dots of blood stained the snow from the nasty cut on his temple. He hadn't lost much blood, but he had what promised to become a sizable, and from the looks of it, painful lump.

Dean's eyelids fluttered and he groaned.

"What's he doing?" Richie asked, panicked.

She held Dean's hands, trying to warm them with her own. "Dean? Can you hear me?"

He blinked slowly several times, finally bringing his eyes into focus. She sat back, relieved.

"You all right?" he asked in a low whisper.

Her laugh sounded suspiciously close to a sob. "I'm fine," she said. "You're the one lying in the snow with a head wound."

He raised his hand and gingerly felt the area around the bump. Grimaced. "Just a scratch," he mumbled.

She braced her arm around his shoulder and helped him sit up. "Any dizziness?"

"Nah." But he spoke through gritted teeth as if fighting back a rush of pain.

"What are you doing?" Richie asked.

She didn't even look at him. "I'm helping him get up."

"No. You've seen he's all right, just leave him."

She bit back the urge to snap at him. "We can't leave him out here in the cold," she said, proud of how rational she sounded. As if she was held at gunpoint every day by someone she used to consider a friend. "He's hurt. He could die."

She could've sworn she saw Dean roll his eyes before he winced. Okay, so he probably wouldn't die, but Richie didn't seem to know that.

Richie was now shivering violently—either from drugs or the cold or both. "F-f-fine. But don't t-t-try to run."

"Can you stand?" she asked Dean.

"Yeah."

She put his arm around her shoulder, shifted onto her heels and helped him get to his feet. Staggering under his weight, she somehow managed to keep her balance. He leaned heavily on her as they shuffled inside. Richie walked backward, kept his gun trained on them. As soon as they were in, he shut and locked the door.

"He can sit over there," the young man said, gesturing toward the far corner of the room. The corner farthest away from any of the exits.

Seemed Richie wasn't all that far gone.

"Can you stand on your own for a minute?" Allie asked when they reached the table.

Dean's face was pale, etched with pain. He nodded, but then hissed out a breath as he shifted, a movement that must've hurt like hell. She let go of him and quickly set a chair down, then helped him sink into it.

"That's good," Richie called from the other side of the pool table. "Now…come over here."

Terrified, she forced herself to straighten. She had to

let him think he was in control, find a way to talk him down before he did something he'd regret.

She had to believe he wouldn't hurt her or Dean more than he already had.

She took a step, but Dean seized her wrist, his grip surprisingly strong. Startled, she met his eyes.

"Wait for my cue," he said almost soundlessly.

Her mind blanked. What was he saying? What did he mean?

"No talking!" Richie shrieked.

She spun back around, her mouth bone-dry. Richie was obviously close to the breaking point. Then the realization hit her and her knees threatened to buckle— Dean wasn't as hurt as he'd made them believe. Make that he wasn't as hurt as he wanted Richie to believe.

"He's thirsty," Allie lied, cursing herself when her voice cracked. "Can I get him some water?"

Richie viciously scratched his neck with his free hand. "No. Just—just get away from him. Come over here."

She hesitated, glanced back at Dean and nodded slightly to let him know she'd heard him before.

"Now!"

Her heart thumping madly, she had to walk away from Dean. Toward Richie.

Everything would be okay. They'd get out of this. All she had to do was keep control of the situation so that no one got hurt.

And if she could, help Richie before it was too late.

"Get the key to the cash register," he told her.

"You...you're going to rob me?" Even though she

knew that had been his intention, hearing his demand still came as a shock. "Do you know what the penalty is for armed robbery? At least ten years in a state prison."

She needed to stop him.

He looked at her as if she'd lost her mind. A distinct possibility, considering she was arguing with a man pointing a gun at her.

"Just get the key!" he shouted, spittle flying from his lips, his face red.

Her legs shaking, she went behind the bar, knelt down and pulled the key from the magnet she kept under the sink. Before she stood, she said a quick prayer that whatever Dean was planning, he'd make his move soon.

"Come on, get up." Richie jerked her to her feet, his fingers biting into her arm. She gasped at the pain. "Open the damn cash register."

Her hands were so unsteady, it took her three tries to fit the key in the lock. The drawer sprang open and he nudged her aside. He tensed, then threw the empty money tray over the bar with a curse.

He turned to her and she took a step back, her hand going to her chest. "Where's the money?" he asked.

"I already put it in the safe." She edged to one side, forcing Richie to turn his back on Dean if he was going to keep her in his line of vision. "You know I don't leave that much cash in the register overnight."

He pressed his hands against his temples. "No, no, no." He focused on Dean, who was bent over, his elbows on his thighs, his head resting in his hands. "We'll…

we'll tie him up. Then we'll go back to the safe, get the money."

"We can't tie him up," she said, drawing Richie's attention back to her. "There's no rope here."

He looked around frantically. "We'll use something else."

"Like what? There's nothing here."

"I don't know!" He picked up the heavy glass mixer and heaved it toward the shelves of liquor. She covered her head as bottles exploded, sending shards of glass flying through the air, stinging the back of her hands. The distinctive smell of liquor filled the room.

Richie was breathing hard, but she didn't dare look to see what Dean was doing. Not if she wanted to keep Richie's attention on her. "You need to stay calm—"

"Shut up!" He pointed the gun at her. "Shut up. I—I need to think. I need—"

"You don't have to do this," she told him, fighting the fear clawing her throat. "It's not too late to end this right now. Before it gets worse. Before you do something you'll regret."

"I didn't want it to be this way. I didn't mean for it to happen." Bits of broken bottles littered his hair and a bead of sweat dripped down the side of his face. He wiped his cheek against his shoulder. "If you hadn't been here—"

"What? You wouldn't have broken into my place? You wouldn't have stolen from me?"

"You don't understand."

Out of the corner of her eye she saw Dean easing up

his pant leg. "So, tell me," she said, edging to the right, away from Dean. "Explain why you'd rather have drugs than a job and friends who trusted you. How you could betray the people who believed in you."

"I didn't want to hurt you. I never wanted you to find out." His eyes welled with tears and he rubbed at them with his free hand. "I just need some money, but this will be the only time. I swear. Then I'll get clean again."

For a moment she felt sorry for him. Then she remembered he was holding a gun on her. Had hurt Dean. Meant to rob her. And she still wanted to help him? She was either pathetic or delusional.

"This isn't you, Richie. It's the drugs."

She licked her dry lips, noticed Dean slowly rising from his chair. Though he'd barely been able to walk, the gun in his hand was steady as a rock.

It was enough to chill her blood, and she shivered. Where did he get a gun? And more importantly, how was she going to stop either of them from using their weapons? How was she going to get them all out of this alive?

"You can still walk away," she said desperately to Richie. "No one's going to hurt you."

Tears streamed down his face and he lowered his arm. But he must've sensed Dean moving behind him, because he suddenly swung his gun around.

"No!" Adrenaline pulsing through her, Allie rushed at Richie, knocking her shoulder into him. The gun went off, the discharge sounding as loud as a cannon in the confined space. Through the ringing in her ears she thought she heard Dean shout. Richie shoved her and she landed hard against the counter of the sink, the breath momentarily knocked out of her. Before she could regain her footing, Richie backhanded her. Her head snapped to the side, fire exploding in her cheek.

Roaring like a cornered animal, Dean jumped onto a stool, then the bar, and with a flying leap, tackled Richie. Richie grunted at the force, his gun skidding across the floor. Allie scrambled through the puddles of alcohol and broken bottles, ignoring the stinging cuts to her palms and knees, her only thought on getting the gun. Helping Dean.

She picked it up, but could only hold it loosely because of the bleeding gashes on her hands, the glass still embedded in her skin. *Just don't drop it,* she chanted silently to herself as she sat back on her butt and aimed the weapon at Richie.

Not that Dean needed her help, since he'd effectively knocked Richie out. She lowered her trembling arms and carefully set the weapon aside. Dean pulled his cell phone out as he straightened from Richie's prone body.

He knelt next to her as he called 911. After a quick, terse explanation of what had happened, he clicked the phone off and gently gripped her chin. His expression turned fierce as he studied her cheek, where Richie had hit her. But that was nothing compared to the fury in Dean's eyes when he noticed the blood on her hands.

He swore roundly, then shifted as if to stand.

"Don't," she said, skimming her fingertips over the back of his hand. Even with that light touch, she could feel the tension vibrating through him.

"Don't what?"

She nodded toward Richie. "He's already uncon-scious. There's no need to pound him some more."

"He hurt you. That's reason enough for me."

"Please. Just…could you just sit with me?"

He glanced at Richie, then at her before nodding. "Yeah, but let's get you out of this mess." He helped her to her feet and smoothed her hair back from her face. "You sure you're okay?"

His tenderness and concern mixed with her own re-lief that they were all alive, making her head swim. "I'm fine." She began to shiver in earnest. "Just more shaken than I'd like to admit. I'm also confused."

He guided her around the bar to the first stool. "You should know better than anyone there's no figuring out why people commit the crimes they do."

"No…I mean…yes, of course I'm curious why Richie would do this. But what I'm really wondering," she said as she searched Dean's face, "is what you're doing car-rying a gun?"

DEAN INSERTED HIS KEY CARD into the lock and opened the motel door. He reached along the wall and flipped on the light. Used to working out of motel rooms, he never went anywhere without first locking all his files in a metal briefcase and making sure his laptop was shut off.

Which was a good thing, considering the way Allie was hovering over him.

"Want to lean on me?" she asked, as if a little bump on the head was enough to keep him down.

He gave her a look. "No."

She followed him inside, shut the door behind her. He didn't want her here. Not when he was feeling so amped up. So on edge.

So out of control.

"What is your problem?" she asked. "First you refuse to go to the hospital—"

"Me? You're the one who should've gone to the hospital instead of insisting the EMT take care of your cuts in the back of the ambulance."

She raised her bandaged palms. "Honestly, it looked much worse than it was." And after they'd taken the glass out of her knees and cleaned the cuts, Jack had given her a pair of Serenity Springs P.D. sweatpants to wear instead of her ruined jeans. "At least *I'm* not in danger of slipping into a coma."

"The EMT said I didn't even need stitches, so I doubt I'm heading into a vegetative state. Besides, what good would it have done to go to the E.R.?" He took his coat off, threw it onto the bed. "All they'd do is tell me I might have a mild concussion and to take it easy."

Even though his head had hurt like a son of a bitch, the four painkillers he'd downed earlier had diminished the agony to a dull ache.

He clenched his fists. He wished the pills would also do something to erase the memory of Allie throwing herself at that maniac. Of that bastard putting his hands on her.

"And now that you've seen me safely to my room," he continued as he sat on the bed and pulled one boot off, "you can go. A shower and a few hours of sleep and I'll be fine."

"Oh, yeah. That's a great idea. And what if you get dizzy in the shower? You could slip and crack your head open. Or be knocked unconscious again."

"I told you," he growled, "I was only out for a few minutes." He threw his second boot across the room and stood. "And I don't need a goddamn babysitter."

She tossed her purse onto the desk. "What has gotten into you?"

"You want to know? How about how, when your brother took our statements, you spun the facts so that while you didn't actually lie, you didn't tell the full story, either. If that's a sample of your skills, you must've been a hell of a lawyer."

"I didn't lie," she said, stepping up to him. "I told Jack what he needed to know. And how about you? You're the one carrying a concealed weapon."

"I have a permit."

"I don't like the idea of one of my employees being armed without my knowledge."

He edged closer until they were nose to nose. "That's the point of it being concealed."

And he could kick his own ass for switching from his preferred—and easily accessible—back holster to an ankle holster. All because she'd almost discovered his weapon that morning in her kitchen when they'd kissed.

"I don't like secrets," she maintained, crossing her arms.

"Oh, really? Then why don't we call Jack? Tell him

some of the facts you left out before. Like how you threw yourself at a gun-waving drug addict!"

She tossed up her hands. "What was I supposed to do? Let him shoot you?"

"If that's what it took to keep you safe, then yes." He wrapped his fingers around her upper arms but resisted the urge to shake some sense into her. "Or did you think it'd be better if you got shot instead?"

She trembled, but since her expression was defiant and angry, he figured it wasn't because she was afraid of him. More than likely the adrenaline rush she'd been riding for the past two hours was waning.

Good. Reality would set in soon.

"I didn't want anyone to get shot. That was the point."

"Next time," he growled, lifting her onto her toes, "do me a favor and don't try to save me."

"Fine!"

"Great!"

Then he crushed her to him and kissed her. After a startled moment that felt more like a lifetime, she threw her arms around him.

Their tongues dueled as his hands raced over her. He couldn't stop touching her, assuring himself she really was safe. Whole.

His head ached but he didn't care. All he cared about was the woman in his arms. He speared his hands into her hair, held her head still while he kissed her deeply. She clawed at his shirt, lifted the hem and drew it over his head.

Pain rocked him and he grunted just loud enough for Allie to hear.

"Oh my God, I'm so sorry," she said. "Maybe we shouldn't—"

He kissed her again. No way was he allowing her to finish that sentence.

He spun them around and walked her backward until the backs of her legs hit the bed. She fell onto the mattress and he followed her down, pressing his hips against hers. He stopped kissing her only long enough to slip her shirt off.

They rolled so that she straddled him, and he reached behind her, unhooked her bra and slid it down her arms. He took one nipple in his mouth and sucked hard. She groaned and arched her back, curling her fingers into his chest.

They flipped again and he tugged her sweatpants down. She lifted her hips to help him, but the fabric bunched, caught on her boots. With a curse, he stood and, grasping them by the heels, pulled them off. She shimmied out of her pants and panties while he took his wallet out of his pocket and kicked the rest of his clothes off.

She scrambled to her knees on the bed, caressing his chest, trailing her unbandaged fingertips across his ribs and down his stomach. She skimmed her warm fingers over him and his hips bucked. She pressed against him, trapping his length between their bodies. He couldn't stop himself from sliding up the silky soft skin of her belly and down again. She scraped a fingernail over the tip of his erection and he bent his head for another voracious kiss even as he dug into his wallet. When he felt the square foil packet, he pinched it between his fingers and tossed the wallet aside.

He ripped open the package and sheathed himself before pushing her back onto the bed and settling between her legs. He pressed his erection between her curls and rubbed against her once. Twice.

"Dean," she gasped, raising her hips, "now. Please."

He gripped her hips and shifted so that he was at her entrance. Her heat, her wetness beckoned him but he held on to sanity, to what was left of his personal morals, long enough to keep from madly plunging into her.

"Allie," he said, sweat beading on his forehead, his arms shaking with the effort to hold himself back, "look at me." Her eyes opened, dark blue and filled with passion. "What's going on between us, what I feel for you, is real. Promise me you'll remember that."

"Dean, what—"

"Promise. Please."

She touched his face. "I promise," she whispered.

He kissed her and slid inside. And it was even better than he'd imagined. He wanted to slow them down, wanted to make it last, but her eyes were at half-mast, her mouth open slightly. A soft flush stained her cheeks and she made a sound of contentment when he filled her.

She was driving him crazy.

When she wrapped her legs around his waist, crossing her feet at the ankles, his control snapped. He pumped into her like a madman. But she met him thrust for thrust. And when her breathing turned to soft gasps, he reached between them and stroked her. She tightened around him, her thighs gripping him, her back arched as her orgasm shook her body. Still he didn't stop. Couldn't. Their skin grew slick with sweat.

She leaned up and kissed him, bit his lower lip, then pushed against him until he rolled over. With her knees on either side of his thighs, she tucked her hips under, taking him deep inside. He gritted his teeth against the need to take control back from her. She bent forward, her peaked nipples dragging against his chest. She kissed him, his neck, his collarbones, his cheeks, her hair cascading around them, cool against his heated skin. Finally, she pressed her mouth against his in a languid kiss, her tongue sliding between his lips to lazily explore his mouth.

He groaned and shoved his hand into her hair.

She straightened and laid her bandaged hands flat on his chest, right above his racing heart. He'd been fighting his feelings for her, but when she smiled at him, he knew he couldn't hold out any longer.

Then she moved.

She undulated against him slowly, so slowly he gripped the bedspread to keep from driving up into her. Her breasts swayed with her movements and he raised his head, catching one pink peak in his mouth. She made a mewling sound in the back of her throat and quickened her pace.

Needing to watch her, he let his head fall back, but replaced his mouth on her breast with his hands. He pinched her nipples and her mouth fell open, her hips working him like a piston.

It was torture. And heaven.

He held on to his control by a thin thread until her breathing accelerated and her nails dug into his chest.

Knowing she was close, he gripped her hips and rocked into her again and again until her body bowed back. She trembled as her second release engulfed her, and only then did he give himself over to the power of his own orgasm, calling her name as he emptied himself inside her.

CHAPTER FOURTEEN

ALLIE KEPT HER HEAD against Dean's chest, listening to the steady sound of his heart. She couldn't believe she wasn't a twitchy, hysterical mess after what had happened between them.

She sighed and snuggled further under the heavy comforter. Dean, having pulled her into his arms and tucked her head under his chin, had fallen asleep a few minutes ago. But his hold on her remained tight. Even in sleep, he couldn't stop touching her.

She wished she could shut her brain down long enough to doze off as well. But that wasn't happening. Not when she was worried about his head injury. She figured she'd wake him every thirty minutes or so to assure herself he hadn't slipped into a coma or something.

Good thing she had so many thoughts flying through her mind. They'd keep her awake.

She'd just had incredible sex with an amazing man.

An amazing man who worked for her. One who held a grudge against his brother—his entire family, really. Who had a hard time seeing more than his own point of view. Someone who kept secrets, such as the fact that he carried a gun.

She should be more nervous. More concerned about

her possible lack of judgment. Should be contemplating how to sneak out of his room. Wondering how she'd be able to face him at work each day.

Instead, she wondered if, when she woke him to make sure he was okay, he'd want to have sex again.

She'd never felt better.

Her stomach growled. Well, except that she hadn't had anything to eat in over twelve hours. When her stomach rumbled again, she remembered the valentine's gift Dean had given her.

She carefully lifted his arm off her and slid out from beneath the covers. Gooseflesh rose on her bare skin and she put on Dean's discarded shirt and her socks. Not wanting to wake him, she picked up her purse and crept toward the bathroom.

A faint buzzing stopped her in her tracks. She frowned and looked down, realizing the sound came from Dean's jeans.

He mumbled something in his sleep and rolled over, the covers slipping down to reveal the strong planes of his back. She shook her head to get her focus off his body.

After a quick search of his pockets she found his phone and took it with her into the bathroom, shutting the door quietly. The name displayed on the screen was Nolan Winchester, along with an out-of-area number. After a few more buzzes, which she tried to muffle by putting a towel over the phone, the noise stopped.

She searched in her purse for the trail mix, opened it and, sitting on the edge of the tub, picked out the chocolate pieces first. Popping them into her mouth, she sighed in pleasure as they melted on her tongue.

Maybe she'd leave Dean a note and run out to get them some lunch. He was bound to be hungry when he woke up. She thought of the ugly bruise on his head. The swelling had gone down, but the skin had already turned an interesting shade of purple, and if she had to hazard a guess, she'd bet it hurt like hell.

She'd pick up some more painkillers, too. God knew they both could use them.

She ate some cranberries, then a few nuts. And because she'd been held at gunpoint not five hours ago and her hands were starting to sting again, she picked more chocolate pieces out of the bag.

When she was done she brushed her fingertips together and dug her own phone out of her purse to scroll through her missed calls. Two from Kelsey. Five from her mother. One from Jack.

Jack obviously hadn't wasted any time letting her family know what had happened.

She glanced at Dean's phone. Speaking of mothers and families wanting to know things… She picked up his cell. Nibbled her lower lip.

On the one hand, it was wrong of her to snoop through his recently received calls. Breach of privacy.

But on the other hand, it wasn't like she was reading his emails or snooping in his underwear drawer. All she wanted was his mother's phone number. The one she'd called him from last night.

Of course, it wasn't Allie's business—or her right—to call his mother about what had happened.

But Dean was hurt. If the situation was reversed and she'd been the one who'd been injured, she'd want someone to let her family know she was all right. And maybe Dean's mother would even have an idea about mending the rift between him and his family once and for all.

Allie flipped the phone open and scrolled through the recent calls until she reached the number listed under Home. Then, with a quick prayer that she had the right number—and was doing the right thing—she pressed the phone button.

The line rang twice before a woman answered, "Hello?"

"Hello, Mrs. Garret," she said, keeping her voice down, "this is Allison Martin from Serenity Springs, New York. I—"

"I'm so sorry, sugar, but I don't accept calls from telemarketers."

"Oh, no. I mean, I'm not a telemarketer. I'm a…friend of your son Dean. We work together at—"

"I had no idea Dean and Nolan had hired someone," she said. "What did you say your name was again, dear?"

Allie frowned. "Uh, Allie…Allison Martin." What was Dean's mother talking about? Him and Nolan hiring someone? "I'm sorry to bother you this early, and I don't want to alarm you, but I thought you'd want to know Dean was injured last night—"

"Is he all right?"

"He's fine. Just a mild concussion."

"I swear," Mrs. Garret said, her sweet Southern accent now steely, "I could skin that boy for putting himself in danger all the time. I thought when he came home from the marines he'd settle on an occupation that didn't turn my hair gray from worrying about him."

A chill climbed Allie's spine. "I'm sorry, Mrs. Garret, but I don't understand. What occupation are you talking about?" *Please be talking about Dean choosing to become a bartender. Please consider tending bar a dangerous occupation.*

"Why, Leatherneck Investigations, of course. Didn't you say you worked with him?"

Even through the roaring in her ears, Allie didn't miss the suspicion in the other woman's tone. "I…I don't work for Nolan and Dean's firm," she managed to say as she blinked back tears. "I'm working with Dean on a, uh, case he's investigating. It's a…a one-time thing." She cleared her throat. "Mrs. Garret, I'm so sorry to cut you off, but I have to go."

"That's fine. Thank you so much for letting me know. And will you please have Dean call me? I'll feel better when I hear from him."

Allie's fingers grew slippery on the phone. She switched ears and wiped her bandaged palm down the front of her—of Dean's—shirt. "Of course," she croaked. "Goodbye."

She didn't wait for a response, just ended the call. Pain welled in her chest, made it impossible for her to breathe. She wrapped her arms around herself and rocked back and forth. Concentrated on inhaling. Then exhaling. Slowly. Steadily.

Dean's mother was wrong. She had to be.

There was one way to know for sure.

Allie picked up her own cell phone and dialed a familiar number. Waited for an answer.

"It's me," she said. "We might have a problem."

"YOU BASTARD."

Dean shot awake and sat up, only to fall back onto the pillow with a grunt of pain as one hundred fifteen pounds of pissed-off female landed on him.

"Allie, what—" He broke off when she went after him with her fists and forearms. He raised both arms but she continued to pummel him. "What's the matter with you?"

"I can't believe how naive I was." She landed a vicious punch above his ear, and that's when he noticed she'd unwrapped the gauze from around her hands. "How stupid." Another blow, this time on his chin, made his teeth snap together.

Jack Martin must've given her self-defense lessons because she had a wicked right hook. She came at Dean with everything she had: fists, forearms, elbows, feet and knees. His jaw throbbed, matching the ache in his temple.

"Ow," he growled when she threw an elbow at his already sore head. "Okay, that's enough. You're going to hurt your hands."

"It won't be enough until you're broken and bleeding," she promised.

Damn but she was bloodthirsty. And considering it was his blood she wanted to shed, he put a stop to it.

He sat up again, throwing her off balance long enough to flip her onto her back. He held both her wrists in one hand and captured her arms above her head.

"Get off," she demanded, bucking wildly beneath him. "I'm not done kicking your ass!"

"The hell you're not," he grunted. She brought her knee up and he rolled in time to avoid being unmanned. He hated when people fought dirty. "Knock it off." He wrapped his legs around hers and pinned them down. "I don't want to hurt you—"

She sobbed softly. "You don't want to hurt me? *I* want to do some major damage to *you*."

But her words lacked the heat she'd come at him with earlier. Worse, tears had begun to leak out, down into her hairline. He met her eyes, caught his breath at the depth of pain he saw there.

His stomach dropped. She knew. He had no idea how she'd found out and it didn't matter. There was no way he'd be able to make her understand. To get her to forgive him.

But he couldn't go down without a fight. "Allie, I—"

"You're nothing but a liar," she said, making it sound far worse than any other name he'd been called. "And I was stupid enough to believe you." She turned her head and shut her eyes. "Now get off me."

He let go of her wrists and rolled to the side. Laid

there staring blindly at the ceiling as she sprang from the bed. *Shit*. He never should have touched her when there were so many lies between them.

Resigned, he stood and put his jeans on. "How did you find out?" he asked quietly

"That you're not a bartender?" She yanked her sweat-pants up over her hips. "That you're a partner in Leath-erneck Investigations, a private investigation firm specializing in missing persons cases?" She snatched the shirt she'd worn last night off the floor. "Your mother told me."

"You talked to my mother?"

"Don't worry, she didn't mean to blow your cover." Allie sat on the chair and pulled her boots on. "Actually, I probably still wouldn't know if I hadn't called to tell her you'd been hurt. I thought maybe the two of us could figure out a way to reconcile you and your brother." She got to her feet, her hands clenched at her sides. "Jack's always saying someday my nose is going to get bent out of joint if I keep putting it where it doesn't belong. He was right."

She picked up her jacket and purse and stalked toward the door. Dean got there first, though, standing in front of it, his legs spread, his arms crossed. "You're not leav-ing until we've talked this through."

"Do you really want to add unlawful imprisonment to your growing list of crimes?"

He felt as if he was losing something vital. Something he'd never be able to get back. And he couldn't prevent it.

"Don't you even want to know why I lied?" he asked almost desperately. "Or who I'm investigating?"

She pulled her cell phone out of her purse. "If you don't move by the time I count to three, I'm calling Jack. One…"

"You don't need to ask because you already know."

"Two…"

Why did she have to be so stubborn? "I don't want to hurt her—I didn't mean to hurt anyone. I want to help—"

"Three." Allie flipped open the phone.

Fine. He'd already lost her; he'd be damned if he'd lose this case as well. He leaned back against the door. "You don't want to do that."

"Oh, yes, I do."

"When Jack gets here to arrest me, I'm sure he'll be very interested in hearing how you helped Lynne Addison escape her husband."

Allie's hand shook as she closed her phone. But she didn't put it away. "I—I don't know what you're talking about."

"Lynne Addison doesn't have custody of her son, and she's wanted for his kidnapping." Dean studied her face, saw the panic. And felt like a total ass for putting it there. But he had to get her to listen. "And you could be charged with assisting in a child abduction."

She sneered. "You're not very good at your job, are you? I told you before, I haven't seen Lynne Addison in almost two years."

He narrowed his eyes. "Now who's lying?"

"You don't have any evidence I helped Lynne. Which

means it's your word against mine. And which one of us do you think Jack is going to believe?"

Dean nodded. "He'll believe you, of course. But who said I didn't have proof?"

HE WAS BLUFFING. He had to be.

But she could see in his eyes that he wasn't.

Her head reeled. What had she done wrong?

She'd trusted him. She should've listened to Jack and Kelsey and never let Dean into her life. Or into her heart.

She slowly lowered the phone. "If you're looking for Lynne, why didn't you just ask me if I knew where she was? Why all the lies?"

"I couldn't take the chance of you tipping her off. I figured she'd get spooked and run again." Dean looked at Allie beseechingly. "All you have to do is tell me where they are. I promise, I'm not out to hurt them."

Her knees almost buckled. He didn't know. Not everything. Not the most important thing—where Lynne and Jon were. *Who* they were.

"It wouldn't have mattered if you'd asked or not," she said, "because I don't know where they are. I didn't help them—"

"You did it to appease your guilt for helping Miles get acquitted." Dean gestured to her phone. "You called several different numbers over the past few months, all to prepaid cell phones—"

"How do you know...?" She felt as if he'd punched her in the stomach. "I didn't lose my phone last week. You took it."

He had the good grace to avert his gaze. "The last prepaid number had a Cincinnati area code. Which is where a woman and child matching Lynne and Jon's descriptions were spotted at a hospital emergency room."

Allie shook her head. "You're wrong."

"Am I? So, you didn't plan for Lynne to stop at that bookstore where one of your ex-clients worked? An ex-client who'd be more than happy to pay you back by helping another woman get away from an abusive husband?" Something on her face must've given her away because Dean's expression softened. "I know about Sarah Lambert. Tell me, how did you do it? Did Sarah sneak the two out the back? Hide them at the store until it was safe for you to smuggle them out of town?"

She began to shake. From anger, she told herself, not because he was so close to the truth.

She was afraid of what was going to happen next. She might not be able to protect Lynne and Jon anymore.

"I—I have to go." She stepped toward the door, but he didn't move away.

"Haven't you done enough? You've carried this responsibility for so long, Allie. You've given her your savings, even gave up your career. You've paid your penance. Tell me where they are." He reached for her. "Let me help you."

She stepped back. "You want to help me? After everything you've done, the way you manipulated me and my feelings, I'm supposed to trust what you say?" She shoved both hands into her hair. "You must think I'm a complete idiot. Well, why wouldn't you? The way I ate up every word you said."

"It wasn't like that—"

"You must be so proud of yourself. And hey, you really went above and beyond. But you didn't have to sleep with me. I'd already bought your act."

"What happened between us last night was real. If we could sit down, talk this through—"

"I don't want to talk to you. I don't want to *look* at you."

"Damn it, Allie, I care about you."

She slapped him. Hard. "Don't," she said shakily, her cut palm stinging. Tears clogged her throat. "Just… don't. Please…let me go."

She didn't know if her slap made him finally move away from the door, or the pathetic plea in her voice. She didn't care. She had to get away from him and figure out a way to fix this before it was too late for Lynne and Jon.

She opened the door and stepped out into the bright sunshine. The cold air.

"I can help you," Dean said from the doorway. "And Lynne."

Allie faced him. "You expect me to believe that? How, by forcing her back to her husband?"

"I'm not working for her husband. I'm working for her mother. And she wants to see her daughter and grandson. She wants to help them."

Allie clasped her hands together to stop herself from

slapping him again. "And that's the last lie you'll ever tell me. Lynne's mother couldn't have hired you," she managed to retort hoarsely. "She's been dead for over a year."

CHAPTER FIFTEEN

DEAN POUNDED ON THE DOOR of the small house. He couldn't believe he'd been so blind he hadn't seen what was in front of his face this whole time.

He banged again and then stepped over to the large window, cupped his hands around his eyes and peered into a tidy living room. No lights. And the driveway was empty except for the tire tracks in the snow.

Was he too late?

He hunched his shoulders and surveyed the neighborhood. It was early afternoon, and the street was quiet. The only sign of life was the smoke rising in a plume from the chimney next door. He'd turned to head back down the steps when a familiar vehicle parked three houses down caught his eye.

He spun back around and hit his open hand against the door. "Allie?" he called. "I saw your car. If you're in there, let me in."

He held his breath as he waited. Finally, he heard the clicking sound of a dead bolt being unlocked, and the door opened.

Allie stood in the doorway in an oversize sweater, jeans, and the boots she'd had on when she'd left his motel room a few hours ago. She hugged her arms around herself. "Guess you're better at your job than I thought."

He didn't reply. Couldn't. Her hair was pulled back into a messy ponytail and her eyes were red-rimmed as if she'd been crying.

She looked...broken. Because of what he'd done.

"Can I come in?" he asked.

She shrugged. "Why not? It doesn't matter what you do now."

He stepped inside and shut the door while she perched on the edge of the worn couch. The room was sparsely furnished—with just a sofa, an armchair, a wooden bench used for a coffee table and an upturned crate by the sofa with a lamp. A small TV sat on an old dresser against the wall by the staircase. There were no pictures on the walls, no framed photos to show who lived here.

Dean pulled the rolled-up folder out of his back pocket and tapped it against his hand. He wanted to sit next to Allie and take her in his arms, to assure her that everything would be okay. But she wouldn't believe him, so what was the point?

She picked up a red Lego piece from the floor. Turned it end over end. "How'd you figure it out?"

"That Ellen Jensen and her son, Bobby, are really Lynne and Jon Addison?"

She nodded once and tossed the Lego onto the table.

"After you left, I asked Nolan, my partner, to figure out who was masquerading as Robin Hawley and why she hired us."

Allie frowned. "You really didn't know she wasn't Lynne's mother?"

He clenched his hands, bending the file. He couldn't believe he and Nolan had been tricked. Or that Allie thought he'd knowingly work for a scumbag like Miles Addison.

"I swear, neither one of us knew." She averted her eyes and he couldn't tell whether she believed him or not. "While Nolan checked out Robin Hawley's story, I thought I'd better double-check everything she'd told us, all the information she'd given us." He pulled out a photo and tossed it on the table beside the Lego piece. "That's when I came across this."

She picked up the color picture of Lynne taken five years ago. Glanced at it and then set it down again. "Lynne Addison doesn't exist anymore."

"No. I guess she doesn't. I knew Ellen looked familiar, but I couldn't place her." Because the last he knew, Lynne was a curvy, fashionable, green-eyed blonde. Not a frumpy brown-eyed brunette. "The eyes threw me the most. Colored contacts?" he asked.

"So, now you know," Allie said, ignoring his question. "What are you going to do?"

He set the file on the table. "Nolan found out that Robin Hawley is actually Sondra Wilkins."

Her mouth popped open. "Miles's secretary?"

Dean gritted his teeth. The idea of him and Nolan being so easily tricked still pissed him off. "Seems her skills are more diverse than just running Addison's office. She's also one hell of an actress. She played the part of repentant mother to a tee."

"Next time you should check out your client's background," Allie said bitterly.

Unable to stop himself, he asked, "Like you did before you hired me?"

He was surprised she didn't shove the Lego down his throat. "I hope you don't have to give back any retainer she paid you. I'd hate for you to be out any money."

Right. More like she hoped he'd drop dead where he stood so she could spit on his cold, lifeless body. "Actually, we told her we were still on the case. In a few days we'll tell her our leads ended somewhere west of the Mississippi. We were thinking Montana or Wyoming."

Her eyes narrowed. "Why would you do that?"

"So, when Addison hires someone else to find her—and I'm guessing he will—it'll throw them off the real trail." He shoved his hands in his pockets. "Nolan and I have a strict need-to-know policy with our clients. Ever since one of our first customers showed up in the same town where we'd tracked his teenage runaway daughter. Once she saw him, our cover was blown and we learned a valuable lesson. So, Lynne—or Ellen—doesn't have to worry about Miles knowing she's here in Serenity Springs."

"Doesn't matter. Because she's not here."

"I know you're mad at me, but you need to stop the act." He jabbed a finger at the picture. "*Ellen* needs to be prepared when the next PI comes looking for her, and I need her to know—" He clamped his mouth shut.

Allie laughed harshly. "You need her to know what? That you're sorry? That you didn't mean to ruin her life?"

"Yes, damn it," he growled. "I am sorry. I didn't mean for any of this to happen."

"Well, you can forget about me passing on your apology. She's gone. And before you ask, I don't know where she went and I doubt she'll be in contact with me anytime soon." Allie picked up a folded piece of paper from the table and threw it at him. It fluttered to the floor at his feet. "Looks like you won't be absolved of this particular sin."

He picked up the paper, unfolded it and read the neat writing: *Allie, thank you for everything but it's time we were on our own.*

He crumpled it in his hand. "Is this for real?"

"The closets are empty. She must've taken off right after I called her this morning." Allie slowly got to her feet as if it hurt to move. "It's over."

He stood frozen to the spot as she walked to the door without a backward glance. He followed, brushing past her and jumping off the porch onto the sidewalk, blocking her.

"It doesn't have to be over," he said. "*We* don't have to be over."

She shook her head. "You're kidding, right? After everything you've done, all your lies, you think there's anything left between us?"

He'd been in worse situations than this, he reminded himself. He'd been shot at, had things blown up next to him. He'd lost his son.

He wouldn't lose Allie. He couldn't.

He swallowed and reached for her hand, but the glare she shot him told him he needed to keep his distance. "Please, Allie."

She inclined her head and he breathed a sigh of relief.

"I'm not proud of any of this," he said. "Not how I allowed myself to be used by that prick to find his wife. And I'm not proud that I lied to you. I actually...I was going to tell you last night—"

"That's convenient."

"It's the truth. When I went outside to warm up the cars I knew I needed to come clean with you. I realized I...cared about you and I didn't want any lies between us anymore." He prayed she believed him. One last time. "But then Richie knocked me out and—"

"And you decided you no longer needed to tell me?" She glanced around and lowered her voice, even though they were alone. "You thought you'd sleep with me instead?"

"I didn't mean for that to happen."

"I trusted you," she declared, shivering in the cold. "I told you things I'd never told anyone." Tears slid unchecked down her cheeks. "You used me. And for what? A job?"

"I was wrong," he said, hating the desperation he heard in his voice. "But I can make it up to you. I know I can."

"You can't," she whispered. "It's too late."

His anger simmered. "So, that's it? You just—" he snapped his fingers "—and we're through?"

"You're the one who lied—"

"You're willing to forgive Richie for holding a gun to your head, but not me."

"That's right, I can forgive Richie. He didn't betray me like you did."

Dean's jaw dropped. "Didn't betray you?" he asked incredulously. "He showed up for work high. He lied to you. He stole from you—"

"He didn't break my heart," she cried. "But you did."

Dean couldn't catch his breath. "Allie, I—"

She ran past him, down the street.

And he didn't know how he'd ever get her back.

MONDAY EVENING NOT even the latest song by Beyoncé, currently blasting out of her portable CD player, could lighten Allie's mood. Not when she'd spent a sleepless night worrying about Lynne and Jon.

And thinking about Dean.

She wiped the back of her hand against her forehead and gripped the edge of the ugly wallpaper, tearing a long sheet off the wall. She was angry—at him for betraying her, at herself for believing him—not because he'd hurt her. For him to hurt her would mean she cared more for Dean than she was willing to admit. It would mean that the tears she'd cried last night were because she'd lost her chance at something special.

The cuts on her palms weren't yet completely healed but she needed to do something to keep busy. It was tear apart either her kitchen or The Summit, and at least she could be alone in her kitchen.

She crumpled the wallpaper and threw it across the room. Persephone gave chase.

"You throw like a girl."

She jumped, glaring at Dillon before shutting the music off. "I'm not in the mood."

"From the looks of it," he said, taking in the torn wallpaper still on the walls and the balls of it littering the floor, "you're in a scary mood."

"Don't you even knock?" she asked, spraying solution on the wall to loosen the glue.

"I knocked," he assured her. "But when you didn't answer, I thought I'd better let myself in."

She really needed to start remembering to keep her door locked at all times. "I'm sort of in the middle of something…" She wiped her sticky hands on her threadbare jeans. "So, unless this is important, can it wait until tomorrow?"

Dillon kicked a pile of scraps out of his way as he crossed to the table. "No. Kelsey asked me to check up on you." He sat down. "She's worried."

Allie's lower lip trembled so she bit it. "I told her when I called that I'm not feeling well. That's all."

"Funny, Kelsey said she tried to get your new bartender to work tonight, but he wasn't answering his phone. Is he sick, too?"

A lump formed in her throat. "I—I don't want to talk about it," she stuttered, keeping her back to Dillon.

"Okay."

She turned and eyed him suspiciously. "That's it?"

"Sure. Hey, you got anything to drink?"

"In the fridge." He got up and opened the door, took out two bottles of beer. "Help yourself," she told him drily.

He grinned. "I got one for you, too."

"I don't want one," she said, not caring if she sounded petulant. She wanted to be left alone.

"Then sit with me while I have mine." He hooked his foot around the leg of a chair and pulled it out. "Come on. You can finish destroying your kitchen as soon as I'm done."

She huffed out an exasperated breath and dropped into the chair. "Fine."

Dillon retook his seat and opened both beers. Slid one toward her. She rolled her eyes and pushed up the sleeves of her baggy sweatshirt before reaching for it and taking a drink.

He raised his bottle as if making a toast. "Nina said yes."

Allie froze, the beer halfway back to her lips. She squeezed his hand. "Congratulations. I'm so happy for you."

He touched his bottle to hers. "Thank you. Now, quit messing with me and tell me what's wrong."

She sat back, placing both hands in her lap. "You said I didn't have to talk about it."

"I lied."

She was too raw. "I can't."

"I'm warning you, if I don't get the story, Kelsey's going to send Jack over here next. The only reason he didn't come tonight is because he's working."

Allie tipped her head back. And wouldn't that be the perfect ending? To have her brother know all about her latest—and greatest—screwup. "I don't want Jack, I don't want *anyone* to know. Not Kelsey. Not Nina. No one."

He nodded slowly. "You have my word."

"I ruined everything," she whispered.

She filled him in on the whole story—from her representing Miles, to helping Lynne and Jon escape, to finding out about Dean's investigation. She managed to get through her confession dry-eyed, but when she finished, she felt as drained as if she'd just run a marathon.

Dillon whistled. "When you break the law, you go all out."

She sipped her beer. "I did it for a good cause. But now Lynne's on the run again and has no one to help her."

"You already gave her money and helped her get away from a bad situation."

"That's what Dean said," Allie admitted. "But it was my fault her husband wasn't in prison where he belonged. What else was I supposed to do?"

"Sounds like you did everything you could." He leaned back. Picked at the label on his bottle. "The cowboy did a number on you, huh?"

And the last thing she wanted was to think about how Dean had made a fool of her. Or worse, her conflicted feelings over him. "He lied to me."

Dillon waited patiently, as if he had all the time in the

world. "He said he didn't want to scare Lynne off," she added. "That he wasn't sure what I knew."

"And if he'd asked, straight-out, if you knew where Lynne was, what would you have done?"

"I don't see what that has to do with any—"

"What would you have done?"

She squirmed, realized she was, and forced herself to sit still. "I wouldn't have told him. But that's different."

"Doesn't seem so different to me. And all this time," her friend continued mildly, "when someone asked you why you quit your job and moved back to Serenity Springs, what did you do?"

Her stomach turned. "I never lied to you or my family."

But guilt pinched her. She hadn't been completely honest in so long, she was afraid she'd forgotten how.

"So, omitting certain information is all right? As long as you're the one doing it?"

Stricken, she sat up. "That's not fair. I didn't want you all to know how I failed."

"So, your pride kept you from telling us what really happened. From helping you during a difficult time?"

She drummed her fingers on the table. "You know, if Jack were here listening to me, at least he'd want to go kick Dean's ass."

"I'm not saying I don't. But if there's one thing I've learned the past few months it's that our fears can keep us from what we really want. They can keep us from living the life we're meant to live. They can even keep

us from being with the people we're meant to be with."
He paused as if letting that wisdom sink in.

But she didn't want it to sink in. She just wanted to
stop hurting. And more importantly, to stop wanting
Dean.

"Did the cowboy say why he didn't tell you what he
was really doing here?" Dillon asked.

"Not that it matters," she said, holding on to her righ-
teous anger as tightly as possible, "but he said he was trying to reconcile a woman with her family. That he didn't
know the client who'd hired him worked for Miles."

"Reuniting a family sounds like something *you'd* do,"
Dillon stated.

Her face heated as she remembered she'd tried to do
exactly that yesterday when she'd called Dean's mother.

But Allie hadn't lied to him. Well, she had, but it had
been for the greater good. She had to keep Lynne and
Jon safe.

Her actions were justified.

Weren't they?

Dillon finished his beer and stood. "I guess I'll be
going, since you've got it all figured out."

"I do." So, why did she feel so sick? So unsure? "It's
for the best that Dean's gone. I can't trust him."

"This isn't about trust," Dillon said, his expression
understanding and—to her horror—pitying. "It's about
forgiveness. And the first person you need to forgive
is yourself. Once you've done that, you'll be able to
forgive him. And maybe, just maybe, you'll also be

brave enough to give him a second chance. To give you both a second chance."

DEAN STEPPED INTO The Summit's kitchen. He'd waited until late afternoon, knowing the bar would be empty, then paid Noreen a hundred bucks to keep Kelsey occupied in the office long enough for Dean to slip into the building unnoticed. He took his hat off and stood in the doorway. Allie had her back to him as she worked at the counter. A sense of déjà vu hit him so hard, he had to grip the doorjamb to remain upright.

It'd been one month since he'd first seen Allie shaking her hips at the stove. And over two weeks since he'd seen her last.

The longest two weeks of his life.

"Hello, Allie."

She spun around, a knife in one hand, a large onion in the other. He drank in the sight of her. Her hair was braided and she had on jeans and a long-sleeved T-shirt. She'd never looked more beautiful.

Or stunned.

She finally blinked and shut her mouth. "Dean," she said, setting the knife and onion back on the counter and wiping her hands down the front of her jeans. "What are you doing here?"

Not quite an enthusiastic response, but she hadn't thrown anything at him or called the cops on him, so things were going better than he'd hoped.

"These are for you," he said as he crossed the room. He held out the bouquet of red lilies he'd picked up at the florist down the block. She made no move to take them so he thrust them at her, forcing her to accept them or let them fall to the floor. "And in case you're thinking about dropping them off at the hospital, I want you to know I already ordered a dozen bouquets of something called gerbera daisies to be delivered there. The lady at the floral shop said they were real cheerful flowers so the patients should like them."

"You sent flowers to the hospital?"

"Yes, ma'am, I did."

She shook her head as if coming out of a trance. "I thought you went back to Texas."

He switched his hat to his other hand. Prayed he wouldn't blow this, not when she was at least listening to him. "That's right. After you walked away from me, I took the first flight I could get. I figured the best thing to do was pretend none of this ever happened." He inhaled deeply but couldn't get rid of the constricted feeling in his chest. "It was easier than staying and risking you not forgiving me."

"And yet here you are," she said softly, but he couldn't tell if she was happy about that or not.

Please, God, let her be happy about it.

"I did a lot of thinking when I got home. Hell, all I did for a week was think about the choices I'd made. I was too scared to work at my marriage and I let my pride and anger keep me from my family for two years." He tossed his hat on the table before reaching for his wallet. He pulled a picture out of it. "I figured since I couldn't fix what happened between us, I should do everything in my power to fix the other aspects of my life. Starting with my family."

He handed her the picture, waited while she set the flowers down on a chair before taking it. Noticed that her hand wasn't quite steady.

He watched her face as she looked at the picture of him holding a little girl. "Is this…"

He nodded. "That's Rene Susan. My niece."

Allie's expression softened. "She's beautiful."

"She is. Which is surprising, since she takes after her daddy."

Allie handed him the picture back and smiled. "Sounds like you made some real progress with your family."

"It wasn't easy," he admitted, sliding the picture back into his wallet. "I thought for sure they wouldn't forgive me. That I didn't deserve forgiveness."

"Is that why you're here? Absolution?"

He swallowed. "I'm here to fight for you."

"What?"

"I can't stop thinking about you. I know it's going to take time to learn to trust me again, so I'm going to stick it out until that day comes." He did what he'd been wanting to do since he first walked into the room—he touched her. Just a light brush of his fingertip down her cheek, but when she didn't flinch, his heart soared. "I want to be with you, Allie," he said huskily. "I want you in my life. No matter what it takes."

She stepped back and his hope waned. "I haven't done much else but think about what happened. Between us.

And with Lynne and Jon. You were right," she said, glancing at him, "I was so scared of not being able to make it up to them that I lost myself. And when I found out the reason you were here I realized I wouldn't be able to protect them any longer. Yet I felt I had to. To make up for what I'd done."

She still blamed herself. He hated that she couldn't see all the good she'd done. "You did all you could for them."

"It doesn't seem like enough. And when I think about them living their lives on the run... I really thought they could settle in Serenity Springs and be safe."

He was suffused with guilt for his part in it, anger for how he and Nolan had been fooled. "And they would've been safe if it wasn't for me."

"No. I wanted to blame you, but I know as long as Miles is searching for them, they'll never be safe." She tucked her hair behind her ear. "I...I appreciate you and your partner sending Miles on a wild-goose chase."

"I hope it worked."

She nodded. Licked her lips. "I've missed you," she blurted, blushing.

His heart raced. "Darlin', you don't know how happy I am to hear that."

He reached for her but she evaded him, crossing to the side table by the back door. She picked up her purse. "You're lucky you got here when you did," she said, rifling through her bag. She pulled out an envelope. "I'm taking a trip tomorrow, and since I wasn't sure how long I'd be gone, Kelsey is going to run the bar for me until I get back."

"Are you returning to New York?" Though he told himself that would be best for her, he couldn't help but wonder if she meant to start over. Without him.

"No. Not New York."

She handed him an airplane ticket. He frowned and then glanced at it. And did a double take when he read the destination.

He caught his breath. "Dallas?"

Her eyes shone with unshed tears. "I was coming after you."

He tipped his head back. "Thank God." Then he pulled her into his arms and kissed her. "I'll never lie to you again," he promised, moments later. "I love you, Allison Martin."

She smiled. "I love you, too, Dean Garret." She fiddled with the button on his shirt and glanced up at him from under her eyelashes. "As a matter of fact, why don't you and I sneak out of here? We can go back to my house, and I can show you just how much I love you...."

He pressed his lips to her forehead. "That's the best idea I've heard in weeks."

He kissed her again and when they drew apart, they were both breathing hard. She was already reaching for her coat. "Oh, and don't forget your hat." The glint in her eyes was wicked. "Unless you have something against wearing it in bed?"

He laughed and settled his Stetson on his head. "No, ma'am, I surely don't."

* * * * *

We hope you enjoyed reading

BEWITCHING

by *New York Times* bestselling author
CARLA NEGGERS and

HIS SECRET AGENDA

by award-winning author BETH ANDREWS!

Both were originally Harlequin® series stories!

Discover more compelling tales of family, friendship and love from the Harlequin® Superromance® series. Featuring contemporary themes and relatable, true-to-life characters, Harlequin Superromance stories are filled with powerful relationships that deliver a strong emotional punch and a guaranteed happily-ever-after.

⬦ HARLEQUIN®

super romance®

More Story…More Romance

Look for six new romances every month
from Harlequin Superromance!

Available wherever books are sold.

NYTHSR0613

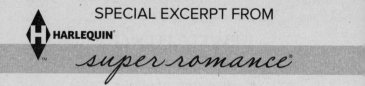
When life doesn't work out for Sadie Nixon,
she has her best friend James Montesano to
lean on. And there's no one better at fixing
things than him. But for once, James is not fixing
anything. In fact, he's changing everything....

Read on for an exciting excerpt of

What Happens Between Friends

By **Beth Andrews**

"You can't hide it from me, James," Sadie said. "I know you
too well. What's on your mind?"

"I'm not sure I want this partnership." He frowned.

What? He'd worked for the family company since high school.
"What do you mean? Isn't that what you've been hoping for all
these years?"

"What if it isn't? What if I want to try something else, be
somewhere else?"

"You? You're steady. Dependable."

He stepped forward and the look on his face startled her,
making her take a quick step back.

"And yet, as steady and dependable as I am, maybe I still want a change." His voice was rough. He didn't sound like James. He sounded, well, sexy. Then he touched her, just his finger trailing down her cheek.

Sadie's mouth was dry so she swallowed. "I guess it's not a bad thing. Change."

But apprehension filled her. Made her think that something was coming. And while she usually was all for the next adventure, she had a feeling she needed to keep her eyes wide open.

Because James was touching her like a man touched a woman, not like a friend touched his good buddy. His eyes were dark with intent.

Sexual intent.

Though he hadn't tugged her closer, she laid her hands on his chest. His solid, warm chest. "James—"

"Did you ever wonder what it would be like between us?"

She opened her mouth but the denial wouldn't come out. Of course she'd thought of it. James was good-looking. How could she not be attracted to him?

But they couldn't act on it. They were friends. It would ruin everything.

Wouldn't it?

Then he kissed her.

Will this kiss change their friendship?
Find out in WHAT HAPPENS BETWEEN FRIENDS
by Beth Andrews, available August 2013 from
Harlequin® Superromance®.
And be sure to look for the other
three books about the Montesano siblings
in Beth's IN SHADY GROVE series.

⬡ HARLEQUIN®

super romance®

More Story...More Romance

Save $1.00 on the purchase of

WHAT HAPPENS BETWEEN FRIENDS

by Beth Andrews,

available August 6, 2013

or on any other Harlequin® Superromance® book.

Available wherever books are sold, including most bookstores,
supermarkets, drugstores and discount stores.

Save
$1.00

on the purchase of
WHAT HAPPENS BETWEEN FRIENDS
by Beth Andrews,
available August 6, 2013 or on any other
Harlequin® Superromance® book.

Coupon valid until November 5, 2013. Redeemable at participating retail outlets
in the U.S. and Canada only. Limit one coupon per customer.

52610859

Canadian Retailers: Harlequin Enterprises Limited will pay the face value
of this coupon plus 10.25¢ if submitted by customer for this product only. Any
other use constitutes fraud. Coupon is nonassignable. Void if taxed, prohibited
or restricted by law. Consumer must pay any government taxes. Void if copied.
Nielsen Clearing House ("NCH") customers submit coupons and proof of sales to
Harlequin Enterprises Limited, P.O. Box 3000, Saint John, NB E2L 4L3, Canada.
Non-NCH retailer—for reimbursement submit coupons and proof of sales directly
to Harlequin Enterprises Limited, Retail Marketing Department, 225 Duncan Mill
Rd., Don Mills, ON M3B 3K9, Canada.

5 65373 00076 2   **(8100)0 11852**

U.S. Retailers: Harlequin Enterprises
Limited will pay the face value of this coupon
plus 8¢ if submitted by customer for this
product only. Any other use constitutes fraud.
Coupon is nonassignable. Void if taxed,
prohibited or restricted by law. Consumer must
pay any government taxes. Void if copied. For
reimbursement submit coupons and proof of
sales directly to Harlequin Enterprises Limited,
P.O. Box 880478, El Paso, TX 88588-0478,
U.S.A. Cash value 1/100 cents.

NYTCOUP0613

REQUEST YOUR FREE BOOKS!

2 FREE NOVELS
FROM THE SUSPENSE COLLECTION
PLUS 2 FREE GIFTS!

YES! Please send me 2 FREE novels from the Suspense Collection and my 2 FREE gifts (gifts are worth about $10). After receiving them, if I don't wish to receive any more books, I can return the shipping statement marked "cancel." If I don't cancel, I will receive 4 brand-new novels every month and be billed just $6.24 per book in the U.S. or $6.74 per book in Canada. That's a savings of at least 22% off the cover price. It's quite a bargain! Shipping and handling is just 50¢ per book in the U.S. and 75¢ per book in Canada.* I understand that accepting the 2 free books and gifts places me under no obligation to buy anything. I can always return a shipment and cancel at any time. Even if I never buy another book, the two free books and gifts are mine to keep forever.

191/391 MDN F4XN

Name	(PLEASE PRINT)	

Address		Apt. #

City	State/Prov.	Zip/Postal Code

Signature (if under 18, a parent or guardian must sign)

Mail to the Harlequin® Reader Service:
IN U.S.A.: P.O. Box 1867, Buffalo, NY 14240-1867
IN CANADA: P.O. Box 609, Fort Erie, Ontario L2A 5X3

Want to try two free books from another line?
Call 1-800-873-8635 or visit www.ReaderService.com.

* Terms and prices subject to change without notice. Prices do not include applicable taxes. Sales tax applicable in N.Y. Canadian residents will be charged applicable taxes. Offer not valid in Quebec. This offer is limited to one order per household. Not valid for current subscribers to the Suspense Collection or the Romance/Suspense Collection. All orders subject to credit approval. Credit or debit balances in a customer's account(s) may be offset by any other outstanding balance owed by or to the customer. Please allow 4 to 6 weeks for delivery. Offer available while quantities last.

Your Privacy—The Harlequin® Reader Service is committed to protecting your privacy. Our Privacy Policy is available online at www.ReaderService.com or upon request from the Harlequin Reader Service.

We make a portion of our mailing list available to reputable third parties that offer products we believe may interest you. If you prefer that we not exchange your name with third parties, or if you wish to clarify or modify your communication preferences, please visit us at www.ReaderService.com/consumerschoice or write to us at Harlequin Reader Service Preference Service, P.O. Box 9062, Buffalo, NY 14269. Include your complete name and address.